“The story is complex [illegible] . . . the characters are [illegible] unusual depth and [illegible]

—Richmond Times-Dispatch

Civil-liberties lawyer Nate Rosen came to Earlyville, Tennessee, to defend the freedom of a fringe religious sect to use rattlesnakes in its worship. But that freedom did not include license to kill local tycoon Ben Hobbes, whose pretty young wife was a convert to the Holiness Church. Suddenly Nate was faced not with upholding the letter of the law but uncovering the secrets of flesh as he followed a trail of ungodly lust, devilish greed, and hellish vengeance to find a killer more deadly than any snake. . . .

THE TRUTH THAT KILLS

“Excellent plotting, terrific atmosphere, with introspective, intelligent Nate Rosen . . . the second entry, after *The Love That Kills*, in a first-rate series.”

—Booklist

“Fascinating, disturbing, remarkable.”

—Mystery News

“FINE, WELL-WRITTEN, COMPLEX . . . A MAJOR TALENT.” ***—Naperville Sun***

RONALD LEVITSKY

THE TRUTH THAT KILLS

AN ONYX BOOK

ONYX
Published by the Penguin Group
Penguin Books USA Inc., 375 Hudson Street,
New York, New York 10014, U.S.A.
Penguin Books Ltd, 27 Wrights Lane,
London W8 5TZ, England
Penguin Books Australia Ltd, Ringwood,
Victoria, Australia
Penguin Books Canada Ltd, 10 Alcorn Avenue,
Toronto, Ontario, Canada M4V 3B2
Penguin Books (N.Z.) Ltd, 182–190 Wairau Road,
Auckland 10, New Zealand

Penguin Books Ltd, Registered Offices:
Harmondsworth, Middlesex, England

Published by Onyx, an imprint of Dutton Signet, a division of Penguin Books USA Inc. This is an authorized reprint of a hardcover edition published by Charles Scribner's Sons under the title *The Wisdom of Serpents*. For information address Charles Scribner's Sons, Macmillan Publishing Company, 866 Third Avenue, New York, NY 10022.

First Onyx Printing, April, 1994
10 9 8 7 6 5 4 3 2 1

Printed in the United States of America

PUBLISHER'S NOTE
This is a work of fiction. Names, characters, places, and incidents either are the product of the author's imagination or are used fictitiously, and any resemblance to actual persons, living or dead, events, or locales is entirely coincidental.

For my mother and father
on their fiftieth anniversary

Serpent handling is a sensitive issue and, for many, a strong personal conviction. The views expressed in this novel are strictly the author's. No disrespect is intended to those who truly believe in the five signs of Mark 16:17-18.

The author wishes to thank the following people: Dr. Loyal Jones, Appalachian Center, Berea College, Kentucky; Dr. Tom Burton, Center for Appalachian Studies and Services, Johnson City, Tennessee; Dr. Charles Wolf, Middle Tennessee State University; the wonderful people of Murfreesboro, Tennessee; and especially my good friend, Steve Cates.

THE FIRST WEEK

Chapter 1

FRIDAY EVENING

The wooden box lay beside the pulpit. It was long with two metal clasps, and across the front someone had painted in black letters, "Mark 16:17–18." As the congregants filed in around him, Jesse Compton sat silently in the third row of folding chairs and watched the box, while sweat trickled under his collar. He wore a two-year-old gray suit, with lapels conveniently out of fashion, to blend with the congregation. Even so, he was overdressed, his sartorial error making him as uncomfortable as the heat. How different this service was, even from the poor Church of Christ he'd visited earlier that week.

Bathsheba sat beside him; the dress smoothed over her knees clung tightly to her long legs. They were beautiful—did she realize how beautiful they were? His own legs were sparrow-thin in comparison. He wanted to gaze into her face, but that would never do—not in church. Besides, he kept glancing at the box. God, he needed a cigarette.

Clapping loudly to the rhythm of an electric guitar, the people sang "Amazing Grace" without songbooks, eyes closed as if reading words written into their souls. The guitar player, standing near the podium, was the only black in the church. His long legs turned inward, like a collapsing marionette, while his hands carefully strummed the hymn. Jesse almost smiled. What would his own friends up at the First Baptist say when he mentioned attending an "integrated" church. He relished the thought like the first sip of an after-dinner cordial.

Looking across the aisle, he recognized one of the congregation, young Claire Hobbes. Her husband had donated a new industrial arts building to the university, the largest such facility in middle Tennessee. She was a pretty slip of a woman with her honey-blond hair, upturned nose, and green cat's eyes, but like the others she wore a long simple dress and no makeup. Ben Hobbes was rich enough to buy into any big old church downtown. Why would his wife mix with these poor folk?

The guitar player put down his instrument and sat in the first row as a man stepped up to the pulpit. Like others in the church, he wore a blue work shirt and dark cotton trousers. He looked about fifty, pale-complexioned, with thick black hair combed straight back. Maybe that's what made his face seem a bit large for his body, or maybe it was the square jaw and dark piercing eyes. Of medium build but with large shoulders and biceps, he was the kind of man whose handshake you'd feel a long time afterward.

Bathsheba whispered, "That's our preacher, Gideon McCrae—my daddy."

From his suitcoat Jesse took a tape recorder, which he balanced on his thigh and switched on.

McCrae lifted a Bible over his head. "John fourteen:six. 'Jesus said unto them, I am the Way, the Truth, and the Life; no man cometh unto the Father, but by me.' " His voice resonated through the room. Resting the Bible on the pulpit, he surveyed the congregation. "You folks know Clark Roberts 'n' his family back there in the last row. Come forty miles to pray with us tonight. Praise Jesus! Clark he tells me the bridge 'tween here 'n' Mayfield been washed out by that awful rain yesterday. Said he had to go downriver 'n' cross, though it took another thirty minutes. I ask why he didn't just try to take his ol' car through the water to save time. Clark says, 'Why, Gideon, only a plumb fool'd do that.' Brothers 'n' Sisters, ain't that the truth!"

Shouts of "Yes, Reverend!" and "That's so!"

"And what did Jesus say? '*I* am the Way, the Truth, an' the Life. No man cometh unto the Father but by *me.*' Did Jesus say that His way was the easy way?"

"No!"

"That it was the quickest?"

"No!"

"No, Brothers 'n' Sisters, I reckon it ain't the easiest or the quickest. 'No man cometh unto the Father but by me.' Some folks'll say that one man's way to God is good as another. That's like sayin' drivin' your car through six feet a' water's same as crossin' a good high bridge. Ain't but one way to follow the Word." He raised the Bible. "That's to follow the Word!"

"Hallelujah! Praise Jesus!"

Jesse glanced at the congregants, saw their rapt expressions, then checked the recorder. What made people respond so fervently? It wasn't the words themselves; he was sure that playing the tape later in his office would provide no clues. Something in the words' power crackled like an electric current between McCrae and his followers. Writing this book was going to be more difficult than Jesse had thought, but he'd do it. The one luxury a Compton never allowed himself was failure.

* * *

It had started easily enough, driving back from the countryside after interviewing a Primitive Baptist, passing through the poor part of town and seeing the sign HOLINESS CHURCH OF EARLYVILLE on a small frame house. He had heard rumors about this church.

"No," the next-door neighbor had said, "ain't nobody t'home. Minister's at the furniture factory, but his daughter Bathsheba's workin' at the Burger King just up on the highway. She'll tell you anythin' you want t'know."

And so she had. Bathsheba was about the same age as his graduate students but looked older in her company uniform, sitting across the table and sipping a Coke. He was thirty-seven, not that great an age difference; his own parents were eleven years apart. Her hair was black and fell in large curls, framing a face with the brownest eyes he'd ever seen. Her skin was a faded tan, and her cheeks dimpled when she smiled, as she was doing that very moment. She was as tall as Jesse; she'd be taller in heels. He imagined her in a white evening gown with emerald earrings shimmering in the moonlight.

"I'm a professor of popular culture at the college," he had said, lighting a cigarette. "I'm working on a book dealing with the churches of this area. The different ways in which people hereabouts worship God."

Bathsheba continued to smile but said nothing. As she leaned back, the smock strained against her breasts.

"I . . ." Jesse's mouth suddenly went dry. He took a long swallow of his diet cola. "I understand that your church is Pentecostal."

"We're a holiness church."

"Yes, that's what I mean. Do people in your church speak in tongues?"

She nodded. "The Bible says, 'And they were all filled with the Holy Ghost, and began t'speak with other tongues, as the Spirit gave them utterance.' "

"Do you?"

"Sometimes . . . when the Spirit moves me." She tilted her head back, eyes half-closed and nostrils quivering. "When the Spirit takes control, you do whatever it tells you."

"I've heard you do other things in church."

"We do all five signs that's spoken of in Mark."

He lowered his voice. "*All* five signs?"

"Yes, it bein' the Lord's Word."

"But aren't you afraid . . . the police?"

"My daddy says the only thing we need fear is the Lord." Bathsheba finished the Coke, her lips glistening. "Would you like to come see a service?"

Jesse watched her through the veil of cigarette smoke. He had to clear his throat again. "Yes, I'd like very much to come."

"Tomorrow night we're havin' a service. It'll start about sundown. I'll be waitin' on you. One thing, we don't allow no tobacco at the service."

Jesse noticed that Bathsheba wore no jewelry at all. How beautiful an emerald necklace would look against her throat. Would the church allow her to wear one?

"You'll excuse me now," she said. "I have to be gettin' back to work."

Jesse watched her walk toward the counter. The brown slacks of her uniform weren't meant to be flattering but still showed her curves and long legs. He knew he was going to church regardless of his book.

* * *

" '. . . after my departing shall grievous wolves enter in among you, not sparing the flock.' "

Jesse looked away from Bathsheba's lap to her father, who paced back and forth behind the pulpit. Sweat glistened on his forehead and darkened under his arms.

" 'Also of your own selves shall men arise, speaking perverse things, to draw away disciples after them.' And so Jesus warned us not to take the wrong path, not to listen to wolves whisperin' 'bout the easy things in life, like some slick game show announcer on the television. You all know the one true way, praise Jesus!"

"Praise Jesus! Hallelujah!"

Eyes closed, some of the congregation stood, their arms and legs jerking. Claire Hobbes was one of them.

Suddenly the black guitar player dropped his instrument, jumped up and turned to the others. He flickered from side to side like a dying fire.

"It's true what the Reverend says!"

"Speak it, Lem!" people around Jesse shouted. "Speak the Lord's truth!"

"You all know the kind a' man I was, before gettin' on the Lord's path. Most a' my life I seen the sun rise through the cold iron bars of prison. Then one day, praise Jesus, a guard gave me the Bible 'n' told me 'bout this church. Bless Reverend McCrae for what he did for me. . . ."

"Hallelujah!"

"Like the good Reverend says, man's gotta be broke down 'n' give up everything, especially that devil Pride, before the Lord'll reach down to lift him up. That's where I was, lower than a snake, when the Lord lifted me up. Now I know, dear

Jesus, You forgive me. I feel the power of Your mercy. Oh, Lord, I feel it washing over me right down, like the cool water of Jordan. Oh, Jesus! Oh, Lord! I feel . . . !"

Everyone was on his feet now, shouting and singing, so that Jesse could no longer hear Lem. He stood also, saw Bathsheba swaying with eyes closed and singing a hymn. Reverend McCrae had been their center, gripping the congregation with his words. Then, as if gravity no longer existed, people spun away from the pulpit, moved toward one another or staggered into the aisles. Some shook as if electrocuted, some fell to the floor, one man jumped up and down as he ran through the church calling the Lord's name.

Claire Hobbes staggered toward Jesse and, as he grabbed her, sounds poured from her mouth. Sounds he couldn't understand. Guttural babbling. Her arms clawed his, so that he couldn't wrench free. He tried to understand—baby talk, bastard German, abracadabra incantations that made no sense. He turned toward Bathsheba for help, but she was gone.

At the pulpit Reverend McCrae held a glass of clear liquid. " 'And if they drink any deadly thing, it will not hurt them!' " He sipped the liquid. "Praise Jesus!"

Jesse had heard of people drinking strychnine at these services. McCrae passed the glass to a wizened old man, with skin hanging around his neck like a wattle. The old man twitched while also sipping the liquid. He placed the glass on the ground and, clapping his hands, shouted, "Glory, Glory, Glory!"

Glancing here . . . there . . . trying to isolate the images, to make sense of this new reality, Jesse felt his mind slipping away. Five . . . ten . . . a hundred voices crying out for something he didn't understand in languages he couldn't comprehend. Wrenching free of Mrs. Hobbes, he rubbed a handkerchief across his eyes, hoping to make everything disappear. Instead, the breath caught in his throat, as what he had both feared and anticipated was finally about to happen.

The wooden box.

Lem bent beside it and, unclasping the locks, lifted the top. Reaching inside he tossed a thick tangled skein, shiny and smooth, onto the floor, something at first Jesse understood as little as the language Claire Hobbes had been speaking. But he didn't need to understand to feel the chill in his spine.

The evil on the floor slowly untangled and tried to slither away, but Lem and Reverend McCrae were too quick. A moment later the minister had stretched a diamondback rattlesnake over his head, while Lem raised his right hand, in which two rattlers coiled around each other like the staff of Aesculapius. Each snake was longer than a man's arm, thick with black markings on skin the color of gangrene, with a half-dozen or more rattles at the end of its tail. Jesse watched, mesmerized, as the snakes looked into the room, into him.

Reverend McCrae walked back and forth behind the pulpit, still holding the snake above his head as if it were a championship belt. Lem slowly separated his two rattlers and handed one to the old man who had drunk strychnine. Placing the snake under his shirt, the old man stroked the animal while it undulated against his skin. Meanwhile, Lem had draped the third reptile over his shoulders, doing a pirouette so that it wrapped once around his neck and coiled its head like a question mark to stare into his face.

Taking the rattler from under his shirt, the old man held it out as a gift for anyone to take. Jesse stepped back, almost stumbling over the wooden chairs, while two hands reached for the snake: Bathsheba's. Turning to face the congregation, she brought the rattler to her breast. Her head thrown back and eyes closed, she smiled as it crawled over her smooth, round shoulders, from one arm to the other. Watching her, the old man clapped his hands and shouted, "Praise the Lord! Oh, praise the power a' Jesus!"

Jesse gripped the chair in front of him and studied their faces—the old man's, Reverend McCrae's, Lem's, and Bathsheba's. He didn't see what he'd expected. He'd thought of McCrae's church as a carny show, like the preachers on television aping for the audience, praying for Jesus and small change. This was different. These people's faces revealed no fear, yet neither did they display a death-defying bravado. Something very private was occurring, a secret not between them and the snakes—they didn't seem to notice the snakes—but a secret with God.

He kept watching Bathsheba, trying to understand, but the din within the church broke his concentration. One sound especially, a slow steady scream, pulled him out of the spell. At first Jesse thought it was one of the congregants caught in her religious ecstasy, but the sound was too insistent. He finally recognized the dull mechanical wail of a police siren.

The others must have heard the sound, yet made no attempt to escape. If anything, realizing the service would soon end, they grew more fervent in their prayers and outcries.

The front door banged open, but, instead of police, Ben Hobbes walked in. He wore the same dusty work clothes as Reverend McCrae and the other men who worked in his furniture factory. In his sixties, Hobbes had a face sharp as a hatchet and a body all angles, as if even an ounce of fat was waste he wouldn't allow. He kept his gray hair closely cropped; his barber claimed to sweep iron filings from the floor.

Hobbes forced his way through the people, pushing them aside when they tried to embrace him. He frowned as he approached Jesse, who instinctively nodded toward Claire Hobbes.

She had fallen to the floor. No longer speaking in tongues, she was breathing shallowly, eyes closed, dried spittle on her chin.

Her husband knelt beside her. His face softened as he touched her shoulder. "Claire . . . Claire, honey, you all right?"

When she didn't respond, he lifted her and, with a torn red bandanna, gently patted her face dry.

Her eyes flickered open, her voice barely a whisper. "Ben? What're you doing here?"

"It's all right, honey. Never you mind. Just as long as you're all right."

Jesse watched them. They might've been father and daughter—not just the age difference, but the story-time-soft way in which Ben Hobbes spoke to his wife.

"I was so worried about you."

Blinking hard, she touched her forehead. "Why wouldn't I be all right in church?"

"Church? You call this sideshow a church?"

"Hush."

"I warned you about this. About all of them. For God's sake, honey, I know what's going on."

"What're you . . . ?"

"I know what they're making you do. The evil, child, I know all about it."

She blanched, tried to speak, but couldn't.

"I don't blame you," he said. "It wasn't ever your fault. It's them, and they'll pay."

From the back of the room a man shouted, "All right, everybody just settle down! This is the police, so let's just keep things orderly!"

Claire asked, "Ben, is this your doing?"

He nodded. "This is just starters, honey. McCrae's gonna pay for what's been done to you."

"Ben, no."

"That's right," the policeman continued, "everybody just set yourselves down!"

Police Chief Whitcomb sauntered down the aisle. About five-six, he was barrel-chested, with huge forearms and hands that gripped a man like lobster claws. Yet, every Christmas Jesse saw him dressed as Santa in front of the courthouse, giggling as the little ones tickled his belly.

"What the hell?" Whitcomb rubbed his eyes then looked again at the pulpit. "You boys see what I see?"

From the back of the room, one of the policemen managed, "Y-yes, sir."

"Pete, go to the car and get me a shotgun." To Reverend McCrae, "You and the others, you put them snakes away now."

McCrae held out his right hand, suspending the rattler before him like a staff. " 'They will pick up serpents'!"

"You're in violation of the law."

The old man beside McCrae hurried to the police

chief. His face twitched hard. "You can't do this. We got our rights under the Constitution."

"Reverend, this is more than just disturbing the peace. We got here a serious violation of the law of Tennessee."

"What law?" The old man's wattle wiggled like Jell-O.

Just then a policeman ran to Chief Whitcomb and handed him a shotgun.

Whitcomb said, "The law against using them rattlers to endanger anybody's life. Now I'm done talking. You best do what I say now." He banged a chair with the butt of his shotgun.

The sudden noise seemed to startle Lem, who, holding his snake between both hands, took a step forward. In doing so, his grip loosened and the rattler's head made a lazy loop, then suddenly whiplashed and buried its fangs into Lem's right shoulder. He jolted, his eyes popping wide, as the snake withdrew and lolled like a drunkard.

For a moment no one moved. Then, grabbing the snake just below its head, the old man dropped it into the wooden box. Reverend McCrae and Bathsheba did likewise with theirs, she letting it slide from around her throat like an unclasped necklace. Closing and locking the box, the old man slid it into a far corner.

McCrae grabbed Lem just as his knees buckled, and guided him to the floor. Jesse joined the other congregants who circled the two men. Ripping Lem's shirt, McCrae revealed two deep puncture wounds, the skin around them speckled with blood. He acted with deliberation, as if participating in a ritual.

"Lord Jesus, send your blessin's upon our

Brother Lemuel and sustain him in his hour of need."

The congregants shouted, "Amen!"

"How you feelin', son?"

Lem swallowed hard, and his eyes were beginning to glaze.

"Lem?"

"Burns, Reverend. Like to be on fire."

"You want us to call a doctor?"

Staring straight ahead, Lem shook his head.

"You sure? If you want doctorin', that's all right. I'll take you to the hospital myself."

"N-no. Let Jesus' will be done."

Whitcomb shook his head. "Pete, call this man an ambulance."

"No," Lem said, biting his lower lip. "Ain't goin' to no hospital."

"You can't make him, Officer," McCrae said. "He's followin' the Lord's will."

"God's will be done," the old man said. "Lookie this." He held up his right hand; the tip of his index finger was missing, the edges blackened and hard. "Rattler did this to me five, six years ago, but I'm all right. It's all God's will."

Whitcomb stared at the young man. "Best stop this foolishness and let me call an ambulance."

Lem shook his head. "Reverend, pray for me. Ever'body, pray for me."

Whitcomb said, "He won't have the time, unless it's from jail. Reverend McCrae, I'm afraid you're under arrest."

"What fer!" the old man demanded.

"I told you already—violating the law against using snakes in a dangerous manner. You better hope nothing bad happens to this fella, because the district attorney might even have a mind to charge you with murder."

The old man almost spat. "Murder?"

"That's all right, Brother Tucker," McCrae said. "John four:twenty-four—'God is a Spirit: and they that worship him must worship him in spirit and in truth.' No one can stop us from worshipin' God in truth. Take Brother Lemuel to my house. Bathsheba'll help look after him. Pray with the others for him while I'm gone. He'll be in my prayers as well."

Whitcomb looked at the congregants standing around him. "In the meantime, I don't want none of you fooling with them snakes. Don't want something like this to happen again. Understand?"

Tucker shook his stump of a finger at the policeman. "Just how're you gonna stop us from followin' the Lord's will?"

Slowly shaking his head, Whitcomb walked through the crowd and stood about six feet in front of the wooden box. Raising his shotgun, he unloaded both barrels, blowing the box apart and splattering bits of snake skin and splinters against the wall.

"I think that'll do it," Whitcomb said. "Come along, Reverend."

The congregants murmured their disapproval but made a path for the two men as old Tucker said, "Brothers 'n' Sisters, let's bow our heads in prayer."

Claire Hobbes grabbed her husband's arm. "Stop them, Ben. You told the police to come. You can stop them."

Whitcomb nodded respectfully. "It's a little late to say none of this happened. A man's been hurt, maybe real bad. I can't just walk away."

"But . . ."

Hobbes pushed his wife behind him, then faced the minister. "There's been a lot more carrying on, hasn't there, McCrae?"

"I don't know what you're talkin' 'bout."

"The hell you don't, you son of a bitch!" He struck McCrae in the face, drawing blood from the other man's lip.

"Ben, no!" his wife cried, and pushed herself between the two men. "I won't let you hurt the Reverend, even if you are my husband."

"Claire, honey, you don't know what you're saying."

McCrae stood ramrod straight. "Mr. Hobbes, I done you no harm. I follow John—'he that keepeth his commandments . . .' "

"Don't you dare quote the Book," Hobbes said. "It's sacrilege coming from your mouth. I know the Bible, too, the way it's taught in a good Baptist church. 'For every one that doeth evil hateth the light, neither cometh to the light, lest his deeds be reproved.' You and this church, you and your seed, I know the evil you're doing to my wife, the horrible, twisted evil. It's . . . I'd like to kill you."

"Stop it!" his wife cried. "I can't stand it, Ben! It's making me . . ."

She swayed, then sank to the floor as Ben caught her.

"Claire, I didn't mean . . . It'll be all right."

Laying a hand on Hobbes's shoulder, Whitcomb said, "Best get her home. Leave the Reverend to me."

Hobbes lifted Claire in his arms. "It's not over. Not by a mile. When I get through with him, the hogs won't even want what's left."

Turning, he carried his wife from the church.

Whitcomb said to his deputies, "Pete, stay with

the injured man. If he changes his mind about medical attention, you see that he gets it right quick. Call me in an hour. Jim, stick around here and make sure everyone else leaves peaceable." To McCrae, "When we get to the station, you can call your attorney."

"What'd I be doin' with a lawyer?"

"You'll be finding out right quick. Let's go."

After they'd left, the people turned their attention to old Tucker, who went back to Lem. The young man was trembling, and his chest heaved. The wound had swelled and darkened around the two bite marks.

Bathsheba said, "Tucker, do like Daddy said. Take him to our house. Have the brothers 'n' sisters pray over him."

The old man nodded. "Where'll you be, child?"

"Huntin' up a lawyer, I guess." She looked around, caught Jesse's eye, and added, "I'll likely drive into Nashville with Cousin Popper. Maybe he knows somebody can help us."

"Don't worry, child, the Lord'll provide."

Jesse blurted, "I'm an attorney."

She stepped close. Her skin, glistening with perspiration, smelled slightly of musk. "Would you help us?"

"I . . . I haven't practiced law for ten years, but I'll do what I can."

"Thank you." Her smile was all the retainer he'd need.

Suddenly he felt a cramp in his right hand and, looking down, saw his tape recorder. The machine was still on and had recorded everything. Thinking about what had occurred during the service, Jesse realized what his words to Bathsheba really meant.

The commitment to defend her father—jail house visits, back room dealings with the state, and maybe even confrontation in court. Criminal law—he smelled it like a rotting carcass. He wouldn't go through all that—what would his mother and his friends say? But he wouldn't abandon Bathsheba. He had to see her again. There had to be some way.

The look in the people's eyes as they huddled around him was sullen defiance in the face of scorn and contempt. Jesse had seen that same look somewhere before long ago. Then he remembered.

"We're going to need help."

"Will it cost much money?" she asked.

"I wouldn't worry about the money."

Her eyes drew him in.

"I wouldn't worry about anything. I know a man who'll help us. This is the kind of case God made just for him."

Chapter 2

SUNDAY AFTERNOON

"Looking out your window," the pilot said over the intercom, "you'll see the Cumberland Mountains, which Daniel Boone and others crossed to settle eastern Kentucky and Tennessee. Descendants of these frontiersmen still live in this beautiful region of Appalachia."

Putting aside the in-flight magazine, Nate Rosen looked through the wisps of clouds to the rolling mountains, dappled green and brown in the afternoon light. In their beauty and immutable strength he always saw God's hand, perhaps as Moses had while receiving the Commandments? Did people living in these mountains feel that same power?

He took the New Testament from his briefcase. Opening the book, he felt like an adulterer. There was pleasure in reading words written two thousand years ago about the people and places of his ancestry. Even more, however, was a sense of guilt, because the words didn't belong to his people.

He had marked two entries and opened to the first—Mark 16:17–18: "And these signs will accompany those who believe: in my name they will cast out demons; they will speak in new tongues; they will pick up serpents; and if they drink any deadly thing, it will not hurt them; they will lay their hands on the sick, and they will recover."

Rereading the passage several times, Rosen shook his head. Who were these people?

"I'd like to see more of that."

The man sitting beside him had spoken. He was middle-aged, dressed in a gray striped business suit, and his face was all smile. The kind of smile that could sell encyclopedias to illiterates.

"Excuse me?" Rosen said.

The man nodded at the Bible in Rosen's hands. "People not ashamed of reading the Good Book in public. You a minister?"

Rosen shook his head, biting the inside of his lip to keep from smiling.

"Even better. A good Christian reading the Bible to himself on Sunday, because he can't be in church. By the way, name's Warren Glenwood." They shook hands. "You live in Nashville?"

"No. I'm going there on business. Actually, to a small town nearby—Earlyville."

"Know it well. My cousin Hank's a realtor there. Live in Nashville myself. I've been to Washington on business."

Rosen glanced at the mountains. "Beautiful country. It's my first visit to Tennessee."

"You'll find middle Tennessee's not quite so hilly but right pretty, just the same. Your first visit? Well, then, here."

He handed Rosen a business card—"Warren Glenwood, President, House of Grits"—and a two-for-one coupon good at any of his restaurants.

"We got five places in the greater Nashville area. You ain't gonna eat no better grits anywhere in the country."

"Thank you," Rosen said.

"Yeah, I was in Washington to see my representative. He's gonna push for a National Grits Day. Shoot, they got official days for just about everything. Might as well honor corn. U.S. grows more of it than any other country."

Rosen turned to the New Testament in his hands.

"I can see you want to get back to your reading. Far be it from me to get between you and the Lord."

"That's all right. Are people pretty religious in this part of the country?"

Glenwood scratched his head. "That's a question, ain't it. Like anywhere else, you got your Bible people and them that's not. But I guess there's more that is. I never miss Sunday church if I can help it."

"Two days ago a man was bitten by a rattlesnake in a church in Earlyville."

"You heard about that, did you? Yeah, my wife mentioned it on the phone yesterday."

"Do things like that happen often?"

He laughed. "Where're you from?"

"Originally, I'm from Chicago."

"Everybody hide when Al Capone's boys come riding down Main Street with their tommy guns blazing? See what I mean? Folks got a picture of a place even when it ain't true. Don't judge us by a few crazy people who go around worshiping snakes. Why, if I was to bring a rattler into church, the pastor'd jump outta his skin. But you go on with your studying."

Turning pages to the second marker, Acts 28:3, 5, Rosen read, "And when Paul had gathered a bundle of sticks, and laid them on the fire, there came a viper out of the heat, and fastened on his hand. . . . And he shook off the beast into the fire, and felt no harm."

From what Rosen had heard, the young man bitten by the snake was seriously ill, maybe dying. It was one thing to believe in miracles, another trying to live them every day. His father tried to live God's miracles, tried to make his sons live them, but Rosen had refused. For him the price had been too high. And now, this small-town church. Again he asked himself, what kind of people were they?

Feeling the plane begin its descent, he put the Bible away and fastened his seat belt.

Glenwood said, "Welcome to the Athens of the South. Sure hope you enjoy your stay."

Walking from the plane into the terminal, Rosen wondered if he'd recognize his old classmate. He needn't have worried. As if the years hadn't passed, Jesse stood and, taking the cigarette from his mouth, nodded hello. He was still thin, thinner than Rosen, and his hair had receded a little. But he was the same impeccable dresser, wearing a camel hair jacket and matching cravat.

They approached each other a little awkwardly and shook hands.

"Nate, it's good to see you. Thanks for coming."

"Hello, Chavrusa."

Jesse smiled. "It's been a long time since I've heard that word. I still like the sound of it. You look wonderful."

"You haven't changed either. Always *GQ*. I still imagine you meeting Cary Grant. First thing you'd do would be to straighten his tie and brush the lint from his shoulders."

Jesse looked him up and down, taking in the old corduroy jacket and faded jeans. "And as Fred used to say, you still look like one of those chihuahuas in a teacup saying, 'Please give me a home.' "

As they walked toward the baggage claim, Rosen asked, "You ever hear from Fred?"

"Not for about five years, since he sent me a new business card announcing his partnership in some New York firm. He also wrote that you had joined the Committee to Defend the Constitution. I wasn't surprised. I always knew you'd get involved in fighting for civil liberties. It's nice to know that Hamlet was wrong—that a conscience doesn't make cowards of us all."

They reached the conveyor just as Rosen's luggage emerged from the chute.

Five minutes later they were on the highway in Jesse's Porsche.

"Very nice." Rosen stretched his long legs while smelling leather and tobacco, like the inside of a private club. "You seem to be doing well. Your father still own the town bank?"

"Daddy died a few years ago. I never wanted to be involved in business and went to law school only to please my mother. My sister's husband took over the bank presidency. I thought it was minimal compensation for their moving into the family home and enduring Mama. I'm afraid I've become a constant disappointment to her."

"You never married?"

"No. There was one young lady I kept company with here in high school and college."

"You used to talk about her—Jennifer Ann."

"That's right. It never did work out. Guess I dragged my heels too long. She ended up marrying the captain of the football team. He used to tease me mercilessly because my idea of sports was a spirited chess game. Well, she bore him six children who are constantly secreting liquids from one orifice or another. Jennifer Ann's now as round as her husband's bowling ball and spends her time saving raccoons from hunters. Not surprisingly, her husband spends his days in a tavern."

"Sad story."

"Yes. It almost makes me believe there's a divine plan after all. Now tell me, how have you been?"

"I'm fine. As you said, I've been working for the CDC for about five years. It's a small organization but growing. I like to think we're doing good work."

"How's Bess?"

"We were divorced four years ago."

For a moment the car slowed. Jesse said, "I still remember your wedding—how much in love you two were. I was more than a little jealous. I am sorry."

Rosen shifted against the door. "That's all right. You'll appreciate the irony. You went to law school to please your mother. One of the reasons I married Bess was because she was the kind of girl my father would've warned me against, had we been speaking. Funny how he was right after all."

"Any kids?"

He smiled. "A daughter, Sarah. She's fourteen. She's living in Chicago with her mother." The smile faded as the thought of missing her throbbed dully like an old wound. "Let's talk about why you called me."

Jesse stubbed his cigarette in the ashtray, and immediately lit another. "As I told you on the phone, it's a case involving a Pentecostal church of serpent-handlers. A member of the congregation was bitten, and the minister's been charged with breaking a law against using poisonous snakes in church. I was at his hearing yesterday. Reverend McCrae's out on five hundred dollars' bond."

"So the judge let him walk for fifty. That's not much."

"If the man who was bitten dies, the police chief

intimated a murder charge. This could be an important freedom of religion case. I assume your organization thinks so."

"Sure, it could be a perfect test case. How did you get involved in this?"

Jesse reddened slightly. "A friend of mine is a member of the church. I wanted to help . . . this person out, that's all."

"A woman, or you would've said 'him.' "

"You're right, as always. See why I called you? We'll be in Earlyville in another twenty minutes."

It was a sunny day in late September, just cool enough for a jacket and tie. While Jesse concentrated on the highway, six fast lanes divided by a concrete median, Rosen's eyes grew heavy from the smooth ride and repetitive scenery. On either side of the road the earth had been sliced clean, exposing layers of weathered limestone, above which tall trees huddled together like hobos over an open fire. The trees' thick foliage obscured the view, but every quarter mile one or more billboards appeared in their midst: MCDONALD'S, COUNTRY MUSIC INN, TACO BELL, COUNTRY COMEDY MUSEUM, HOUSE OF GRITS, HOLIDAY INN—a roll call of roadside America. Interspersed with these commercial advertisements were smaller, hand-lettered signs announcing: CHURCH OF CHRIST OF MELBA'S CORNER, HOLINESS CHURCH IN JESUS' NAME ONLY, FIRST BAPTIST CHURCH OF CRICKET HOLLOW, and a dozen others.

Rosen shook his head. "There're as many churches in Tennessee as Wisconsin has taverns."

Turning onto the Earlyville exit, Jesse said, "Lots of people take their religion personally. You've got churches splitting off churches all the time, like some theological chain reaction. Memberships of three or four people. Daddy the minister, momma and kids the congregation."

"That small?"

"It doesn't make religion less important to them. As Thoreau said, there's power even in a majority of one."

"I didn't mean . . ." Rosen felt his own face grow warm and almost whispered, "I know." Wanting to change the subject, he nodded out the window. "Who's that?"

The road had narrowed to two lanes and wound through an open field with low rolling hills in the horizon. Two figures walked slowly across the field, an old man with severe features and a pretty young woman. They walked beside each other without ever quite touching.

"The Hobbeses," Jesse said, "going on their daily constitutional."

"Father and daughter?"

"Husband and wife."

"He looks like an Old Testament patriarch walking with his handmaiden."

"It may've started like that; Claire worked in Ben's furniture factory. Since they've been married—about a year—he'll do anything for her. Well, almost anything. She was at the serpent-handling service Friday night when he came for her, along with the police. He was very angry with Reverend McCrae, even threatened him. He doesn't want Claire involved with the serpent handling and other goings-on at the church."

Rosen stared at the couple. "Is Hobbes's wife your 'friend,' the one who interested you in this case?"

"No, I don't really know either of them too well. That's his furniture factory over there, the largest employer in town."

They passed a spur that led directly to a huge wooden building, its paint peeling, so that it looked as much brown as white, with piles of lumber stacked in an adjacent work yard big as a ballpark. A large semi with the company name was slowly wheezing to a halt in the yard, while a half-dozen forklifts glided toward it.

"Some place," Rosen said.

"Ben and his brother Simon own it. It's been in their family for over a hundred years and makes some of the best furniture in the country. They say Jack Kennedy's favorite rocking chair was a Hobbes. A lot of people depend on the factory for their livelihood." He gave a sidelong glance. "There've been rumors about problems among the Hobbeses."

"Because of the marriage?"

"There's always some of that. Pretty young thing marrying a rich old man . . . you can imagine the stories. More importantly, there's been talk of selling the factory or even closing it down. A shutdown could ruin this town."

Passing a field ripe with corn, they reached an intersection indicating Earlyville two miles ahead. Instead, Jesse turned left, drove about a mile, then turned into an entrance proclaiming CENTRAL TENNESSEE COLLEGE, HOME OF THE HOUNDS. The road meandered past several buildings of brick and glass shaped like sticks of butter, with an occasional cluster of trees to break the monotony of closely clipped grass.

They continued to the end of the campus, where Jesse parked in front of an old frame building with a pair of rockers on the porch. A sign nailed onto the porch balustrade read POPULAR CULTURE CENTER/DR. JESSE COMPTON, DIRECTOR. Through an open window Rosen heard a scratchy recording of guitar playing and someone singing.

"We're home," Jesse said. "I'll get your luggage. You'll be staying with me."

"I thought you were a practicing attorney. You never mentioned being a college professor."

"Didn't I?"

Jesse led Rosen into a small hallway. The large area on their right, which must have served once as a living room, was now a work area. Bookshelves filled to capacity covered the wall directly ahead. An adjacent wall contained racks of phonograph records and boxes of cassettes. Stepping into the room, Rosen saw, to his left, a small partition dividing a wooden desk from a series of file cabinets. The fourth wall was covered with old music posters advertising A. P. Carter and other country singers.

Several folding tables, placed end to end, bisected the room. Two college students, a boy and a girl, sat at one end of the tables listening to music coming from a tape recorder. The boy kept starting and stopping the tape, while the girl scribbled on a legal notepad.

Jesse whispered to Rosen, "Two of my grad students. They interviewed an old-timey local musician, Willie Duncan. He wrote a lot of songs about life during the Depression. They're transcribing the lyrics for a book the center's doing."

Rosen asked, "You're not practicing law?"

"I gave that up a few years after returning to Earlyville. I never much liked the idea of corporate law and I'm afraid criminal law's beneath a Compton. Noblesse oblige only goes so far."

"So you chose the ivy walls of college life."

"I got my Ph.D. in history and have been here six years. It's a small school, but I'm happy. The college has let me develop a popular culture program, one of the few like it in the country. We're saving history."

"I'm sure you're doing good work."

Jesse smiled. "It's a bit selfish, really. What else does the Compton family have besides its history? As a psychologist might say, my work allows me to self-actualize the same way your civil liberties organization lets you."

"What do you mean?"

Instead of answering the question, Jesse said, "We'll get you settled, then review the case. I've gathered some initial research."

Climbing upstairs, Rosen smelled the stale odor of tobacco. The second floor contained three rooms and a bath. Jesse led him into the third room and put his luggage down. The room contained a bed, night table, chest of drawers, and rocking chair—antiques beautifully handcrafted of dark wood. A diamond-patterned quilt of red and green hung above the bed, and another quilt was folded neatly on the bed. A half-dozen framed photographs of Jesse's ancestors were arranged on the wall with the window.

"I hope you'll be comfortable," Jesse said.

"It'll be like sleeping in the Smithsonian. Are you sure you trust me with all these antiques?"

"This house survived a whole pack of Yankees long before you, during the Civil War. I'll see you in my office, the room next door, when you're ready. No hurry."

After unpacking, Rosen pushed up his pillow and lay on the bed. As always when traveling to a new town, he took a few minutes to settle in, finding what the new place had in common with home. Usually it was easy. He kept his apartment in Washington nearly as Spartan as the dozens of hotel rooms to which, over the years, he'd grown accustomed. This room was different. It was home and family and deep roots and, for the first time in years, reminded him of his tiny bedroom as a boy, the aroma of his mother baking challah and the sound of his father and grandfather chanting holy words deep into the night.

His hands trembled, and his forehead had broken into a cold sweat. Rubbing his eyes, as if trying to erase the memory, Rosen went into the bathroom and washed with cold water. Then he walked into Jesse's office.

A computer center built of oak—with printer, modem, telephone, answering machine, and a cassette player—ran the length of the right wall. The remainder of the room was taken up with rows of bookshelves and two straight-back rocking chairs resting on an American Indian throw rug woven in blues and reds.

Jesse sat at the desk and tapped an ash from his cigarette. "Try one of the rockers, both turn-of-the-century Hobbes. I think you'll find them surprisingly comfortable."

Rosen settled into the chair. "Very nice."

"Before we start, there's a message for you on the answering machine. Here."

Jesse punched a button, and Rosen immediately leaned forward. His daughter, Sarah, was speaking.

"Hi, Daddy, it's me. I called your boss, Mr. Nahagian, and he said I could reach you here. Don't worry, this isn't an emergency. I didn't get shot or get a C on my report card or anything. I just need to talk to you. Call me real soon, please. 'Bye."

Thinking about why she might have called, Rosen missed what Jesse was saying. "Sorry."

"I was just wondering if she's as pretty as she sounds."

"Prettier." He showed his friend pictures of Sarah in his wallet. "Fortunately, she takes after her mother."

"Not totally. She has your eyes."

"Think so?"

"Yes, and that's the most important feature. As the poet said, 'The eye is the mirror to the soul.' "

Taking back his wallet, Rosen studied Sarah's face. "I'd like to think so. Do you mind if I call her?"

"Of course not. Use the phone here. I have to check on my students downstairs. Take all the time you need."

Moving to the desk, Rosen lifted the receiver and hesitated. Whenever Sarah told him "Don't worry" there was something to worry about. When he finally dialed her number, he knew he was right.

Chapter 3

"Hello," Bess said.

"It's Nate. I got a message that Sarah called. Is she all right?"

"Are you in D.C.? I tried reaching you myself, but your answering machine said you were out of town."

"I'm in Tennessee on a case. What's wrong?"

"Nothing. I mean, Sarah's fine."

"Why did she call?" The other end went silent for several seconds. "Bess?"

"Nothing's wrong. I'm . . . getting remarried, that's all."

Now it was Rosen's turn to grow silent. Finally, he asked, "Who is he? It's not the one Sarah told me about last year, the one with dandruff who kept adjusting his underwear in public."

"No, someone else. I've been seeing him for almost eight months."

"What is he—an accountant or a doctor?"

"A doctor." Again she hesitated. "I suppose Sarah will tell you anyway. He's a podiatrist."

"You're marrying somebody who makes a living fondling other people's feet? Don't you find that the least bit disgusting?"

"Go ahead, Nate, get it out of your system. Then we can talk about Sarah."

"You said she was all right."

"She is. I mean . . . you know how she never really accepted the divorce. She fantasized that somehow we'd get back together again. Now she has to realize it won't happen. It's been hard on her. She's seeing the school psychologist."

"Is it that serious?"

"You know Sarah, she keeps most things inside. She's grown even less communicative with me. I want her to get to know Shelly—"

"Shelly's the foot massager?"

"He has two children from his first marriage, but they're grown. I want the three of us to be a family. Not for him to replace you with Sarah, but at least they should get along."

"I still don't understand. Why a psychologist?"

"Like I said, she doesn't talk much to me anymore. She cut a class—you know how seriously she takes school. And Mrs. Chang, her piano teacher, says she's not concentrating. The Young Performers' Competition is next semester. Did Sarah tell you what she did several weeks ago at an all-school assembly?"

"No."

"She was playing her Chopin piece. It was so beautiful. Suddenly, she broke into Duke Ellington's 'Satin Doll.' In front of all those people—I could've killed her. When I asked her why, she said, 'Chill out. Daddy would've liked it.' "

He couldn't help but smile. "Maybe I would have."

"That's just what I expected from you! I thought for Sarah's sake . . . Look, let's not fight this time—please, Nate."

"Sure. Let me talk to her."

"She's not here now. I'm certain she called you

to talk about Shelly and me. I want you to do something—not for me, but for her."

"What?" Rosen already knew the answer.

"I want you to make her see things the way they are, about Shelly and me and about you and me. Sarah will listen to you. She always does. Will you do that, Nate? Please, for Sarah."

He imagined Bess sitting in the kitchen, holding the receiver while wiping the counter or checking a roast in the oven. She had the same long dark hair as their daughter. Rosen remembered how it tangled in his fingers when he drew her to him and they made love.

"Nate?"

"Sure," he replied without thinking. "Sure, I'll talk to her. When are you getting remarried?"

"In a few months, during Thanksgiving vacation."

He wanted to say, "One more turkey shouldn't make any difference," but instead managed, "Well, congratulations."

"Thanks. I'll tell her you'll call Tuesday night. She'll be back very late this evening, and tomorrow Shelly and I are taking her with us to dinner. It's Shelly's birthday."

"What do podiatrists eat—fillet of sole?"

"Very funny. Thanks again, Nate. Good-bye."

Rosen held the receiver, as if through it he could see Bess at the other end. Pushing up her sleeves, she probably paddled in those fluffy slippers upstairs into bed and, sipping a Coke, finished grading papers for school tomorrow. She always waited until the last minute. He wondered if she still wore his old flannel pajamas at night. No, Shelly wouldn't like that.

"All right to come in?" Jesse asked from the doorway. He held two tall glasses.

Nodding, Rosen hung up and returned to the rocker.

Jesse sat at the desk. "Is your daughter all right?"

"Yeah."

"If you'd rather we put this off . . ."

"No, let's get right on it."

"Here, I thought you'd like some iced tea."

"Thanks, Chavrusa."

Rubbing his eyes, Rosen turned his attention to the case but knew it would take time to learn what his friend had to say. In law school, when they'd worked together, Jesse would inevitably be late with his part of the assignment. Lighting a cigarette, he would say, "It's my Southern upbringing. You all are just too caught up in your Yankee rat race." Yet, both outsiders, they were drawn to one another—Jesse as a Southerner and Rosen as one who had been raised as if in a Russian ghetto in another century. After a while, Jesse became his unofficial *chavrusa,* study partner, like the one Rosen had had in the yeshiva of his youth.

Rosen took a long swallow of tea. "This is good. Helps to wash down that science experiment the airplane called lunch. Now, about the case?"

Jesse handed Rosen a file of papers. "I've had some of my students compile a background on serpent handling. The practice began here in Tennessee in 1909, at a place called Grasshopper Valley. A farmer named George Hensley read Mark sixteen, verses seventeen, and eighteen: 'And these signs shall follow them that believe . . .' "

" 'They shall take up serpents,' " Rosen said, scanning the pages in the file. "So this Hensley began to handle rattlesnakes at his church, and others in his congregation joined in."

"Yes. From there it spread to neighboring states.

In 1938 in Harlan, Kentucky—that's coal mining country—three members of a serpent-handling church were arrested but acquitted."

"No one was hurt. I see here in 1968, in Virginia, a minister put two rattlesnakes against his temples, was bitten and died the next day. One church member was convicted by the Virginia Circuit Court of Appeals."

Jesse lit another cigarette. "That was a strange case. Apparently the man had to take the oath on the witness stand with his left hand. His right had been amputated years before, after being bitten by a rattler. There was another conviction in 1973, in Carson Springs, Tennessee. Two people died . . . not from snakebite but from drinking poison."

"Swallowing poison, not snakebite?"

Jesse nodded. "Strychnine. Remember what it also says in Mark: 'And if they drink any deadly thing, it shall not hurt them. . . .' During Friday's service, I saw Reverend McCrae and another man drink what I think was poison. Nothing happened to them."

Rosen crinkled his eyebrows. "You saw this?"

"Yes. There were other things, too. People going into fits, speaking in tongues. I didn't see it, but these churches also lay on hands to cure the sick and even handle fire without feeling pain or being burned."

Rosen stared at the paper before him, but the words were blurred. What kind of people were these serpent-handlers? The man on the airplane had called them crazy. Another nutty religious cult, but what if it wasn't? What if it was something else . . . something more familiar?

"Nate, are you all right?"

"Go on, what else?"

"Even though the two men died from drinking

strychnine, the co-pastors of the church were convicted under the 1947 Tennessee law against the use of animals, including snakes, that endanger the life or health of any person. The state supreme court upheld the conviction. In 1987 near Greeneville, Tennessee, a man drank poison and died. No one was charged with a crime. There've been at least thirty recorded cases of folks dying from snakebite or poison during church services. Even George Hensley, the man who started it all, was bitten to death in 1955. It reportedly took him a long time to die. Snakebite's real painful."

Laying the file on the floor, Rosen walked to the window. Students slowly crisscrossed the campus, going to class or lunch. They were normal kids, probably thinking about a ball game or getting a date for the weekend—anything but a few holy rollers putting rattlesnakes to their temples and drinking poison. If serpent handling were mentioned to those kids, Rosen imagined the looks on their faces. That was normal; that was the way he should feel. Why didn't he?

"Nate?"

Rosen turned to his friend. "Sorry. Guess I'm a little tired."

"Maybe we should continue this . . ."

"No, I'm all right. Jesse, you were at Friday's service. How did it strike you?"

Jesse took a long draw on his cigarette. "The truth? I don't ever remember being so frightened. It wasn't just because of the rattlesnakes, although that was unpleasant enough. It was losing control. That part of the service—how long was it, five or ten minutes?—seemed compressed into one long moment, as in a dream, where impossible things are not only possible, they're the norm." He shivered. "But this was a nightmare. Handling snakes, drinking poison, babbling in tongues."

Rosen wet his lips so that he could speak. "You didn't find any of the service . . . truly spiritual?"

"Lord, no!" Jesse laughed nervously, drawing on his cigarette. "That's like asking a rape victim if the man who attacked her had sensitive eyes."

Rosen watched his friend smoking, then asked, "How do you see us approaching this case?"

Jesse glanced down at the file. "It appears to be a straight Amendment One freedom of religion issue. Article One of the Tennessee Constitution declares that no one can interfere with the rights of a person's conscience."

"Yet your state supreme court upheld those 1973 convictions."

"There's always the U.S. Supreme Court. It refused to hear the appeal on that case. Maybe it would agree to rule on this one. Your organization would certainly like that, wouldn't it?"

Rosen said, "That's why it sent me here when you called."

"So it's really that important a case?"

"Could be. Times are changing for the worse. Our courts aren't the great defenders of the little guy anymore. Christian Scientists being convicted of manslaughter when their child died without being given medical attention, members of the Native American Church being penalized for taking peyote in a religious service. Life's getting much harder for those who are different. This won't be an easy case."

Jesse said, "Remember those mock trials in school? You always had us take the 'loser side,' as you called it. I loved watching you argue with the others. You always could argue real well. That's why I called you."

Rosen returned to the rocking chair. "Was it? Who's the woman connecting you to this case?"

"See the way you cut through subterfuge? I called you for two reasons. The first is, quite frankly, I can't handle a case like this alone. I've neither the experience nor the inclination. I'm happy running this popular culture center. It's let me remain an outsider. That's what I meant by self-actualization. That's my perfect role, the observer, the interviewer. You've always been an outsider, too, but you're a fighter. The greater the odds against you, the better."

Rosen looked away for a moment, then nodded. "All right. What's your second reason?"

Jesse leaned closer. "This woman, Bathsheba McCrae. She's young, backwoods, unscrubbed, and I find myself . . . Let's say I'm attracted to her in a way I've never felt toward a woman before."

"Jennifer Ann?"

"As Mark Twain once said, that's like comparing a lightning bug to lightning. I tell you this—you alone, because you're the only person in the whole world I can trust not to laugh at me. If my family or friends were to find out . . . it's unthinkable. Do you understand?"

"Yes."

"Besides," Jesse added, leaning back, "the case itself should be reason enough. Instruct the American people on how to respect the Constitution. What's that your rabbi used to tell you about teaching?"

Rosen smiled. "From Hillel. 'Even when I strive in my own behalf to do the right thing, have I fulfilled my obligation? Certainly not—for I must still strive to teach others the right way.' "

"That's right, Nate. Teach Earlyville the right way."

Rosen felt his heartbeat quicken, and his hand, as if an independent being, picked up the file and began thumbing through the pages. Reviewing the case, planning strategy—as always, he was excited by the battle ahead.

He began to think aloud. "It could be a question of intent. These people, these serpent-handlers, aren't using poisonous snakes with the intent of injuring themselves or anyone else. Are their actions any more dangerous than those of a race car driver who knowingly risks his life for a profit or a boxer who could well be killed in the ring? I wonder how many boxing fatalities there've been compared to people killed by snakes or strychnine . . . we'll have to find out. Perhaps there's even more than the 'intent' question. Do these people even think of what they're doing as dangerous? If it's the Lord's will . . . Jesse, we're going to need to talk to members of the congregation, especially those who were eyewitnesses to Friday's events. We need to know exactly what happened."

Jesse said, "We can arrange that this evening. And maybe the tape will help."

"Tape? What do you mean?"

Jesse reached into the top drawer and took out a cassette. "I taped the service as part of my research."

"What're you, Richard Nixon? Why didn't you tell me? Let's hear it."

Rosen leaned close to the desk, while Jesse turned on the recorder. For the next hour Rosen listened intently to the service, trying to imagine, from the sounds of preaching and praying, what had gone on. At one point he heard a woman talking distinctly, yet in a language he couldn't understand.

"That's Claire Hobbes," Jesse said. "She was speaking in tongues."

Rosen felt the sweat beading on his forehead. There was something familiar about what he was hearing, something he refused to acknowledge. Not now. The case . . . concentrate on the case. Returning his attention to the tape, he heard the police siren and the police chief's call for order. A few minutes later there was a loud bang, followed by a great commotion.

Jesse said, "Chief Whitcomb hit a chair with the butt of his shotgun. Then the rattlesnake bit Lemuel Banks."

Leaning even closer Rosen listened until Reverend McCrae was led away, then replayed that part of the tape. He had Jesse carefully recount all the events after the police arrived.

Finally, he sat back and rocked slowly while wiping his face with a handkerchief. "Those two kids downstairs, can you have them transcribe the tape now? I'll also want them to take down and type what you've just told me."

"Of course, if you think it's urgent. Is there anything else you need?"

"Make an appointment with the district attorney for tomorrow morning. Then I'll need to call the airport. I want to see if there're any flights back to Washington tomorrow afternoon. My boss isn't going to be happy about this, but at least you'll impress the hell out of your girlfriend.

"What do you mean?"

Rosen sighed softly. "Jesse, you didn't need me. This case is never going to trial."

Chapter 4

SUNDAY EVENING

If patience was indeed a virtue, then Earlyville was preparing Rosen for sainthood. He had wanted to grab some fast food and see Reverend McCrae, but Jesse insisted upon cooking dinner. While Rosen browsed through the library downstairs and the two graduate students transcribed the serpent-handling tape, their host grilled chicken in the backyard. So heavy was the aroma of barbecue sauce, it could've been cut and served on a plate. When Jesse finally struck the dinner bell, he didn't have to ring twice.

They sat at a table on the porch. The students were both sandy-haired, freckled, and polite in a "please pass the potatoes" kind of way that Rosen rarely encountered. They spoke mostly of their work at the popular culture center. Tired and absorbed in his meal, he listened not so much to what they said but to how it was phrased. Their words came in the same gentle, earnest manner that he himself had used in yeshiva discussing the Talmud with his rabbi.

Finishing his second helping of chicken and salad, Rosen said, "Best meal I've had in a long time!"

Returning from the kitchen, Jesse placed a pecan pie on the table. "My aunt Harriet made it yesterday. She's a blue ribbon winner at the county fair.

I'm cutting all three of you a right nice slice. Don't you insult my aunt by leaving any on your plate."

After the dishes were washed and stacked, Rosen said, "It's six-thirty. Can we meet Reverend McCrae now?"

"Just give me a few minutes to clean up."

A half hour later Jesse came downstairs, freshly shaved and smelling of cologne. He had changed into a burgundy cashmere sweater and gray slacks. "All set," he said, smiling.

The Porsche drove slowly through the campus, turned right on Jackson Street, and passed several blocks of nineteenth-century homes. Before each house stretched an emerald lawn with arching trees and neatly trimmed bushes. Everything was old yet looked new, like polished silver. Jesse nodded at one of the larger homes, a symmetrical two-story building with balcony and colonnades. At either end of the house was a white one-story addition, mostly full-length windows.

"That's Ben Hobbes's place. It's been in his family for at least a hundred years. Of course, around here that's not particularly old. We passed his brother's house on the last block. Not quite as big, but it'd do nicely for most folk."

They continued past the enormous First Baptist Church of Earlyville, its tall white columns resembling those of an ancient Greek temple. A series of shops led to the old county courthouse in the town square. More white columns, in front of a bell and clock tower, and in a corner of the square, the statue of a lone Confederate soldier pointed his rifle north.

Jesse said, "The statue's supposedly modeled after my great-grandfather, who saved the town from Yankee marauders during that late unpleasantness between the states."

"You mean the Civil War?"

"Hush now, you want to get lynched?"

Jesse swung the car past another dozen stores, continuing on Jackson, until a half mile later the houses hunched closer together and peeling wood replaced polished brick.

Rosen said, "I take it that Reverend McCrae isn't one of Earlyville's wealthier citizens."

Jesse shook his head. "He's probably dirt-poor, or mighty close to it. We talked for a few minutes yesterday after the hearing. He's originally from West Virginia and, like a lot of mountain folk, moved here to make a living. He worked in Nashville doing some carpentry, then came here and got a job in the furniture factory. Some of his church people moved along with him; others joined the congregation in Nashville or here in town."

"Ben Hobbes's wife?"

"I believe she's from Nashville."

They passed small slat houses. Men in rocking chairs smoked on the front porches and women hung laundry, while their children swung in tires roped over old tree limbs or played kick-the-can with neighborhood dogs. Crossing the highway, they drove into a large development of modest town homes, four to a building, each with a postage-stamp lawn decorated with flower pots and wind chimes. Jesse parked in front of the second building, where a solitary pink flamingo tilted as if nursing a broken wing.

"Reverend McCrae lives around the corner," Jesse said, getting out of the car. "This is a state housing project built about twenty years ago. Folks here nicknamed it the Last Resort but keep up the place pretty well. Since we're in the neighborhood, I thought we'd visit Aunt Emily."

"Are we going to have enough time to interview McCrae?"

"This'll just take a minute. Aunt Emily'd never forgive me for being so close and not stopping by."

The door was answered by a stout old black woman who wore a brightly colored dress and a matching scarf around her head. Pulling Jesse inside, she hugged him tightly.

" 'Bout time you come visit. Been over a month since I seen you last. Sit yourself down."

The living room was taken up by a vinyl orange couch, a coffee table, and two chairs. A few Woolworth landscapes decorated the wall, as did a framed newspaper photograph of the Rev. Dr. Martin Luther King, Jr. Jesse sat on the couch, and Rosen took a chair.

Jesse said, "This is Nate Rosen from Washington, D.C. We went to law school together in Chicago. Aunt Emily took care of me up until the time I went away to school."

"And a more troublesome child I never want to meet," she said, then laughed. "Nice to meet you, Mr. Rosen. You all just hold on a second." She walked slowly into the kitchen.

"Aunt Emily was with my family for over forty years. Raised three of her own kids—two are teachers and one's a bank officer. She always called me her fourth and biggest problem child."

Aunt Emily returned with a tray of lemonade and cookies. She placed them on the coffee table and settled on the couch beside Jesse. "My grandchillen was here last week, so look what I got. Still your favorite . . . them Oreos with the double fillings."

"We just had some pecan pie. I'm afraid I'm full up."

"Skinny thing like you! Why, Mr. Rosen, I was

ashamed to admit caring for this child, thin as an old rooster chased outta the hen house."

They laughed, and Aunt Emily said, "You, too, Mr. Rosen. Not much meat on them bones. You ain't got no call to be shy."

He took the lemonade and a cookie. "You have a very nice home."

"Thank you. This whole development was started by the government. Coulda bought an old house closer to town but who'd wanna be messin' with everything that'd need fixin'? Besides, I always wanted somethin' that wasn't a hand-me-down, somethin' brand-new."

"I understand that Reverend McCrae is one of your neighbors."

Her brow crinkled. "You talkin' 'bout the snake man? Yeah, he musta bought the place from Lettie Baines's family, after old Lettie died. You remember her, Jesse? Her daddy run that fillin' station on Crockett."

Rosen asked, "What kind of man is McCrae?"

"Don't know and don't wanna know. Tell you one thing. If he come 'round here with them rattlesnakes, I'd be hollerin' for help from the roof. What kind a' man calls hisself a Christian and be temptin' God like that?"

Rosen looked into his lemonade. "I was hoping you could tell me."

"Man like him gimme the willies. That daughter of his, though, sure's pretty enough. I see her walkin' to Burger King or sometimes drivin' her daddy's beat-up ol' car."

The color rose in Jesse's cheeks as he said between bites, "She must have lots of boyfriends."

Aunt Emily winked. "Sometimes in the evenin' sittin' on my back porch, I seen the girl sneakin' out her back door. Down the block somebody musta' come pick her up."

Rosen asked, "Why do you think she was sneaking around?"

"Ain't hard to understand with a daddy crazy as hers. 'Sides, you expect the girl to invite her boyfriend inside with all them snakes crawlin' around?" Aunt Emily shivered. "Told my grandchillen to stay far away from that house. Rattlesnakes—the very idea!"

"Has Reverend McCrae caused any disturbances in the neighborhood?"

"Man keeps pretty much to hisself. But you musta heard about that poor boy who was bit the other day. Radio said he wouldn't go to no doctor. Just prayin' for a cure. Like the Lord's gonna waste His time lissenin' to some fool who ain't got sense enough to stay away from rattlers in the first place. And this McCrae calls hisself a man a' God."

"Have you ever seen him with the snakes?"

"Lord have mercy! I tol' you nobody'd get close enough to me with them devilish things! You sure is askin' a lotta questions. You ain't one a' them snake people?"

Jesse said, "No, Aunt Emily. Mr. Rosen is Jewish."

"Jewish?" She crinkled her brow. "Like that Mrs. Shapiro who owned the clothes store in town, then died and done give away all her money to the county orphanage?"

"That's right."

"She was a good old woman. Come from Russia or some such place. Wouldn't have nothin' to do with no snakes, you hear me!"

"It's all right, Aunt Emily. You just calm yourself."

"I am calm! You ain't havin' any dealin's with the snake man, is ya?"

"We just need to see him for a few minutes on legal business."

"Legal business? 'Bout gettin' rid a' them snakes, I hope."

"Don't worry. You know I'd never let anything happen to you. Now, what's this I hear about Miss Simms telling her nieces to go to blazes?"

For the next fifteen minutes, Jesse gossiped with Aunt Emily about old friends and relations, moving so easily between living and dead that Rosen wasn't sure which was which. Births were mentioned, baptisms, marriages, and funerals; everything seemed recorded in some great magical town Bible that all the residents, like Jesse and Aunt Emily, had memorized. As he had at dinner, Rosen remembered long ago studying with his rabbi and how the old man would speak of Hillel, Rashi, and other great sages of the past, as if at that very moment they sat around the table sharing their wisdom. And so, settling back in his chair and sipping the lemonade, Rosen listened to the wisdom of Aunt Emily.

Finally Jesse glanced at his watch. "Eight o'clock already? We best be going. Still have that business with your neighbor to take care of. I'll come again real soon. I promise."

"See that you do," Aunt Emily said, "and bring this nice man with you."

As they left her house, the sun was just setting. Rosen yawned and stretched, enjoying the cool evening breeze against his face.

Jesse said, "Let's walk. After pecan pie and cookies, I could use the exercise."

Approaching the corner, Rosen saw the curb crowded with automobiles, mostly old "beaters" with bumper stickers proclaiming: HONK IF YOU LOVE JESUS. A lone police car was parked in front of a fire hydrant.

Three men lounged on the steps of the second town house. They looked like a Norman Rockwell painting in their flannel shirts rolled to the elbows and baggy gray work pants. They were speaking softly to one another about the best signs under which to harvest corn, as they nodded politely and moved aside for Rosen and his companion.

The living room, similar in size and furnishings to Aunt Emily's, was crowded with people of all ages. A crying toddler was taken up by the nearest woman, petted, and cooed, then passed along to someone else. A platter of sandwiches nearly filled the coffee table, which also offered boxes of cookies and lemon squares. Standing beside the coffee urn, a young policeman carefully balanced a pyramid of chocolate chip cookies on his paper plate.

Jesse said, "Deputy Pete Higgins, this is my friend Nate Rosen. Is Lemuel Banks getting any better from the snakebite?"

The policeman chewed thoughtfully. "Time and the Lord will tell. He's pretty much the same as yesterday. Here, you all got to try one of these cookies. Miss Ann Hensley, daughter of Jake, the hardware store owner, baked them."

Jesse took one and handed another to Rosen.

"Umm," Jesse said, "tastes so good it must be a sin. We'd like to see Reverend McCrae. It's real important."

"He and a few others are with Lem in the Reverend's bedroom. Go ahead—last room on the right."

Rosen asked, "All these people members of the congregation?"

The policeman nodded.

"How have they been acting?"

"Like normal folk worrying about one of their own." He lowered his voice. "I didn't want Chief

Whitcomb sending me over here. Didn't know if some rattler'd be popping out of the sugar canister like one of them peanut brittle joke cans. But everything's been right civilized so far. Still and all, I'm chewing my food real careful."

Rosen and Jesse squeezed through the hallway and stopped at the bedroom door. Heads bowed, three men and a young woman stood around the bed. Nearest the headboard, a broad-shouldered man with thick black hair and a square jaw led the others in prayer.

". . . and that, if it be Your will, to make the bite on Brother Lemuel's shoulder as harmless as the viper's that fastened onto the hand of Paul. For he shook it into the fire 'n' felt no harm."

"Amen," the others said.

"For Brother Lemuel has shown that same love and tried his best to walk in the path of our Lord Jesus."

"Amen." One of the other men, much older, added, "Praise the Lord and His mercy."

While the prayers continued, Jesse whispered to Rosen, "The man praying is Reverend McCrae. That's his daughter, Bathsheba. Old fella's named Tucker. Don't know the third man."

Rosen stepped closer to the bed and, over the woman's shoulder, saw Lem's walnut-colored face. His hair was plastered against his head, his eyelids half-closed, his mouth twisted into a grimace, teeth biting into his lower lip. A heavy woolen blanket covered Lem up to his armpits. His upper body was naked, and the wound in his right shoulder was black and swollen.

Soon the small congregation said a final "Amen," and Bathsheba wiped Lem's face with a cool damp cloth.

Jesse asked, "How's he doing?"

The old man said, "I seen a lot worse. It's the Lord's will, but I believe the boy will pull through."

"That's real good to hear. Reverend, this is the attorney I spoke to you about—my friend Nate Rosen."

They shook hands; McCrae had a powerful grip. He looked Rosen straight in the eyes and, unlike most people, didn't smile. He was sizing up Rosen at the same moment he was being judged.

After a long moment, McCrae turned to introduce the others. Nodding shyly, Bathsheba stepped back. She was a beautiful woman, and despite her shapeless dress, Rosen guessed that her figure was striking. Easy to see why Jesse was attracted to her and, considering her surroundings, why he wanted his feeling to remain a secret. Rosen wondered if the attraction was mutual; was she even aware of Jesse? He saw no word or gesture pass between them.

The third man was McCrae's cousin from Nashville, James Johnston, and, indeed, they were the city mouse and his country cousin. Johnston looked about the same age and his face bore a striking resemblance to McCrae's. However, he wore an embroidered cowboy shirt, jeans, and Western boots. Besides having a slighter build, Johnston wore his hair long like a rock star's and sported a gold earring.

"Call me Popper," Johnston said, grinning, while pumping Rosen's hand. "Everybody else does." Johnston was an easy man to read, the kind whose soul carried a sample case.

Rosen said, "Reverend McCrae, we'd like to speak to you about the case."

Old Tucker shook his head. "Didn't you hear what I said 'bout Brother Lemuel?"

"Even if the boy recovers, there's still the charge

of violating the state ordinance against using poisonous snakes in a dangerous manner."

"But the boy . . . !"

"That's all right, Tucker," McCrae said. "You and Sheba tend to Brother Lemuel. Mr. Rosen, let's us all go to the back porch. Popper, I expect you'll want to set with us. This way."

In the kitchen several women were washing dishes and mixing pitchers of lemonade. McCrae stopped beside one of them, a petite blonde who smiled weakly. There were lines under her eyes and her hair was disheveled.

Taking the woman aside, he spoke to her softly. "You shouldn't be here, Sister Claire. You already done enough. Best go home."

She shook her head. "I told the Lord I was going to stay all night or until Lem gets better. Everybody in this house is a witness to my promise. Ain't his pain been caused by me?"

"You stop such talk."

"If Ben hadn't called the police, then maybe . . ." She swallowed hard, her eyes glistening. "No, it's more than that. I've been bad, Reverend. Unclean."

"What're you talkin' 'bout? What's happened ain't your fault or your husband's. It's all God's will, you know that. Now I don't want our church to come between you and Ben."

"I don't wanna go home . . . can't. Ben's working late anyway. Ain't nobody for me to be home for."

The Reverend put his hands gently on her shoulders. The woman seemed so fragile that McCrae's powerful grasp would crush her. Instead, his hands seemed to uplift Claire. She stood straighter, and some color returned to her cheeks.

He said, "Go home 'n' get some rest. Make peace with your husband."

"But I promised. . . ."

"The Lord don't want that kind a' promise, seein' the pain it causes you. You go on home."

She nodded. "In another hour or so, I promise. Thank you, Reverend."

"Lord bless you, child," he replied, then led the other men through a screen door to the back porch.

They sat in creaking wooden chairs around a card table. Above the screen door a single naked bulb, obscured by dirt and swarming flies, filtered a grayish light over the men. Rosen could barely distinguish McCrae sitting across the table but felt the Reverend's eyes staring into him. In the backyard fireflies intermittently pinpointed the darkness, reminding him how tenuous his existence was in the great black void of God's endless night. A man like McCrae walked through that void certain that, in the valley of the shadow of death, there was no evil to fear, for God walked beside him. Rosen's father had walked with that same certainty, as Rosen once had, but so long ago he barely remembered.

Jesse said, "Nate is with a civil liberties group, the Committee to Defend the Constitution. He came here at my request to help defend you against what happened in church last Friday evening."

McCrae replied, "We're simple folk and don't wanna agitate the law, but nothin's gonna stop us from followin' the word a' God. It's all in the Bible, plain as day. If'n we gotta fight for the Lord's way, His will be done."

Popper said, "Amen. Gentlemen, you don't know the hardship Gideon's faced preaching the Word. His church was burned down in West Virginia. Why even here in Earlyville, there've been problems. Tell them about the break-in."

"Weren't nothin'," McCrae said. "Last week, when we was at church, somebody broke in here. Messed up my room 'n' Sheba's. Turned some drawers inside out. They didn' take nothin'—ain't got nothin' worth stealin'."

"Just more harassment. Ain't that a violation of our First Amendment rights?"

"Possibly," Rosen replied, taking the transcript of the tape from his inside coat pocket. "Reverend McCrae, I don't think you'll have to go to court, not unless you want to."

"I don't understand."

"Did you know that Jesse tape-recorded the service?"

"No, but we got nothin' to hide."

Flipping several pages, Rosen leaned close and could barely read the words in the gray light. "This section . . . after the police chief and his deputies entered the church. Up until that moment, no one was hurt by the rattlesnakes . . . is that right?"

"Yes."

"Then Chief Whitcomb told everyone to stop, that they were violating the law. He's handed a shotgun by a policeman and says he's talking about 'the law against using them rattlers to endanger anybody's life. Now I'm done talking. You best do what I say.' It's at that moment Lemuel Banks is bitten. Did Whitcomb make a menacing gesture with the shotgun?"

McCrae said, "Mister, a man holdin' a shotgun on you ain't exactly the Christian kiss."

"I understand he struck a chair, startling Mr. Banks and making him lose his concentration."

"That's right."

Rosen stretched back in his chair. "There it is. Jesse has already scheduled a nine o'clock meeting tomorrow morning with the district attorney. *If* we present this transcript, a copy of the tape, and depositions signed by Jesse and those others who attended the service, I don't think the state of Tennessee will want to take this case to court. We can argue that the service was peaceful, orderly, and nonthreatening *until* the police came. That, in fact, by his aggressive words and actions, Chief Whitcomb actually caused Lemuel Banks to be bitten. That would leave his department open to several potential lawsuits, including defaming the church and its minister, as well as a suit for personal injury by Lemuel against Whitcomb. Not that it would ever go that far. As I said, once the district attorney sees the potential damage to the state, he'll back off."

For a minute no one spoke. Finally McCrae said, "Ain't sure I follow you. You're sayin' there ain't gonna be no court case?"

Jesse nodded. "That's right, Reverend. Once we have your permission, all Nate and I have to do is speak to the district attorney. There shouldn't be any trouble at all."

McCrae spoke directly to Rosen. "Nothin's ever easy as it seems. A minute ago you said, '. . . if we present the transcript. . . .' Why wouldn't we? Why the 'if'?"

Rosen almost smiled; there was something much more to the man. "Jesse told you I work for a civil liberties group. I was sent for the sole purpose of constructing a First Amendment defense—that the Tennessee statute against serpent handling is itself a violation of your constitutionally protected religious freedom."

After a few moments of silence, McCrae said, "You wanna put the law on trial. That it?"

"That's it exactly. Or that was it, until I heard the tape and a probable way of avoiding a trial altogether."

"Makin' your trip down here for nothin'."

Rosen shrugged. "Tomorrow morning Jesse and I will talk to the district attorney and—"

"Does it have to be that way?" Popper Johnston asked.

"What do you mean?"

"Couldn't Gideon go ahead with that freedom of religion defense and have his day in court?"

"Of course he could, if he wanted to ignore the police chief's actions and agree to make this a test case of the statute. We'd probably lose in the Tennessee courts but appeal as far as possible, even to the U.S. Supreme Court. It would take a long time, years, and require quite a personal commitment on Reverend McCrae's part. What's your interest in this case, Mr. Johnston?"

"Call me Popper." His fingers drummed the table. "Guess I could tell you a pack of lies but, as Cousin Gideon knows, I'm done with lying. Lying, smoking, drinking, gambling, drugs—done with all them, thanks to Cousin Gideon and the church. He saved me, just the same as pulling me out of the fire."

"The Lord saved you," McCrae said.

"Well, you were sure His instrument. And it's my intent to help you spread the Lord's word the best way I know. This here trial Mr. Rosen's talking about could help."

"How's that?" Rosen asked.

"I used to work in Nashville managing singing groups. Maybe you heard of the Taylor Family, the Jonesboro Outlaws, Grandma Sara Salter. No . . . well, I made good money handling them. One thing I learned in the music business, it pays to advertise.

Last few months I've been trying to convince Cousin Gideon that religion can work the same way. You seen all them preachers on television who don't have near the power of the Lord over them. I'm working right now on a deal with a local network that could send Cousin Gideon's message to thousands of folks. And that's only a start. Course, it's hard for a newcomer breaking in."

Rosen said, "That's where a court case could be very useful. All that free publicity . . ."

"Yeah."

". . . putting Reverend McCrae at the forefront of the struggle for religious freedom. All those news articles, talk shows . . ."

"Exactly!"

"I can just see him and his snakes with Geraldo Rivera."

Popper clapped his hands. "You understand my meaning exactly." Turning to his cousin he added, "See how this could spread the Word of the Lord? See what this could do for all of us? What do you say?" His fingers drummed the table nervously.

McCrae looked at Popper, until the other man's hands fell to his sides. Then he said, "I appreciate what you're doin' for the church, as long as you never forget that it's for the church 'n' not any one man in it. As for this here trial, like I said before, I ain't one to go botherin' the law. A man's gotta fear the Lord first, then respect the law, otherwise what kind a world would there be? You see enough a' Sodom on any city street. Drinkin', gamblin', women dressed like whores 'n' call it fashion, fornicatin', men layin' with men—shameless, all shameless! It's a wonder God don't wash the whole world away like hosin' out a stinkin' garbage can."

He stopped to rub a shirtsleeve across his forehead, while his breath grew slow and heavy. Coughing loudly, he added, "Let these here gentlemen fix things quiet-like so there's no fuss."

"But Gideon . . ."

McCrae shook his head. " 'But he made hisself of no reputation, and took upon him the form of a servant, and was made in the likeness of men. . . .' If our Lord and Savior chose to humble hisself, then that's the path we all must take." To Rosen, "I want to thank you kindly for your help, you and Mr. Compton. Will you need me to come down with you to the district attorney?"

"No, but Jesse and I had better be going. We have that nine A.M. meeting with the D.A. If all goes according to plan, the charges against you should be dropped. That means I probably won't be seeing you again."

The four men stood; once again he shook McCrae's hand. The Talmud said never rush to judgment, and Rosen hadn't. Still, he hated to leave town without knowing the kind of man McCrae really was. The man who wound serpents around his arms for the same reason that he, as a boy, wound the leather phylacteries around his. Was that same God he had fled still so close? Looking into McCrae's deep, dark eyes, did Rosen see mocking him that old reflection of himself?

Chapter 5

MONDAY MORNING

District Attorney Paul Grimes was a thin man with hands like talons. His balding pate accentuated a large hooked nose and, sitting behind a mahogany desk, he moved his head from side to side while reading, as if both eyes couldn't focus together. His eyes were the color of autumn drizzle.

Across from Grimes, Jesse lit a cigarette and was glad that Rosen sat beside him. The D.A. had admitted them immediately; that was the least he could do, since he and Jesse belonged to the same country club. Grimes seemed a bit nervous, idly jotting a few notes. It was damn awkward. At least Rosen could do most of the talking and take care of this unpleasantness as quickly as possible. Closing his eyes for a moment, Jesse thought of Bathsheba and how, after dropping Rosen at the airport, he'd drive to her house with the good news. They would go for a walk, perhaps he'd ask her out and she'd agree. The movies, if her church permitted it, then . . .

"Sorry to keep you gentlemen waiting," Grimes said, folding his hands on the desk. His fingers didn't quite fit together. "Hello, Jesse. How's your mamma? I hear she's still in the hospital."

"Doing as well as expected. Pneumonia is very dangerous at her age."

"What isn't?"

They both smiled.

Grimes said, "I must admit my surprise at finding your name as defense counsel for this . . . Gideon McCrae. I didn't realize you still practiced law. It's been years, hasn't it?"

"I've always thought that law was like riding a bicycle. Once you learn, you never forget."

"Yes, well, I mean, in a case like this . . ."

"Paul, this is my friend Nate Rosen. He works for the Committee to Defend the Constitution."

"Don't believe I've heard of that organization."

Rosen said, "It's similar to the ACLU."

The D.A's smile faded like snow under a hot sun. "I have another meeting at ten o'clock. Shall we get down to business?" He turned to Jesse. "I take it you're representing this Gideon McCrae."

Rosen said, "*Reverend* McCrae."

"I'm afraid my department's going to pursue this case. It's more than a simple disturbing the peace. Your Mr. McCrae was in clear violation of Tennessee law by bringing poisonous snakes into his church. That's assuming Lemuel Banks doesn't die. If he does, then the charges may—"

"Banks's condition is improving," Jesse said. "He should make a full recovery."

"Let's hope so. If you're here because McCrae wants to plead guilty and save the state some time and money, maybe we can talk about a reduced sentence. But he needs to stop breaking the law. We don't want any more trouble from him or his church. In fact, he might consider leaving the county."

"Reverend McCrae has assured us that he doesn't want to make any trouble."

"Well, he's showing good sense."

Rosen asked, "Mind if I play through?"

"Excuse me?"

"I get the feeling you both think you're at the country club and regard Reverend McCrae as a little unpleasantness, like a shower on the eighteenth hole."

"I really don't understand. . . ."

"Why is it so important to bring this case to trial?"

The D.A. shuffled some papers as his skin slowly turned the color of cold shrimp. "He broke the law."

"There's more to it than that. Reverend McCrae and his people weren't even disturbing the peace. They were inside a house of worship minding their own business."

"You're an outsider, Mr. Rosen. Where're you from . . . New York?"

"Washington, D.C."

He shook his head. "What'd you think when you first heard about McCrae and his rattlesnakes? I'll tell you. 'What do you expect from a bunch of redneck crackers?' Well, that's not what we want folks thinking of Tennessee. We don't go rolling 'round on the floor, frothing at the mouth, ripping off our clothes and screaming 'Jesus! Jesus! Jesus!' That kind of behavior's more common to the crackheads of Washington, D.C. Heroin, cocaine, street gangs with Uzis—you got yourself a real jungle there."

Jesse said, "Now, Paul, you must admit we have our share of problems in Earlyville. What about that story in the paper about a man arrested for selling marijuana two blocks from the courthouse?"

"I'd hardly equate a little problem with marijuana to the hell that's breaking loose all over the country."

"I didn't mean . . ."

"Besides, that's not the reason you're here."

Rosen said, "I agree. We're here to discuss the Constitution and Reverend McCrae's First Amendment rights."

"Don't give me that crap. Want to play first-year law school? What if your religion commands you to make human sacrifice? We're talking about a man who endangers others with poisonous snakes. You know damn well any freedom can be restricted when you threaten the community."

Grimes and Rosen stared at each other like two gunfighters.

Jesse crushed a cigarette butt, then lit another. "Nate, shouldn't you show Paul the transcript and my deposition?"

From his inside coat pocket, Rosen handed the papers to the D.A., as well as a copy of the cassette. "Jesse was at the church Friday night. As part of a research project, he recorded the entire service, which has been transcribed. We'd like to call your attention to pages sixteen and seventeen, where I've marked them, as well as the last page of Jesse's sworn deposition."

Grimes reworked the crease down the center of the papers until the manuscript lay flat. He began with page one, bending forward and shifting from eye to eye every few pages. After he finished, he returned to page sixteen and reread the next two pages. Then he carefully reviewed Jesse's deposition.

The intercom buzzed, and his secretary said, "You've got that ten o'clock appointment with the zoning commission over at the courthouse."

Rubbing his eyes, he replied, "Tell Bud Henshaw I might be a few minutes late. Hold any calls." He looked at Rosen. "I don't see this making a bit of difference. On the contrary, it establishes that poisonous snakes were used in the service conducted by Gideon McCrae and that Lemuel Banks was bitten by one of them."

Rosen said, "You're not having your calls held to tell us that."

Sighing as if bored, Grimes began collecting a set of papers, placing them in his briefcase. "Why don't you enlighten me? Just what does it mean?"

"It means the service was peaceful until Chief of Police Whitcomb disturbed the congregation and made menacing gestures with his shotgun. His striking the chair startled Banks, so that he lost control of the snake. One could argue that the police caused the disturbance and Lemuel Banks's subsequent injury. The statute itself is vague, using the term 'to endanger the life or health of any person.' Reverend McCrae and his congregation certainly don't believe their lives were endangered in any way . . . that is, *until* the police broke in on their service. If the state decides to prosecute, the church or Lemuel Banks individually may wish to take legal action. This could be very messy for your office, and you'd lose."

Grimes folded his hands and tilted his head, looking at Rosen as though he were looking at a piece of carrion. "So much for your high-minded principles, eh, Counselor? You're a wiseass . . . a real wiseass. What happened to the constitutional issues involved?"

"My organization would love nothing better than a test case, but in the interest of our client—"

Grimes's intercom buzzed. "Sorry to interrupt, sir, but Chief Whitcomb's on line one and says it's urgent."

Keeping his gaze on Rosen, the D.A. picked up the phone. "What is it?"

As he listened, Grimes's eyes grew wide. "Yes, just terrible." A minute later, "Is the press there?" Then, "Don't let them get on to anything until you see me. Everything goes directly through me. I'll cancel all my afternoon appointments. As soon as you finish, come right over. I don't have to tell you how important it is to do a thorough job."

He hung up, absently stroking the receiver as if it were a kitten. "Terrible, just terrible."

Jesse asked, "What is it?"

Taking out a handkerchief, Grimes wiped his forehead. "Ben Hobbes died last night in his home."

"Good Lord! What happened?"

"Whitcomb says—" The D.A. caught himself. "The investigation's just begun. We'll know much more after the lab work and medical examiner's report."

Rosen asked, "You're not assuming it's natural causes?"

As Grimes stared at the attorney, the corners of his mouth rose slightly. "You can read all about it in the newspaper." Holding the transcript of the church service, he added, "I really must thank you all for bringing me this information. It should prove most enlightening. Now, I must be going. Jesse, remember me to your mother. Good day, gentlemen."

They left the new county building in silence. Several times Jesse was about to speak, but his friend seemed a world away, occasionally shaking his head. It was nine forty-five; Rosen's plane was scheduled to depart at one. Inside the Porsche, Jesse turned on the engine, then cut it abruptly.

"What is it, Nate?"

"Will we pass Ben Hobbes's house on the way to the airport?"

"Sure, but . . ."

"Let's go."

As they drove up Jackson Street toward the college, traffic slowed considerably. Near the corner where Ben Hobbes had lived, a police car with its flashing red light blocked the oncoming lane.

"Turn here," Rosen said as they reached the intersection.

Jesse had to drive another half block, past several police cars, before finding a space. He parked just beyond the alley that ran behind the homes facing Jackson.

"What's back here?" Rosen asked.

"Garages. The alley gives the people on Jackson access—also for deliveries and garbage pickup. What's this all about? Why're we here?"

Rosen strode up the block. Shaking his head, Jesse followed his friend to the corner. A crowd had gathered behind a yellow wooden barrier, while a policeman directed traffic around the squad car blocking the lane. Chief Whitcomb stood on the front steps of Hobbes's home conferring with someone facing away from Jesse. When Whitcomb returned inside, the other man, holding a camera, turned and walked toward them.

"Hello, Cousin Bobby," Jesse said.

As the photographer stepped around the barrier, the two men shook hands. "Been a long time, Jesse. Not since Aunt Harriet's birthday. You haven't seen the pictures I took of the party. You look mighty good in that herringbone jacket."

"I'd like you to meet an old friend, Nate Rosen. Say, what's going on?"

"Ben Hobbes died last night. Won't that make folks around here jumpy, what with all that talk about closing the factory?" He shook his head. "Glad to be outside. Poor Mrs. Hobbes having to sit in there with her brother-in-law, as if she hasn't suffered enough."

"How'd Ben die?"

Cousin Bobby glanced at the crowd. "Come over to my car."

They walked back to an old green Toyota. He lowered his voice. "I don't rightly know what happened."

"You took pictures of the body."

"Yeah, but . . . he was lying on his belly across his bed, covers all twisted around him. Phone off the hook, glass of milk knocked onto the floor. I don't know, Jesse."

Rosen asked, "Were there any marks on the body—gunshot, knife wound, punctures?"

Bobby shook his head.

"Did it seem like he'd been struggling with anyone?"

"I don't think . . . you know, maybe I shouldn't be talking to you all. I could get in trouble."

"Why? Is there anything to hide?"

"I don't know, mister. Lab boys come and gone. Police dug samples from the carpet. I don't know. I better get going. Chief Whitcomb wants these pictures this afternoon. Remember, Jesse, I expect you next week for little Peggy's confirmation."

As Cousin Bobby pulled away, Rosen said, "We've got to get inside."

Jesse crossed his arms. "I'd surely appreciate you telling me, why in the world are we here?"

"Because I'm such a wiseass. I think we'd better try the back way."

"Wait. . . ."

But Rosen didn't wait, and once again Jesse followed him. They walked down the alley and stopped in front of the Hobbeses' two-car garage. The door was up, revealing a battered pickup truck beside a new white Corvette. Next to the garage, a wrought-iron fence enclosed the backyard with its trimmed hedges, gazebo bowered by a pair of giant oaks, and a policeman standing guard on the porch steps.

"Let's try going through the garage," Rosen said.

The door to the house was unlocked and opened into a small hallway that, in turn, led to the kitchen. As large as most folks' living room, the kitchen was an odd combination of traditional wood cabinets crafted from deeply veined oak alongside the latest built-in appliances. A trestle table with six chairs stood on a polished plank floor of tongue and groove, the kind it felt good to walk on in stocking feet.

In contrast to the kitchen's quiet dignity, the table was covered with Styrofoam cups, pieces of stale doughnuts and cigarette butts squashed like brown beetles inside tin ashtrays. A rough oak two-by-four leaned against a counter near the sink.

Looking at the mess, Rosen said, "Police central."

They walked through the doorway into a formal dining room with its crystal chandelier, china cabinet, corner hutch, and an eight-foot table filled with more garbage, including a half-dozen Dunkin' Donut bags. They continued into the hallway, only to be pushed back by two policemen.

One was black, the other white—both young and clean-cut, the type who might advertise underwear in a Wal-Mart flyer. All four men looked at one another, not quite knowing what to do.

Rosen said, "Mr. Compton and I have just come from the district attorney's office. We're here to see Chief Whitcomb." He handed his card to the black officer.

The policeman studied the card, then said to his companion, "I'll go tell the chief. You'd better watch them."

A few moments later Rosen brushed past the second policeman. "There's something I've got to tell Whitcomb. Come along, Officer."

Again Jesse followed and found his friend in the foyer beneath another large chandelier. The walls were paneled in dark wood, with an old-fashioned umbrella stand in the corner. The two policemen flanked Rosen, and he faced Chief Whitcomb, who scratched his head while looking at the lawyer's business card.

"How in the world you get in here?"

"The garage door was unlocked. We thought it best to enter unobtrusively, so as not to alert the press. We know how District Attorney Grimes wants to keep the lid on this."

"My deputy here says you just been with the D.A."

"That's right. We're representing Reverend McCrae and his church concerning the incident that occurred Friday evening. You know my colleague, Jesse Compton."

"Oh, Jesse. How are you?"

"Nice to see you, Chief."

"I didn't quite follow what this here feller was saying. You're doing some lawyering again?"

"A little."

Rosen said, "Mrs. Hobbes is a member of Reverend McCrae's church. We wanted to offer her any help that she might need."

"I still don't understand."

"We'd like to see Mrs. Hobbes."

"I don't believe I can allow that. Mr. Grimes gave strict instructions—"

"We've just been with the district attorney."

"That true, Jesse?"

He didn't like this; Rosen was close to causing a scene. Still, it was too late to back down. He nodded.

Whitcomb said to one of his men, "Please ask Mrs. Hobbes to step out here for a moment."

"Which one?"

"The young one."

A minute later, Claire Hobbes walked into the hallway.

"Someone been asking for me?" Steadying herself like a drunkard, she stared at Jesse, her brow furrowing slightly. "I know you?"

He nodded, barely recognizing the woman. Her pleated bathrobe of robin's-egg blue was buttoned awry, so that she seemed a pale scrawny bird breaking from its shell. Her face was lost behind eyes raw from crying.

Jesse said, "I was at the church service Friday night."

Her head cocked slightly as she walked toward him. "That's right, you were there. You must be a friend of Reverend McCrae. He sent you here to comfort me."

"Well . . ."

"Yes," Rosen said. "You could say we're here because of Reverend McCrae."

"Is he coming?"

"He probably doesn't know what's happened."

She shivered and, moving closer, clutched Jesse's arm as she had during Friday's service. He was afraid the woman would again fall into tongues, but she pressed her lips together and spoke only with her eyes, red and glistening.

"Perhaps we'd better stay," Rosen said. "Mrs. Hobbes appears to be in no condition to face this ordeal alone."

Whitcomb glanced from the woman to Jesse. "I wanted to call her doctor, but she wouldn't let me. I don't like seeing anyone in such pain." He paused. "All right, you two can sit with her a spell, but I'd appreciate you not interfering with my men. Mrs. Hobbes, best if you joined the others."

She wouldn't let go of Jesse as they walked into her living room.

The plank flooring, paneled walls with built-in bookcases, and stone fireplace at the opposite end identified it as a "man's room." On either side of the entryway stood an antique grandfather clock and a rolltop desk. Straight ahead a leather couch and love seat were arranged kitty-corner around a dark oak coffee table. Three Hobbes rocking chairs drew near the table. Behind the couch, two large windows faced Jackson Street. Between them hung a magnificent quilt with patches of brown and green hunter's hues. At the far end of the room, adjacent to the fireplace, a doorway led into what appeared to be a greenhouse.

Claire Hobbes joined Jesse on the love seat near her in-laws. Simon, Ben's younger brother, sat with his wife on the couch, while their son Danny stretched lazily in a rocker. Simon was a softer version of his brother, his sharp nose and close-set eyes modified by a double chin and rounded belly. His hair was as gray as Ben's but longer and styled. He wore a powder-blue seersucker suit, with a white shirt open at the throat, and puffed a pencil-shaped black cigar. Smoke trailed from its tip thin as a spider's thread.

His wife, Ruth, clasped her hands, rough from working in the garden. From Kentucky, she was what people called "a handsome woman"—broad-shouldered, with high cheekbones, a broad nose, and laugh lines at the corners of her dark eyes. Her skin was copper-colored like her grandmother's, a full-blooded Cherokee. She kept her long raven hair up with a tortoiseshell comb. As a boy, Jesse remembered walking past her backyard and watching Ruth, wearing a halter top, wash her hair in a large basin. It would spill over her shoulders like quicksilver and, when she stood, cling wet and gleaming all the way to her waist.

Danny was about thirty, the youngest of three children: a married daughter lived in California while the older boy, a Marine, had died in Lebanon. Danny had inherited Simon's light skin and sharp features, but his dark hair and wide-set eyes were his mother's, giving him an Oriental cast. His tight polo shirt and jeans emphasized a strong muscular frame. Not that he was used to physical labor. People said the only thing he worked hard at was sex.

Rosen and Whitcomb sat in rocking chairs across the table from the Hobbeses. Taking out a notebook, the police chief flipped through the pages.

"Let's see here. Looks like I got everything from you folks. You all can go on home. I'll let you know if there's anything else we need you for."

Simon Hobbes folded his arms. "What do you mean, we can go home? You still haven't told us what the hell happened here . . . what really happened."

"Medical examiner needs to run tests on the

body. Once we get his report plus results of the lab workup—"

"Cut the crap, Whitcomb! Something ain't right here."

"Until we can prove otherwise, it looks like your brother had a stroke around midnight, give or take a few hours."

"Bullshit. My brother was never sick a day in his life."

Danny said, "It could've happened that way, Daddy. Sometimes those things just—"

"Shut up. Ben was too mean to die of natural causes. You put a double round of buckshot into him, he'd spit out the pellets and ask for dessert. Something ain't right. Are you gonna tell me, or do I have to see Grimes myself?"

Whitcomb looked as if he had just tasted spoiled chicken salad. "Sorry, Mr. Hobbes, that's all I can tell you now."

Ruth touched her husband's arm. "Leave the man alone. He's just doing his job."

"Hmph. Maybe *these* fellers know something. You two more cops?"

She said, "Don't you recognize Bedford and Lilian Compton's boy? How are you, Jesse?"

"Just fine, Miss Ruth. Real sorry about this."

"Compton?" Simon Hobbes repeated. "What're you doing here?"

Jesse glanced at Rosen, who said, "We're here at your sister-in-law's request."

"And who're you?"

"My name's Nate Rosen."

"I don't understand. You a friend of this here woman?" He nodded curtly at Claire.

"We're representing Reverend Gideon McCrae

concerning an incident that occurred in his church last Friday evening. I'm sure—"

"Damn it! I knew that snake man was somehow mixed up in this. I warned Ben. Course he couldn't see past this here young female he picked outta that church. She blinded him . . . her and that snake man. Whitcomb, there's something ain't right."

The police chief stared at his notes. "There's nothing I can tell you—don't know nothing yet. That's the Lord's truth."

Ruth Hobbes leaned forward. "We ain't lookin' to make your job hard, but something's peculiar. Else why all these folks taking pictures and scraping Lord knows what from the floor?"

"Like what?" Rosen asked.

She nodded past him, toward the opposite wall, where two windows faced the backyard.

He asked the policeman, "Can I take a look? I won't touch anything."

"Guess it wouldn't hurt."

Whitcomb led Rosen to the wall. Both windows were built of the same dark wood used to panel the walls. The right window was broken near the sill; a few bits of glass lay on the sill and floor. Jesse watched his friend examine each window carefully. Rosen tried to raise the unbroken window, but it was latched at the top. He squatted and pointed to where a dirt mark had darkened the floor directly below the right window. His finger followed traces of dirt that grew fainter as they led from the wall.

"What's outside?"

The police chief said, "Flower bed."

"Anything disturbed?"

"I'd rather not say right now, but we're doing a thorough investigation."

"Did you remove any glass from the floor?"

"No." Bending closer, Whitcomb half whispered, "Sure looks like somebody broke in. Can't be sure, just yet, that the intruder killed Ben Hobbes, but sure is suspicious."

Rosen shook his head. "If someone broke in from the outside, he would've cracked the glass much higher. Where it's broken, he couldn't reach through and get his hand high enough to unlock the clasp. Besides, most of the glass is on the outside, meaning the force of the blow came from inside the room. Someone wanted you to think this was a break-in."

Rosen studied the marks, then once again looked at the floor. He asked, "Will you let me take a look upstairs where the man died?"

Whitcomb was studying the window intently and scribbling furiously into his notebook.

"Chief, can I look upstairs?"

"Uh, sorry. No way, unless you get clearance from Mr. Grimes. I believe it'd be best if you left. Ain't nothing you can do for young Mrs. Hobbes. She needs a doctor or a preacher . . . well, a doctor anyways."

Jesse glanced back at Claire. She looked so fragile, a dying flame consumed by its own grief. Why was he here, a voyeur spying upon a family's misery? Why had Rosen insisted upon coming?

"Nate, let's go. You don't want to miss your plane."

"All right," Rosen said softly, still looking at the window and floor as if waiting for them to tell him something. "All right."

They walked across the room to the foyer. Jesse paused and nodded good-bye. Simon Hobbes lit another cigar and waved him away, while young

Danny uncurled from his rocker and watched Claire dabbing her eyes. He seemed about to walk toward her, when his mother bent close and whispered something, making him settle back into the chair.

The two men left the same way they had entered, through the garage. Reaching the Porsche, Rosen sat on the hood and looked back down the alley.

Jesse said, "Your plane."

"I'm not leaving today. Could you put me up a little longer?"

"Of course. What's this all about?"

Rosen shook his head. "I'm not sure, but that business with the window. I think Ben Hobbes was murdered."

"No." When Rosen didn't respond, Jesse continued, "Even if it's true, why'd you want to come here? What do we have to do with it?"

"Whom did Ben Hobbes hate? Whom did he recently threaten?"

"You mean Gideon McCrae?"

Rosen nodded. "Maybe McCrae took those threats seriously. Maybe he decided to do something first, before Hobbes carried out his threats."

"That's nonsense."

"Is it? Your cousin Bobby said there weren't any marks or signs of violence on the body. How else can you kill a man?"

"I don't know . . . poison?"

"What did you see McCrae sipping last Friday night?"

Jesse leaned heavily against the car. "Oh, Lord." He suddenly felt dizzy and broke into a sweat. "Maybe the police don't know about all that."

"Sure they do. We told them. Remember the

transcript, and how 'enlightening' Grimes said it might be?"

"That's right. No, I can't believe Reverend McCrae could do something like that."

"It doesn't matter what we believe. If the D.A. can make a case against McCrae, he will. Who better to put on trial than the leader of a snake cult? A little bit of California right here in Tennessee. Won't Grimes just eat it up."

"What're we going to do?"

Rosen gave a short, hard laugh. "I don't know. But I'm such a wiseass. I'll think of something."

Chapter 6

TUESDAY MORNING

Rosen awoke to a soft ringing, like an alarm clock slowly running down. Reaching toward the night table, he fumbled for the alarm that wasn't there. The noise was a telephone somewhere down the hall. He glanced from his watch, which read 9:05, to the light melting like butter around the edges of the shade.

Yawning, he sank back in bed and tried to recall his dream. Something about his ex-wife, Bess. They were walking in a park, like the one in her old neighborhood where he had proposed. He had been trying to tell her something. What was it?

"Nate?"

Wearing a burgundy silk robe, Jesse stood in the doorway. With a towel he was wiping some shaving cream from his cheek.

"That was Popper Johnston, Reverend McCrae's cousin, on the phone. You were right—it's a murder charge. He wants me to come right down to the courthouse."

Rosen swung his legs over the bed. "That damn transcript must've supplied the motive. Johnston want you to arrange bail for McCrae?"

Jesse began to nod then shook his head. "No, you don't understand. The police have arrested Claire Hobbes, not McCrae."

Rosen remembered her from the day before, thin and frightened and half out of her mind. What were the lab results? How had Ben Hobbes died?

Jesse said, "It's been a long time since I've done any criminal law. I'd appreciate your coming along."

"Sure."

"Are you going to wear your corduroy jacket?"

Rosen rubbed his eyes. "What?"

"You wearing the same jacket as yesterday?"

"Uh . . . I guess so."

"I've got a paisley tie that will make it almost presentable."

Rosen smiled. "I feel better already."

A half hour later they arrived at the courthouse in downtown Earlyville. Gideon McCrae and Popper Johnston sat on a bench a few yards from the entrance. The Reverend wore a green work shirt and slacks; Johnston sported a sharkskin suit and cowboy boots.

"Thanks for coming," Johnston said, pumping both their hands. "Sister Claire was arrested around eight this morning. The one call she made was to Cousin Gideon. We need to have you gentlemen arrange bail."

McCrae took Rosen's arm. "Popper, you 'n' Mr. Compton do what has to be done. I need to talk to this man here."

Jesse hesitated, but Johnston said, "I know exactly where to go. We can get Sister Claire processed real quick. Come on."

After the other two men went inside, McCrae said, "None a' my congregation never been in trouble like this. Want ya t'know that Sister Claire is an upright woman. Wouldn't hurt a fly."

"I hope you're right."

"The Lord knows she's innocent, but that don't seem enough for the state a' Tennessee. That's what I wanted to tell ya. Now about your fee . . . ?"

"There's no fee."

"I appreciate that, but we don't take no charity."

"Reverend McCrae, my organization is privately funded for the purpose of protecting people's constitutional rights. That's what brought me to Earlyville—the serpent-handling charges against you. If the D.A. drops those charges, I don't know how long I'll be able to stay. Perhaps a day or two."

"Well, then, the Lord will provide." He extended his hand.

McCrae spoke with a quiet dignity common among working men, but again there was something more. Rosen saw it in the Reverend's dark eyes and felt it in the grip of his handshake.

It unsettled Rosen, so he said, "When Jesse first told me someone had been arrested for murdering Ben Hobbes, I thought he meant you."

McCrae's expression remained unchanged, as did his tone. "Why's that?"

"Because of what Hobbes said at Friday's service. How you were hurting his wife and that he'd get you for it."

"We're used t'threats and mockery. That's why the Lord warned us t' separate from unbelievers. Ben Hobbes was an unbeliever. Couldn't stand that his wife loved the Lord even more'n she loved him."

It was maddening, the way McCrae diverted Rosen's questions with talk of love and God. Too simple an answer for anyone but a simpleton or a saint, and Rosen didn't believe the Reverend was either.

"Don't you think Ben Hobbes had the right to

protect his wife from harm—the poisonous snakes?"

"When Daniel went into the lions' den, did he have anything t'fear? When the Lord's hand is on your shoulder, what can hurt you?"

" 'The Lord is my shepherd,' " Rosen half whispered.

"That's right. You do understand."

Rosen turned away to stare at the statue of the lone Confederate soldier. In a way they were the same, the granite rifleman's resolve and McCrae's simple faith in God's will. The more desperate the situation, the greater their belief. He shook his head. It seemed so perverse, and yet . . .

Johnston appeared in the doorway. "They're bringing Sister Claire to the judge now."

"Already?" Rosen asked.

"When we mentioned the name Hobbes, everybody jumped. Besides, the district attorney was real nice about moving things along. He and Jesse seem right friendly. Jesse went to get Sister Claire."

A wide hallway stretched the length of the interior, with courtrooms on either side. Plaster walls were painted a green that had faded to the color of old dollar bills. Near the entrance, Rosen expected to find policemen standing beside an X-ray machine, ready to search briefcases and purses, but instead an old man with red suspenders sat behind a newsstand with boxes of candy on the counter.

"We're in Courtroom B," Johnston said, pointing to the second door on the left.

It was a handsome old room. Fluorescent light emanated from an overhead circular fixture about ten feet in diameter. Beneath its soft glow, six rows of benches led to a railing with a swinging gate. A crescent-shaped wooden barrier separated the jury box, to the left, from the two attorney's tables. Flags of the United States and Tennessee, droopy as sails under a listless sky, stood on either side of the judge's bench.

About a dozen people sat in the courtroom, the usual assortment of defendants, attorneys, and witnesses. Women in matching blouses and skirts clutched their purses, hoping to beat a parking ticket; another in a supermarket uniform snapped her gum, probably waiting to testify in a shoplifting case. A short stocky man with a thin blond mustache stood with his lawyer and a young prosecutor before the judge, getting a continuance on a charge of selling marijuana.

As the defendant and his lawyer walked up the aisle, Johnston whispered to Rosen, "I got to run an errand or two. I'll be waiting for you all in the lobby."

A side door opened to admit Jesse and Claire Hobbes, followed by District Attorney Grimes carrying a manila folder. Grimes whispered something to the young prosecutor, who sat down. While the D.A. handed the folder to the judge, McCrae took a seat in the back row and Rosen approached the bench.

The nameplate read JUDGE WILBUR HALLECK. He was a small round man with mint-green eyes who peeked over the bench like a frightened rabbit. His nose wiggled, trying to adjust the bifocals he peered through. Reading the folder he cleared his throat. "My, my, this is a serious charge."

Grimes's left hand gripped the lapel over his heart, and he cocked one eye toward the judge. The fluorescent light encircled his balding head, as if he were some beatific vulture awaiting sainthood.

"That's why I personally wanted to bring this

matter to Your Honor's attention and ask that the accused not be allowed to post bond. The state believes she killed her husband in a cold-blooded fashion. Moreover, she is a relatively recent member of our community and, therefore, has no real roots in Earlyville. One might even call her a transient. She may have access to her late husband's wealth, using it to flee the state's judicial system. In addition . . ." He paused for emphasis. "This woman is a member of an unsavory cult. We all know what kinds of perversions these people can perpetrate. Remember Charles Manson."

The judge's eyes widened—Rosen expected him to disappear under the bench. "Uh . . . who is representing the defendant?"

Jesse said, "I am, Your Honor."

"Jesse Compton? Why, I haven't seen you here in years. I didn't know you still practiced law."

Grimes said, "I've been told it's like riding a bicycle."

"What's that?" The judge scratched his head. "I do hope your mamma's feeling better. You give her my regards."

"Yes, Your Honor," Jesse said.

"Fine man, your daddy. I do believe he was about the best bridge player I ever did see."

"Your Honor, this is Mr. Nathan Rosen, an attorney from Washington, D.C. He'll be assisting me."

Rosen said, "Your Honor, we ask that this woman be released on her own recognizance. Contrary to what the district attorney has said, Mrs. Hobbes was married to one of the most prominent citizens in Earlyville and has established roots in this community."

Grimes gave a long shake of the head. "They'd barely been married a year. Up until that time, to the best of our knowledge, she was a transient, traveling with her church like it was some circus sideshow."

"Your Honor, our client resents this constant reference to her church as something unsavory or evil. Her church is not on trial—"

"We'll see about that," Grimes cut in.

"Because the district attorney has nothing else to use against our client, he resorts to guilt by association, linking her to a church that, though unpopular, has not been convicted of any criminal act. It is patently absurd to refuse bond to someone like Claire Hobbes."

"Well, well," the judge muttered, pulling the papers toward him. "Mr. Rosen does have a point. Of course, this is a most serious offense and, therefore, a bond of some significance does seem to be in order. Shall we say . . . one hundred thousand dollars? I trust you gentlemen will find that satisfactory."

"As Your Honor wishes," Grimes said, nodding slightly. "We ask that the preliminary hearing be set as soon as possible."

Rosen nodded. "The sooner we hear the specific charges the better."

Judge Halleck smiled, pleased he could make both sides happy. "Of course. Shall we say a week from tomorrow at . . . uh . . . nine o'clock? Good." Turning to the bailiff he said, "Next case."

A policeman touched Claire's arm, about to lead her back through the side door.

Rosen said to her, "We need to discuss posting bond."

She looked at him with vacant eyes.

"Mrs. Hobbes?"

Turning, she let herself be led away.

Jesse said, "Come on, Nate. We'd better talk to Reverend McCrae. He'll get through to her."

As the three men left the courtroom, they found Grimes waiting near the door. He drew Rosen into an alcove, then took a gold watch from his vest pocket, as if considering how much of his valuable time he could spare.

Finally Grimes said, "I have some good news for your client—your other client, that is. We sent a doctor to examine Lemuel Banks. It seems he'll fully recover. Therefore we've decided to drop the charges against Reverend McCrae."

"Was it because you knew the case was a loser, or because you figured to take care of McCrae and his church by putting Claire Hobbes on trial for murder?"

" 'Why' isn't important. You just run along and tell McCrae the good news. Then keep running all the way back to Washington. With the serpent-handling case closed, your organization's services are no longer needed."

"Aren't they? I'm not so sure. That crack to the judge about Claire Hobbes belonging to a cult and that little dig about Manson. You are bringing her church into the murder case."

"That's no longer any of your affair."

Feeling his face grow warm, Rosen fought hard to control his temper. He was angry at the D.A.'s arrogance but, even more, angry at his own complicity. That damn transcript he'd given Grimes . . . Rosen was certain it figured in the charges against Claire Hobbes. And the fact that Grimes was handling the case himself meant two things—it was a big case and he thought it was a sure thing.

Rosen said, "This must be an election year."

The D.A. pursed his lips, then allowed a small smile. "Isn't it always?"

Rosen had taken the wrong tack trying to put Grimes on the defensive. "Look, I may be here another day or two to help Jesse Compton prepare a defense. Would it be possible to see the evidence against Mrs. Hobbes? The medical examiner's findings, the police and lab reports?"

"They should be available for Mr. Compton this afternoon."

"Would we be permitted to examine the crime scene, Ben Hobbes's bedroom?"

"Yes. We took the seal off this morning. Look around to your heart's content."

"You made a very quick arrest. The evidence must be—"

"If you're planning to pump me for information, I can save us both some time. On the night of the murder, Mrs. Hobbes came home about nine-fifteen; we have a witness to substantiate that. Her husband arrived about a half hour later. He died from poison in his milk—strychnine, to be precise. The same kind of poison used in the serpent-handling service. Claire Hobbes had both motive and opportunity, and we have physical evidence to back up the charge. She's guilty as sin."

Rosen asked, "Has she confessed?"

"No, but how many murderers do? I'll tell you something strange—she didn't deny the charges. Didn't say anything."

"You must have more than that. You said you have a motive. What is it?"

"That Mr. Compton will learn at the preliminary hearing. I don't want to take away all the surprises. You'll excuse me." The D.A. took a step then paused. "You know, Rosen, I wouldn't mind you working on the defense. Jesse Compton's too new at this. Besides, we move in the same circles, and there are proprieties. But you bring in a certain foreign element."

"You mean I'm a Jew."

"Let's just say, an out-of-town lawyer, from Washington no less. You'd stand there like a lightning rod taking everything I threw at you, until your case just finally burned itself up. Ashes to blow away in the wind."

While Grimes walked away, Rosen bit his lip to prevent some bit of sarcasm that would only make things more difficult for his friend.

Reverend McCrae stood at the candy counter with Jesse, who bought a roll of breath mints. Popper Johnston was grinning, emerging from a telephone booth in the corner.

"I talked with Ben Hobbes's banker. Hobbes and Sister Claire shared a joint checking account. Banker wouldn't tell me how much, but there must be plenty. I explained the situation, and he's sending someone over with a cashier's check for ten thousand dollars. That'll take care of the bail, and she'll be out within the hour."

Rosen said, "For a layman, you seem to know a lot about the legal system."

"I been in court more'n most lawyers. I seen it from the other side. Course, that's all in the past."

"When Mrs. Hobbes is released, Jesse and I will take her home. We need to look over the house, especially the bedroom where her husband died."

"You want Cousin Gideon and me to go along?"

"No, that won't be necessary." Depending on what they found, Claire Hobbes might need to stay away from Reverend McCrae during the trial.

"Just as well. I wanted to drive into Nashville

with Cousin Gideon. We're gonna talk serious business with some folks about expanding his congregation."

Rosen said, "I almost forgot. The district attorney's dropping all serpent-handling charges against Reverend McCrae."

McCrae shrugged. "Don't seem to matter much, seein' the mess Sister Claire's in. This mean you'll be leavin' town soon?"

"I don't know. I don't like the way Grimes tried to link Ben Hobbes's murder with your church—guilt by association. I'd like to monitor the case at least for the next few days."

Johnston said, "We may hold on to you for a spell after all. Like the Good Book says, the Lord works in mysterious ways."

Fifteen minutes later a well-dressed young man carrying a leather slipcase scurried into the building. Putting his arm around the bank clerk, Johnston led him up the stairs, Jesse and McCrae following closely.

Rosen walked from the courthouse, blinking in the sudden morning light. He sat on a bench and, looking past the statue of the lone Confederate soldier, saw downtown Earlyville spread before him like an open hand. The old-time drugstore, the Country Inn, antiques shops, white-haired gentlemen taking deliberate steps with their canes, children tumbling from the soda shop—as if he were thumbing through a box of old postcards.

Rosen understood such a world, for he had been born into one like it, although the people he watched on Jackson Street wouldn't have understood. He had once performed his own daily rituals—prayer and studies—with the same quiet devotion. Perhaps that's why the murder angered

Rosen; it didn't belong in Earlyville. There was, of course, the moral indignation against taking a human life, but also a sense of violation—like a poisonous snake suddenly striking on a path that had always been safe.

Fifteen minutes later the four men walked from the building with Claire Hobbes. While Johnston chatted about "liquidity" with the young banker, McCrae placed his hands on the woman's shoulders and spoke softly. Nodding to Rosen, he led his cousin and the banker toward Jackson Street.

Rosen joined Jesse and Claire Hobbes. This was the first time all morning he'd really noticed her; earlier he'd been too busy sparring with the D.A. She was probably attractive, but that would've been after a good night's sleep, a little makeup, and a skirt tailored to show off her figure instead of the shapeless green dress she was wearing. Her skin looked waxy; the only color was the red of her eyes, red like open sores. It was as if a leech had attached itself to her soul.

Rosen sat in the front seat of the Porsche and, while Jesse drove to her house, glanced at Claire through the rearview mirror. She stared at the wadded tissue in her hands, occasionally dabbing her eyes and wincing. Did she even know where she was?

She was like a little girl, reminding Rosen of his daughter. He was supposed to call Sarah tonight. What would he say—should he practice his arguments as he did before a case? She had been hurt so much already. He couldn't add to that pain.

Jesse stopped the car at Claire's backyard gate but kept the motor running. "I thought this would be better, Mrs. Hobbes. No one to see you come home. Give you some peace and quiet."

"Good idea," Rosen said, helping Claire from the car. "Aren't you coming, Jesse?"

His friend's cheeks darkened. "I have to run a few errands. I can pick you up later."

"That's all right. It's such a beautiful day, I'll walk home."

Rosen led Claire through the backyard into her house. They stepped into a narrow utility room, where a doorway opened to the kitchen. The mess made by the police remained on the table, stale cigarette odor hanging in the air. The rough piece of oak still leaned against the counter. Opening a window, Rosen watched as Claire stuffed the table litter into one of the doughnut bags. She worked absently, as if from habit.

"Claire, do you know who I am?"

She kept cleaning. "Uh-huh. Some lawyer."

"My name's Nate Rosen. I've been working to help Reverend McCrae."

At the mention of McCrae, the woman looked at Rosen hard. Blinking several times, she relaxed a bit. "Reverend told me not to worry, to trust the Lord. I'm sorry, Mr. . . . ?"

"Nate."

She looked around, then rubbed her forehead. "Where's my manners? Please sit down. Can I get you something?"

"Actually, I am hungry . . . went off this morning without breakfast. It looks like you could use something to eat as well."

"Let me fix you something." She tried to smile. "Ben was always bragging on my cooking."

"That would be fine. While you're making breakfast, do you mind if I go upstairs and look at the room where your husband was . . . where he died?"

Swallowing hard, she said, "First bedroom on the left."

"Could you give me a scissors and some plastic wrap?"

A stairway led from the foyer to the second floor. The hallway displayed rows of old photographs, tracing the Hobbes family back before the Civil War. Rail-thin frontiersmen with their dour-faced wives stared at the camera as if it were a gun.

Opening the bedroom door, Rosen thought at first he'd made a mistake. The small room, almost monastic, contained one twin bed with curved head- and footboards resembling a sleigh, a chest of drawers, a night table with a telephone beside the bed, and a closet with a few changes of clothes. The walls were bare. Above the night table, a single window overlooked Jackson Street.

There was nothing to indicate murder. Only the bedsheets, twisted and touching the floor, appeared out of the ordinary. Examining the bed, he saw a few small stains where liquid had spilled onto the sheets, then dripped to the floor. A small piece of sheet had been cut out and the floor scraped, no doubt by police looking for evidence. Taking the scissors and plastic wrap, Rosen did the same thing, putting the samples into his shirt pocket. While on his knees, he noticed a tiny shard of glass, which he also took. Something else. Glancing at the electric socket and phone jack below the night table, he saw that the telephone wire had been cut.

He looked out the window. A man was standing on the sidewalk in front of the house. Wearing a cheap green suit tight at the shoulders, he appeared solid as a ham shank. He noticed Rosen, and for a moment their eyes locked. He had thick coppery hair and a broken nose, and his eyebrows looked like pieces of Brillo pad. Checking his inside coat pocket, the man took a step toward the house, paused, then walked away.

Rosen checked the other three bedrooms on the second floor. One was used for storage, another for guests, but the third—by far the largest—would have suited the Queen of England, with a canopied bed, long chests of drawers, full-length mirror, and two rocking chairs—all furniture handcrafted in the early-American style that was the Hobbes trademark. The brush and comb on the dressing table were silver, and the open closets displayed enough clothes to fill a boutique.

Also on the dressing table lay a copy of Elizabeth Barrett Browning's *Sonnets from the Portuguese*. Rosen turned to the bookmark, at Sonnet XXXV:

> If I leave all for thee, wilt thou exchange
> And *be* all to me? Shall I never miss
> Home-talk and blessing, and the common
> kiss. . . .

A sheet of paper was tucked under the book. Someone had begun a poem:

> My heart can only beat when I'm with you,
> To no one else will I ever be true.
> If we two are kept apart . . .

He wondered whether Ben Hobbes was the kind of man who would appreciate her poetry. Rereading the sonnet, he felt a sudden chill—was Claire's poem intended for her husband? What would her next line have been?

Walking downstairs, Rosen smelled the aroma of freshly brewed coffee mixing with that of ham sizzling in the pan. He should have told her . . . no . . . what was the difference? After all these years, what was the difference?

She was standing by the stove, spearing slices of ham and dropping them onto a platter. She had placed two settings on the table, and he sat in front of a steaming bowl of what appeared to be mush. After pouring the coffee, Claire sat across from him.

He asked, "What's this?"

"Haven't you ever eaten grits before?"

"No . . . I . . ." He remembered his conversation with the man on the airplane. He tasted a spoonful—bland but filling.

"You might like some butter on it. Hope it's smooth."

"Yes, just fine."

"Ben always said how nice and creamy my grits tasted. The kind you get in restaurants got lumps big as your knuckle." She served the meat. "I suppose you never did eat real country ham."

Rosen shook his head. "I didn't grow up eating pork."

"Why not?"

"My religion. I'm Jewish."

"Oh, like that Mrs. Shapiro folks tell about. Gave all her money to an orphanage. All I can say is that you sure been missing some good cooking. Sorry I ain't had time to bake. Got drippings in the pan there for some red-eye gravy that'd be right good with biscuits." Her eyes began to glisten. "How Ben loved my cooking."

The ham tasted sweet, with a trace of salt. Every time he ate pork, Rosen imagined an angel in heaven putting another tick mark against his name. How would the angel score Claire Hobbes? Was the woman really as innocent as she seemed? "You liked cooking for your husband?"

"Ben said I cooked good as his momma. Meals was our best time together. Breakfast and supper here at home. I'd bring his lunch to the factory, and we'd walk a spell after."

"Is that where you first met, in the factory?"

She nodded. "I grew up in Nashville. That's where I met Reverend McCrae and some other church folk. I came with them to Earlyville. Most of us got jobs in the furniture factory. I worked in the kitchen. Ben courted me in the old-timey way, flowers 'n' all. His first marriage. Imagine, at his age."

"Was it also your first marriage?"

"Yes."

He didn't ask about her poetry; it seemed too intimate a question. But in time it would have to be explained.

Instead, he asked, "You and your husband got on well? I couldn't help notice upstairs that you each had your own bedroom."

She looked into her plate. "Ben's idea. He bought all that nonsense to pretty up my room but said it was too delicate for the likes of him. Why're you asking?"

"The prosecution will want to know your relationship with your husband—how well you got along, that sort of thing. Claire, why do the police think you killed your husband?"

When she looked up, her eyes grew wide, but there were no more tears to cry. "I heard them talking about poison. That I put poison in the milk Ben drinks before going to bed."

"Let's back up. The night of the murder I saw you at Reverend McCrae's house shortly after eight.

He told you to go home and get some rest. What time did you arrive home?"

"The police asked that. It was around ten. Ben was already home."

"Don't you mean you came home before your husband?"

"No, it was after."

"The district attorney has a witness who claims you arrived home at nine-fifteen, a half hour before your husband. According to what you're saying, you must've stayed at McCrae's until about nine forty-five. Can anyone who was with you confirm the time?"

Claire shook her head. "Everybody was so worried about Lem, nobody paid any heed of time. I was out back by myself for a spell, thinking things over, then kinda slipped away without telling no one. I felt bad about leaving Lem, but the Reverend said I should be with my husband. I only know when I got home, 'cause the time was on the car radio."

Rosen said, "Let's put the time discrepancy aside for now. When you arrived home, did you speak with your husband?"

"No, but I saw a light under the door of his room." She glanced at the rough oak board against the counter. "He even brought that home, fixing to make me a shelf above the sink for my flowers. Since it was so late, I thought we'd talk in the morning."

"Did you usually prepare his milk?"

"Uh-huh, but not that night. I come home too late."

"And what did you normally do, just heat it?"

She nodded. "He drank this special kind of milk—acidophilus—took me three months before I could say the word right. I started to get his milk. I saw a new carton in the refrigerator; delivery boy must've brought it earlier that afternoon."

"You called in a grocery order?"

"Uh-huh. Do that from time to time. Our next-door neighbors, the Duncan sisters, let the delivery boy in. We was out of milk and a few other things, so I called the grocer from Reverend McCrae's about three o'clock. Didn't want to leave poor Lem to go shopping."

Rosen said, "So you didn't arrive home until that night, long after the groceries were delivered."

"That's right. When I got home, I went to the refrigerator and started to take the carton out but saw Ben'd already opened it. Figured he'd fixed his own milk. The police found a glass broke all over the floor next to his bed. They were talking poison."

"Do you keep any poison here, like an insecticide?"

"I . . . I don't think so. How could they think I killed Ben?" Suddenly she stared at Rosen, as if seeing him for the first time. "I'm scared."

Rosen sipped his coffee. "Last Friday night at the church service, your husband threatened Reverend McCrae. He accused McCrae of doing something to you, something evil. Do you know what he meant?"

Claire shook her head hard, but over his coffee cap, Rosen watched her knuckles grow white clutching the table edge.

"How could they say I killed him?" she demanded.

"I don't know," he said, putting down his coffee. "Let's finish breakfast, then try to find out."

Chapter 7

TUESDAY AFTERNOON

After dropping off Rosen and Claire, Jesse returned to Jackson Street. Near the corner a big man with a crooked nose stood beside an old Ford Granada with Davidson County license plates—maybe a salesman from Nashville. Crossing the highway into the Last Resort housing project, Jesse parked in front of Reverend McCrae's house. He straightened his tie in the rearview mirror and popped two breath mints into his mouth.

Lemuel Banks sat alone on the front porch steps. The black man wore a sleeveless T-shirt that exposed arms thin as chicken wings. The swelling in his neck and shoulder had gone down, but the wound still appeared irritated, black at the center. Head bent over his guitar, Lem strummed the melody of an old Negro spiritual, "Lord, Take This Burden," while half singing, half humming the words.

"That's a beautiful old song," Jesse said. "The center has a recording of Hattie Daniels singing it."

Lem continued playing softly. After a few minutes he stopped and looked up. His face looked more like a skull, with his skin tight at the forehead and dark in the hollows of his cheeks.

"I know you?"

"Jesse Compton. I was at the Friday evening service. I'm an attorney representing Reverend McCrae. You looked mighty poorly Sunday night. Glad you're feeling better."

Lem shrugged. "Lord wanted me healed. I praise Jesus for His mercy."

"That was mighty brave of you to refuse medical aid. You must have a powerful faith."

"I can read, mister. Bible come right out and tell a good Christian to follow the five signs a' Mark. That all I be doin'."

"Yet you were bit."

"Yeah." Strumming the guitar softly, Lem continued, "My fault. Sometime I get so carried away by the preachin' 'n' singin' that I don't wait for the Power to come over me. That's what happened. I touched the serpents without the Power comin' over me 'n' got hit. Reverend McCrae always warnin' us be careful. Never mix your own will with that a' the Lord. If'n you do, you be askin' for trouble. Guess I know better next time."

Lem played another old spiritual, his soft humming almost a moan. For folks like him and Reverend McCrae, music was the same as religion—simple, deeply rooted, and intensely personal. A man read the Bible and followed its dictates. That was all, and that was everything.

Jesse said, "I have good news. The district attorney's decided not to prosecute Reverend McCrae for what happened to you."

"Sure glad to hear it. Any trouble brought on him was my doin'. Now there be more trouble. I feel bad for Sister Claire. Ain't no way she'd hurt anyone, especially her own husband. You her lawyer, too?"

"Well, yes, at least for now. Say, is Reverend McCrae's daughter around? I need to talk to her."

Avoiding the other man's gaze, he added, "It's very important. Legal business."

Lem looked down at his guitar. "She busy."

"I won't take much of her time. I came down from the courthouse to give her some important information. Is she inside?"

Lem adjusted one of his guitar strings, playing the chord until it sounded in tune. "Guess it'd be all right, you the Reverend's lawyer 'n' all. She out back."

Jesse walked around the house to a small yard. The area was scrubby with patches of dry grass, a few dandelions providing the only color. A chicken-wire fence surrounding the yard had long ago rusted, and its posts tottered every which way like a group of giggling schoolgirls.

The screen door opened, and Bathsheba walked barefoot down the porch steps. She wore a long lemon-colored dress with sleeves rolled up to the elbows, and her arms cradled a large wicker basket, upon which lay a folded blanket.

"I heared you talkin' t'Brother Lemuel, so I went inside 'n' fixed us a nice lunch. Thought you might like goin' on a picnic." He watched her dimples grow as she smiled.

"Why, I'd love to go. I don't have to teach a class until this evening."

"Good. I gotta work later this afternoon, but we got us a few good hours till then."

"I came to let you know that the state's dropping all charges against your father. He won't be prosecuted."

"Your doin'. I knew you was a good lawyer. We're all beholden t'ya." Her smile faded. "How's Sister Claire?"

Jesse wondered if Bathsheba expected him to

free the woman with as much ease. "It may be a difficult case."

"My daddy says t'trust the Lord, but I'm awful worried. Since Friday's service, she's been in such a sorry state."

"Nate Rosen and I will do everything in our power to help her. I don't want you to worry."

"Looks like we're beholden to ya again."

Jesse didn't know what to say, so he nodded and lit a cigarette. "Here, let me help you with the basket—looks pretty heavy."

"That's all right. You could fetch what's over against the porch. Yeah, that's it."

He picked up an odd-looking contraption. Its handle was long and thin, similar to a golf club, but at the end was a leather loop. He didn't like the way it felt in his hand. "What is it?"

Again she smiled, walking with him to the front yard. "We call it a snake-catcher. Use it for rattlesnake huntin'. Ooh, I ain't never been in a fine car like this."

Jesse was afraid to ask anything more about it, afraid he might jeopardize their being together. After all, he was on a date with Bathsheba; she'd actually invited him. After all those hours worrying how he'd ask her out. Maybe she was joking about the snakes. There weren't any rattlers in these parts . . . were there?

Bathsheba leaned out the window, so that the breeze gently tousled her curls. When her hand went across the soft leather of the backrest, he imagined her touch on his own skin.

He asked, "Where to?"

"That field by the furniture factory. It's pretty, lots a' wild flowers 'n' a stream."

"That's Hobbes private property. Isn't there a wire fence . . . ?"

"That's back a ways, stretches across a cornfield leading up t' the holler. There's plenty room off the highway. 'Sides, don't that land belong partly t'Sister Claire? Seems like her friends got just as much right t'use it as anybody."

Jesse turned onto the highway and drove toward the factory. He couldn't imagine her father or anyone else from her church saying what she just did, acting . . . well . . . acting pushy. Bathsheba was dirt-poor and uneducated, but during the few times he'd seen her, she seemed different. Jesse's own mother acted that way all the time—parking next to a fire hydrant, chatting with her friend during the middle of a movie, or putting $10,000 in a shoebox so it wouldn't be taxed. But those were things rich folk did, not someone coming barefoot down from the mountains.

Bathsheba reached down to scratch her thigh; the dress rode up and stayed above her knees. Her skin was incredibly smooth and tan; in comparison his was fish-belly white. Staring out the window, did she notice him glancing at her legs? An oncoming truck rumbled close, its horn blaring for Jesse to stay in his lane. A few minutes later the Porsche reached the open field.

She said, "Pull in there . . . that's right."

Jesse parked where the overgrown grass had been beaten down by numerous tire ruts. A NO TRESPASSING sign tilted on its post. About a half mile to their right stood the furniture factory. Straight ahead the land, mostly prairie with a few clumps of trees, merged into a cornfield that sloped toward a ridge just below the horizon.

She said, "Why don't you leave your jacket in the car? It's mighty warm."

As they stepped from the car, Jesse looked at the ruts. "Have you been here before?"

"A time or two. Mostly Lem come out here huntin'." She gave the basket to Jesse and took the blanket and snake-catcher. "You mind walkin' some? Stream up yonder's mighty pretty."

"Fine." He looked down at her bare legs and feet. "But if there are poisonous snakes in the area . . . shouldn't we be careful?"

"Don't pay them rattlers no mind. It's the hottest part a' the day. S'long as we stay away from any paths or shady places, we'll be fine. Here." She put her hand on his arm. "Just stay by my side. This way."

Jesse felt the sweat slide under his shirt as they passed the NO TRESPASSING sign. He'd never broken the law; as a boy he'd never even been late for school. He was a little afraid but, even more, excited by her hand upon his arm. She stepped lightly over the uneven ground, while he occasionally stumbled in his attempt to keep up. Every few minutes she paused, without complaint, to let him catch his breath. Finally they reached a small stream that meandered down from the ridge. Bunches of blue and yellow wildflowers played hide-and-seek among the tall grass.

"This'll do fine," she said, beating down an area about four feet square and spreading the blanket. As she and Jesse sat, two honeybees buzzed lazily above them. "Hope you like what I brung."

Opening the basket, Bathsheba took out bread, a platter of ham and cheese, macaroni salad, cookies, and a large fruit jar filled with lemonade.

"Oh my," Jesse said, "this is some spread."

"Lots a' folk brung food during Lem's sickness. We ain't never gonna eat it all. 'Sides, you look like a man who needs some good cookin'."

He wiped his face with a handkerchief. "That ham sure does look good."

"Here, let me fix you a sandwich."

Bathsheba sat, legs tucked under, and made his lunch. Mouth parted, the point of her tongue licked her lower lip as she handed him the plate. One of her curls had become tangled just above an eyebrow. He longed to smooth it back into position but didn't dare. Besides, maybe if he touched her, this would all disappear as if a dream. It was beautiful, that curl, black and lustrous and coiled like a . . .

Suddenly he put his plate down.

"Jesse, you all right?"

He nodded. Taking out his handkerchief, he wiped his face again.

"You went all white real quick-like. The food's all right?"

"Yes, it's fine." He took a long swallow of lemonade.

While Jesse ate his sandwich, she nibbled bits of ham and cheese. For a long time neither spoke. They listened to bees humming among the flowers near the stream and watched a few clouds puff like smoke in a pale blue sky. As a boy he'd sat on the edge of a stream day after day waiting for the fish to bite. Not that he'd enjoyed fishing, but there had been nowhere else to go and nobody else to be with. In all that time, he never remembered hearing the bees or watching the clouds. Eyes turning inward, all he'd seen was what he'd felt—the sweet pain of his own unhappiness. Whenever things had grown too difficult, he would sit very still, feel that sweet pain and everything bad would go away for a little while. Now, staring at Bathsheba's smooth brown legs tucked under her body, he was feeling that pain, only it had never been more intense.

"You're awful quiet," she said. "Sure you're feelin' all right?"

He took another drink of lemonade. "I've just been enjoying the day. You were right about this place—it is beautiful. As a boy I used to go fishing in a stream like this . . . no, it was never like this. Never as beautiful."

Bathsheba tilted her face toward the sun, fluffing her hair so that one tangled curl shook free. Her moist skin glistened, and he thought how soft and warm it would feel.

"It's like this back home," she said, stretching her legs so that they were almost touching him. "Used to go off into the woods 'n' spend the whole day pickin' berries. Swimmed naked in the river. Course, that was before Daddy found the Lord 'n' became a preacher. His life turned whole around. Guess mine did, too."

Jesse tried not looking at her legs. "What was your father like before?"

"A mean man, rough as a cob. Used to drink a lot. He come down hard on lots a' men. I saw him once break a feller's head fightin' over a woman. But one day that changed. Friend took him to a church meetin' out in a field, under a brush arbor. Know what that is?"

"Yes, I've seen them. It's a frame made of branches and covered with leaves and such."

"My daddy heared the Lord that day. The power come over him like lightning, knocked him to the ground, shook him around 'n' left him sweatin' like he was dying a' fever. 'God shook me like a rag doll!' he told folks. After that day he never did touch no drop a' whiskey or swear or break any a' the Commandments."

"When did that happen?"

"I reckon 'bout ten years ago. He's been upright ever since."

Her brow crinkled slightly; perhaps too much sun. The sun was hot. Jesse felt a bit light-headed, as if he'd been drinking. "And you?" he asked. "Do you share the same beliefs?"

Bathsheba turned away, so that he couldn't see her face. "Ever'body knows the answer to that question. It's in the Bible plain as day. 'Honor thy father.' "

Jesse nodded. " 'And thy mother.' You've never talked about your mother."

Staring into the horizon she almost whispered, "And I never will." She slowly rose to her knees and put the food and dishes into a plastic bag, leaving the basket empty.

"How 'bout we take a walk," she said, reaching for the snake-catcher.

Suddenly Jesse felt the same chill he had in church, when the wooden box was opened. He lit a cigarette and inhaled deeply. "Are there really rattlesnakes in this field?"

"If there wasn't before, there is now. Last Friday, man my daddy knows come to Earlyville from east Tennessee. Brought a crateload a' rattlers—eight big 'uns. We used three in the service you was at. After seein' what that policeman's shotgun did to those three, the feller dumped the rest in this here field. Best way he figgered t'hide 'em. Lord knows, it's sure gonna be hard enough findin' 'em."

"Aren't you afraid?"

"Why? They's just poor dumb critters. I'd rather

hunt rattlers than cross the highway when them college kids get liquored up." She stood, the basket in one hand and the snake-catcher in her other. "If you'd like t'stay here, I won't be long."

"No." He struggled to his feet, brushing the crumbs from his lap. "I don't want you to go alone."

"All right. Can't say I mind the company." She handed him the basket. "Just stay close t'me and watch the ground real careful. You'll be fine."

They wandered toward the ridge. The land rose unevenly, filled with thick clumps of grass and gopher holes from which Jesse expected a rattler to appear at any moment. The only sounds were crickets humming and an occasional fly buzzing around his ear.

"I wish there was a path to follow," he said.

"That's where they'd be, all right, waitin' for some critter to come along. Let's try over by them trees. It's shady there. They do like their shade."

As they approached the trees, something dashed through the grass just past Jesse's foot.

"Jesus!" he shouted, jumping back.

He fell heavily on one leg and almost knocked over Bathsheba. Trying to regain his balance, he grabbed the woman, feeling her heavy breasts tight against his chest. Her laughter made him quickly pull away.

"Only a poor little rabbit. Nothin' t'worry 'bout. Lord, you sure did scoot, like the cow jumpin' over the moon."

He laughed, retrieving his cigarette from the ground. "I suppose I looked rather silly."

"Never you mind. Ever'body's touchy first time doin' this kinda thing. Man'd be a fool if'n he wasn't. You want t'go back?"

He shook his head.

"C'mon, then. Just make sure—"

Bathsheba was interrupted by another noise, this one loud and coming from the ridge. About a quarter mile ahead stood a fence of heavy-gauge wire about four feet high. Past the fence a field lay thick with tall, green corn, through which a man hurried toward them shouting. He passed through an open gate, then locked it.

"Hey! Don't you know this is private property! Didn't you all see the No Trespassing signs?"

It was young Danny Hobbes. He wore a sleeveless T-shirt, torn jeans, and an old pair of boots, the laces frayed. His clothes were dirty and stained with sweat. Danny's gaze lingered on Bathsheba, then narrowed at Jesse.

"Compton, what're you doing here?"

"We're just out for a walk. Had a picnic . . . see." He held up the basket. "I guess we missed the sign. Sorry."

Danny moved closer to the woman. "That's all right. No harm done. Who's your lady friend?"

"This is Reverend Gideon McCrae's daughter." To Bathsheba, "Danny's the nephew of Ben Hobbes."

"That's right," Danny said, grinning. "Our family owns all this land. Guess that makes it mine." He ran a hand through his hair, and Jesse smelled the sweat from his body. Bathsheba must've smelled it, too. Danny stood matchstick close to her and said, "I got a powerful thirst. Any cold beer in that picnic basket?"

Bathsheba shook her head, then brushed back her curls. "We ain't got nothin' you'd want."

His grin widened like a crescent moon. "Don't know about that. Thought I knew all the pretty ladies in town, but guess I was wrong."

"Reckon you don't know much 'bout anything."

"Well, I wouldn't . . ."

"Leastways, that's what I hear from your aunt."

"Who?"

"Aunt Claire . . . your Uncle Ben's widder."

Danny took a step back and suddenly grew pale. He glanced around, then balled his hands into fists, not to attack but, rather, to protect himself. With his back hunched, for a moment he actually seemed smaller than Jesse.

"What do you know about Claire? What she tell you?"

Bathsheba looked at him like a mother about to scold her child, but said nothing. Her power grew, as their eyes locked and the silence lengthened. Just as Jesse had watched, during Friday's church service, the serpents gazing back at him while slowly uncoiling their smooth lithe bodies.

Finally Bathsheba turned toward Jesse. "Maybe we oughtta walk back toward the water."

Jesse asked Danny, "You don't mind us being here, do you?"

As if cold, the other man rubbed his arms. "Guess it's all right. Just stay away from the fence. I put in some hybrid corn and don't want nobody messing with it."

"We won't be going over there. I didn't know you farmed."

Smirking, he stretched back his shoulders and moved his legs apart. He reminded Jesse of Elvis. "Most folks think I can't do a damn thing. Take my daddy and my uncle Ben. They give me this piece of land like throwing a bone to a stray dog, and me their own flesh and blood. My daddy, he probably thinks this is something else of mine that'll likely go belly-up, but I'll show him. I'll show 'em all."

He took a step toward them, saw that Bathsheba's expression hadn't changed, and stopped suddenly. "I got to be going. Mama's got lunch ready."

Danny strode away toward the factory, glancing back to see they hadn't followed him. In a few minutes he disappeared from view, but Bathsheba continued to gaze in that direction.

Jesse cleared his throat. "Shouldn't we be getting along?"

Nodding, Bathsheba walked back toward the stream. She seemed preoccupied, flicking the snake-catcher against the tall grass while humming softly. Jesse had expected the worst—she and Danny walking away together, maybe to lie upon the blanket and make love, while he stood in the middle of the field, as he used to sit alone fishing the day away. But she hadn't left him; instead, Danny was the one who scurried away like a frightened rabbit. She had actually sent Danny away. Why?

He hurried beside Bathsheba and recognized the tune she was humming, an old mountain ballad called "Rose in Winter." As a boy he remembered Ruth Hobbes singing it as she washed her long black hair:

> Who'll take a thread of sunlight
> And weave it for my glove;
> Who'll bring a rose in winter
> And be my own true love?

He almost murmured, "I will."

She skipped over a rock. Following her, Jesse

nudged the rock and heard a loud rattle. He froze as the snake drew its head back to strike. Before the rattler could hit, the leather loop flicked over its head, pulling it back. Still unable to move, Jesse watched Bathsheba twist the loop tight around the snake just below its jaws, then lift it halfway off the ground. It was about a yard long.

"Little feller," she said. "If it was a fish, I'd throw him back. Open the basket."

Jesse's eyes were transfixed by those of the rattler, endless pools of darkness. It was only after a long time that he realized he wasn't staring at the snake but at Bathsheba.

"Jesse."

Blinking hard, he placed the basket on the ground. He opened it, then stepped back. "Do you need any help?"

She had already positioned the snake directly above the basket. The reptile hung motionless except for its tail, which twitched idly, the sound soft as the turn of a fishing reel. Balancing the snake-catcher's handle under her left arm, Bathsheba lowered the rattler into the basket, closing and securing the lid with her right hand. She handed the contraption to Jesse.

"I'd better carry our friend here. We'll head back now. Guess you had enough huntin' for one day. Watch where you're walkin'. Like they say, 'Where there's one, there's two.' "

Gathering the basket between her hands, she led him back toward the stream. Jesse followed closely.

Stretching back with eyes closed, Bathsheba lay on their picnic blanket, the basket about a foot from her head. Jesse sat beside her. She raised one knee, and her lemon-yellow dress slipped halfway up her thigh. His eyes followed the line between the fabric and her skin, which, in contrast, appeared even darker. As if responding to his gaze, her leg stirred slightly, the dress edging up farther.

Jesse touched the place where her skin met the fabric; his finger traced the line that seemed to melt under his touch. He moved his hand higher and found she wore no underwear. She pushed him away and, with the same motion, pulled her dress over her head. He had never seen anything so perfect; she could have been carved from stone.

But she was warmer than stone, warmer and more yielding. One arm drew him to her, another reached around his head as his lips touched her open mouth. Her teeth felt sharp, cutting his face. Tasting the blood made him stronger, and they wrestled together. He heard her breathing heavily, which made him ravage her body until, unashamed, he cried out. A few seconds later she pushed him off and, as they lay still together, Jesse realized it had not been Bathsheba's passion he'd heard. The sound came from the basket above her head. Somewhere behind the wicker—a soft steady hiss.

Chapter 8

TUESDAY AFTERNOON

Rosen had always prided himself on his memory; he could still quote sections from the Talmud, not recited since childhood. The passages were often constructed with initial letters forming a pattern, and he continued to use the same mnemonic device for other needs, like directions. "C-L-C-L-C-L": from *Claire's* house go *left,* past the *college,* then turn *left* at the *corner* with the *light.* That, Claire had said, would take him to the main highway, from where he could see the factory. She even lent him her new Corvette, which purred along Jackson Street like a kitten licking its paws.

At breakfast, once Rosen said he would help her, at least for the next few days, Claire calmed down and even smiled while reminiscing about her husband. No, the age difference hadn't mattered, maybe even made some things easier, ". . . like the way he loved me so unselfish-like." The smile tightened around her lips when she'd said that.

Rosen wasn't sure why he was still on the case. As soon as his office learned the state had dropped its charges against Reverend McCrae, he'd surely be ordered home. "Simple murders are as commonplace as corn in Kansas," his boss was fond of saying. The purpose of the Committee to Defend the Constitution was for something much more important.

Maybe he felt sorry for his friend Jesse, who alone wouldn't be able to handle a criminal case like this. Maybe he thought District Attorney Grimes would use the serpent-handling ceremony against Claire and, therefore, make her case a First Amendment issue. But the real reason, the one he'd been avoiding all along, had nothing to do with Ben Hobbes's murder. He wanted—needed—to know if Gideon McCrae was merely another Bible-thumping charlatan or if his faith was real. What did he see when he closed his eyes and held the serpent high above his head?

Rosen grimaced; it wasn't like him, letting this weakness seep into his soul. *Stay with the case—a woman's life hangs in the balance.* If only he understood Claire Hobbes better. Was she so simple and innocent? Because of his upbringing, he couldn't read women as easily as men. All those years studying with the rabbi and the other boys, knowing no women except his mother. Claire seemed a little like his mother, the way she felt at home in the kitchen, the way she depended upon a man while at the same time dominating him. That must've been her relationship with Ben Hobbes, and it was their relationship that ultimately would explain the murder. That was why he was driving to the Hobbes furniture factory.

Reaching the highway, Rosen saw the factory in the distance. After passing an open field, he slowed the car, then turned and parked on the soft rutted ground next to Jesse's Porsche. Taking a few steps he called "Jesse!" but received no answer. The Porsche was locked and seemed undisturbed; there were no signs of violence. Rosen shaded his eyes and gazed into the distance. A soft wind combed the tall grass as the land sloped toward a great ridge just below the horizon.

"Jesse!" he shouted. A few crickets hummed their reply. Probably nothing to worry about; maybe his friend was gathering mint leaves to make the perfect julep. He'd check back later, after finishing his visit.

Rosen drove another half mile and followed a large company truck inside the work yard, where it backed into a loading dock. He continued up the driveway that wound into a parking lot, pulling between a pickup and an old sports car, its front end as battered as a punch-drunk boxer.

He walked back through the work yard. The area was bustling with activity—forklifts rearranging piles of wood and transporting crates of furniture; men in hard hats, rough work gloves, and boots carrying lumber inside; a thickset man, holding a clipboard, standing by the trucks and checking through bills of lading. Behind them the factory stood tall and wide, a square city block, its barn-sized double doors yawning open.

Next to the factory was a small building labeled OFFICE, its clapboard walls freshly painted brown. Rosen walked inside to the reception area. Along the room's perimeter were pieces of Hobbes furniture—cabinets, chests of drawers, tables, folding screens, and, of course, the famous rocking chair. The back wall contained three doors to inner offices. In the center of the room, a secretary sat behind a magnificent antique desk of dark oak. She looked about the same age as the desk. Her nameplate read: MRS. VERA ATWATER.

Adjusting her glasses, which were clipped to a

turquoise cord hanging around her neck, she smiled. "And how may we help you?"

"I'd like to see Simon Hobbes."

She glanced at her calendar. "Do you have an appointment, Mr. . . . uh?"

"Rosen." He handed her his card. "No, I don't, but I was hoping Mr. Hobbes would see me." He bent closer; people tended to cooperate when they believed they were taken into his confidence. "You see, it's about his brother's death. I'm working on the case, and there are some rather important questions I need to ask Mr. Hobbes, questions I'm sure he'd rather answer in the privacy of his office. You do understand, Mrs. Atwater."

The old woman examined his business card as carefully as if she were playing bingo. "Yes, I do understand, Mr. Rosen. However, it is most unusual for Mr. Hobbes to see anyone without an appointment."

"Mr. Hobbes is in, then?"

"One moment please."

She walked to the middle office, knocked, and went in, leaving the door slightly ajar. Rosen smelled the heavy aroma of a good cigar.

As Mrs. Atwater reappeared, her boss shouted, "And keep him outta here! Keep him away from me, you understand!"

Closing the door, the secretary returned to her desk. She lowered her glasses and tried to smile. "Mr. Hobbes . . . uh . . . I'm afraid, Mr. Rosen, that he . . . uh . . ."

"That's all right. I couldn't help but overhear. By any chance, is Mrs. Hobbes available?"

"She's not in her office. I believe she might be in the factory, but I don't think it would be wise—"

"Thanks very much. You've been a great help."

Leaving the office, Rosen walked to the factory entrance and stepped through the open doors. It was not at all what he'd expected. There were no great conveyor belts or assembly lines manned by sallow workers with curved spines. No swirls of dust, deafening noise, or pervasive odor of oil mixed with metal.

He stood in an area the size of a small warehouse with a fifteen-foot-high ceiling from which a series of fluorescent lights cast a warm glow through the roomy interior. Attached to every piece of heavy machinery, piping carried sawdust up to exhaust fans, while propellers high up on the wall circulated a cool breeze. Each workman had his own station—a large wooden worktable with clamps, vises, and a power saw; a complete set of tools hung on the wall behind each man. Every set shone as if freshly polished.

Beside each workman lay several pallets, some stacked with lumber, others with pieces of smaller unfinished furniture. In one corner an old man was planing a drawer for a magnificent dresser resting beside him. Several younger workers stood in silence around him, watching his skillful hands speak a language they understood intuitively.

Watching the old man, Rosen grew at ease, smelling old parchment among the wood shavings, and for a moment the old man became a rabbi, the younger ones his students and the factory a yeshiva. No . . . he shook his head, forcing himself to see the scene before him as it really was. He would not reconcile so easily with the Great Prosecutor. All this talk of God's love and the miracle of the serpents had made him soft. What did these people know . . . really know about God's "love"? If he told them what he knew, would they dare touch a cross, much less a rattlesnake?

Rosen turned as someone shouted, "Hey, mister!"

The stocky man who had been outside with a clipboard walked toward him. "Can I help you?"

"Yes, thank you. I'm looking for Mrs. Ruth Hobbes."

"If you'll check in the office . . ."

"Already have. Mrs. Atwater said Mrs. Hobbes was probably somewhere in here."

He ran a hand through his hair. "It's getting on lunchtime. She usually meets her boy in the cafeteria. Let's check over by the loading dock first. You a salesman?"

As they began walking, Rosen shook his head. "Do I look like one?"

The other man laughed. "Nah, your cologne ain't strong enough. Most of them fellers make you want to put on a gas mask. Let's take a look in here. Why, you're in luck. See her?"

"Yes, thanks very much."

Rosen walked into the loading dock. Straight ahead a half-dozen workers rolled heavy wooden crates into a truck. To his left, an open area about the size of a classroom contained four long tables. Sitting on the end of each table, legs opened like scissors, one young woman faced another. Each was handweaving bark strips of oak or darker cherry into a wastebasket frame. Moving closer, he saw that the women wore cutoffs and Central Tennessee College T-shirts.

Walking among the tables, Ruth Hobbes looked as young as the others, her figure firm and lithe. She wore a sleeveless top and jeans, but what set her apart was her thick black hair falling to her waist.

From a far corner, a paint-spattered radio blared country music. All the women were laughing and chattering across tables. Mrs. Hobbes moved easily among them, putting her hand on one woman's shoulder while pointing to the spacing of bark on a basket, nodding when another asked a question.

Seeing Rosen, Ruth Hobbes held out her hand. It felt rough, and her grip was strong as a man's. "You're that lawyer feller. Friend of Jesse Compton's we saw yesterday at Ben's house."

"You have a good memory. My name's Nate Rosen."

"What can I do for you?"

"Nice of you to offer. I've just been to see your husband—or, should I say, tried to see your husband. I couldn't get past Mrs. Atwater."

She laughed, and Rosen liked the sound of it—strong and unashamed. "That's Simon, all right. Like folks say around here, he'd rather peck shit with the chickens than talk to a lawyer. No offense, Mr. Rosen."

"None taken. I feel the same way about most lawyers. The district attorney, for example."

"Old Paul giving you a hard time, is he? Well, he's just one to look after himself. Not half as ornery as the man before him, but you ain't here for that. This is all about Ben's widow, Claire, ain't it?"

He nodded.

"Poor Claire. She didn't kill Ben. Ain't in her to hurt anybody. She's more a child herself, poor little lamb."

"You're quite fond of her."

"With my own daughter living so far away, guess I do take kind of a mother's interest. Best I can tell, Claire don't have no family of her own. She's a gentle creature—spends hours reading poetry."

"Writes it, too."

"There, see what I mean? Anything I can do to help her, you let me know. As for Simon . . ." She shrugged.

Rosen said, "I can understand your husband being upset by his brother's death and not wanting to talk about it. However, I do need to ask him, as well as you and your son, some questions. Mr. Hobbes will have to answer them in court. It'd be better for everyone if he spoke up now."

Mrs. Hobbes glanced back at the young women, then said to Rosen, "Let's walk a little. Already enough stories being told around this here place."

They walked toward the loading dock, where the workmen were putting away their dollies. Rosen checked his watch—five minutes to noon and lunch. Passing the young women, the workers didn't even turn their heads.

"Amazing," Rosen said, "not even a wolf whistle."

"Won't allow it," she replied. "Any feller bothering one of my girls can best collect his things and head downtown to the unemployment office."

"Your girls?"

"While they're here under my roof. They're college girls working part-time to help pay their expenses."

"That's very nice of you."

She boosted herself onto the back end of a truck and slapped its fender. "This here was my education. My daddy was a fix-it man—could do anything with his hands. We were from Kentucky, mining country, but he didn't want to work underground, sucking in that black dust like his brothers. So we all packed into an old pickup truck—Mama and five young 'uns—and did a fair amount of traveling. Nobody had much time for schooling, never was in one place long enough. I promised myself two things when I growed up—to get some learning and have a piece of land to sink some roots into."

Rosen leaned against the truck and looked from her callused hands to her soft brown eyes. "You wanted what's been the dream of the Jewish people for centuries. I bet you got it."

"It wasn't easy, but I surely did. We come here to Earlyville when I was eighteen. Hobbes Factory needed a skilled furniture maker. Daddy figured what he didn't already know, he could learn right quick. I worked weaving baskets, just like those girls back there."

"That's where you met Simon Hobbes?"

She nodded. "We hit it right off. Oh, the two of us ain't much alike, but maybe that's what makes it work so well. Simon loves to holler and have his own way, but that's just the Hobbes in him. He's really sweet as molasses. Right after we was married, he let me finish high school. I practiced my talking so's he wouldn't be ashamed to take me places—not that he ever let me think he would be. Then I took some courses in accounting. Up until we got those newfangled computers, I did a pretty fair job with the books. Too much for me now, but he let me do what I wanted. Now I spend most of my time with my garden. You're gonna have to see it."

"I'd love to. Your husband sounds like a generous man."

"He sure is, and not just with me and the children. He helped set up a new hospital wing, filled the church pantry at Christmas, and . . . well, he wouldn't want me braggin' on him too much."

Rosen looked away but watched her from the corner of his eye. "All that takes quite a bit of money. The business must be doing very well. That right, Mrs. Hobbes?"

"Call me Ruth. I gotta be getting to the kitchen."

Hopping off the truck, she stumbled into Rosen.

He held her wrists gently. "We were talking about the company finances." When she hesitated, he said, "It'll all come out in the probate of your brother-in-law's will."

Ruth sighed, almost a shiver. "I know. There's something else, too."

"The rumors about selling the company?"

She stared at him. "You already heard about that? Guess I might as well tell you—papers'll be getting hold of it real soon. An offer's been made for the company." She lowered her voice, as if ashamed. "A real good offer."

"Those things happen all the time. There're constantly mergers and buy-outs. . . ."

"Not for Hobbes Furniture, a family business that's been right here in Earlyville for a hundred and nine years. The offer's been made by one of them big Japanese outfits."

"What did your husband and brother-in-law decide to do?"

"They didn't. That is, they decided two different things. Simon was for selling. Ain't no one left to carry on with the business. Our oldest, Skip, died some years ago. Betty's in California, and Danny, well, he just ain't the type to handle something this big. He'd ruin it, and it'd ruin him."

"What about Ben?"

"The pair of them, stubborn as mules. Ben wouldn't hear any talk of selling. Said that for the first time he had to think of his own family—that him and Claire might even have a baby one day.

There'd be someone to carry on the name and the business."

Rosen said, "I suppose the two of them, being so strongwilled, had some serious arguments."

"Ooh, did they."

"Maybe even violent."

"Why, one time—" She stopped suddenly and glared at Rosen. "That was a cheap lawyer trick you just pulled. I ain't saying no more about nothing."

He felt ashamed. She was right; it was one of his "cheap lawyer tricks," putting someone at ease, then suddenly grabbing for the jugular. He had always defended the practice as being in the best interests of his client, the prosecution having most of the advantages anyway. Someone like Grimes, the D.A., probably used the tactic often enough himself, which only made Rosen more ashamed. Ruth Hobbes wasn't Grimes. She had been honest with Rosen, and he had treated her honesty as a weakness.

She pulled her hands from his grasp, but her eyes softened a little. "Guess you're just doing your job—helping Claire and all. I best get my boy's lunch ready."

"Do you mind if I walk a little with you?"

She hesitated. "Please yourself."

They returned to the large area that Rosen had first entered. All the workers had left for lunch. Ruth stopped where the old man had been working on the chest of drawers.

She ran her hand lovingly along the contours of the unfinished wood. "Sure is something, ain't it?"

Rosen said, "You don't see craftsmanship like that anymore."

"That's what the name Hobbes means. My daddy never did like working anyplace so much as this here factory. Said it made him think of his granddaddy building things the old-timey way. He sure loved this place. Worked over in that corner right until he died."

Rosen touched the chest of drawers. For some reason it reminded him of the worm-eaten steamer chest in his parents' room, the chest that had carried the Torah from his grandfather's village in Russia.

"Your father was lucky. Not many of us get to live our lives without compromising belief of principle."

She laid her hand over his. "Somehow it'd be a shame to sell out. Them Japanese sure is clever, but they'd be putting in robots and computers and take the soul right out of the wood."

Rosen had always been afraid to open the chest. From all the old stories about Russia, he had expected that, if given the opportunity, demons would've leaped from the wooden box and stolen his soul. How was a young boy to know it would happen so differently?

He jerked, startled.

Ruth was shaking him gently. "You all right, Mr. Rosen?"

He smiled weakly. "I'm fine. Call me Nate."

"All right, Nate. Looks like you could use a good meal. This way."

He'd never seen a cafeteria like the one they entered. No partitions separated the kitchen from the dining area. The cooks carried platters of sizzling fried chicken and potatoes from the stove to a long serving table, where the workers simply stepped up and helped themselves. They poured water or lemonade from large pitchers. No money was exchanged. The men sat on benches at long trestle tables, similar to the one in Claire Hobbes's kitchen.

Ruth led him to the serving table, "Help yourself. Don't you be bashful."

"There's no cashier," Rosen said.

"When my husband's granddaddy built this factory, he wanted things to stay the same between him and his workers. You know, back then when a man worked for you, he ate at your table. That's another part of the Hobbes tradition. You understand why lots of folk around here think this place's kind of special and don't want it to change. But here I am talking, while you must have a powerful appetite. Go ahead."

Surveying the table, Rosen shook his head. "Thanks, but I had breakfast at Claire Hobbes's a little while ago. Sure looks good, though." He half whispered, "No grits?"

"Oh, you like grits?"

"Well, I had my first taste this morning."

"Claire made 'em for you, did she? Bet you had some country ham."

He nodded.

"With that good red-eye gravy?"

"Well, no, she said . . ."

"Shame on her. After Ben's funeral tomorrow, you come over to the house. I'm fixin' country ham, red-eye gravy, and cracklin' bread."

Against his better judgment, Rosen asked, "What's cracklin' bread?"

"You know that brown sticky mess left in the kettle after the hog's butchered and the fat's made into lard?"

His throat began to tighten as he shook his head.

"Well, that's cracklin'. You cut it into small pieces and mix it with your cornbread. When Mama made it, one bite and no matter how bad the day was, your mouth started smiling."

Rosen felt like anything but smiling.

She patted his arm. "You don't look so good. Appears you don't take to our kind of food. What in the world do you eat?"

Pouring some lemonade, Rosen drank half a glass and felt much better. "Why, there's nothing like going down to Lake Michigan and catching a bunch of gefilte fish. What a fight them little fellers'll give ya. Cook that up with a mess of matzo balls—Lord, that's what I call good eatin'."

Her brow crinkling, Ruth stared at him for a few seconds, then smiled. "Why, Nate, I do believe you're teasing me a bit."

He smiled back. "Only a bit."

"That's all right. I mean to get some red-eye gravy and cracklin' bread down your throat yet. Well, here's my boy! Whew, were you wrestling with the hogs?"

Danny Hobbes had walked into the cafeteria. He slouched somewhat, ambling like a dog. Even though his shirt and jeans were covered with dirt, his mother hugged him tightly.

She said, "All that working in the fields, I bet you got a powerful hunger. Made something special for you." She called to one of the cooks, "Jenny, please fry up that piece a' peach pie I brought over! How this boy loves his fried pie."

"Hello, Danny," Rosen said.

The young man narrowed his eyes but shook hands. "I know you?"

"We met at your uncle's home yesterday morning. I came with Jesse Compton."

"Just saw Jesse yonder in the fields."

"I noticed his car parked there on my way to the factory. What's he doing?"

The other man suddenly broke into a grin. "Says he was out on a picnic with some fine-looking woman. Too fine for the likes of him, if you ask me."

"What woman?"

"That snake preacher's daughter."

Ruth said, "You stay away from her. You know how your daddy feels about Reverend McCrae."

"Yes, ma'am."

"Now go wash up before you touch any of this good food. You look like my uncle Zeke coming out of the coal mine."

Drawing himself to his full height, he said, "I already put in a full day's work. Probably more work than Daddy's done in a week, sitting back in his easy chair, puffing on them cigars, shuffling—"

"Hush now. Get along and clean yourself up. Don't want your pie to get cold."

"Yes, ma'am." He left the room.

Ruth turned to Rosen. "Danny ain't had much luck with work. His daddy's been a might hard on him. You have children?"

"A daughter."

"Girls is different. After our older boy died, Simon expected a lot from Danny, maybe too much. The boy never did like working in the factory during summers. When Simon tried teaching him the money end of the business, it didn't do too good. God didn't give the boy no mind for figures. But, bless him, Danny kept trying. Got his daddy and uncle to let him use some of the land by the factory. Land never was much use to anybody. Simon's granddaddy grazed cattle. During the Second World War, army tried growing plants to make rope. Before he died, my older boy, Skip, thought of raising Tennessee Walkers. Course, that never did happen."

"But Danny's making a go of it?"

"He's been farming for the past few months, working by the sweat of his brow, as the Good Book says. Won't let any of us help him. Wants to make it on his own. Wants his daddy to be proud of him."

Rosen smiled. "I can see you already are."

Ruth began to blush and quickly took the plate of fried pie from the cook's hands. When she cut into the crust with a fork, the air filled with the warm heavy sweetness of peaches.

Holding a forkful of pie in front of him, she said, "I don't care what kind of food you're used to, I reckon you're gonna like this. Now open that lawyer mouth a' yours."

"Yes, ma'am," Rosen said, and he did.

Chapter 9

WEDNESDAY MORNING

Jesse let his alarm clock run down before opening his eyes. He was trying desperately to remember a dream—a beautiful woman lying in his arms and moving under him. Realizing it hadn't been a dream, he grinned and stretched broadly, running his hands over the blanket as he had over Bathsheba's smooth skin. She had been with him yesterday afternoon, more beautiful than he could've imagined, and more exciting. He didn't know what those few hours had meant to her, but they had changed his life forever. The file lying on the floor beside his bed proved it.

He had set the alarm for eight-thirty; Ben Hobbes's funeral service began at ten. Walking down the hallway, he noticed that Rosen's room was empty. He hadn't seen his friend last night, but the bed had been slept in and the window shade was raised. Rosen was probably already downstairs having breakfast. Stepping into the bathroom, Jesse turned on the shower full blast and began singing:

> Who'll take a thread of sunlight
> And weave it for my glove;
> Who'll bring a rose in winter
> And be my own true love?

After shaving and splashing on his good French cologne, Jesse returned to his bedroom and put on his double-breasted gray suit, the one he'd worn to his father's funeral. Looking at the mirror on the door, he knotted his tie in a double Windsor. It was paisley and, like all his ties, patterned in shades of muted blues and grays. Winter colors, dead colors. He would buy a new tie today—something forest green or, even better, red. Picking up the folder near his bed, Jesse walked downstairs while humming "Rose in Winter." After all, it was their song.

Rosen sat at the kitchen table, the *Tennessean* spread before him. Sipping a cup of tea, he idly turned the pages. He wore a navy blue blazer, a gray button-down shirt, and a blue knit tie. The outfit would do equally well for a funeral or faculty meeting.

"Good morning, Jesse. I didn't hear you come in last night."

"I didn't want to wake you." Jesse lay the folder on the table. "I had my Tuesday night seminar. Right afterward I consulted with some students about their independent projects, then went for a walk. It was a beautiful night with one of the constellations—Orion, I believe—shining so close, reaching up a man'd be afraid of burning his fingers. Didn't get home till almost midnight."

Rosen turned to the sports page. "I understand you and young Miss McCrae frolicked in the field yesterday afternoon."

Jesse's cheeks began to burn. "Where did you hear that?"

"Damn. Cubs lost in the ninth. Can't get any relief pitching. I'm sorry—you were saying?"

"We went on a little picnic. I wanted to tell her that charges against her daddy were dropped."

"Sure." Rosen scanned the baseball story. "I met Danny Hobbes yesterday at the factory. Says he saw you two and that your body language was more than lawyer to client."

What had Danny Hobbes seen? What had he told people? If Bathsheba's father found out, what would he do to her . . . to him?

Jesse spoke very slowly, as if each word were a bullet being loaded into a gun. "What did Danny say?"

"Hmm . . . oh nothing. Just that he saw you two with a picnic basket. What did go on between you two?"

Swallowing hard, Jesse fumbled for his cigarettes. "I . . ." He waited to light up. Then he didn't know what to say.

Rosen put down the newspaper. "This is a small town. If there is anything between you and the McCrae girl, it won't take long for your family and friends to find out. Have you thought of that?"

Jesse leaned against the counter. "I don't want to think about that now. I'm happy, Nate, for the first time in a long while."

"I'm just worried. . . ."

"Don't. Thanks, but don't. I called you because you wouldn't laugh. That doesn't mean you can't be happy for me. All right?"

Rosen stared at him for a long time, then smiled. "Say, that bread on the counter's awfully good. Did you get it from a bakery?"

"Uh, no. Miss Wilona Applebee left it on the porch yesterday. She's a cousin on my mother's side. Bakes every Monday. What that woman can do with a piece of dough. And you should taste her fried pies."

"Are you going to have breakfast? The service starts in forty-five minutes."

Jesse thought about the spread Ruth Hobbes would surely serve after the funeral. "I'll just have some bread and tea. There'll be plenty later."

"I'll bet. Ruth Hobbes threatened to inflict something called 'cracklin' bread' on me."

"Umm. S'good."

"What did you do after your date—I mean, appointment—with Ms. McCrae?"

Buttering a piece of bread, Jesse sat across the table. "I stopped to see my cousin at the county building. You know, Cousin Bobby Simmons, who works part-time as police photographer—you met him at—"

"Sure. I remember."

"Then I visited my mother in the hospital. Afterward I had a graduate class to teach. When I returned home, you were already in your room, and the light was off. I didn't want to disturb your sleep. Glad you're comfortable here."

Rosen poured Jesse more tea, then refilled his own cup. "It's all this fresh air and country living. Early to bed and early to rise."

"Aren't you going to ask what I saw Cousin Bobby about?"

"A new recipe for red-eye grits?"

"That's gravy. No." He handed the folder to Rosen. "I thought this might be of some help to our case."

Rosen opened the folder and immediately leaned over it, pushing the newspaper off the table. After flipping through the pages, he stared at Jesse. "How'd you get a copy of the D.A.'s file on Ben Hobbes's murder?"

"Cousin Bobby's wife's sister works in the D.A.'s

office. I asked Bobby to do me a favor. I did have to push him a little, but after all, I helped to get his little brother a scholarship to the college. You see, when their father died . . ."

"Hold on, I can't keep up with your family. Is there anyone in town you're not related to?"

"Black folk . . . well, some of them."

Studying the file, Rosen muttered, "Mr. Compton, such tenacity on your part. I'm impressed. You never were this ambitious in law school. What's gotten into you, or do I already know?"

But Rosen didn't wait for an answer; he was already deep into the file, removing the papers, then jotting notes on the inside of the folder. And if he had waited—what would Jesse have said? Something cornpone like "Love has made me strong"? Was that what'd happened? He'd read old Indian legends about eating the heart of one's enemy to gain his courage. Lying in the green field with Bathsheba, what had he drawn from her?

Watching his friend busily taking notes, Jesse closed his eyes and remembered their days together in law school. The others arguing a point of law, the debate growing louder, while Rosen silently flipped pages and scribbled notes. When he spoke, his voice was the softest of all, yet always silenced the others. Sometimes he didn't convince everyone, but how they listened, like children around their teacher. Jesse had been right to call him.

The scribbling stopped, and Jesse opened his eyes. One side of the open folder was covered with notes, the other had been organized into several short sections—he counted six.

"This the case against Claire Hobbes?"

Nodding, Rosen leaned back and nudged the

folder across the table. "As they say in poker, read 'em and weep."

Jesse read each section carefully:

1. *Motive*—Ben Hobbes threatened Rev. McCrae at Friday's service; Claire threatened her husband at same service (did she really love McCrae?); Simon's family said Ben was thinking of changing his will, with Claire (and McCrae's church?) the big loser.
2. When did Claire arrive home?
   a. Claire says after her husband.
   b. Celia Duncan (neighbor) says Claire arrived before.
3. *Problem*—only Claire's prints (+ delivery boy's) on the milk carton—how could this be if she's innocent???
   delivery boy dropped milk off with a few groceries at 4:30 in afternoon—no one home (Duncan sisters had key to let him in).
4. Murderer knew Ben Hobbes's habits (Claire?).
   a. two cartons of milk; only acidophilus milk (Ben's milk) poisoned; Claire's milk o.k.
   b. only bedroom phone line cut, probably to stop a poisoned Hobbes from calling for help; killer knew Hobbes would go into bedroom to drink milk.

5 Poison used to kill Ben was strychnine.
a. type of poison used in McCrae's serpent-handling services.
b. open box of rat poison (strychnine) found in garage of Hobbes's home.

6. Break-in clumsy attempt to conceal "inside job"—sign of an amateur and someone under emotional stress (Claire?).

Jesse reread the reasons several times. He felt their weight like six great stones around his neck, yet Rosen had seen them so clearly and, seeing them, would know what to do. Just as in their law school days, he would make it all right. Jesse began to smile, but the smile froze on his face as he remembered that Rosen might soon be leaving. Then the case would be his responsibility—his alone.

"Nate, about the case. Is it possible you could stay a while longer to work on it with me? Maybe your organization would let you—"

"Oh, I forgot to tell you. My boss called last night. I hadn't told him the charges against McCrae had been dropped, but he already knew. Seems he received a call from a Mr. James Johnston."

"Popper, Reverend McCrae's cousin?"

"The very same. Mr. Johnston explained everything about McCrae, the subsequent murder of Ben Hobbes, and the arrest of his wife. He argued very persuasively that Claire's arrest might, in part, be linked to her membership in McCrae's church—the freedom of religion angle. My boss agreed to let me stay on the case."

Jesse said, "That's wonderful! Popper must be some salesman."

"Of course, he had a little help. McCrae's church made a five-thousand-dollar donation to the Committee to Defend the Constitution, to help defray my expenses."

"Five thousand dollars? Where did their church get that kind of money?"

"You can't guess?"

Jesse thought for a moment. "The only person who'd have that large a sum would be Claire Hobbes, if she had access to her husband's money. They did have that joint account, the one she used to make bail. You think the donation was Popper's idea?" Rosen only stared at him, and Jesse said, "Of course."

"I don't like it. Once the D.A. finds out, and he will, he'll use the donation to link Claire and McCrae's church even more closely. That only strengthens her motive to kill Ben. The state already has your tape to prove Claire put the church's welfare ahead of her husband. Simon Hobbes and his family are ready to testify that Ben was thinking of changing his will at the expense of his wife and, one could argue, her church as well." He nodded at the folder in front of Jesse. "What do you think of our chances?"

Again Jesse scanned the outline. "Doesn't look good, does it? How can Claire's fingerprints be the only ones on the milk carton, besides the delivery boy's, if her husband poured his own glass of milk that night, like she said?"

"Claire told me that she touched the carton, saw it had been opened, and assumed her husband had already poured his own milk."

"Then why weren't his prints on the carton?"

Rosen shook his head. "That's pretty impressive physical evidence. The milk was delivered with a bag of groceries about four-thirty that afternoon. No one was home, but a neighbor let the delivery boy in. The boy put the groceries away—he did that whenever no one was home. Something else bothers me even more." He pointed to number two on the folder. "This discrepancy over when Claire came home. If she's innocent, why would she lie about the time? Her next-door neighbor puts Claire's arrival about a half hour before Ben's. What can you tell me about her neighbor, this . . .

Celia Duncan? She's the same woman who let the delivery boy in."

Jesse smiled. "She's one of the ABC Sisters. Lives with her sisters Abigail and Beatrice. They're getting on in years—Miss Celia, the youngest, must be about eighty-five. I believe Miss Abigail's confined to bed."

"When you're that old, I'm not surprised."

"It's not age. She's a school crossing guard, and a bus hit her. All three are real characters. Miss Abigail was a Marine in World War Two and saw most of the world by the time she left the service. Miss Beatrice was a civil rights leader back in the fifties and sixties, led Earlyville's first sit-in. For years Miss Celia ran the radio station their daddy owned. She used to read selections from D. H. Lawrence and Henry Miller—drove folks crazy and got her arrested. I remember one time the police had to break the radio station's door with an ax while she was reading James Joyce's *Ulysses.* Guess all three ladies were ahead of their time."

Again Rosen pointed to number two on his outline. "If we could substantiate that Claire arrived home *after* her husband, we'd have a start toward lending credence to the rest of her story. Could this Miss Celia be a little senile—maybe confused about the time?"

"I haven't spoken to the sisters in almost a year, but they're all pretty sharp—especially Miss Celia. I don't think even you'd get very far tripping her up on the witness stand, and the jury wouldn't like you trying."

"Fair enough, but we'll need to speak with her. Will she be at the funeral?"

"I expect so. The Hobbeses and Duncans go way back. Speaking of the funeral, we'd better get going." As they stood, Jesse added, "Nate, I'm glad you're staying on. This case isn't keeping you from anything else you've planned?"

Rosen put the file back inside the folder. "My schedule's been cleared. I owe you for a long-distance call I made last night—a personal call."

"Forget it. I hope everything's all right."

Rosen hesitated then said, "Bess is getting remarried."

"You called your daughter. That's why you're upset."

"Yeah. You know, I'm not sure how *I* feel about it, but Sarah's hurting bad. I tried talking to her."

"How'd it go?"

"I went around the issue like a lawyer arguing a case he can't win."

"Sometimes these things just take time."

"Maybe. I promised to call her in a few days." Rosen tapped his knuckles on the table. "Well, enough of my triumphs. Let's go."

The day was beautiful; a few wisps of cottony clouds only gave depth to the powder-blue sky above the horizon. Turning onto Jackson Street, Jesse lowered the car windows to enjoy the cool air. With the breeze came those street sounds one could hear any morning in Earlyville, but which he'd heard—really heard—only on those somber days he drove to a funeral service. Leaves rustling, birds singing, mothers calling after children. The sounds he'd heard as a little boy walking to his grandfather's funeral. Funerals of other grandparents, aunts and uncles, his own father, then cousins and friends not much older than he. On all other days of his life, time passed. He grew older, made his small failures, like burnt recipes quietly scraped into the trash, and endured. But on these few days reserved for remembering death, the trees rustled in the breeze, birds sang, and mothers called after their children. Would he hear the same sounds from under the ground, when others drove to his funeral?

Yet, today was not quite the same as before. On all those other days Jesse never had Bathsheba to think about, and for a few moments, instead of the sounds of the town, he heard her breath soft against his ear.

"Watch it!" Rosen warned, and Jesse quickly applied the brakes.

Traffic was slowing as they approached the First Baptist Church, where the service for Ben Hobbes would soon begin. The church parking lot would certainly be full, so Jesse drove into an alley behind a small medical building. He parked in its private lot.

"Belongs to our family doctor. He's visiting his daughter in Connecticut."

They crossed Jackson and joined the crowd of well-dressed men and women moving slowly toward the church. Jesse checked his watch—9:56. Those standing at the top of the long stone steps, between the Corinthian columns, walked through the church's open doors, gradually lowering their voices. The organ music resonated loudly through the entranceway like the outcry of a mourner who forgot that, after all, this was a First Baptist funeral. Someone would no doubt be talking to the new organist, and, in fact, a minute later the music softened considerably.

The two men found seats in the third pew from the rear. The church was filled to capacity, probably more than five hundred people. Other old Earlyville families sat near the Hobbeses, as well as the lieutenant governor, a state supreme court justice, and local political leaders, including District Attorney Grimes.

Jesse nudged his friend. "Do you see those two elderly ladies across the aisle and two rows up? Beatrice and Celia Duncan. Miss Abigail must still be laid up in bed. You want to see them after the service?"

Rosen nodded as Reverend Taylor walked to the pulpit.

Although he had been minister to the First Baptist Church for over thirty years, Reverend Taylor didn't look much different now than when he'd first come to Earlyville from a Detroit seminary. As always, he wore a gray suit that hung a bit loosely over his lank frame, his blue eyes still shone brightly, and his hair had whitened so slowly that Jesse always remembered its being that color. It had taken people a long time to get used to him and his ways. He often joked that, even after all this time, his tombstone would read: "That preacher feller from up north."

Reverend Taylor surveyed the entire church and smiled gently. His soft voice, carried by the amplifiers, seemed to speak personally to each of the congregants.

"In our conversations over the years, you and I have defined a Christian as one who emulates Jesus. Our Savior is often portrayed as being gentle, loving, and filled with forgiveness. And so He is. But He is also a complex individual, as all of us are complex. He had great strength, which He used in behalf of righteousness—witness His actions against the moneylenders, his confrontation with Satan, and above all, during His Passion, when He sacrificed Himself to save us all.

"Ben Hobbes was a good Christian, because he did indeed emulate Jesus. Although a gruff man, he showed great love for his neighbors and workers in the generous actions he did on their behalf. And, in the last year of his life, he came to know the blessings of marriage. His wife can attest to the tenderness and love within his heart."

As Jesse listened to the eulogy, he felt his body relax against the back of the pew. Reverend Taylor's voice always said welcome like a soft pat on the shoulder. How different from last Friday's service, with its shouting, falling on the floor, speaking in tongues, and serpent handling. Just thinking of those things made him shiver. He tried to concentrate on the minister's words but kept hearing Claire Hobbes's babble and saw the rattlesnake slowly undulate over Bathsheba's shoulders onto her soft breasts, breasts that he himself had caressed. Growing warm, he took out a handkerchief, wiped his forehead, and leaned forward.

Jesse continued to listen and learned of a man who, as Reverend Taylor had said, was more complex than most folks realized. A man who loved his brother's family like his own, who with Simon gave generously of the Hobbeses' fortune—to the college, to the church's social programs, to his workers. A man who worked side by side with the carpenters in his factory, making beautiful furniture with his hands, exactly as his father had done. "Has Jesus not been called a carpenter's son?" the minister asked.

Jesse scanned the church. Brows furrowed slightly, shakes of the head—many of the congregants must've been posing the same question he asked himself, "Why would anyone murder such a man?"

He wondered if Reverend Taylor would mention the way in which Ben Hobbes had died, but the minister concluded his eulogy with a prayer of comfort for the deceased's widow, family, and friends.

As the congregants said "Amen" and began rustling in their seats, Reverend Taylor added, "As many of you know, Ben's widow is not a member of our church. She has requested that her minister be permitted to say a few words of comfort. Therefore, if Reverend McCrae would like to take the pulpit . . ."

The church grew silent as heads turned. Jesse looked up and down the aisles.

Again the minister asked, "Would Reverend McCrae please come up to the pulpit?"

He was in the last row; maybe he'd been there during the entire service. Bathsheba and Popper Johnston sat beside him and remained seated, while McCrae slowly stood and walked up the center aisle. He wore an old black suit, shiny at the elbows and knees, which seemed tight around his shoulders. His footsteps echoed in the silence as he approached the stairs that led to the pulpit.

There was a loud scuffling in the front pew. Wearing a long black dress, Claire stood and clutched at a handkerchief. Breaking away from a series of arms reaching up to stop him, Simon Hobbes stumbled toward the stairs. Reverend McCrae reached out to help him. Hobbes pushed the other man away, started up the steps, then turned and clenched his fists.

McCrae said something softly, which only made Hobbes angrier. He seemed ready to strike the other man when Ruth Hobbes stepped between them. Holding her husband's wrists she spoke rapidly while he shook his head. Reverend Taylor also tried to calm him. Hobbes stood very still for a moment, as if deciding what to do, then strode to the pulpit.

Leaning over the microphone, he barely restrained his anger. "This funeral service is in honor of my brother Ben, a man who loved this town and was loved by the people in it. I don't want anybody to forget the beautiful words Reverend Taylor just said about Ben. I'll tell you all one thing. Nobody"—he paused to glare down at Claire until she sat down—"nobody knew Ben like I did. He'd sooner ask the devil himself to come up here and preach, as have *that* man"—he pointed to McCrae—"take the pulpit. Nobody here's said how my brother died. Nobody's used the word 'murder' this morning. Well, now *that* man's in our church, I'm saying it. 'Murder'! I don't know for sure who killed Ben, but I know the way he felt about that snake church his wife was mixed up in. And I believe with all my heart, it's that snake church responsible for my brother's death."

Jesse's gaze shifted to Reverend McCrae, who turned on the steps to face the congregation. His face showed a serenity different from the calmness Reverend Taylor displayed. This was something deeper, a brooding reminiscent not of Jesus but of God of the Old Testament. Although McCrae spoke without amplification, even in a back pew Jesse had no trouble hearing him.

"I was asked here t'give comfort to a widder, but it appears even in a church this big, there ain't enough Christian love to honor her wishes."

"Get out of here!" Simon Hobbes shouted.

"I'll be goin', but nothin'll stop me from prayin'

with my brethren for Claire and the soul of her poor husband."

"Amen!" someone shouted from the rear of the church. Jesse turned to see Popper on his feet, clapping and once again shouting, "Amen! Praise Jesus!"

Just inside the church doorway stood two television news teams with their video cameras running. One of the reporters worked for a national news affiliate broadcasting from Nashville. How long had the media been there—during the entire service, or had they just recorded Simon Hobbes's outburst? What a story that would make for the evening news.

Without glancing at the cameras, Reverend McCrae walked down the aisle and through the church doors. Claire ran after him, stumbling to the floor just in front of the reporters. She looked up desperately in Jesse's direction, and Rosen took a step forward. But she stared past them both, and a moment later Bathsheba was at her side, lifting Claire easily and stroking her hair.

As the two women walked outside, the video cameras, like a pair of obedient hounds, turned to follow them. The organ softly played "Resting in His Everlasting Love." Men faced their wives and each hesitated, not knowing quite what to do. Then the voice of Reverend Taylor once again flowed through the amplifiers, reminding everyone where the burial was to be held and giving a few more pertinent announcements—the same voice most had been hearing in church since they could remember, the voice that made everything better.

Shaking one another's hands, as they always did when services concluded, the congregants turned and, finding their smiles, walked from the church.

Chapter 10

THURSDAY MORNING

"Come in, Nate. I'm almost ready."

Claire stepped back, admitting him to the foyer of her home. He stood where he'd first seen her, that morning of her husband's death. The woman whose grief had moved him, despite what his rabbi once said: "When all other gates are closed to her, the gates of a woman's tears are opened." Even as it had moved him, Rosen instinctively distrusted his grief; now he grew even warier. She was smiling, and he smelled the faintest aroma of perfume—expensive perfume.

Claire wore a black dress that showed her figure. The skirt fell just below the knee, and her nylon stockings, sheer black, were more suited for a cocktail party than widow's weeds. She wore no makeup; her soft face was framed by blond tresses combed back from either side of her forehead. Her body had lost its tenseness; standing erect, she actually appeared a few inches taller than he'd remembered.

"Thanks for coming. After what happened in church yesterday, I couldn't face Ben's family alone."

"Sure. Besides, one of your attorneys should be present at the reading of your late husband's will.

Jesse couldn't come—he has a class to teach at the college."

"I like Mr. Compton and all, but I'm right glad you're here."

"I didn't know your church would allow you to wear such a fashionable outfit."

She blushed, coloring her cheeks and making her even prettier. "You're right. Guess I don't follow every bit of the Reverend's teachings. Ben bought me this outfit—always said it was one of his favorites. I thought he might like me wearing it now and then."

"I can't argue with that." Rosen checked his watch. "The reading's at ten. I understand the attorney's office is in downtown Earlyville."

"That's right."

"We've got twenty minutes. I've got Jesse's Porsche outside—shouldn't take us nearly that long. Do you mind if I go upstairs and check your husband's room again? I want another look at the physical evidence."

"Go right ahead. I haven't touched his room since he was . . . just ain't had the heart. I'll go into the kitchen and put my breakfast dishes away. Meet you back here in a couple minutes."

Climbing the stairs, Rosen walked into Ben Hobbes's bedroom. Bedsheets remained draped halfway onto the floor, where a few scrape marks had been made, first by the police, then by Rosen, to collect samples of the milk that Ben had spilled. He squatted near the bed and reached under the small night table. The telephone cord had been cut cleanly, probably by a sharp scissors or knife. After taking the poison, Hobbes would've been in great pain; the cut cord would've prevented him from calling for help.

Leaving the murder scene, he walked down the hall, through an open doorway, into Claire's bedroom. The way she'd looked in the foyer, the way she smiled at him—this was the room Rosen really wanted to see.

Her bedroom was beautiful. Almost too delicate for real life, the furnishings seemed suited for a dollhouse. He thought of his daughter, Sarah, and the dollhouse he'd bought that Hanukkah before the divorce. How her eyes widened as he unpacked it. The three of them spent all evening putting it together. How they laughed. It was the last time he remembered laughing with his wife. Yes, there'd been a canopy bed and little rocking chairs for the dolls, but not . . . He sniffed the air. Not that.

It was the kind of smell that caused Rosen's stomach to tighten and made him ashamed to be thinking about his daughter. It was perfume, the fragrance he'd noticed on Claire but much stronger, as if the bottle had been spilled. He walked toward the bed and smelled something else among the rumpled bedsheets, something all the perfume in the world couldn't make sweet. The heavy odor of sweat in an unholy bed. He shook his head and heard his rabbi's voice whispering, "*'Yetzer ha-ra.'*" "The evil impulse"—the one that made man no better than an animal. No, he was a lawyer, not a trembling yeshiva boy. Look for the truth! And glancing over the bedsheets, he saw the truth, one he didn't yet understand.

On the top sheet near the pillow curled a hair—raven-black, about two inches long and wavy. Not Claire's. Gideon McCrae had a thick mane of black hair combed straight back. Rosen had seen the two of them together, at the Reverend's house, caring for Lemuel Banks. McCrae had rested his hands upon her shoulders and spoken soothing words until her tenseness ebbed. Was the bedroom another way of comforting the grieving widow? What had Ben Hobbes said to his wife about the church: "I know what they're making you do. The evil, child, I know all about it." Was this the "evil" Hobbes had been talking about?

Maybe the lab in D.C. could tell something from the strand of hair. As he put it into a fold of his handkerchief, Claire walked into the room.

She looked puzzled, then her face flushed. "I just come to get my gloves. You said you wanted to see *Ben's* room."

"I was just there. I couldn't help peeking in here. It's so beautiful—the bed, the rockers, everything. It reminded me of a dollhouse I gave my daughter a long time ago. I don't get to see her very much, and . . ." He shrugged, slipping the handkerchief into his pocket. "Sorry."

Rosen watched her watching him, but she was an amateur at that kind of game. He wouldn't flinch, and she'd either have to call him a liar or accept his explanation. After a moment of indecision, she smiled and picked up a pair of black satin gloves from her dressing table.

"Course it's all right. Now, we'd better get going. After you, Nate."

It was a five-minute drive to Ben Hobbes's lawyer, whose office was located two blocks past the First Baptist Church.

As they passed the church, Rosen said, "It was a beautiful service. I'm sorry Reverend McCrae wasn't allowed to speak."

Claire bit her lip, then shrugged.

"The funeral itself went well," Rosen continued.

"I can't believe all the food that was served afterward. What a spread."

"It was nice of Ruth to offer her home. She's right handy in the kitchen. Course, lot of folks helped her out. You can see how popular Ben was."

"You did some cooking, right? The fried chicken?"

"Uh-huh. I used to waitress some in Nashville. Old woman named Ethel taught me how to cook. I tell you, people came a long way for her chicken."

Rosen grimaced. "Ruth made me eat some of that cracklin' bread."

"Mmm, wasn't that a bit of heaven."

"Bread soaked in hardened pig fat? That and the salted ham, deep-fried chicken, and fried pies. I'd love to be a cardiologist in this town. I'd give out coupons offering two-for-one bypass specials."

"You didn't like the food?"

"Actually, that was the best fried chicken I've ever had. Jesse's going to take me into Nashville and show me the sights. I'd sure like some more. What's the name of the restaurant where you used to work?"

"Patty's Place. Over near the river on—" She stopped suddenly. "I don't think it's there no more."

"Too bad. Ham, fried chicken, biscuits and gravy, cracklin' bread—the unhealthiest food in the world, yet everyone around here seems to live to a ripe old age. Quite a paradox. Must be due to small-town clean living. Following the Good Book, the Ten Commandments and all. Like what Reverend McCrae teaches in your church. He must be a great spiritual leader."

For a moment she looked out the window, then suddenly turned toward him. "I ain't been perfect. I know that better 'n' anybody. Reverend McCrae's church is God's church—that I truly believe, but it's a hard faith to rest on. I can only try. Nate, I do try." Her eyes began to glisten.

The gates of a woman's tears. Rosen looked at the road straight ahead. "At last Friday's service Ben said that the church was doing something evil to you. What was he talking about?"

She sniffled. "Don't know. He . . . he just didn't like the church. That's all there was to it. Park right there. The lawyer's a few doors down."

A block before the courthouse, Rosen pulled into a space in front of the Country Inn. A wizened old man sat on a bench, under the restaurant's window, reading a newspaper and spurting tobacco juice into a spittoon.

"Mornin'," he said, showing a mouth half filled with amber-colored teeth. "Grits is awful smooth this mornin'. Ol' Beverly's cookin'. She got a right nice touch with them grits."

"Thanks. We're not eating just yet."

"Suit yourself." The old man spat a wad the size of a small mouse. "They got meat loaf for lunch. That's what I'm waitin' for."

"Be sure to save us a seat."

Rosen and Claire walked a half block farther. She stopped in front of a small two-story office building, white frame with emerald-colored awnings over each of the four windows. Next to the door two metal nameplates read: JOSHUA PERRY, D.D.S. and HARLAND GARNET, ATTORNEY-AT-LAW.

"Mr. Garnet's on the second floor," Claire said.

Entering a small reception area, they were greeted by a tall woman of about fifty who had what lingerie ads described as a "full figure." She came around the desk and put her arm around Claire.

"We're so sorry about your husband. You let us know if there's anything we can do." She held out her hand. "You must be Mr. Rosen. I'm Harland's wife and secretary, Angela. Can I get either of you coffee or tea—no? You'd better go right in, the others are already here."

The inner office was quite large, with built-in bookcases lining the walls, a massive oak desk, a couch, and four rocking chairs. Rosen recognized Hobbes craftsmanship in all the furniture. Simon Hobbes, his wife, and son sat on the couch. Ruth held her husband's hand tightly, as much a restraint as a sign of affection. Reverend Taylor and another man, older and even thinner, sat in two of the rockers. Near the door stood Popper Johnston, wearing a seersucker suit with a string tie and cowboy boots.

Harland Garnet stood from behind his desk and nodded. Balding, with a salt-and-pepper mustache, he looked a few years older than his wife and several inches shorter, with the trim body of a runner. He gestured for Rosen and Claire to take the two empty rockers.

"Now that you all are here, we can begin." Garnet spoke with a rich Southern drawl. "I must apologize for moving this along, but I'm due in court at eleven. Let me introduce everyone—Simon Hobbes, his wife, Ruth, and their son, Danny, Reverend Henry Taylor of the First Baptist Church of Earlyville, President Gilbert Shelby of Central Tennessee College, Mrs. Claire Hobbes and her attorney, Nathan Rosen. Back against the wall is Mr. James Johnston, representing the Holiness Church of Earlyville. Sure we can't get you a chair, Mr. Johnston?"

"I'm fine," Popper said, waving his hand.

Simon grumbled, "Don't know why he's here. Should be just family."

Garnet put on a pair of reading glasses. "You're all here representing either yourselves or institutions as beneficiaries of Ben Hobbes's will. I invited Reverend McCrae, but he preferred not to come and sent Mr. Johnston in his place. I'd like to read the will in its entirety. It's fairly short and to-the-point, Ben insisting that I take down his words exactly as he said them. This document has been duly witnessed and notarized. Of course, my wife, Angela, has made copies for all of you."

Garnet was right. Dictated by a simple and direct man, Ben Hobbes's will took about five minutes to read. Rosen was surprised to learn how wealthy the deceased had been. The college was endowed with a Chair of Furniture Arts in honor of Hobbes's father. The First Baptist Church received one of his investment portfolios, worth a little over $150,000. Danny Hobbes received $50,000 with the promise of another $50,000 after marriage and the birth of his first child. Certain personal family mementos, like his father's gold watch and great-grandfather's set of tools, went to Simon. Reverend McCrae's Holiness Church received the deed to the house in which they conducted their services, as well as a gift of $10,000. Everything else, the bulk of his estate, which included his home and a one-half interest in the Hobbes Furniture Company, went to ". . . my beloved wife, Claire, who's brought more happiness to me since we've been married than I've had in all the rest of my life put together."

The attorney began reading the final clause. If Ben Hobbes were to die childless, then his half of the business could be bought back from Claire by Simon, at three-quarters of its fair market value, ". . . in order to keep the company under the family name."

Looking up, Garnet said, "Of course, we can only estimate how much the company is worth. An audit will have to be made within the next few weeks. Now, the other part of the final clause reads as follows."

"What the hell!" Simon shouted, struggling to his feet while tearing free of his wife's grip. "This ain't none of what Ben wanted! You know that, Harland! You know he wanted to cut her and them snake people out completely! He told us he talked to you! What the hell's going on!"

"Calm down, Simon."

"If this is some damn lawyer trick a' yours . . . !"

"I said, calm down before I put you back in that sofa." The veins in the back of Garnet's neck grew taut, and his face reddened. "You've got no call saying something like that. After all the years our people go back."

Ruth said, "He didn't mean nothing, Harland."

She pulled her husband's hand until, grimacing, he sat beside her. At the opposite end of the couch, Danny leaned as far away from his father as possible.

Garnet nodded curtly. "It is true that a week ago, Ben told me he was thinking about changing his will. He mentioned cutting out Reverend McCrae's Holiness Church as beneficiary, but he said nothing about altering any provisions regarding his wife. As far as I know, he never wrote another will. I certainly didn't draw one up, and I've been doing all his legal business for almost twenty-five years."

Ruth repeated, "Simon didn't mean nothing. You go on and finish."

Garnet read the remainder of the final clause. If,

at his death, Ben Hobbes was a father or Claire was pregnant, then his half of the furniture factory remained in her hands, ". . . the purpose being to continue the family business for the child or children of Ben Hobbes."

The attorney looked up, taking off his glasses. "You all know what that means?" He stared at Simon.

"Don't mean a damn thing," Simon retorted. "Ben and her never had no children."

Garnet shook his head. "That hasn't been determined yet—not *quite* determined, if you know what I'm saying." To Claire, "You do know what I'm saying?"

"I think so," she replied.

"Normally this'd be nobody's business but yours, but because of the way in which the last clause is phrased, we're going to have to know if . . . well, if you're with child."

Simon gave a hard laugh. "My brother was almost seventy. Of all the fool—"

"I believe I am," Claire said.

The room grew quiet. Rosen watched Simon's jaw drop but was more interested in the reaction of Danny Hobbes, sitting beside his father. The young man's eyes grew wide as he stared at Claire, then slowly drew a hand through his hair. His long, thick black hair.

Garnet asked, "What do you mean, you 'believe'? Have you been to a doctor?"

"No, not yet. But I missed . . ." She blushed violently and almost whispered, "There's ways a woman can tell."

"We'll need to have your doctor run some tests immediately. Is that all right with you?"

She nodded. "Dr. Butterworth . . . he's just around the corner."

"That ain't all right with me!" Simon shouted. "I don't know what kind of trick she's trying to pull, but the business belonged to my brother and me! With him dead, it's mine to do with as I please!" He was back on his feet. "I've got a deal on the line!"

His wife stood beside him. "Simon, that's enough. We best be going. Ain't nothing more for Harland to say. Good-bye, everybody."

Simon tried to push her hand away. "But I ain't—"

"Oh yes you are." Steering her husband through the doorway, she added, "Come along, Danny."

The young man stood awkwardly, his gaze moving from Claire down to his shoes. Hands in his back pockets, Danny followed his parents from the room.

Garnet waited a minute, as if to be sure the Hobbeses weren't returning, then said, "I think our business is concluded. Reverend Taylor, Mr. Shelby, and Mr. Johnston—I have a few papers here for you to sign."

As the three men approached the desk, Rosen whispered to Claire, "Let's get out of here."

They slipped out the door, nodding to Mrs. Garnet as they left the waiting room.

It was only when Rosen was driving from town that he noticed how flushed Claire was. She slumped against the car door, her eyes closed and her breathing labored. He was about to say something but hesitated, watching her from the corner of his eye. Was this an act for his benefit? Gradually she opened her eyes and dabbed the perspiration from her forehead. Turning the corner, he parked near the alley leading to Claire's garage.

Across the street and a half block down, an old

brown Granada faced them. The man with the broken nose sat inside reading a magazine. He peeked over the pages occasionally, then resumed his reading.

Rosen nodded toward the car. "Do you know who that is?"

"I don't think so. Can't see him too well, though."

"He's got Davidson County license plates. Where's that?"

"Right close. Nashville's in Davidson County."

"Nashville—that's where you're from, right?"

Ignoring his question, she led him down the alley. "Might as well go in through the garage."

After she unlocked the garage door, Rosen rolled it back. Her Corvette and Ben's pickup truck rested side by side. Near the door to the kitchen was Ben's worktable. A pair of work gloves, a tape measure, and two sheets of sandpaper lay piled together at the nearest corner of the table.

"Your husband's things?"

"He must've brought them home to make my shelving. I still haven't taken that wood out from the kitchen. Maybe you could do it for me. Take those gloves so's you won't get no slivers."

"All right." As Rosen took the gloves he noticed a dark circle and a small dribble stain that had dried beside it. "What's this?" When Claire shook her head, he examined the stain more carefully. Then they went inside into the narrow utility room.

From the kitchen came a scraping sound followed by the banging of drawers and cabinets, as if someone were conducting a search. Gently pushing Claire behind him, Rosen opened the kitchen door slightly.

An old woman, not much over five feet, stood on a chair and peered into a cabinet above the sink.

Below her, the wood plank leaned against the counter. Rosen had never seen anyone her age wearing a tank top, blue jeans and sandals. Her hair, the color of frost, was still thick enough to be bunched into a tight bun. Opening the door wider, he and Claire walked into the kitchen.

The old woman glanced at them while continuing her search. "Hello, Claire. Gentleman with you that lawyer friend of Jesse Compton's?"

"Yes, Miss Celia. Anything I can help you with?"

"Well, you know we made it to the funeral yesterday—lovely words by Reverend Taylor, but we missed the burial. Bea and I had to take Abigail to the hospital for some more tests. The way they've been sticking her, I'm surprised she has any veins left."

"I hope she's feeling better."

"I believe so, dear. She's beginning to get around. Says if the city won't give her back the crossing guard job, she'll sue them for age discrimination. Bea knows all about those kinds of lawsuits from her civil rights days. Maybe this young fella will take the case. How about it, Mr. . . . Rosen, isn't it?"

"Yes, ma'am," he said. "If your sister's anything like you, I'd guess the city would be happy to settle out of court."

The old woman hopped down from the chair. "Your tongue's oily as a lawyer's all right. Not that I minded the compliment. I'm Celia Duncan. My sisters and I live next door. The Hobbeses and Duncans been neighbors for years."

"Why are you here now?"

She held her hands straight out, fists clenched. "Put the cuffs on, Copper, you caught me red-handed. I was looking for a box of low-salt oatmeal I lent Ben last week. When I cook it nice and lumpy, it's one of the few things Abigail can chew without any teeth."

Claire said, "It's over on this shelf above the refrigerator. Let me get it. Nate, would you please take care of this here wood?"

"Sure. Don't leave just yet, Miss Celia. I'd like a word with you.

Putting on the gloves, he carried the wood into the garage, sliding it under the worktable. Again he noticed the dried stain in the corner and, taking out a penknife, scraped a few bits into another fold of his handkerchief. Something else for the lab in D.C. to check. Leaving the gloves on the worktable, he returned to the kitchen.

The two women sat at the table while a pot of coffee percolated on the stove. Rosen took the chair between them.

The older woman said, "I've got some tasty leftover pork chops at home. It's cruel leaving them in the house for Abigail's gums to drool over. Why don't I cook you both some lunch?"

Rosen shook his head. "Thank you, but I'm meeting Jesse Compton for lunch."

"Besides," Claire added, "Nate doesn't much favor pork. He's Jewish. You know, like that Mrs. Shapiro who gave all her money to an orphanage."

"Lord, child. I know what a Jew is. I used to read Allen Ginsberg on my radio station. Besides, people have that all wrong about Judith Shapiro. What she said was, better her rotten children were orphans than depend on her for any money. She left them her entire estate anyway."

Rosen said, "If we can return to the night of Ben's death. Miss Celia, could you clarify a discrepancy between your testimony and Claire's? It's regarding the time Claire arrived home on the night of her husband's murder."

"What's the problem?"

"According to the district attorney's records, you stated that Claire came home at nine-fifteen and her husband about a half hour later."

"That's right."

Claire said, "I believe I got here closer to ten. Ben was home before me. His truck was in the garage. I heard him in his room, I swear I did."

Rosen asked, "Miss Celia, how are you so sure about the time and sequence of events?"

The old woman rested her hand on Claire's arm. "I don't want to cause you any more grief, dear girl, but I know what I know. I was sitting on the front porch, listening to the radio, and saw you coming down Jackson, then turn at the corner heading for the alley. That was about fifteen minutes after I'd given Abigail her nine o'clock medication."

Claire got up for a moment to pour the coffee.

Rosen said, "Excuse me, Miss Celia, but isn't that distance too far for you to see the driver?"

"I didn't have to see the driver. I know Claire's car—that snappy Corvette—well enough."

"But you didn't actually *see* the driver."

The old woman clicked her tongue. "Young man, I know what I know. Later, Bea and I were sitting in the kitchen. About a quarter to ten, we heard Ben's truck. Claire, you know what a terrible racket that muffler of his makes."

"And you didn't hear anything else from the Hobbeses' house?"

She shook her head. "Is this discrepancy about the time that important?"

"We just want to make everything as clear as possible. You let in the delivery boy the afternoon before the murder. That was about four-thirty?"

"Yes. Ben gave us a key to the house years ago. He'd call an order to the grocer's, and one of us would let in the delivery boy. We'd do the same thing for Claire when she was busy with her church business."

"That's right," Claire said. "Like I told you before, I called in the order about three from Reverend McCrae's. We was all so worried about Lem."

Rosen asked the old woman, "As far as you know, no one else entered the house until that evening around nine-fifteen, when someone in a Corvette drove here?"

Miss Celia nodded. "But if it wasn't Claire, who was it?"

"Good question. Claire, could anyone have borrowed your car while you were at Reverend McCrae's?"

"No," she said almost too quickly. "Keys were in my purse in a closet with the other women's purses."

"Then someone could've taken them."

"Nobody would've done such a thing. Just ain't possible."

They stared at each other. This time she played the game well, barely blinking. Finally Miss Celia got up to leave. Checking his watch, Rosen saw it was nearly twelve; he was supposed to meet Jesse for lunch on campus. He and the old woman left through the garage. She continued to her house, while he walked down the alley to Jesse's car.

Rosen drove the Porsche slowly down the street. Concentrating so much on what Miss Celia had said, he almost didn't notice that the brown Granada was still parked in the same place. The driver's face was buried in his magazine. Through the rearview mirror, Rosen saw the other man leave his car, walk up the street and around the corner toward Claire's front door. The man was heavy—he had to hike up his trousers—but broad-shouldered, with a short, muscular neck. The build of someone who'd once been an athlete, many years and a boatload of beer ago.

Turning his car around, Rosen parked two blocks down from the Granada and waited. He thought of the families of Earlyville, of Ben and Claire Hobbes; Simon, his wife and son; Reverend McCrae, his daughter and cousin; even Celia Duncan and her sisters. Somehow, despite their arguments and the murder, he felt the connection among them. The one to the other and all to the land, this speck of Tennessee called Earlyville. Not unlike the families of his little street in Chicago that once made up his world, from the yeshiva at one end of the block to the kosher butcher shop at the other. A world that he'd been forced to leave long ago, yet that still traveled with him wherever he went. Damn! He missed his daughter. He saw his grandmother's face in her, and a little of that world. What would he say when he phoned her?

The man was returning to his car. Fifteen minutes had passed. Rosen started the Porsche and crept about a block behind the Granada, as the man turned left on Jackson Street. Passing the entrance to the college, Rosen kept going. The big man was heading toward the highway. Rosen decided to keep following him; it was the only fresh lead he had. He hoped Jesse would understand, but lunch would have to wait.

Chapter 11

THURSDAY AFTERNOON

Leaving Earlyville, the big man took the highway leading west. Rosen stayed three or four car lengths behind and jotted the Granada's license into a small notebook.

Last Sunday he had driven this same highway from the airport. Six fast lanes with a concrete barrier median; along either side trees rose above exposed layers of brownish limestone. With traffic so light, had the other man spotted him? Because the Granada couldn't possibly shake Jesse's Porsche, would the big man panic, would it lead to a confrontation, or was he after all only a vacuum cleaner salesman trying to peddle a deluxe sweeper? Rosen smiled and shook his head. Maybe it was nothing, but why had the other man waited for Rosen to leave before approaching Claire's house?

Twenty minutes later they passed the airport and, after another five miles, the big man took the exit marked "Downtown Nashville." Rosen moved a little closer. The Granada made a right onto West End Avenue, an area filled with fast-food restaurants, sports shops, and Laundromats, which usually signaled a college campus. Sure enough, two blocks down on the right Vanderbilt University began, its dark brick buildings presenting themselves with the quiet dignity of old money.

Across the street, Centennial Park stretched into the distance—past majestic trees, multicolored flower beds and an artificial lake—until reaching the Parthenon, the only exact-size replica in the world of the ancient Greek temple. No wonder Nashville was called the Athens of the South. Couples worked small paddleboats across the little lake, while families spreading blankets over the lawn shared picnic lunches.

The images stayed with Rosen long after he passed the park. Had he yielded to the terms set by his father or, years later, those of his ex-wife, maybe he would've had a family to take to the park. But long ago he'd turned his back on his father's God, and his father turned his back on him. If only Bess could've settled for what he was, but she couldn't. So he traveled to places he didn't know, like this one, to be a stranger among strangers. He'd come to accept it. Still, it would've been nice.

Rosen followed the Granada into the business section of town. Banks alternated with offices and hotels; occasionally a nineteenth-century building asserted itself like a stubborn old relative. He passed Union Station, a customs house, and the bell tower of some church long since vanished. The people Rosen had met in Earlyville were like this city, the past holding on with the same clawlike grip as the Duncan sisters.

The intersections were numbered in descending order. Past Fourth Street, adult bookstores and peep shows peppered the neighborhood. A few women lounged in the doorways, stretching their long legs like bait. Eyes averted, men walked close to the storefronts. Rosen stared at them, wondering who would take this kind of lonely walk where all was flesh and no spirit. He looked a moment too long.

At Third Street, just as the light changed to red, the Granada suddenly turned left. Rosen could only jam on his brakes and watch the other car disappear in the traffic.

There was no chance of catching the big man, so, when the light changed, Rosen followed the street to the river. Parking, he walked past a reconstructed fort of log palisades. Opposite the water, old warehouses of gray brick lined the next few blocks; some had been converted into condominiums. Places where, long ago, cotton bales and human beings had been sold. Rosen couldn't understand slavery, just as he could never understand the stories his grandfather had told of the pogroms in Russia, Cossacks bashing in the skulls of babies with the same casualness as cracking an egg.

A half block farther, he walked into a branch of the post office. Tearing a sheet of paper in half, he taped the pieces into two small packets. From his handkerchief he removed the evidence, the black hair from Claire's bed and scrapings of stain from her garage worktable, placing each in a packet, then enclosing both, with a short message, in an Express Mail envelope. His office in D.C. would receive the evidence tomorrow, which meant that with luck he could get the lab results early next week.

After posting the letter with the clerk, he asked, "Do you know a restaurant called Patty's Place? It's supposed to be near the river."

"You betcha. Go back to Second and turn left. Can't miss it. If you like fried chicken, you're gonna love Patty's."

Second Street acted as a boundary between the renovated riverbank, with its tourist attractions like the old fort, and the seedier area he'd passed earlier. Patty's Place was a few doors up the street, an old narrow building squeezed between a used-record store and a pawnshop. Its bricks were painted lime green, but large patches had peeled off to reveal an earlier coat of brown, the entire effect one of camouflage, as if the restaurant were ashamed to show itself in such a neighborhood.

Inside, Rosen was surprised at the restaurant's length. A row of about a dozen booths ran along the left wall, ending at a jukebox in the far corner. Across a narrow aisle stood the counter, filled with at least twenty people in suits, cowboy garb, hard hats, T-shirts, even a jogging outfit. Nobody talked much; the customers hunkered over their plates and sucked chicken bones while listening to a lugubrious country-and-western record. Something about a woman running off with her husband's best friend's hound dog. Rosen slid onto the last vacant stool.

Snapping her gum, a young waitress waited for his order.

He said, "I didn't get a menu."

Rolling her eyes, she nodded at a chalkboard hanging over the coffee urn. It read: "Today's lunch—Chicken, Chili, Chitlins" and listed the prices.

"Chicken, chili, chitlins," he repeated. "No chopped liver?"

"Huh?"

"Fried chicken will be fine, and hot tea."

The waitress called in his order, then brought a pot of tea. She wore too much makeup; her hair, dyed henna, was too red; her outfit too short and too tight. The whole effect made her look like a comic strip character. Glancing from their plates, the customers watched her body wiggle behind the counter. She must've known they were watching. Did she count on it for bigger tips, for the come-ons and good times later? Claire said she'd worked here. Was this the way she'd dressed and moved for the customers? Rosen couldn't imagine her acting that way, yet she'd called herself bad. Was this what she meant?

Five minutes later the waitress served him a plate heaped with fried chicken, steak fries, and cole slaw.

"Looks great," he said. "I've heard a lot about this place. Have you worked here long?"

Rosen realized immediately he'd said the wrong thing. How many times had she heard that line before? She looked him up and down, studying his potential as a one-night stand, while he felt his face burning.

"I didn't mean it like that."

"No?" She smiled, leaning forward. "What did you mean?"

"A friend of mine used to work here. Maybe you knew her."

"Maybe. What's her name?"

"Claire." He remembered her maiden name from the D.A.'s report. "Claire Daniels."

The woman's brow furrowed. "Don't know her, but I only been working here little over a year."

"There's a cook named Ethel . . ."

"She's the one who fried your chicken, which you'd better start eating before it gets cold. Unless you got something else on your mind."

Her gaze held him for a moment. Looking away, Rosen saw the man next to him smirking.

"Could I see Ethel?"

"Not now. She's too busy cooking. Maybe later this afternoon. Well, if you need anything else, you let me know."

As she moved with her coffeepot down the counter, Rosen stared into the plate and ate his lunch. The fried chicken was delicious, better than Claire's; biting through the crispy skin, he tasted the hot tender meat sprinkled with spices. The potatoes were just as good. In ten minutes he'd finished the meal. Too fast. The food lay heavy in his stomach. Shifting carefully from his stool, he left a tip, paid his check at the register, and stepped outside, adjusting his belt.

He went around the building to a narrow alley behind the restaurant. Garbage cans lined the back wall. Flies swarmed like dark clouds over the graveyard of chicken bones or buzzed against the kitchen's screen door, where the smell of more chicken and hot grease made Rosen's stomach feel even heavier. Waving away the flies, he quickly stepped inside, shutting the screen door tight.

The temperature jumped twenty degrees; air crackled with the sound of frying chicken. Down the center of the kitchen stood a wooden table. Along the length of one wall ran stainless steel vats of hot oil, above which hung wire baskets filled with chicken or potatoes that the cooks lowered into the sizzling oil, raised, then dumped into trays back on the table.

All five cooks were black and wore long aprons stained with grease and blood. The oldest, a woman about sixty, was short and heavy, with arms like half-filled balloons and legs the size of ham hocks. A few wisps of silver hair peeked from under a red bandanna. She stood at one end of the table, cutting the chicken, then shaking spices from an unmarked tin can with a mesh top. She worked with a singleness of purpose that reminded Rosen of an automaton. The heat, the sight of all that raw chicken, and the smell of hot oil unsettled his stomach even more. He mopped the sweat from his forehead.

At that moment the woman looked up. "You another one a' them health inspectors?" Rosen walked toward her and waited for a wave of nausea to pass. "Thought Cal took care of them violations. Boys all been washin' their hands after goin' to the bathroom. You'd think their mamas woulda' learned 'em better when they 'uz young. Hey you don't look too good. Ozzie, bring me a little a' that cookin' brandy."

Rosen took a few sips, which settled like a warm blanket over his bubbling stomach. "Thanks, that is a little better. I'm not the health inspector. Is your name Ethel?"

She grasped the cutting knife. "Who wants to know?"

His smile, when it came, felt like wet plaster on his lips. "I'm here about Claire Daniels." When Ethel didn't answer, he repeated, "Claire Daniels. She worked as a waitress here a few years ago."

"I know who you're talkin' 'bout. Poor child. Been seein' all the bad news on TV. You more a' that bad news?"

"No. I'm Claire's attorney."

"A lawyer? God help us all. I ain't talkin' to no lawyer, so you might as well just—"

"Not even if it's to help Claire? She told me that you were her friend."

Ethel nodded, as if daring him to say otherwise.

"She had no mama. Somebody had to tell her what to do."

"What do you know about her?"

"She was a decent child, maybe a little mixed up, but who could blame her? Her mama'd been sick a long time. Finally died a few months after Claire come to work here. Never talked 'bout her daddy. Don't think the poor girl ever knew who he was. Worked her whole life but never was like some a' the white trash you find 'round here. She done studied her books, always readin' that pretty poetry. Maybe she was a little mixed up, but that church sure helped straighten her out, even if it did mess with them snakes."

Rosen asked, "Do you know how she first became involved with Reverend McCrae's church?"

"No, and I didn't wanna have nothin' to do with them snakes. Preacher and that girl a' his—they was awful nice to Claire—come 'round sometimes for lunch, after she started goin' to their church. For a while it was right across the street, where that plumbing supply place is now."

"Is there anyone who could tell me something more about Claire, especially how she became involved with the church?"

"Hmm, now that be a problem. Tania, another waitress who was a good friend a' hers, got married and moved up to Kentucky. Course there's that old boyfriend a' hers. Still see him around."

"Who's that?"

Before Ethel could answer, a door opened near the corner by the stove, and a man walked out. He was white, about thirty, and wore an apron like the other cooks. Tall and sandy-haired, he was strikingly handsome, his body just beginning to grow soft from too much fried food. He held up his hands, like a doctor after scrubbing, and gave an idiot grin.

"See, I washed my hands after taking a pee, just like that other feller told me to do. No need to be comin' back for six months. Now if it's more money—"

"Shut up, fool!" Ethel shouted. "He ain't another health inspector. He's Claire Daniels's lawyer. Come here to ask some questions, that's all." To Rosen, "That's Cal. He's the owner's grandson."

"Assistant manager," Cal said.

"Manager?" Ethel shook her head. "Boy can't remember to wash his hands. When he was little, all the time he be sloppin' grease and chili all over his clothes. His granma got so worried, she was gonna put him in a rubber suit." The woman laughed, her whole body shaking.

"That was a long time ago. Now you'd better get back to work and stop gabbing with—"

"Don't you be tellin' me what to do. When you was a baby, I changed your diapers right here on this table, and I can still lay a hand across your backside."

Rosen resisted the thought of dirty diapers mixed with his fried chicken. "I won't take much more of your time. You mentioned someone who might tell me more about Claire."

"Oh yeah. That be Hec Perry. Fella plays the local clubs. I still see him around."

Cal said, "Guy's a loser. Half the time he's hopped up on something. Claire was smart to dump him. Don't know what she saw in him in the first place."

"Hush, now. You's just jealous she didn't pay you no mind."

"Look at me, mister. Why would any woman

rather go out with some doped-up third-rate musician?"

Ethel said, "You loves yourself so much, you don't need no woman."

Cal slowly shook his head. "It ain't that, really it ain't. It's just . . . well . . . something was always funny about her, that's all." His face grew red, and after a moment he added, "Looks like we're getting a little behind here." He began cutting potatoes.

Rosen asked the woman, "Where can I find Hec Perry?"

"He used to live above a bar called Here's How. Claire say he played there at night to pay his rent. For all I know, boy's still there. Place is right up this here street. You can't miss it."

"Thanks."

"That's all right. You give Claire my love 'n' tell her I'm prayin' for her. Newspapers been spreadin' a pack a' lies. I know she's a good girl."

"I'll tell her," Rosen replied, but his gaze lingered on Cal. The other man was cutting potatoes dangerously close to his fingers, his mind somewhere else.

Opening the screen door, Rosen hurried through the alley past the clouds of flies until reaching the street, where he breathed deeply the clean air. It was good to be walking. He'd been sluggish, not just from the fried chicken. Each day something new had been revealed about Ben Hobbes's murder—whether relating to cause of death, motive, or suspects—but it all seemed to be heading nowhere. Now he had a fresh lead.

Ten minutes later he stood in front of Here's How. Its facade had been designed as an old-style saloon, the bar's name written across the top of a plate glass window in letters formed as branding irons. The letters were chipped and faded, and the glass itself was taped in two of the corners where it had cracked. On the other side of the window along a low counter lay a collection of Western paraphernalia—boots, lariats, and two ten-gallon hats—all covered by a thick layer of dust. In the center of the window, a large beer sign flickered neon like an anemic lightning bug. Above the saloon was a second floor with four dusty windows.

Stepping inside, Rosen let his eyes adjust to the dimness. In his travels he'd seen hundreds of bars; Here's How could've been any of them. A half-dozen tables, a dart board, a pinball game with an Out of Order sign, and a silent jukebox glowing softly in the far corner. The only other customer sat near the cash register and chatted with the bartender. Both were old men with curved backs and large eyes, as if their bodies had adapted to this environment of whispers and darkness. Rosen sat a few stools down. Sighing, the bartender trudged toward him.

"What'll it be?"

"A beer—whatever's on tap."

After the old man drew the beer, Rosen raised his glass. "Here's how."

The bartender grimaced and started walking back to his friend.

"Wait a second. I'm looking for someone who works here."

The old man leaned wearily against the countertop. "I'm the only guy working here. My wife helps out at night."

"Somebody else. A musician named Hec Perry. Is he living upstairs?"

"Just who are you?"

"I'm an attorney. Mr. Perry isn't in any trouble.

I simply want to ask him some questions, but I need to see him immediately."

The bartender rubbed his face, then looked at his friend, who nodded.

"All right," the old man said, "but I ain't got nothing to do with him. You're wrong about him working for me."

"I thought he paid his rent by playing for the customers."

"That was a long time ago, before the place started going downhill. My wife's idea—she's got a soft heart. Goes along with her soft head. Said it would give the place some class, because Hec plays such beautiful music. Well, I got to admit he does that, don't he, Lou?"

Again his friend nodded. "Prettiest music you'd ever want to hear."

"Funny thing is that Hec don't work much. He don't seem to do anything, yet the rent's paid every month. Go figure that one."

Rosen said, "So he does live here."

"He's probably upstairs right now. Leastways, I ain't seen him leave all day. Take the stairs. Hec's room is last door on the left."

"Thanks." Finishing his beer, Rosen paid for the drink and stepped down from the stool.

The old man added, "You sure Hec ain't in any trouble? Not that I care. It's my wife. It'd upset her if anything . . . you know."

"I only need a little information. Thanks again for your help."

The narrow stairway led to a corridor as dim as the barroom; the only light filtered through a dust-covered window. As Rosen approached the end of the corridor, he heard music. It suddenly occurred to him that he didn't know what kind of instrument

Hec Perry played. He'd assumed it was guitar, but the music was smoother and more melodious, closer to a harp. When he knocked on the door, there was no reply—only the sweet music. Rosen turned the knob.

At the far end of the room, Hec Perry sat beside the window strumming a dulcimer on his lap. He was thin, almost ethereal, with long blond hair tied in a ponytail and delicate features that might have been a girl's. He was naked except for a pair of torn blue jeans. Eyes half closed, looking up toward the ceiling Perry continued to pass his hands over the strings and play such bittersweet music. Watching the musician, Rosen thought of the shepherd David at his lyre singing his psalms. He felt a deep longing—for what, he wasn't quite sure. His childhood, his ex-wife, for the lives he hadn't chosen to live?

"Mr. Perry?" The musician seemed not to hear. "Mr. Perry, I'd like a few words with you. It's about Claire Hobbes . . . Claire Daniels."

Perry looked in his direction; it took a moment for his eyes to focus. He continued to play, motioning for Rosen to sit on the bed next to him. The room reeked of tobacco and the more pungent odor of marijuana. A bed, night table, and chest of drawers—none of which matched, one suit in the closet and a laundry basket overflowing with dirty clothes. The night table contained a half-empty whiskey bottle with a half-filled glass, an open pack of Camels, and an ashtray with a pyramid of cigarette butts.

Rosen sat beside Perry and cleared his throat with a heavy cough. "You play beautifully."

The musician smiled vacantly. " 'A damsel with a dulcimer in a vision once I saw. It was an

Abyssinian maid, and on her dulcimer she played.' "

"I don't . . ."

"Coleridge. Welcome to my Xanadu. Would the weary visitor like some refreshment?"

"No, thanks."

"You don't mind if I indulge." He stopped playing, took a short drink, then lit a cigarette. Faded needle marks dotted his arm.

"I understand you used to date Claire." Perry's eyes squinted as he took a long drag on his cigarette. When he didn't reply, Rosen continued, "I'm Claire's attorney. You know about the trouble she's in—the murder charge."

"You want me to be a character witness for her?" He laughed sharply. "I'm afraid I'm what you lawyers call an impeachable witness."

"Why, because you dated her?"

"No, because I'm still dependent on her. Since her marriage, she sends me a couple hundred each month to keep me going."

"Why?"

His face twisted into a smile. "Because she's an angel."

"You two must've been close."

"Yeah, she gave me everything . . . well, almost." He took a long drag on his cigarette. "Look, I'm not really in the mood for conversation."

Rosen filled the other man's glass. "Just a few more questions. How did you and Claire meet?"

He shook his head.

"At the restaurant where she worked?"

Perry hesitated, then went for the drink. "Yeah, I saw her there a couple times, but we started going out later. I was with a group called Black River Hollow. She came around with her minister, his daughter, and their cousin Popper Johnston. Popper was my group's manager—talked about having us record some Christian music for this Reverend McCrae. You know, Jesus rock and roll. Can you believe it, Jesus and Popper? The man was more into—" He stopped suddenly and looked away. "Well, nothing never did happen with the music, but Claire and I started going together. We had six good months. I cleaned myself up—no drugs, cut down on the drinking. My music was never better."

"What happened?"

He shook his head. As Perry reached for the glass, Rosen grabbed his arm. "What happened?"

The musician was trembling, but Rosen wouldn't let go. Finally Perry stared into his eyes. " 'A damsel with a dulcimer in a vision once I saw. It was an Abyssinian maid. . . .' "

Rosen shook Perry's arm.

"Ask the Abyssinian maid," Perry said, and his eyes began to grow glassy.

Rosen shook him harder.

"Leave the boy alone," someone said from the doorway.

It was the big man, the one Rosen had followed from Earlyville. He stood just inside the room, arms folded, and slowly shook his head. He had the scarred face of a prizefighter, flattened bridge of a broken nose and cauliflower ears.

As Rosen stood, he thought again of David; was this how the young shepherd had felt facing Goliath? The man looked like a bully, and bullies were like dogs. You couldn't show them any fear.

Rosen crossed his arms. "I'm glad you came by. Saves me the trouble of looking for you."

The big man smiled, showing teeth the color of

Indian corn. "My friend wants to be left alone. I think you'd better leave."

"Hec and I are having a private—"

"You can walk out or crawl out—makes no difference to me, but you're leaving now. Just keep your hands where I can see them." He opened his suit coat to show his shoulder holster, then walked toward Rosen.

"Take it easy. I'm not armed."

The big man stood in front of him. "I never take any chances. That's why I've stayed alive for so long."

"Who are you?"

He handed Rosen his card. It read: "Albert Aadams, Private Investigator" with a phone number and Nashville address.

Rosen said, "A double *a* for Adams?"

"Yeah, had my name changed. Puts me first in the phone book, ahead of Acme Detectives. Pretty smart, huh?"

"Brilliant."

"Thanks," Aadams said, lifting Rosen like a chair and carrying him to the hallway. "Now go on home, and you won't get hurt."

"I still need to ask Perry a few questions."

"Why?"

"That's privileged information between me and my client."

"You mean Claire Hobbes? You'd better get your facts straight, buddy. Claire Hobbes is *my* client."

"What?" Rosen asked. "What do you have to do with her?"

"That, Mr. Lawyer, is privileged information," Aadams replied with a grin, before closing the door in Rosen's face.

Chapter 12

THURSDAY AFTERNOON

"In ancient Mesopotamia, for example, the serpent was especially favored by the god Ningishzida, who guarded the door of heaven. And what did the pharaohs wear upon their foreheads to symbolize their authority? The asp. The snake whose bite on the milky breast of Cleopatra proved so deadly."

Jesse paused to survey his students. Leaning over their desks, they eagerly took his words as golden threads to be sewn into their notebooks. He smiled. That was as it should be in his world, bound by four cinder-block walls and a blackboard. For a forty-five-minute tick of the universe, the marks his chalk made were as significant as those carved into the tablets of Moses. And as Moses was never challenged, neither was he.

Walking down the center aisle, he continued his lecture. "Even on our own continent, the snake has been revered for its mystical powers. In Aztec lore the great god Quetzalcoatl was depicted as a feathered serpent and his high priest was known as Prince of Serpents. As part of their rain dance, the Hopi Indians put live rattlesnakes between their teeth."

"Sort of like what's going on here," one of his students said. Kenny, the short, earnest-looking boy in the back row.

"What do you mean?"

"The snake-handling group here in town. Isn't that what your lecture's leading up to?"

"This is a class in folk religion."

"Yes, sir, but what I mean is . . . you seem to be portraying snake handling—"

"The people who practice it prefer the word *serpent*."

"Whatever . . . you seem to make it natural. But to me, it's nothing but—"

The boy stopped suddenly and looked past Jesse, as did the other students around him. Jesse turned to see Bathsheba edging into the classroom. She wore a long green dress with sleeves and a high collar, its color faded from too many washings. Smiling shyly, she sat in the corner and folded her hands on the desk top.

Jesse felt her stare like the heat of an open fire. He said, a little too loudly, "Kenny, what's your point?"

The boy's eyes were focused on Bathsheba.

"Kenny!"

"It's just . . . the snake is evil. We all know what the Bible tells us about the snake tempting Eve. That's what caused man's fall, the start of all our troubles."

"The Bible's a big book, and there are other significant passages you need to recognize. Because it sheds its skin, the snake has been a symbol of immortality—and not just the staff of Aesculapius. In chapter three of John, when Moses lifted his standard engraved with a serpent, this was the foreshadowing of Jesus' being lifted upon the cross, so that we might have eternal life. Does anyone know the words of Jesus in Matthew ten, verse sixteen?"

Just then the bell rang, but no one stirred.

Bathsheba said, " 'I send you forth as sheep in

the midst of wolves, be ye therefore wise as serpents and harmless as doves.' "

"That's right," Jesse repeated, their eyes locking, "be wise as serpents."

Whispering to one another, the students glanced at Bathsheba, who remained seated while they filed out the door.

When the two of them were alone, she said, "You teach real good."

"What're you . . . why did you come here?"

"I ain't never been to no college before. When I finished work over at the Burger King, I said to myself, I drive by that college most every day but never s'much as take a look-see. That was before I knowed you. Had t'ask three people, till one told me where t'go. I hope it was all right. Me comin' here, I mean."

Before he could answer, she added, "You sure was somethin', standin' up there like a preacher man. You got yourself a golden tongue, all right."

Jesse glanced at the open doorway to be certain that no one was eavesdropping. "I'm glad you came." As she stood, he added, "Have you ever thought of going to college? This is a state school, and you're a resident of Earlyville. I'm sure arrangements could be made to . . ."

He lapsed into silence as she walked past him to the front of the room. She moved laterally a few inches from the blackboard, gazing as if it were the deep green expanse of the Cumberlands. She picked up a piece of chalk and rolled it slowly between her palms.

He asked, "About school?"

Placing the chalk in her left hand, Bathsheba began sketching in long broad strokes. Jesse moved behind her to watch the drawing take shape. As it became more definitive, he grew to hear his own heartbeat.

"Whaddya think?" she asked, stepping back to admire her work.

It was his caricature, a thin man in a suit, kicking up his heels and waving both arms. But it was what lay between those lips that made the breath catch in his throat. A large writhing rattlesnake.

Bathsheba said, "Just like you was talkin' 'bout to your students. Them Injuns dancin' for the Lord t'pour down His blessed rain."

He was trembling.

"That's what you saw at our service. Me 'n' the others prancin' with them serpents wrapped 'round us like the Lord's lovin, arms. 'Cause that's what they were. When you're under the power, ain't no evil. No matter what it looks like"—she chalked a circle around his caricature—"ain't no evil."

Jesse stared into his own face for a long time, and it grinned back as if about to tell a dirty joke. Was that what had frightened him at Friday's service? Had he been afraid to let himself go the way Claire Hobbes had babbled in tongues or Bathsheba caressed the rattlesnake? He shook his head, almost laughing. That wasn't it, not it at all. He'd lost control lying with her in the field. That's why the face on the blackboard—his own idiot face—leered back at him.

He felt her fingers cool against his cheek.

"Sorry," she said. "Didn't mean nothin' by it. Just my way a' jokin'."

"It's all right." His gaze remained fixed on the board.

Gently she turned his face toward hers. "Can you get away for a spell?"

"Uh, yes. I don't have a class until this evening.

Would you like to go for some coffee? We could go into town or maybe you'd like to see the student center. If you've never seen the campus, I'd be happy to show you around the—"

"I was thinkin' we might go back to the field. It's right nice this time a' day. Cool breeze 'n' all." She took his hands.

The room was hot, stifling. Bathsheba's hands felt cool, yet he was still sweating.

"I'd like a cool breeze, but I'm afraid I lent my car to Nate Rosen."

"That's all right. I got my daddy's car. Just an old clunker, but it works."

Lowering the car's windows, he let the wind slap his face until his cheeks tingled. He tried not to look at her, at her tan ankles, or to think about the implications of their ride. She was his girl, that's all, and they were going for a drive in the country.

She said, "I like your tie, and that pretty red silk handkerchief stickin' outta your pocket."

"Thank you. What we talked about back in class—I meant it. I could help you get into college."

"Imagine, me in college."

"Of course, you might have to take some prerequisites. There are special tutoring programs for disadvantaged students."

"I'm afraid you're dreamin'. My daddy'd never allow it. College is what he calls a den a' iniquity, like a bar or a whorehouse. You seen the way them girls dress in their shorts, with all that makeup on. He'd never allow it. 'Sides, he don't think women need any kind a' learnin' 'cept what's preached to them from the Good Book."

"Is that what you believe?"

She shrugged. "Don't much matter what I believe."

"You're wrong. There's so much more of the

world than the four walls of your church. I really could help."

"Don't want you troublin' yourself. You already done so much for us folk."

"It's been no trouble. Besides, you've helped me with my research. Today's lecture, for example, was leading up to Pentecostal serpent handling. I plan to interview members of your church about the other signs—speaking in tongues, casting out demons, drinking poison, and healing the sick. Other customs as well. Foot washing, for example."

"We do that, too."

Her mouth twisted into a small smile.

She turned onto the highway, drove another half mile, and parked on the edge of the field, not far from where they had stopped a few days ago. The NO TRESPASSING warning tilted nearby; each gust of wind shook the sign as if it were the last drunk at closing time.

As they walked into the tall grass, the din of highway traffic softened to a murmur. In the distance stood Danny Hobbes's cornfield, which gradually disappeared into the thickly wooded ridge just below the horizon. The sun was strong and, slanting over Jesse's left shoulder, polished the yellow grass golden and sent sparkles of light over it. Everything was transformed from what it had been before. Walking with a stronger step, he had no difficulty following Bathsheba's long strides. The wind kept disheveling her curls, so that she'd lift her arms to untangle them, showing the swell of her breasts. It felt good walking beside her; he could've kept on as long as she wanted.

She stopped by the stream where they'd picnicked. The water, too, seemed clearer and cleaner as they sat beside it. Dabbing his forehead with his new handkerchief, Jesse heard his own heartbeat for the second time that day.

He watched the bees dancing among the sunflowers. "I'm glad we came. It's a beautiful day."

"Sure is. Perfect time of day for snake huntin'." Seeing him shiver, she laughed. "Just teasin' again."

"That's all right. As you might've noticed, I'm not a very brave person."

"I didn't mean . . ."

"No, it's all right. I have no illusions about myself. I have my mother to thank for that. My father, the good banker, was the perfect gentleman. How everybody loved him, and with good reason. His business, clubs, charities, he gave so much of himself to all of them. Perhaps that's why he never had anything left for me. But, you know, that was better than being reminded by my mother daily what an exalted name I had inherited. Whenever I disappointed her, she'd roll her eyes toward heaven and intone, 'How sharper than a serpent's tooth is an ungrateful child.' Daddy and Momma—what a pair they made."

Jesse glanced at Bathsheba. She sat facing him, legs tucked under the long skirt, her shoes nearly touching the water. Her eyes had widened, and her face revealed the same rapt attention as a child listening to a favorite fairy tale.

He said, "I'm sorry to ramble on. It's easy talking to you."

"I'm sorry for you. Reckon there ain't nothin' worse than a man who won't do right by his young 'un. Maybe your mama was just tryin' t'do your daddy's job as well as hers. Don't be too hard on her."

"It sounds as if you're speaking from experience."

Bathsheba took a stone and threw it hard into

the water. It didn't skip but quickly sank to the bottom.

"Don't like t'talk on it. Ain't much t'say anyways. She was young, and she died when I was young."

"So you didn't get to know her too well."

"Well enough. She was a good woman, better'n most."

"Like your father, from the mountains?"

"No, from town. Her folks was . . . different. Didn't mix with his. He didn't want me. It was him named me Bathsheba—said my mama tempted him. Well, that's the way he tells it anyways. Then it was plain Sheba—said it suited me better."

"Your own father didn't want you? I don't believe it."

Her eyes narrowed. "That was a long time ago, before he catched religion. Like they says, 'Old sins forgiven to the holy livin'.' "

"Still, it's hard to believe. . . ."

"Don't wanna talk 'bout it no more."

Suddenly she took off her shoes. Scooting closer to the stream, she raised her dress to her knees and kicked at the water.

"Hey!" he shouted, trying to protect himself from the splashes.

"C'mon! Take off your shoes 'n' have yourself a good time!"

He hesitated a moment, then removed his shoes and socks. His big toe tested the water; it was cold.

"Go on," she said. "Look!" Her legs churned the water, scattering a half-dozen frightened birds skyward.

He joined in her play, dipping his feet into the stream, making small circles, flapping them harder until the water roiled. They laughed together so hard the tears came, and he put all his heart into their play. She kicked at him and he at her, water spraying high above them into a fine mist colored seashell pink by the dying sunlight.

After a while they both grew tired. Jesse dabbed himself with his red silk handkerchief and noticed how Bathsheba's dress, nearly soaked through, clung tightly to her body.

Taking the handkerchief from him, she wiped her throat. "That sure was fun."

He nodded, watching her throat.

"Like you was sayin' before," Bathsheba continued, folding the cloth between her hands, "there's more my church can teach you."

"The five signs?"

"Yeah, that 'n' other things. You asked about foot washin'. You know what's in John thirteen? 'He took a towel and girded himself. Then he poured water into a basin and washed his disciples' feet and wiped them with the towel he was girded with. If I, your Lord and Master, have washed your feet, you should wash each other's.' You know about that, don'tcha?"

He nodded.

Bathsheba dipped his handkerchief into the stream. Kneeling before him, she took his right foot and slowly moved the wet cloth across it. He shivered.

"Too cold?" she teased.

Tingling, Jesse shook his head, not wanting her to stop. When she did, it was only to begin on his other foot. Closing his eyes, he grew disembodied, except for the ankle that Bathsheba's delicate fingers were now touching. He had been almost electrocuted once as a child, plugging in a radio with an exposed prong. That was her touch—hot and jolting and totally inseparable from his being.

When she finally released him, he looked down to see that she'd gathered the hem of her dress to dab his feet dry. Straightening the dress down to her ankles, Bathsheba leaned back on her hands. She shook her head once, so her curls fell back into place.

"So you never done foot washin' before?"

"No."

"Does it make you feel any more Christian?"

He didn't care what she said, only that she'd touch him again.

"We ain't but half done with the ceremony. Lord said we was t'wash each other's feet. You know, so that no one'd be above the other."

His red silk handkerchief lay heavy and damp on the ground. Shifting his weight to his knees, he took the cloth and timidly dabbed at her foot.

"Do a right good job," she said. "Remember, as my daddy'd say, you're on the Lord's business."

He dipped the cloth into the stream and, cupping one of her feet, stroked it softly.

"That's nice," she said dreamily, "real nice."

Was it a dream? Releasing one foot, he sponged the other. Her body pulled away slightly, and he noticed Bathsheba had leaned back upon the ground. Slowly she pulled her dress above her ankles, and the cloth in his hands followed. He caressed her skin, watched it glisten under the droplets of water. Was it a dream?

Like water the dress was receding, leaving her tan legs bare to the knees. Clutching the wadded handkerchief, his hands followed the contour of her calves, then dropped the cloth. He gripped her knees and waited.

Jesse thought he heard something, perhaps her laughter, but the blood pounded too loudly in his ears. His mouth followed where his hands had been, then Bathsheba's legs split open as easily as he'd seen men gut a fish. She held him, his face nuzzled against her thigh, her dress covering him, his nostrils filled with her. And suddenly Jesse realized that he was the fish, her legs and hands playing with him, slipping the line, then reeling it in. A flapping fish hooked under the gill. Be a fisher of men, Jesus had said, and she was.

Was it a dream?

Later, when she pushed him away, Jesse closed his eyes tightly and shivered from the cold wind. Thinking about his hands on her legs, he grew excited again and wasn't ashamed to let her see. Would she let him touch her again?

What was that? He heard something, something in the grass not far away. Low, dull, now sharper . . . a hissing. Hissing in the grass.

He started, sitting up and opening his eyes wide, the breath catching in his throat. "Rattl—!" he tried to shout, to warn her.

Bathsheba sprawled on the grass beside him, the dress tangled so tightly around her ankles that she appeared to have no legs.

She smiled crookedly. "Hsssss!"

He shook his head, running a hand through his hair while waiting for it to clear.

"Still scared a' them snakes." Her laugh came short and hard but, when she finally touched him, her voice softened. "Ain't nothin' t'worry about. Now best get dressed, or you'll catch a chill."

Jesse felt cold, a numbing cold that made it difficult to pull up his trousers. Two buttons had been torn from his shirt, and his tie was crumpled and grass-stained. He stuffed it into his pocket.

"Aren't you gonna smoke?" Bathsheba asked.

"Don't folks smoke after they done what we just did?"

"I don't know."

"Go on. I like watchin' you smoke."

"All right."

It calmed him, doing something he always did without thinking, simple as breathing.

"There now, you look right handsome."

"Hardly," he mumbled, feeling his face grow warm.

"Well, you sure do look like one a' them college fellers, all right. You must be awful smart."

"Am I?"

"You're a teacher and a lawyer. You saved my daddy from jail."

"Nate Rosen did most of the work."

"And you're helpin' Sister Claire. You'll get her off, too, just like you did Daddy."

Jesse took a few more puffs. The tobacco cleared his head. "We're doing everything we can, but it won't be easy."

"Why not?"

"There's a great deal of evidence against Mrs. Hobbes. Her fingerprints on the milk carton. Her neighbor placing her in the house before her husband's arrival. The bad blood between your father and Ben Hobbes, and Claire's threat to her husband at last Friday's service. Even poison containing strychnine was found in her home. If you put all that together, I'm afraid the district attorney has a very strong case." He paused to take the cigarette from his mouth; it was a gesture he'd often used in class for its dramatic effect. "Did you ever stop to think that your friend might be guilty?"

Bathsheba sat up, crossing her legs into a lotus position. "Sister Claire wouldn't hurt a fly. I can't believe she done it. Ain't there any other people who'd wanna kill Ben Hobbes? That brother a' his—the way he carried on against my daddy at the funeral. He's sure a mean one."

"I didn't know Ben Hobbes well but enough to know he was a hard man. I imagine there are plenty of people with grudges against him. Nate went with Claire this morning to the reading of the will. That may tell us something, such as who else benefited financially from his death."

"Sure do hope so, because—"

A loud crack interrupted her sentence. Jesse looked up, thinking it might've been thunder, but the sky was clear.

Bathsheba stared past him toward the ridge. "I been around squirrel hunters enough to know a rifle shot when I heared it. Came from over there. We'd better have a look-see."

She was far ahead of Jesse by the time he struggled to his feet and brushed his clothes. His legs were stiff and, hobbling along, he lost her in the tall grass. One moment she was there; the next she'd vanished. He moved faster, almost stumbling over the knotted undergrowth. Not far from the fence protecting the cornfield, he found Bathsheba on her knees bent low. She wasn't alone.

She looked up at him, her eyes glistening. "Oh Lord, it's Lem. He's been shot. I think . . . Lord, I think he's dead."

Jesse forced himself to stare at the body. Lemuel Banks lay awkwardly on his belly, like a rag doll thrown by an angry child. Blood had soaked the back of his shirt from a bullet hole where the middle of his spine used to be. More blood was collecting in a pool under his armpit. He wasn't moving, didn't look as if he was breathing.

Beside him was a gunnysack. Jesse bent close, when a gust of wind sending a chill through his body made him draw back. An instant later a rattlesnake slithered from the bag, quickly sliding into the underbrush. Bathsheba angrily shook the bag, but nothing else fell from it.

"Snake huntin'. Somebody shot him just for snake huntin'." She was sobbing.

"The No Trespassing sign. Do you think . . . ?"

"For snake huntin'!"

Jesse looked into the cornfield, from where the shot must have been fired, and locked eyes with Danny Hobbes. The young man stood behind the open gate, his body turned back toward the field. Seeing Jesse and Bathsheba, he approached the body in that low-slung walk of his.

Before he could say anything, Bathsheba pounced on him like a great cat. He stumbled back, falling to one knee, while her nails clawed his face and neck. Although a big man, Danny couldn't stop her, his biceps straining to hold back the long fingers that cut him.

"Stop it, you crazy bitch! For God's sake, Compton, get her off me!"

"You k-killed him!" she screamed, choking back the tears.

"I didn't touch him! I came running when I heard the shot! I swear!"

Catching Bathsheba off balance, Danny pushed her to the ground and stepped back, balling his hands into fists. Blood trickled down his cheeks from the deep cuts her nails had made. "Don't care if you are a girl. You come at me again, I'll smash your face in."

Springing to her feet, she shouted, "You killed—"

"Didn't do no such thing! Told you, I was working in the field when I heard a shot. Come running and saw you."

"Liar!"

"Then where the hell's the gun I was supposed to use!" He held up his hands. "Where is it?"

When Bathsheba hesitated, Jesse said, "Somebody'd better get the paramedics. And the police."

Dabbing his face with a handkerchief, Danny winced. "I'll call from the factory. You and this crazy bitch stay with him. I'll be right back with help."

Bathsheba stared at Lem's body, blanketed in the first shadows of twilight. Her shoulders sagged; at that moment she had the same beaten dog look as Danny. Maybe the wind was picking up—Jesse buttoned his jacket and rubbed his arms together. It didn't do any good. He just couldn't get warm.

THE SECOND WEEK

Chapter 13

FRIDAY MORNING

"Thank heavens your father's not alive to see his family bear this shame. It's bad enough I have to face our friends and neighbors."

Jesse knew that's what his mother would say when she found out. He would sit across from her bed in the hospital and wait quietly; while arching her eyebrows, she let her coffee grow cold to emphasize her displeasure.

"It's bad enough that you're defending a murderer, but to be mixed up in a murder yourself. . . . How am I to bear the shame?"

Once again, he would endure her words and her face tight as a mask. But, for the first time, that didn't bother him. Nor did he mind sitting in Police Chief Whitcomb's office and being questioned about Lemuel Banks's death.

He had just given his account of the murder and waited while Whitcomb's secretary left to type a copy for his signature. He felt a little groggy, probably from last night's sleeping pill. Across the desk, Whitcomb cracked walnuts in his powerful hands. His thick, stubby fingers had a hard time picking pieces of nut from the broken shell.

Jesse turned to see, through the large window behind him, the station buzzing with activity. Beside one desk, a rough-looking character in a denim jacket stood handcuffed while staring at the ceiling. In the next aisle, a man and woman shouted at each other; the police had to separate them when the lady began kicking her companion. Another officer brought in Keeley, an old man who sang moonshine ballads for liquor money in front of the courthouse. Jesse could see Keeley's face lifted in song, but no one paid the least bit of attention. They'd heard him often enough.

Whitcomb's office seemed out of place, more like a man's den at home. A small television set rested on a snack table in the corner. Bookcases were half filled with penal codes and professional manuals. The rest of the shelving displayed old-time model trains, each car shining like new. On the walls hung framed copies of old Earlyville train schedules and prints of nineteenth-century locomotives. A cuckoo clock read 11:07.

Returning to the room, Whitcomb's secretary placed Jesse's statement on her boss's desk, then stood quietly beside the TV set. Sweeping the walnut shells into a wastebasket, Whitcomb leaned over the statement as if it were dinner and read each word carefully. Again Jesse glanced back into the squad room. Old Keeley was sitting alone in a corner, his trembling hands holding a cup of coffee.

The police chief grunted. "Looks in order." Handing the papers to Jesse, he added, "It don't tell us any more than you said yesterday afternoon in the field. Heard a shot, then found the body. That's about it." He took a folder from his desk drawer and removed what appeared to be another statement. "Your account's the same as the McCrae girl's."

Jesse slowly straightened in his chair. "I take it that Bathsheba has been here already?"

"Oh, yeah. She come in real early, about seven-thirty. Said she was on her way to work—dressed in one of them fast-food outfits."

"I was hoping to . . ." What could he say? That he no longer cared about his family name or what his mother thought? That he'd come down to the police station gladly, thinking only of seeing her again? He was even—God forgive him—grateful for Lem's death, if it could bring him and Bathsheba closer together.

Rosen walked into the office. Rubbing his eyes, he sat in a chair beside Jesse.

"Rough morning?" Whitcomb asked.

"I had another go-round with your supercilious district attorney. Grimes called me into his office just to gloat. Claire's going to be charged with first-degree murder. When I said she's pleading not guilty, he smiled. He wants this to go to trial."

"Well, your friend's finished here."

"Just for the record, I take it that neither Jesse nor Bathsheba McCrae is a suspect in Lemuel Banks's murder."

"I'm sure Jesse told you last night, we tested him and the girl for gunpowder residue. No traces on either of them."

"What about Danny Hobbes? He was there, too."

"We found the murder weapon near the body, just inside the fence by the corn. Ordinary hunting rifle. Most folks in this county own one or two. Ain't gonna help us much—no fingerprints."

"I asked about Danny Hobbes. Did you find traces of gunpowder on him?"

Taking Jesse's signed statement, the police chief busied himself placing the papers in the folder.

"Did you even test him?"

"Well, no. He sort of disappeared after calling in the murder."

"You mean he's in hiding?"

"Don't mean that at all. You lawyers are pretty good at putting words in a feller's mouth. What I said was we couldn't find him. I called his house last night and left a message asking him to come in this morning."

"If it's not too much trouble, that is. Don't you think it's a little suspicious, Lemuel Banks being murdered on Hobbes property? The killer was probably standing in Danny Hobbes's corn, and after the murder Danny disappears."

Whitcomb balled his great hands into fists. "You saying I ain't doing my job?"

"What I'm saying is—"

"Because being at the scene of the crime works both ways. Why was Jesse and that woman trespassing on Hobbes's property? Were they out for a roll in the grass or maybe up to something funny with the victim? He was hunting rattlers; maybe they was hunting them, too. Maybe the two men got into a fight over the woman. That McCrae girl sure is fine-looking, ain't she, Jesse? Good-looking enough for a man to fight over, maybe even kill for."

Jesse reached for his cigarettes. "We were just out walking—discussing her church for a research project I'm doing. That's all. Is it all right if I smoke?"

Whitcomb glared at Jesse, then suddenly broke out laughing. "Course. Ashtray's under a pile of them papers. See how folks can get riled up when there's no cause. After all the dust settles, Banks's death will probably turn out to be another one of them hunting accidents."

Rosen furrowed his brow. "What?"

"Kids is always out hunting rabbit or squirrel. It was late in the afternoon, getting dark. They probably heard a rustling, shot first, and seeing what they'd done, dropped the rifle and ran scared outta their minds."

"You don't really expect—"

"Why, Miss Ruth!" the police chief said. He quickly pushed himself from his chair. "Thank you for coming by. Hello, Danny."

Ruth Hobbes and her son walked into the office. She wore a short leather jacket over a red turtleneck and jeans. Her black hair was pulled back into a long thick braid, which emphasized her Indian features, high cheekbones and dark eyes. Danny's hair was wet and matted, as if he'd just come from the shower.

She put a hand on Jesse's shoulder. "What a terrible thing, seeing somebody murdered. Danny told me all about it. How're you feeling?"

"Fine. Well, I'm a little tired. It was hard getting to sleep after everything that happened."

"Course it was."

Whitcomb pointed to his chair. "Sit down here, Miss Ruth."

"Thank you." She motioned to her son, who slouched against the door. "Come over here, honey, and tell Chief Whitcomb what you know."

Like a boy being dragged before the principal, Danny stepped forward. Whitcomb's secretary, perched on a corner of the desk, wrote what the young man said, then left to type it into a formal statement. Danny mentioned nothing concerning his whereabouts after the shooting.

Folding his arms, the police chief nodded. "Seems in order with what Jesse and Bathsheba McCrae said in their statements. Wouldn't you agree, Jesse?"

But it was Rosen who answered. "Some things need to be clarified."

"Such as?"

"Lemuel Banks was shot in the back and fell facing the highway, toward Jesse. That means whoever murdered him was standing in the cornfield. Since the rifle was dropped at the edge of the field, the killer was close by. Neither Jesse nor Bathsheba saw anyone running away. Danny came up from the field very quickly." He stared at the young man.

Whitcomb asked, "What're you getting at?"

"Danny must've seen whoever killed Banks. He'd have had to. Unless . . . Danny was never tested for gunpowder residue, was he?"

Miss Ruth asked, "What're you all talking about?"

"Where did he—" But before Rosen could finish, Danny Hobbes bolted from the room.

"What's this about gunpowder residue?" Miss Ruth repeated.

Whitcomb looked down at his shoes. "Just a way to check if somebody's fired a gun. Nothing for the boy to worry about."

"No," Rosen agreed. "He's already had plenty of time to wash his hands."

"What are you saying?" she demanded. "You can't possibly believe that my son . . ."

"Course not," the police chief said. "There's not the slightest proof. . . ."

"Where was Danny last night?" Rosen asked.

Whitcomb walked over to him and flexed his hands.

Rosen looked up at the other man. "Need a walnut?"

"I think your head'd be about the right size. You best leave this woman and her family alone."

"You know, they should videotape your work here and start a new television show, 'Interrogations of the Rich and Famous.' "

"What're you getting at?"

Before he could answer, Miss Ruth stood. "I'd like to go now."

Stubbing out his cigarette, Jesse also rose. "I think that's a good idea."

Whitcomb's face reddened in anger, while his hands, balled into fists, struggled to stay at his sides. Rosen stood tense and expectant, his lips almost smiling.

Jesse pulled Rosen by the arm through the police station, until they stood on the outside steps.

"You shouldn't have spoken to Whitcomb like that. It only made him angry."

He braced for Rosen to lash out at him, but his friend suddenly smiled. "That's how I wanted him to react. If he knows someone won't let the investigation slide, maybe he'll look harder for Banks's murderer."

"You mean my son." Ruth Hobbes stood beside them. "Do you really think Danny could've done such a thing?"

Rosen's smile faded but didn't quite leave his face. He hesitated, as if searching for the right words. "I honestly don't know if your son's involved. I think there's a connection between the two murders, and I have a duty to find out the truth."

"A duty to your client, Claire?"

Again Rosen hesitated. This time he didn't answer. Instead, he asked, "Do you need a lift home?"

"Thank you, but it's such a nice day, I'm going to walk."

Located directly behind the old courthouse, the police station was shaded by a giant oak. The edges of the tree's thick green leaves had begun to blush, as if hearing the breeze whisper "Autumn" like an indecent word. It was a "lover's breeze," that slight chill in the air making girls cuddle closer to their sweethearts. Lighting another cigarette, Jesse wished he was walking with Bathsheba. Arm in arm, they would stroll past the courthouse, while other men would turn their heads and think how lucky he was. Pausing before the statue of the old Confederate soldier, he'd explain how it was modeled after his great-granddaddy, who rode with Nathan Bedford Forrest. Then, as she looked up at the statue, her face warmed by the sun and her curls gently tousled by the breeze, he would pull her close; they would kiss and whisper their love for each other. His hands upon her shoulders, pulling her close. . .

"Jesse, are you all right?" It was Rosen.

"Uh . . . yes." He flicked an ash. "I was just thinking about something."

"It's almost noon. How about some lunch at that restaurant you've been bragging about?"

"Huh?"

"You know, down the block by that lawyer Garnet."

"You mean the Country Inn? But I never . . ."

"Sure, that's it. You'll join us, Miss Ruth?"

"Thank you, but I think I'd best be going."

"Please." Rosen touched her arm just above the elbow. "There are still a few questions I'd like to ask you. We could clear up several things that might help Danny."

"Well . . ."

"Maybe the restaurant has some more of that good grits and cracklin' bread."

She laughed. "I know you're joking, but I'll make a real Southerner out of you yet. All right."

The Country Inn was bustling with its usual lunchtime activity. There was no counter, but three tables pulled together and placed near the cash register served the "regulars"—those elderly gentlemen who came for coffee at mid-morning and usually remained several hours. Jesse recognized a few old friends of his father, probably on their fifth cup, as lackadaisical as the restaurant's ceiling fans. After retiring, his father had sat at the chair nearest the cash register, holding court as he had all those decades at the bank. When he died, no one used that chair for over a year. "That's *respect,*" his mother had said, as if the word were foreign to him.

One of the old men, who had been a foreman at the furniture factory, nodded to Miss Ruth. She patted his shoulder, and they exchanged a few words. Scanning the room, Jesse saw that the booths along the wall were filled, as were the dozen tables taking up the floor checkerboard fashion.

"Looks pretty crowded," Jesse said. "It's not really worth the wait. You said I recommended it? Don't know why I would."

Rosen lowered his voice. "You didn't. I wanted to speak to Ruth Hobbes. We still don't know where her son went after reporting Banks's murder."

"Do you really think Danny could be involved?"

Rosen looked at Miss Ruth and almost sighed. "Yes. If he didn't kill Banks, he must've seen who did. And there's a connection to the murder of Ben Hobbes—"

Suddenly a hand shot up from a back table near the swinging kitchen door. Two men sat together. The hand waved them forward.

As they moved closer, Jesse recognized Popper Johnston as the man signaling them. Johnston's hair was combed back into a ponytail; he wore a buckskin jacket over an embroidered shirt and a string tie. Besides the gold earring in his left ear, Popper's right hand flashed a large turquoise ring. In contrast, the other man, pasty-faced, with the heavy jowls of a hound dog, was dressed in a conservative gray business suit. Fiddling with a cigarette, he shifted uncomfortably in his seat.

"Nice to see you all," Popper said. "Please join me. Phil was just leaving."

Rosen shook his head. "Thanks, but we don't want to disturb you. I'm sure a table will open up in a few minutes."

"No trouble at all." To his companion, "I believe we've covered everything. You've got the agreement signed and sealed."

"We're all set to go."

"Fine. See you next week then." When Phil hesitated, Popper said. "Anything else?"

"The deposit. I need . . . ah . . . the five hundred dollars. I'm afraid the check will have to be certified."

Grinning, Popper took out a money clip thick with what appeared to be hundred-dollar bills. He peeled five from the top, handing them to the other man, who, wide-eyed, held them like a child with an ice-cream cone. "No need for a receipt," Popper said. "We're both God-fearing men. Ain't that right, Phil?"

Nodding, the other man counted the money twice before tucking it into his wallet. He stood and made a slight waving motion with his cigarette. "Like I said, my crew will be out a week from today to set things up. As long as you're sure about the permit."

Pointing to Rosen, Popper said, "I believe this man's gonna help me with that. Shouldn't be no problem. After all, this is America, land of the free. See you in a week."

After the other man left, Popper said, "I insist you all sit down. Lady and gentlemen, lunch is on me."

Rosen took the chair across from Popper, while Jesse sat opposite Miss Ruth. Bringing their menus was Emma Teasdale, the oldest waitress in Earlyville and probably the United States. At least once a day she'd ask the owner why he didn't charge a nickel for a Coke, "like your granddaddy did."

"Hello, everyone," she said, looking through her bifocals. "Why, if it ain't young Jesse Compton. How's your mama?"

"Feeling better, Miss Emma. Wish she could get around as well as you do. When you going to retire?"

"When they elect a good Democratic president like Mr. Roosevelt. Now what can I get for you all?"

"I've got a friend here from up North. I want him to have a taste of real good Southern cooking. What do you recommend?"

"I recommend he come over to my house for supper. Why you want to bring him here? Cooks don't listen to a thing I say. Norman overcharges everything. You know how much a Coke costs these days?"

Rosen studied the menu. "Fried chicken, fried

catfish . . . all this fried food. Ah, here. I'd like the hot turkey sandwich. And some tea, please."

"You want that with the fried apples?"

After everyone else had ordered, Popper said, "Lucky I ran into you, Mr. Rosen. I might need your professional services."

"I'm already representing Claire Hobbes—you helped to arrange that. Besides, my specialty is constitutional law. I don't think you'd be needing—"

"Oh, but I might. You see, I have a permit for Reverend McCrae's church to hold a social at Cottonwood Park next Friday. That's that big park on the other side of the college."

"What's the problem?"

"At the social, the Reverend McCrae plans to hold his usual Friday evening service."

"You mean serpent handling?"

Popper nodded.

"You know what to expect. I assume Chief Whitcomb will be there with his shotgun. There is a Tennessee statute against handling poisonous snakes—we've been all through that."

"I know. My question is, can they stop us from meeting in the park?"

"If, as you say, you have a proper permit to hold your church social—no. Once you take out the snakes, that's a different matter. Then you're subject to arrest."

"The thing is . . . what if the authorities knew in advance that's what Reverend McCrae was planning to do?"

"Are you saying they will?"

From inside his buckskin jacket, Popper unfolded a large handbill and laid it on the table.

Even before Jesse read the words, he saw the

drawing of a rattlesnake curled around Bathsheba's shoulders. Both the rattler and the woman stared at him with the same cold eyes. She was smiling. The picture ended just where her breasts began to swell. The drawing excited him, as it would any man who saw it.

"You can't be thinking of putting these all over town?"

Popper clapped his hands. "Oh, yes I am, and not just in Earlyville, but throughout the county. Need as big a crowd as we can get. You remember a few years back, that bestselling poster of a boa constrictor slithering next to some naked actress? Was she anything compared to our Bathsheba? A poster, yeah, that's coming next."

Rosen asked, "What about T-shirts or a music video?"

"Why not? There's nothing you can't do once you set your mind to it. That man who just left—he's an electronics contractor from Nashville. He's wiring the park for another fella who's gonna videotape the service. I've already bought time on one of the local religious channels. If all goes well, we can syndicate it."

"Syndicate what? What are you talking about?"

Popper stretched out his arms. "The Gideon McCrae Ministry of Healing."

The words seemed to die slowly, like distant thunder. No one spoke for the next minute. Then Emma brought lunch.

"You all look a might pale," she said, putting down the plates. "Folks usually don't get that way until after they've eaten this sorry excuse for food. More tea, young feller?"

They ate in silence. Jesse barely touched his sandwich while, across the table, Miss Ruth picked at her salad. Like him, she kept glancing at the handbill of Bathsheba and the snake. In contrast, Rosen seemed to relish his meal. Only his furrowed brow betrayed what Jesse had often seen during law school. His friend was thinking hard, evaluating not only what Popper had just said but also its implications. It was only after he'd finished his meal that Rosen returned to the subject.

"Popper, you're taking a chance."

"In what way?"

"Once the authorities see those handbills and know definitely what you're up to, they can ask a judge to rescind your permit."

"What about the First Amendment—free speech and right of assembly?"

"As your district attorney is fond of saying, there's no such thing as an absolute right. A number of years ago the village of Skokie, Illinois, refused to allow the Nazi party to march through the center of town. The village was worried that the march would not only cause psychological damage to its Jewish residents but that violence might ensue. Given what happened at Reverend McCrae's serpent-handling service last week, Earlyville might have the same worry about, at the very least, a disturbance of the peace." He paused to drink his tea, then added, "Of course, that's what you want."

Leaning back in his chair, Popper signaled for the check.

Rosen continued, "The police breaking up the service—on video. That's just the touch you'd need. You already have that certain bizarre quality with the rattlesnakes. Crawling over a beautiful woman like Bathsheba—how Freudian can you get? And that final touch, Chief Whitcomb and his shotgun.

It's like Billy Graham meets Madonna. Sure, I'd say you could syndicate the program."

"No!" Jesse blurted, grabbing the handbill with both hands and crumpling it into a ball. "You can't do this to her. I won't let you."

Popper scratched his head. "All we're doing is following the word of God. It's a free country, Mr. Compton."

"Jesse's right," Miss Ruth said. "This thing you're planning ain't right. It's real bad for the town."

Popper asked Rosen, "Will you help us in case the town tries to rescind the permit?"

"Does Gideon McCrae know everything you have planned? The posters, the television show?"

"He knows I'm helping him reach out to others in need. He's agreed to let me handle the business end. He only has to worry about preaching the true Word."

"Those news cameramen suddenly appearing to film Ben Hobbes's funeral service—that was your idea, wasn't it? You knew how Simon Hobbes would react to Reverend McCrae taking the pulpit. A cheap way of getting publicity for the church."

"Not cheap—free. That's the best kind. In fact, after lunch, I'm going over to our local paper, the *Earlyville Sentinal,* demanding they run an editorial about Brother Lemuel's death. I believe he was killed by somebody who hates our church, just 'cause we worship differently. Maybe now you'll see us folks just tryin' to practice our religion."

Rosen stared at the other man for a long time, then asked, "Where'd you get the money to finance this?"

The question came suddenly and seemed to catch Popper by surprise. As angry as Jesse was, he'd never have asked it. It wasn't a "Southern" question—too direct, but it was exactly what a good lawyer would ask. Just then Emma brought the check.

"I was able to find some very generous backers." Popper took the check and, pulling out his money clip, left a tip almost equaling the cost of lunch.

Miss Ruth asked, "What kind of businessmen would invest in a church?"

"The kind who want, as their only profit, the spread of God's Word. There are such men." Fingering the wad of money, he added, "You haven't answered me, Mr. Rosen. Can I retain your services?"

"No."

Popper waited for an explanation. When none came, he grinned and walked to the cash register, then out the door.

Watching him leave, Jesse felt the ball of paper hot in his fist. He looked down and, past his whitened knuckles, imagined the rattlesnake coiled tightly around Bathsheba. He wouldn't let that happen. Pushing back his chair, he hurried through the restaurant, not caring that others, watching him, clicked their tongues and probably whispered, "That Compton boy—what's wrong with him?"

Outside, Jesse looked in both directions, but Popper was gone. Jesse sat on the bench in front of the restaurant, as the pigeons scattered. Moving his hand to wipe his brow, Jesse saw it was still clenched. He relaxed it and unrolled the handbill. Looking into Bathsheba's eyes, he felt somebody staring through the window of the restaurant. His father's friends, the old men who came there every day to gossip, because there was no longer anything in their own lives worth discussing.

Bathsheba was looking at him and smiling, as if

to say, "Why do you care what they think or say? When two people are in love, nothing else matters."

"That's right," Jesse said to himself. "When you're in love, nothing else matters," and smoothing the handbill over his knee, he smiled back at her.

Chapter 14

SATURDAY EVENING

Walking into the popular culture center, Rosen smelled the roasting meat and the spices of the simmering potpourri. He called out, "I've got the wine!"

"In the workroom!" Jesse replied. "Everything's almost ready! They should be here in twenty minutes!"

Rosen walked into the workroom and stopped suddenly, blinking hard. He'd been gone most of the day, doing research in the county court building, and wasn't prepared for the room's transformation. One of the two worktables was gone; the other, stripped of its piles of papers, proved to be a handsome trestle. It was surrounded by four straight-back chairs carved from the same dark wood as the table. The dishes were fine china, the napkin rings and candlesticks silver. Two serving bowls, cut from blue glass, matched the centerpiece vase, filled with marigolds.

Jesse was lighting one of the candles. Through the window the sun's rays flowed obliquely, casting half his body in dark shadow, like a Rembrandt. He seemed to belong to that era, as gentleman and master of the house, instead of to a world that preferred hamburgers to roast duckling.

He stepped from the shadows. His light gray suit,

a European cut, made his movements appear even more graceful. He could've been Fred Astaire.

"What kind of wine did you get?"

"I told the clerk . . ."

"Charles prefers to be called a wine merchant."

"Then he should wear a tuxedo instead of an apron. I told him what you wanted. He said they were temporarily out of stock." Rosen handed Jesse the bottle. "He thought this might do as well."

"Hmm, I did want something robust, but this may be a bit too bold for the ladies."

"Oh, let's be bold. Besides, it looks all right."

"And how would you know?"

"It doesn't unscrew. What a beautiful table. You'd make somebody a great wife."

Jesse smiled. "It is nice having company. I don't entertain much. I've grown apart from my mother and sister and, consequently, the family friends. I put in an occasional appearance at the club, but those men might just as well be strangers." He cradled the wine gently. "I've been thinking about her, Nate."

"Bathsheba?"

"I've been thinking of asking her to marry me. If I did and she said yes, we'd have to move. Do you think she'd understand? It would take a miracle for the people of this town to leave us alone. Those kinds of miracles just don't happen."

"Couldn't you say the hell with them?"

"If I had your courage. I know you did that to your father." He paused. "And I think I know what it cost."

Rosen started to turn away.

"Sorry, Nate, I shouldn't have said that. It's just . . . I can't imagine living without her."

"Suppose she won't leave her church? Don't these Fundamentalists lead a pretty strict life?"

Jesse thought about their time together in the field and suppressed a smile. "I don't believe she's entirely orthodox. Besides . . . there's something about her church I find appealing."

"Sure, its long legs."

"I'm serious. I took down my Bible today and read through it. Thinking about Reverend McCrae's church, the earnestness of his congregation's song and prayer, made the words come alive for the first time."

"What about the snake handling?"

"At least those people felt something inside. Do you know how long it's been since I've felt anything real?"

"You sound a little lovesick."

Jesse's hands gripped the wine. "Yes, Bathsheba's part of it, but only part. I thought, of all people, you'd understand."

Rosen shrugged. "I'm sorry. Guess you touched a nerve when you mentioned my father. I didn't mean to . . ."

"No, I'm the one who should apologize. I shouldn't have brought all this up. We're supposed to be carving a delicious dinner tonight, not our souls."

"Forget it. Look, I'm going upstairs to change. I'll even put on my good suit."

Jesse shook his head. "And I said I didn't believe in miracles."

Twenty minutes later, Rosen walked downstairs just as the doorbell rang. "I'll get it!" He opened the door and saw yet another Claire Hobbes.

She wore a black silk blouse with pleated skirt and black stockings. The string of pearls and matching earrings looked real. Her makeup, artfully applied, highlighted her eyes and made her lips fuller. She really was an attractive woman, yet still had that childlike vulnerability. As in the way she clutched her purse with both hands. No wonder Ben Hobbes had been so taken with her; she was that irresistible combination of a woman to love and a girl to protect.

"Hello, Nate. Thanks so much for inviting me. Such a nice thought." Her voice lilted.

"It was Jesse's idea, really. He's needed a reason to show off his cooking since I arrived. By the way, I tried to reach you at home yesterday evening."

"Yesterday . . . oh, I was in church. Our Friday evening service. Don't worry, there weren't any snakes."

A second car rolled up the drive—a black Lincoln Continental.

Rosen continued, "I wanted to tell you that I met a few of your friends Thursday."

"Really?"

"Yeah, from Nashville."

The smile froze on her face.

"They had some very interesting things to say about you."

As if she hadn't heard, Claire said, "Why, Ruth, how pretty you look!"

Ruth Hobbes walked up the steps as the Lincoln began a wide circle, then paused. Ruth's son, who was driving, glanced from his mother to Rosen; then his gaze rested on Claire. She shifted slightly, as if a spider had crawled upon her, and stepped into the hallway. Danny suddenly accelerated, screeching tires kicking up dust as the car sped away.

"Be careful!" Ruth called after him, then shook

her head. "Guess boys will be boys. Evenin', everyone."

She wore a long dress, the color of pewter, and silver earrings. A silver comb flashed in her thick black hair, which fell straight back almost to her waist.

Claire said, "I could've driven you, Ruth."

"That's all right. Danny had some things to do in town. He'll pick me up later. I don't drive so good at night, especially after a few glasses of wine. Well, here's our host now."

Jesse stepped into the hallway holding a tray of hot hors d'oeuvres—stuffed mushrooms, bacon wrapped around water chestnuts, and various cheeses bubbling over crackers.

"Oh, this is elegant," Ruth said. "Thank you so much for the invitation."

"Yes, Jesse," Claire added, "this is so nice."

"It's my pleasure. With all the pain Claire's been going through, I thought she could use a bit of cheering up. Now, why don't we all sit down and relax. The wine's already decanted. Dinner should be ready in a few minutes."

They walked into a small room on the other side of the hall. It had probably once been a bedroom but was converted into a comfortable drawing room. It had the same handsome wooden furniture as upstairs—rocking chairs, couch with a blue Williamsburg print, coffee table, and built-in bookshelves. The authors ranged from the classics to the great Southern writers, like Faulkner and Flannery O'Connor. Another dozen of Jesse's dour ancestors, in framed photographs, stared down from the wall. Looking into their eyes, Rosen understood why Jesse's family would never understand a marriage to Bathsheba.

The two ladies sat on the couch, while Jesse poured the wine, then took a chair beside Rosen. "I hope you enjoy this. It should prepare us nicely for the more full-bodied dinner wine."

"This is wonderful," Ruth said, "but I'm afraid it's spoiled on the likes of me. When we was raised up back in Kentucky, all we had was my Uncle Alvin's moonshine."

"That had an art all to itself, the same as fine wine."

"You're right as rain. I remember Uncle Alvin getting into a fight with a customer who accused him of rigging up some tubing made outta tin. Old Uncle Alvin swore he'd only use copper tubing. Said any man who didn't use copper oughta be hung. Funny, ain't it, how my uncle never minded breaking the law by running a still, yet had his own laws about making 'shine that he'd die before breaking?"

Jesse shrugged. "That's not so strange. History shows us a number of people who followed their own law, even when it went against the government. Some of them most folks admire, like Thoreau and Gandhi and Dr. King."

Rosen said, "Then there're those like Son of Sam and Ted Bundy, whose law told them to murder as many people as they could get their hands on."

Ruth took a long sip of wine. "That's sure a lawyer's answer, sticking up for the law. But people make the law. Don't you guess that sometimes they make mistakes that others see, like Dr. King?"

Rosen rubbed his eyes. "Sure. There is one immutable law, the law of God. That's what Dr. King was following."

"But even God's law could be some pretty rough justice."

"You mean like stoning adulteresses?" He glanced at Claire, who turned away to look into her wine. "Perhaps, but what happens when you ignore God's law? Are you willing to risk being swallowed by a whale or drowned in the Great Deluge?"

"I won't argue with you, Nate. You sure do sound like a preacher."

Jesse said, "He studied to be a rabbi."

"Is that right? You woulda been a good one. What happened?"

"My father and I had a disagreement. Like you, Ruth, I questioned the severity of God's laws. My footsteps didn't quite fit into the ones my father had laid before me. We had a parting of the ways. To this day, he hasn't forgiven me."

Jesse muttered, " 'How sharper than a serpent's tooth,' " then caught himself. "I'm sorry. Just something my mother says about me came to mind."

Claire looked up. "That's Shakespeare—*King Lear*."

"Do you like Shakespeare?"

"Uh-huh, especially his sonnets." She walked to the bookshelf and took down *The Complete Works of William Shakespeare*. Flipping through the pages, she read:

"Shall I compare thee to a summer's day?
Thou art more lovely and more temperate;
Rough winds do shake the darling buds of May,
And summer's lease hath all too short a date."

She closed the book. "Sure is pretty."

"Yes," Rosen said. "I've often found that people who enjoy reading poetry also write it. Do you write any poetry?"

She blushed, looking even more fragile and endearing. "It's not very good."

"Would you recite some for us?"

"Oh, yes, please," Ruth said.

"No, I can't. I'd be too embarrassed, especially after reading Shakespeare."

Rosen asked, "You write sonnets?"

She nodded.

"Then they must be love poems. Were they to your husband?"

Her cheeks darkened even more, and for a moment, her jaw set tight. Finally she said, "Like I told you before, I'm a little embarrassed. Rather not talk about it."

"Maybe you wrote them to Hec Perry."

The book almost fell from her hands.

He continued, "As I was telling you before, I met some of your friends in Nashville Thursday. Hec Perry wanted me to say hello, but then, you still see him from time to time."

Returning the book—at the same time hiding her face—she replied, "We're old friends, that's all."

"What about one of your new friends, a man named Aadams?"

"Who?"

"Aadams with a double *a*. He's the kind of guy mothers point at to scare their kids into behaving."

"I don't know who—"

"He's a private detective who says you're his client."

"Oh, that man. Yes, well, he offered to investigate Ben's death. I thought it wouldn't hurt to have someone else helping you and Jesse on the case. He showed me good credentials."

"The kind of people writing him a recommendation think a 'pen' is a prison. What's the real reason?"

"I don't think I like the way this conversation is turning."

"Then why don't—"

"I believe that dinner is ready," Jesse blurted. "Claire, if I may have the honor." Taking her arm, he led her from the room.

Ruth said to Rosen, "I guess that means you're escorting me, unless, with the mood you're in, you'd rather go a few rounds."

He pursed his lips, about to tell her his suspicions, then shook his head. "I'd never stand a chance. If I may have the honor."

He sat across from Ruth at the dining room table, with Jesse and Claire on either side. They ate their salads quietly.

Feeling guilty for causing the change in mood, he cleared his throat. "I can't wait to see what Jesse's prepared. He wouldn't let me into the kitchen."

Jesse poured the wine. "Well, after hearing you cast aspersions on our Southern cusine . . ."

"Me? Never."

"I think Jesse's right," Ruth said, smiling. "I still haven't seen you eat any of our good cracklin' bread."

"You mean that pig grease?"

Jesse stood. "I believe it's time."

He walked into the kitchen and, returning a moment later set on the table a deep serving tray.

"Smells great," Rosen said. "What Southern delicacy is it?"

"Yankee pot roast."

They looked at one another, then burst out laughing. Jesse brought out a casserole and bread.

"Miss Ruth, would you do the honor of saying grace?"

"Of course."

As she prayed, Rosen fought back the memories of blessing the wine and bread. His father's soft words when speaking to the Lord, the aroma of his mother's freshly baked challah, his older brothers jostling one another under the table. He'd never felt as warm or as safe. He'd never feel that way again.

Music was playing; the tape machine was on. He recognized the instrument, a dulcimer as sweet as Hec Perry had played.

Ruth clapped her hands. "Why, that's Will Stevens. I ain't heard him since I was a little girl. He's from my grandfolks' time. Come outta the same hills as us and worked the coal mines, too. All that black dust finally killed him. Jesse, you knew he was from the same parts as me. That was right nice a' you."

"I'm glad you like it. Our center found a few of his old records in somebody's attic. I made this tape for you to take along home."

"Lord bless you. And what's this casserole? Why, Nate, I do believe you are in for a treat after all. That there's cheese grits." As Jesse served the casserole, she asked, "Do you melt the cheese first, before stirring it into the grits?"

"Is there any other way? I add a touch of garlic. What do you think?"

"Mmm, delicious," Ruth said. Claire nodded in agreement.

"Nate?"

Rosen took a bite and chewed it carefully. "Not bad. Actually, it's pretty good."

Again Ruth clapped her hands. "Well, success at last!"

"One question," he asked. "These grits are supposed to be Southern cooking?"

"Sure enough."

"Then why aren't they fried?"

Laughing, they chatted about food, music, the work of the popular culture center, and Ruth's growing up in coal mining country. She and Jesse did most of the talking. Occasionally Claire glanced at the tape recorder, as if Hec Perry was sitting a few feet away playing his dulcimer. They finished dinner with a dessert called huckleberry cobbler, made by another one of Jesse's inexhaustible supply of cousins. Like everything else he'd served, it called for a second helping.

Afterward Ruth said, "My buttons are popping!"

"Yes, Jesse, so good," Claire agreed.

"I'm glad you all enjoyed it. Now shall we adjourn to the drawing room for a cordial? I have a rather fine selection of liqueurs."

As they stood, Rosen said to Jesse, "Really a terrific dinner. If you'll excuse me for a few minutes, I need to make a call. I tried to get Sarah yesterday, but she was out."

"Of course. Take all the time you need."

He walked upstairs and, sitting at Jesse's desk by the telephone, noticed he'd carried his wine. For a devout Jew wine could be good when sanctified at the meal. Like sex, when it was between a man and wife in love. Sarah was a sanctification of what had been his love for Bess. Is that why he felt so sick inside when he dialed his ex-wife's number?

Sarah answered. "Hello."

"Hi, Shana." That was his pet name for her; it was Yiddish for "dear one." "Glad I caught you. I've just had the best dinner."

He spoke for a few minutes about Jesse and

Ruth, and a little about the case. Usually Sarah listened eagerly, interrupting him with repeated questions. She was quiet, however, patiently waiting for him to finish his small talk. Finally she did interrupt.

"Daddy, why did you call, really?"

"You know. It's what we started to talk about last time. About your mother getting remarried."

"Why bother? There's nothing I can do about it. And you . . . you won't do anything."

He didn't expect her hurt to come out so fast. He said softly, "Shana, there's nothing I can do. Your mother has the right to live her own life."

"You can—"

"There's nothing I can do."

"You *can* do something. Mom always said you thrived on lost causes. What else would you call our family?"

She was damn smart. He'd try another tack. "Shelly, your mother's friend, how does he treat you?"

"He touches people's feet all day long."

"Better than being a proctologist." She didn't laugh. "You know what a proctologist—"

"I know. Just like Mom used to say—you and your stupid jokes."

Suddenly he saw the three of them together, the way it so often used to be in their small suburban home. His legal work would be spread on the dining room table, while Bess graded papers and Sarah, between them, did her homework. They'd listen to classical recordings, what Bess herself had listened to when first taking up the piano. Every so often Rosen would slip in a Thelonious Monk album, and she would shake her head at his "stupid joke" while he and Sarah laughed. Bess didn't mean anything by it, not at first; he remembered how, late at night, she'd laugh softly in his arms and whisper her love. How they'd loved each other, but that was before his ambition proved to be as small as their home, and for her as confining.

He felt the old hurt coming on. It had been four years since the divorce, yet still it happened. Sometimes when he saw a family walking from church, or a schoolteacher carrying a bunch of papers, or a woman pushing up the sleeves of her sweater as Bess always did, or when he awoke suddenly in the middle of the night and reached over to her side of the bed. God, was that it? Was he really afraid, not for Sarah, but for himself?

"Daddy?"

"I'm sorry. Tell me about . . . Shelly. Is he a nice man?"

"I don't know."

"Be fair."

"I guess so. He tries to be nice."

"What about the big question? He's not a . . . you know."

She finally laughed, and a little of his pain went away. "No, he's not a White Sox fan. At least he won't admit it. He's going to take Mom and me with his sons to see the Cubs play the Mets."

"Great. Sit in the bleachers, and if he doesn't throw back the New York home runs, you have my permission to beat him with my autographed Ron Santo bat."

"Oh, Daddy, I wish I could stay with you. Then maybe Mom getting married wouldn't be so bad."

"Would you . . . like to visit for a while? Maybe when your mom and Shelly go on their honeymoon—it's supposed to be in November, right? We'll spend Thanksgiving together."

"A lot we'd have to be thankful for."

"We'd have each other."

"I'm sorry, Daddy, I didn't mean . . . Can I come? Mom was going to have me spend the time with Grandma and Grandpa. You know how much fun a week with them can be."

"What do you mean? You're probably the only fourteen-year-old girl in the world who's an A-rated player in mah-jongg."

Again she laughed. "Oh, Daddy. I can stay with you, can't I?"

"Sure. I'll talk to your mother."

"She's out with Shelly tonight. You know, you and I haven't really settled anything."

"Yes, Miss Freud, I know. But it's a start."

"Just a second. I think Becky and Tina are at the door." She came back a minute later. "We're going to pig out on pizza and watch this video *All That Jazz*. You ever hear of it?"

"Are you kidding? It's great."

"The title reminded me of you."

"You always have the right comeback. You sure you want to be a concert pianist and not a lawyer? Have fun, honey. I'll talk to you soon."

"I love you, Daddy."

"Love you too, Shana. 'Bye."

Putting down the receiver, Rosen stared at his glass, then finished the wine in one swallow. He was sweating and took out a handkerchief to wipe his forehead. Glancing at his watch, he saw he'd been talking for almost twenty minutes. They'd be wondering what happened to him. He stood quickly and left the room but, at the head of the stairs, suddenly felt light-headed. Almost stumbling on the first step, he grabbed the handrail and sat down heavily.

His face lay against the cool wall while he listened as the blood pounding in his ears gradually subsided and his heartbeat slowed to normal.

"Nate? Lord, are you all right?"

Ruth hurried up the steps and sat beside him, putting her hand over his. "Are you all right?" she repeated.

He nodded. "Is this what cheese grits does to you?"

"What happened?"

He hesitated but, looking into her face, saw the same soft brown eyes as of his old rabbi. Her hand holding his was as gentle, and she waited patiently, as the old man had always done, while he gathered the courage to speak.

"I'm not exactly sure. Something that's been buried deep inside finally crawled out."

"Something back home? Jesse said you were calling your daughter. I got a mite worried when you didn't come downstairs. Sure you're all right?"

Loosening his tie, Rosen inhaled deeply and nodded. "My wife's getting remarried. It's upset Sarah, my daughter, quite a bit. Part of me's always felt bad about never being there for her."

"I bet you try."

"I do—doesn't make it hurt less."

Ruth shifted to give him more breathing space but still held his hand. "I bet you do better than you think. I told you about my oldest boy, Skip, dying overseas. You talk about hurt. At least your girl's alive. You'll see her grow up, get married, have a family of her own. Ain't a day goes by that I don't cry a little inside for my boy. It's an awful ache—like a man whose leg's been cut off but he's still got the feeling it's there."

"I never would've brought this up if I'd thought you'd be hurt. . . ."

"It's all right." She squeezed his hand. "Good for me to have somebody to talk to 'bout this. Simon, he don't want to hear Skip's name no more. Hurts too much, and Danny ain't exactly been his pride and joy. You all right to go back now?"

"Sure." He hesitated, then added, "You know what's funny, Ruth? Part of me's sad for how my ex-wife's remarriage is affecting Sarah. The other part—it's what you just talked about. Our marriage has been dead for years, yet I keep feeling it."

"Do you think you still love her?"

Holding the railing, Rosen pulled himself up. "In love with Bess? God help us both if I am."

Chapter 15

SUNDAY MORNING

Rosen stared into the open casket beside the pulpit. Dressed in a cheap blue suit, Lemuel Banks lay on the cushion like a scrawny fighting cock. The young black man's soul had long since fled its body to rest in heaven; that was as it should be. Yet, Rosen wished he could pull it back for one minute. Once he wouldn've dared asked the unaskable—"What was the Face of God?" Now, his unregenerate self thought only of the case and wondered, "Who murdered you?"

Upon Banks's chest lay an open Bible, a passage underlined from Mark: "They will pick up serpents." As if that answered all questions.

Rosen turned to join Jesse in the front row, along with Claire, Reverend McCrae, his daughter, and the old man named Tucker. Their church was filled to capacity, about seventy people, men wearing old suits shiny at the knees and women in long print dresses. It wasn't much of a church, just the old house Ben Hobbes had willed to McCrae's congregation. Several interior walls had been knocked down to create one big room for worship with rows of folding chairs to serve as pews, cracked windows instead of stained glass, and an old wooden podium. But the building didn't matter; it never mattered to those who truly loved God. Like Rosen's ancient ancestors, forced to wander the earth, whose synagogue was never really a place but a people.

In a corner past the pulpit, a man played the guitar, while the congregants clapped in time to the music. Four policemen mixed with the crowd, while near the front door Chief Whitcomb held a shotgun in his huge hands.

A few minutes later, Tucker stepped behind the pulpit, and the guitarist stopped his playing. As the old man began speaking, the loose skin under his neck jiggled, and he wiped his eyes with the back of his hand.

"I knowed Lemuel Banks 'bout as good as anybody here. Sure knowed what he loved best—the Lord, his brethren sittin' right here, and the sweet music his guitar played. Brother Clay pickin' on Lem's guitar a minute ago—that was right nice. We're lookin' t'hear more of it soon enough. You all . . . you all know Lem had a hard life. Found the Lord in jail, but that's all right. Like it says in Acts, 'Repent and be baptized every one of you in Jesus' name, and you'll receive the g-gift of the Holy G-ghost.' " He stopped to wipe his eyes again. "Brother Lemuel got that gift, praise Jesus!"

"Amen!" the congregation shouted.

Taking out a handkerchief, the old man blew his nose and coughed hard. "Brother Clay . . . why don'tcha play some more a' Lem's favorites. Let's all join in the spirit. Hallelujah!"

The guitarist resumed playing, and the congregation clapped louder, swaying to the rhythm and singing. Even Jesse sang, glancing at Bathsheba, who stood beside him. The song had something to do with Jesus' everlasting arms, and no one needed a hymnal to know the words. No one except Rosen.

He edged along the wall past a policeman until he reached the front entrance. Cradling his shotgun, Whitcomb stood against the door frame. Rosen jerked his head, and the two men stepped onto the front porch, closing the screen door behind them.

"Expecting trouble, Chief?"

Whitcomb smiled. "Maybe a little more target practice, that's all. District attorney ain't taking any chances about another disturbance by these people. Don't want no snakes popping out of the casket, like it was some trick can of peanut brittle."

"Maybe your guns should be pointed out there, not inside the church."

"Why's that?"

"Maybe Lemuel Banks was murdered by some fanatic who hated Reverend McCrae's 'snake-cult.' At least that's what some people say."

Whitcomb screwed his face tight. "What people?"

"The congregation inside. Friday afternoon I ran into Popper Johnston, Reverend McCrae's cousin. He's of the same mind. He was on his way to the newspaper office and said the church wasn't going to take this lying down."

"Don't like him. He's on the make—him and his Nashville ideas. Wouldn't be surprised if he didn't try to make McCrae into a cross between Jesus and Elvis. Know what I'm saying?"

Rosen laughed. "You may be right. Have you learned anything new regarding Banks's death?"

"Not much. The bullet that killed him matches the rifle we found near the body, but we guessed as much. Like I said before, probably just a hunting accident."

"You know that Danny Hobbes is lying."

"What makes you think that?"

"Jesse said, after he heard the gunshot, no one ran past him across the open field. The only other way of escape was through the corn. If Danny didn't shoot Banks, he must've seen who did."

Whitcomb rubbed his jaw. "Maybe not. Lot of land under the plow, and corn's pretty tall. The killer could've got past the boy." When Rosen shook his head, the police chief said, "Damn it, it could've happened that way! I've known Danny all his life. He couldn't do such a thing."

"Did you test Danny's father for gunpowder residue or ask if he had an alibi at the time of the murder?"

"You crazy? Why should I suspect him?"

"Who in this town hates McCrae's church more than Simon Hobbes? At his brother's funeral service, he practically accused McCrae of murdering Ben. He was pretty open with his threats and, after all, Lemuel Banks was killed on Hobbes's property."

"The boy was trespassing. Hunting for rattlesnakes, of all things!"

"Is murdering a poacher legal in this county?"

Whitcomb gripped the shotgun so hard his knuckles whitened. "You get smart with me, I'll find an excuse to kick your ass back to wherever you come from. I can't suspect someone like Simon Hobbes of murder without no evidence. Let's leave it as a real bad joke."

"But you haven't answered—"

"I said, best let it be. I'm going to check the service. Do yourself a favor, and just keep out of my way." Walking inside, he snickered, "Simon Hobbes—the very idea."

As the screen door banged shut, Rosen sat on the front steps. The day was sunny and warm. Unbuttoning his jacket, he noticed the torn lapel where that detective Aadams had grabbed his coat before throwing him out of Hec Perry's room. He had stood outside Perry's door for a few minutes, then left, intending to return the next day. That was before this second murder. Here he was again outside the door, always the outsider looking in, like the wandering Jew of old. Listening to old Tucker preach and the congregation shout their "Hallelujahs," Rosen remembered that the anniversary of his grandfather's death would be in a few days. He would have to light the *yahrzeit* candle of remembrance; the one thing he still did, no matter where he was. Bowing his head, he whispered the Kaddish, both for his grandfather and Lemuel Banks.

He felt tired and a little dizzy. Of course he was dizzy; he'd been running blindly through a maze whose paths didn't lead home but, rather, in convolutions from the house of Ben Hobbes, whose murder had started the investigation. The paths seemed to lead nowhere, like the one to the furniture factory where Simon Hobbes refused to talk, the cheap apartment where Hec Perry played his mournful songs, or the field's tall grass where Lemuel Banks had been murdered. Rosen considered the path that had led him to this church and the people inside. Claire and the McCraes, Gideon and Bathsheba. Did Claire really commit the murder; if so, was she acting alone or merely as a servant of her preacher's will? Was McCrae for real, or was the D.A. right in portraying him as another Charles Manson?

Shaking his head, Rosen heard the congregation's hymn. He stood on the porch steps and stretched stiffly. Wherever he was in the maze that had begun with Ben Hobbes's death, he was certain the correct path lay somewhere through those church doors. And so he returned to the service.

He stood against the back wall, next to Whitcomb, who shifted his shotgun while scanning the congregation. He nodded to his deputies on either side of the room. One policeman rested a hand on his holster. Looking at the shotgun, Rosen remembered why Whitcomb was at the service. He felt a chill in his spine—would the snakes come out? His gaze followed Whitcomb's toward the pulpit.

Tucker was no longer conducting the service. Reverend McCrae stood behind the pulpit, arms outstretched and eyes closed in prayer.

"Matthew nineteen: 'Oh, Lord, we've forsaken all to follow you. What shall we then have?' And Jesus, in His sweet mercy, answered, 'You shall sit in the throne a' his glory, and you all shall inherit everlastin' life.' That's what He said, praise Jesus, 'everlastin' life'!"

"Amen!" the congregants shouted.

"Not only that, but He also said, 'He who's first shall be last, and he who's last'll be first'! Ain't that somethin'!"

"Sure is, praise Jesus!"

McCrae lowered his hands to grip the podium and stared into the congregation. He seemed to be looking directly at Rosen. "What does that have t'do with Brother Lemuel stretched out in front a' us? Why, everything in the world. Lem called hisself a miserable sinner, just like us all. But he also believed, with all his heart, in the sweet mercy a' Jesus. That makes every bit a' difference, because he shall inherit everlastin' life. That's why this here service ain't no time for cryin'. Brother Lemuel's soul's bein' rocked by the lovin' arms a' Jesus. We should be happy for him. Ain't that right?"

"Yessir, Reverend! Amen!"

"As for the man who killed him—whoever that man may be—don't let your heart be filled with hatred. Pity him as you would a traveler who's lost the right good road and stumbles blindly in the storm, only gettin' stuck deeper 'n' deeper in the black mud a' sin. Pray for his soul to find the right path, just as Lord Jesus forgave sinners such as ourselves. Amen."

"Amen!"

"Let's have some singin', then, just like Brother Lemuel woulda' wanted. Brother Clay, take up that guitar a' his, and play somethin' joyous. We're celebratin' the Lord raisin' up the spirit of a good neighbor and friend. 'You shall sit in the throne 'n' have everlastin' life.' Oh, glory of our Lord Jesus! In His name only shall ye live!"

Hands began clapping even before Brother Clay began to play. He sang something about the Lord's abiding light, but soon his voice was lost among dozens of other singers whose hands beat time to a guitar they could no longer hear. From his front row seat, old Tucker stood and walked down the aisle shouting "Praise Jesus!" like a train conductor announcing the next stop.

Other people also stood. They blocked Rosen's view but, walking along the side wall, he saw McCrae's daughter, Bathsheba, stand, her lithe body swaying. She held out her hands. Claire took one and stood beside her.

A moment later, Jesse took Bathsheba's other hand. He sang louder, his body moving awkwardly to the music. Suddenly he began trembling in fits and jerks, his face flushed and sweating, while his mouth struggled to form words. Unable to speak, he sank to his knees, both hands grabbing Bathsheba's. Rosen wanted to run to his friend but found his own hands gripping the back of a chair, as if that alone kept him afloat in an endless sea.

The service continued for another fifteen minutes—singing and clapping and praying to the Lord. Gradually the music diminished, until only a few voices sang the hymn. Then only the gentle strumming of Lemuel's guitar played by Brother Clay, until that, too, ceased.

From the pulpit, Reverend McCrae glanced at the coffin. "That was right nice. I believe Brother Lemuel was joinin' us from up there in heaven. Remember, everybody, the burial's at Deer Creek Cemetery at noon. That's in about an hour. Afterward, you folks are all invited back here for eatin'. The sisters have cooked up a mess a' good food. We expect t'see you all. Lord bless you. Amen."

"Amen," echoed the congregants, who turned to shake one another's hand or to embrace. A few left; most, however, remained to chat. They spoke of the weather, broken automobiles, a new family that had joined the church—everything except Lemuel Banks's funeral.

Standing near the pulpit, Whitcomb ordered two of his deputies to the burial, "Just in case."

When the police chief finished, Rosen said, "Guess the show's over."

"Wasn't much of a show, except for your friend there. Who'd a' thought Jesse Compton . . . ?"

"Chief, can we keep this about Jesse between the two of us, at least for a while? He's been under a lot of stress lately."

Whitcomb rubbed his jaw. "Hell, why not. I'll speak to my men."

"Thanks."

"You best get Jesse to a proper service, like the

one Reverend Taylor gives downtown at the Baptist Church." He stretched. "Guess I'll be able to go home to a right good lunch and watch me some football. You like the Bengals?"

"I don't follow football too much. I'm a Chicago Cubs fan."

"Cubs? Hell, if you like Chicago, at least go for the Bears. They're winners."

"Thanks, but I always seem to drift toward the losers."

"Like McCrae here and his bunch. Well, I'm dropping by the burial later to make sure everything stays quiet. Probably see you there."

"I expect so. Enjoy your lunch, Chief."

After the police left the church, Rosen turned to Jesse, who still sat on the floor, his hands clutching Bathsheba's.

Kneeling beside his friend, Rosen said softly, "Come on, let's sit in a chair. I'll help you."

Flushed and glassy-eyed, Jesse stared straight ahead, his breathing shallow. Gripping one of his arms, Rosen struggled to lift him. Bathsheba helped, and together they dragged him to a chair in the front row.

"Jesse?"

For a minute there was no response; then he blinked, suddenly aware of his surroundings, and sagged forward, elbows on his knees.

"Jesse, you know where you are?"

He nodded, inhaling deeply and wiping his forehead with a trembling hand. He shook his head hard, then managed a weak smile. "If my dear mother could only see me now. What do you think she'd say about my carrying the Compton name?"

Rosen said nothing. There was nothing to say, only to sit quietly with a hand upon his friend's arm and wait until he became himself again. After another few minutes, Jesse leaned back and ran a hand through his hair.

"It was . . ." He swallowed hard and looked away.

"Yes?"

"It was like being hit by lightning. I saw this flash . . . not with my eyes, but behind them . . . inside my head. It grabbed me here"—he cupped the back of his neck—"and jerked me around like I was a kite in the wind. Hot, so hot, yet I was shivering. What was it? Nate, do you really think it could've been . . . God?"

This time it was Rosen who looked away. Was the question so difficult? In law school the answer was always in some book—easy enough to find. So it was when seeking God. As a boy, Rosen remembered his father warning him against those who only danced and shouted their love for the Almighty.

"God will not be found like a drunken man at a wedding," he would say, tapping the parchment of the Torah. "He is to be found here, only here." Always the Book, his father had insisted with that same certitude through which he viewed all things. The same certitude that had driven Rosen away.

For a moment he was afraid to look at the man opposite him, expecting to see his father's eyes, hard as flint. Instead, Jesse gazed back at him expectantly.

Rosen grew angry. "What do you want me to say? I don't know what happened to you. You want me to tell you God's hard of hearing and nearsighted, that you have to scream and jump around to get his attention? That's not—"

"I didn't mean—"

"That's not the way it is. A man doesn't scream to get God's attention."

Rosen felt a hand on his shoulder. "That's right." Gideon McCrae stood over him. "A man don't need t'shout for the Lord. Don't even need t'whisper. All you got t'do is say with your heart, 'Jesus, I accept You.' "

"You'd be amazed what's been done to my people in the name of Jesus," Rosen said.

"I know well enough the evil that's in man. But that ain't the Lord's fault. After all, He was one a' the chosen people, just like you."

Rosen bit his lip but said nothing.

McCrae continued, his strong hand surprisingly soft on Rosen's shoulder. "I come from minin' folk. Ain't a much harder life than that. Didn't have time for learnin' as a child. Went to school as a man t'learn to read the Bible. Read it through many a time, and all of it's the pure truth. But sometimes I think the words can get in the way a' the spirit. Know what I mean?"

Rosen saw himself with the other yeshiva boys, bending over the Talmud to learn the meaning of each and every holy word.

"Why do folks make it so hard on themselves? Don't take even a whisper: 'Lord Jesus, I accept You with all my heart.' "

How easy it seemed—how logical. As if he were back in yeshiva with McCrae his older *chavrusa,* breaking down a complex passage into its obvious meaning. Hadn't Rosen done the same thing for Jesse so many times in law school? Yet he wouldn't accept the Reverend's logic, even if it was against his old enemy, the God of his father. He was a defense attorney and did his fighting with the truth, not counting on mercy. McCrae's gentle words were appealing, so easy to accept, yet he would not betray his people. And so he sat there, like the man his rabbi once spoke of, who neither swallowed his mother-in-law's cooking nor spit it out.

"That's all right," McCrae said, as if reading Rosen's mind. "Whether you accept Him now or not, I believe you're doin' the Lord's work. I'll pray for you."

Jesse said, "I believe, Reverend McCrae. I believe the Lord's accepted me."

"Then He has, Brother Jesse."

Music had begun again, and clapping. Not bothering to return to their chairs, people carried on where they stood. This time there was something different in the singing—more than just the volume, which had grown quickly to a din, but the participants' fervor. Heads tilted back and eyes shut tightly, with God's love radiating upon them like a summer sun. Mouths raced to sing the words and, moving too quickly to pour out their love, slurred into indistinguishable speech. Claire was one of them, falling to her knees and chanting something almost Hebrew.

And the bodies, even the primmest matrons, swayed to the rhythm of their song. In front of the pulpit, Bathsheba lifted her arms and, nostrils flaring, called out the name of the Lord. Her heavy breasts and long thighs strained against her cotton dress, growing damp with perspiration. As she undulated, Rosen thought he'd never seen any woman so sensual and, growing ashamed, tore his gaze from her.

Instead, he watched a skinny man hold a bottle with a burning rag as a wick. The man passed the bottle under his open hand then let the licking flame rest under his chin. He was laughing, shouting, "Praise the Lord! Praise Jesus!"

Trembling, Rosen wanted to escape, to grab his friend and run from the church. Yet, Jesse stood singing with the others, a certitude in his manner Rosen had never seen before; had his friend finally found a place of his own choosing where he belonged with all his heart?

Again Rosen stood alone as an outsider, unable to join the celebration, unable to leave. Edging from Bathsheba and Jesse, he jostled the casket. He grabbed its side with both hands, looked into the coffin, then jumped back, his scream lost among the shouts of the congregation.

Two rattlesnakes lay upon the corpse, one crawling down a leg while the other curled itself around the open Bible. They seemed interested neither in him nor in those shouting the name of the Lord.

Suddenly two pairs of hands reached in to lift the snakes. Turning, Rosen saw Reverend McCrae and Tucker, the rattlers over their heads, parading in front of the pulpit. The old man treated the serpent like a plaything, curling it around his arm, then unwinding it to tuck it under his shirt, so that its head appeared between the buttons.

The Reverend was more solemn, holding the snake a few inches from his face. McCrae and the creature stared at each other, until the rattler leaned back and looked away. McCrae passed it to his daughter, who let it slink across her breast.

Once again ashamed to watch Bathsheba, Rosen turned back to the old man. Instead, it was Jesse holding the serpent, making it crawl along his arms and around his neck. He was not afraid, as if he'd become someone else. As if he'd been . . . born again.

Watching them all—the shouting, the writhing, holding death between their hands—Rosen wondered if this was what Moses had seen coming down from Mount Sinai. Was dancing before the golden calf any more dangerous, any more seductive than this?

Moses had cast his staff to the ground and created a serpent strong enough to swallow those of his enemies. But Rosen could only find the courage to watch and try to understand. After all, had his father not said the day he sent him away, "You will never be another Moses"?

Chapter 16

MONDAY MORNING

"Thanks for coming right over, Nate. I'm so excited, I just had to tell somebody. And I knew we'd have to get in touch with that lawyer, Mr. Garnet."

Claire sat beside him on her living room couch. Dressed in a white blouse, gray skirt, and white stockings, she seemed more girlish than she'd been Saturday night. More girlish and far too innocent to be involved in murder.

"Congratulations," Rosen said. "You must be very happy."

"Oh, I am! They say a pregnant woman glows. Am I glowing?"

"Like a hundred-watt bulb. Do you have any cravings for pickles and ice cream, or fried pie with red-eye gravy?"

"Not yet, but that may come in time. I've never been through this before. I only wish Ben was alive. It was all he really wanted, somebody to carry on his name and the family business."

"This is going to have a great impact on the company. Does your brother-in-law, Simon, know about your pregnancy?"

"No. I was hoping you'd come with me to tell him. Then maybe you could take care of the legal work with Ben's lawyer." She handed him an envelope from the coffee table. "I had the doctor write out everything. He says the baby's due at the end of April, right about when spring begins. I like that. Please give it to Mr. Garnet. I don't want to worry about all those legal things. Just want to be left alone to have my baby. You understand—don't you, Nate?" She looked down at her lap, while her fingers pulled at a loose thread on the couch.

"Sure. When do you want to take care of all this?"

"Well . . . I was hoping you'd go over to the factory with me now. Simon's sure to be there." Her voice brightened. "And Ruth. She's been awful good to me. I know this'll make her happy. I ain't got no folks, and she's been almost like my mama. I made a decision this morning. If I have a boy, course his name'll be Ben. If it's a girl, I'm gonna name her Ruth."

"She'll be very proud. What about Danny?"

Claire tore the thread from the couch. "What do you mean?"

"How do you think he'll feel about having a new cousin?"

"Oh, that? I don't know."

"You two are family and about the same age. I thought you'd be pretty close."

"Danny's always been off on his own. He never did get along too good with his daddy."

"I've noticed that. He's supposed to be quite a lady's man. Is that right?"

She shrugged. "That's what some folks say."

"You think the stories are true?"

"Guess maybe so."

"Earlyville's a small town. Wouldn't you know if . . . ?"

"Why're you asking me all these questions about Danny?"

Rosen shifted toward her and paused. Did he hesitate feeling guilty about interrogating a pregnant woman, or was it merely another one of his psychological ploys—to let her stew a little? Whatever the reason, he needed to find out certain information. The case came first. It always came first.

"On Thursday, after Danny called the police to report Lemuel Banks's murder, he disappeared for the evening. Do you know where he went?"

Claire's turn to hesitate. Biting her lip, she shook her head.

"He's never mentioned any hangouts, or women?"

"Told you I don't know, and I'm beginning to resent—"

The telephone rang. Claire walked to the rolltop desk, just inside the living room entrance, and lifted the receiver. "Hello." As soon as she heard who it was, she glanced at Rosen, then lowered her voice.

"Yes, all right. When? . . . I can't. . . . No, wait. . . . All right. . . . Yes, I'll be there. Yes, I'll bring . . ." Again she glanced at Rosen. "All right. Good-bye."

She returned almost timidly to the couch. "I'm afraid we'll need to postpone going to the factory. Maybe later this afternoon, if you're free."

"Sure. Can I drive you to wherever . . . ?"

"No, I'm fine. I'll call you later."

"Was that by any chance—"

"No, it wasn't Danny!"

"I was going to ask if that was Gideon McCrae."

"Oh." She rubbed her arms as if cold. "No, not the Reverend. Somebody else."

"I wanted to talk to him about yesterday's service. The second one—after the police left. The one with the rattlesnakes."

"Reverend didn't want any trouble, so he waited

for the police to leave. The service was something we all felt had to go on for Lem's sake, to see if anybody felt the Lord's power that day. Some folks did."

"Like Jesse Compton?" How was Rosen going to put it; how could he explain the look on his friend's face? "Since the service Jesse's been acting very strange."

"He's been quiet, sort of to himself?"

"Yes."

"Kind of like his eyes were looking at something inside his head. Like that?"

He nodded.

"I know the feeling, Nate. Been through it myself, like most folks in the church."

"You've handled snakes?"

"No. We each do what the Lord tells us to. I speak what the Spirit moves me to say. The words . . . what I say . . . most folks can't understand."

"Then how do you know the words come from God?"

"Others can tell the meaning—that's an even greater gift. Like Bathsheba. She knows what I'm saying."

Most people would have laughed at what Claire was saying, or become angry over what happened to Jesse. He could've accused McCrae's church of brainwashing his friend, causing him to suffer a nervous breakdown—but Rosen knew what Claire was talking about. The ineffable power had shone over Jesse as a blinding light, warm and golden and radiating love, while not one glimmer reached the dark corner where Rosen had sat alone.

Smiling, Claire touched his arm. "I do thank you for coming over and for all your help. You're the first person I called to tell the news."

Rosen put his hand over hers. "Again, congratulations. There's no greater happiness than a child. I know."

"That's right—you have a daughter. Well, one day right soon you'll have to tell me all about her. Kind of give me an idea of what I have to look forward to." Her gaze drifted from him to the telephone. When she looked back, her smile was gone. "I really got to be going. I'll call you this afternoon at Mr. Compton's."

Five minutes later Rosen was in Jesse's car, a half block from the alley leading to Claire's garage. From the moment she had canceled their visit to the factory, Rosen had planned to follow her. Another man might be the real father of Claire's child. He remembered her rumpled bed, the smell of sex, and the black hair. The evening of his death, Ben Hobbes had threatened Gideon McCrae, but Claire's lover could've been Danny. Either way, with the birth of her child a lot of money was at stake. Enough for murder.

In another few minutes Claire's white Corvette emerged from the alley and turned left on Jackson. Rosen followed, a few car lengths behind, past the college to the highway. Instead of crossing into Gideon McCrae's subdivision, Claire turned onto the highway leading toward Nashville.

Rosen had expected as much. Earlyville was a small place and Claire was well known, especially after being charged with her husband's murder. An assignation would be easier in the big city.

It wasn't quite eleven. Highway traffic was light; traffic here was always light compared to Washington's Beltway. A painter's beat-up station wagon, with its ladder and clanging paint cans, stayed between him and the Corvette. Claire drove in the right lane, which moved as quickly as the other two. If people here only knew what big-city life was really like, they'd . . . They'd realize how lucky they were.

Jesse hadn't chosen a bad life, living in the town of his ancestors where everyone knew everyone else. Where people still cared for one another, as McCrae's church had cared for Lemuel Banks when he'd been bitten or, at his funeral, when they'd sung and trembled beneath the Hand of God. McCrae, Bathsheba, Claire, even Jesse. Funny—in law school his friend was always searching for the answers, the ones that came so easily to Rosen because they lay in books. Now Jesse had the Great Answer and Rosen—still the wandering Jew.

He passed the airport. Only a few more minutes to the Nashville exit. Rosen turned on the radio but heard only country music, cowboys singing about the trucks they'd loved and the women they'd driven away. He flicked to one more station, and suddenly a miracle. Billie Holiday was singing "God Bless the Child," while Lester Young's saxophone cried softly, sending chills up his spine. She was always "The Voice" to Rosen, just as Thelonious Monk was "The Piano."

Lady Day's song was followed by Art Tatum's magic on the keyboard with "Body and Soul." Tatum was a genius, a blind man whose fingers swaggered over the keys like John Wayne walking into a saloon. Rosen could use some of that sureness now. Concerning the case, he was as blind as Tatum and had no idea where his next step would lead, other than Nashville.

Claire took the first exit into the city. Rosen followed two cars behind, while Joe Williams sang "Don't Get Around Much Anymore." Humming along, he adjusted to the slower downtown traffic and enjoyed the sights. Centennial Park was filling with the lunch crowd; businessmen and -women sat on benches or upon blankets spread on the verdant grass. A busload of schoolchildren scampered toward the Parthenon, their teachers hurrying after. To his right, Vanderbilt students, dressed much better than those on Jesse's campus, strolled between the buildings.

Rosen had driven the same route while following Aadams last Thursday. Maybe the detective was Claire's destination. She turned left on Third Street, as Aadams had, but this time no traffic light interfered. Rosen followed her around a corner and quickly pulled into an open space while she parked at the end of the block, behind Aadams's beat-up Granada.

As she stepped from her car, Rosen rubbed his eyes. Had they passed in the street, he wouldn't have recognized her. Wearing sunglasses, Claire had changed into a green turtleneck sweater, designer jeans, and sneakers. A Louis Vuitton purse with a long strap hung from her shoulder. She walked back up the block while checking addresses. Rosen was about to duck below the windshield when she hesitated in front of a building, then stepped inside.

The once fashionable neighborhood had become run-down and was now one of those magical streets where a Porsche left overnight would vanish by morning. Locking the car doors, Rosen walked up the block. On either side, buildings of mouse-colored brick rose three or four stories. The tallest was a hotel that rented by the day or hour—"Cash Only, In Advance." Another, the Friendly Finance Company, protected its windows with heavy iron bars. A few buildings were nailed shut, the boards rotting and splintered.

Rosen stood before the door that Claire had entered. Near a broken metal rod, from which an awning must've once hung, a sign read: THE LAVERGNE BUILDING. Inside, a stairway corkscrewed to the upper floors, and a row of mailboxes listed the tenants. "Albert Aadams, P.I.—302." The elevator, perpendicular to the mailboxes, looked rickety enough to scare a coal miner. Rosen trudged up the stairs.

The hallway was narrow, smelling like a wet book, with four offices on either side. Aadams's was to his right, between Cupid Escort Service and Madame Tallulah, Psychic. A slight woman of about sixty, with orange-colored hair and wearing a purple pantsuit, opened the psychic's office. Two well-dressed ladies, probably mother and daughter, stepped from the room.

"You'll see," the orange-haired woman said in the same Yiddish accent as Rosen's grandmother's, "he's not going to divorce his wife. He's just using you."

The mother nodded. "I knew he was no good. Thank you so much, Madame Tallulah. You saved Carol from a terrible mistake."

"Don't thank me. Thank the stars."

The two women took the elevator downstairs.

Seeing Rosen, the psychic clasped her hands. "Come in, young man. I can feel you are in need of great help."

"No, thank you, I'm here—"

Grabbing his arm, she pulled him toward the door. "I know. You're here to see me but are a little nervous. That's all right, everybody's like that the first time. It's not a little thing—pouring out your heart to a stranger."

"No, really. I came to see—"

"You're troubled. Troubled by . . . a terrible financial decision."

"No."

"An illness."

Rosen shook his head.

"A woman." When he didn't answer, Madame Tallulah clapped her hands. "Aha, of course! Didn't I tell you I know all?"

He stayed her hand as she reached for the doorknob. Glancing at Aadams's office, he asked, "What do you know about your next-door neighbor, the detective? Is he a *zhlub*?" Rosen used the Yiddish word for "ill-mannered person."

She crinkled her nose. "A real *momzer*—you know what I mean?"

Rosen nodded; she was calling Aadams a bastard.

"You're not mixed up with him? It is over a woman. Your wife—he's following your wife. . . ."

"No."

"Then you're mixed up with someone else's wife, so the big jerk's following you." Rosen was about to shake his head when she added, "Of course not, a nice boy like you. Want me to read your palm?"

He pressed a twenty-dollar bill in her hand. "Why don't you look into your own palm and tell me more about Mr. Aadams."

Rubbing the bill, as if her fingers could tell the denomination, she smiled. "So all right, that's worth one session. You want I should tell you about the *momzer*. He thinks he's some hot-shot detective, a regular James Bond, but, if you ask me, he don't know his . . . excuse the expression . . . ass from a hole in the ground. I passed by his door once when it was open. He was feeling up some mousy little man who wanted to hire him. Not feeling up, exactly, he was checking if the man had a gun."

"You mean frisking?"

"That's right—frisking. 'Cause I wouldn't want you to get the wrong idea about him, bad as he is. He goes for the women, that one. Notice I don't say 'ladies.' " She nodded down the hall to the escort service. "Pays a regular visit to that place. Only kind a' person he lets get close to him gotta be wearing a size-D cup—if you know what I mean."

"I understand. Is he the kind of man who might resort to blackmail?"

Madame Tallulah glanced at Aadams's door, then rolled her eyes toward the sky. "That man would do anything for a dollar. *Kineahora,*" she added as a protection against the evil eye. "He once came to see me, wanting to know if I had any information on my customers he could use to get money. Said we'd split it. I turned him down, of course. I'm a professional. I got my ethics."

Rosen watched Aadams's door. Coming upstairs, he wasn't certain what he'd do. There was the possibility of confronting Claire with the detective, but that could do more harm than good, especially if the big man was prone to violence. At the very least, Rosen wanted to "case the joint"—to infer something about Aadams's character from his surroundings. Madame Tallulah had helped Rosen do that and more. If Claire caught him there before he knew why she'd come, he'd look stupid, the one character defect a lawyer couldn't afford.

"Thanks, Madame Tallulah. You've been a great help. May your business prosper."

"From your lips to God's ear. My little mensch." She squeezed his cheeks. "And the name's Ida."

Rosen walked downstairs and out of the building. Passing Claire's Corvette, he slid into the Porsche and leaned back in the seat, hoping the wait wouldn't be long.

Five minutes later a taxi pulled up in front of the LaVergne Building. A tall brunette showing a lot of leg left the building and got into the cab, which drove away. She was probably an employee of the escort service. Then Claire stepped out, fumbling to slip on her sunglasses. Rosen ducked down. Checking her purse, she lifted something halfway out. Hard to tell at such a distance, but it appeared to be a folded manila envelope. She also fumbled with her keys but, once inside the car, squealed from the curb, leaving a pair of tire tracks in her wake.

Rosen drove to the end of the block, Second Street, and looked in the direction she had turned. Her Corvette was long gone. He let the Porsche purr contentedly while deciding what to do. Claire had taken the turn leading to Broadway; from there the highway returned to Earlyville. He could follow her and perhaps even beat her home. But maybe Claire wasn't going home—not just yet. She was close enough to make one stop, and Rosen thought she would.

Turning right, he drove down Second, across Broadway and past Patty's Place. The restaurant was filling with the lunch crowd, and the smell of fried chicken lay heavy in the air as if spread with a trowel. It made Rosen hungry; he'd eaten nothing since his morning tea. He was tempted to stop but wouldn't give in to his appetite. Instead, he thought about what the envelope in Claire's purse might contain. Whatever it was, the odor of blackmail hung in the air stronger than even Patty's fried chicken.

The only paper possibly that important to Claire was Ben Hobbes's second will, if such a document existed. If it did and, as Simon Hobbes contended, if it eliminated Claire from a share of the factory, that piece of paper would be worth a great deal, even Ben Hobbes's life. Rosen didn't want to believe Claire was involved in her husband's murder. Not just because the woman was his client, or because she was pretty and petite, or because she appeared to be vulnerable. He'd had plenty of clients lie to him, both in words and appearance, and more than one had been guilty as charged.

No, that wasn't it, and he'd been fighting the real reason all along. Even now, alone in the car, he was afraid to admit the truth. He imagined himself on the witness stand, staring at the prosecutor and seeing his own face. If Claire was involved, probably her church was, too, and Rosen didn't want that.

"No, I don't want that."

There, he'd said it. If he couldn't make his peace with God, at least there were those who could. The world was filled with Bible-thumping phonies who spoke of heaven as a fur-lined Cadillac, but Gideon McCrae wasn't one of them. His faith was real. Rosen had seen faith shining in Jesse's eyes and had been happy for his friend, happy and jealous. It wasn't Rosen's fault—would never be. Yet, if others could find their way back, there might be a chance for him.

A few blocks from the restaurant, just as he suspected, Rosen saw Claire's car parked in front of Here's How. She was stopping to see her old boy friend, Hec Perry. Rosen pulled in a few spaces behind her Corvette.

Even though it was almost noon, it was twilight

inside. Flickering beer signs behind the bar floated their spider-light through the smoky darkness. At first the room seemed deserted. However, at the far corner, in the warm glow of the silent jukebox, the old bartender slumped in a chair. Head thrown back and mouth wide as a bass's, he snored contentedly, shifting occasionally in the straight-back chair.

The stairway leading to the second floor yawned before Rosen like an abyss. In the distance whispered the rustling that wind might make through an empty canyon. He shivered momentarily, then was no longer cold, for a dulcimer, playing the soft, sad music of lost souls like himself, murmured to him.

The music drew him upward, the pull irresistible, when suddenly something grabbed him. He was jerked back like a dog on a choker and stumbled down the stairs. Again he stood at the bottom of the steps and, looking up, discerned a big man outlined in the bar's twilight. Aadams patted Rosen down, checking for a weapon, then lifted him by the lapels nearly off the floor.

The detective smelled of liquor. "Ain't this getting to be a regular habit, you and me meeting in this bar?"

Rosen wouldn't answer, not yet. Not while Aadams had him twisting in the wind like a hanged man. He struggled against the big man, pushing with all his strength, until his jacket ripped. At least he was free. Now he was ready to talk.

"You followed me here."

"Yeah. I saw you in that beautiful Porsche watching Claire Hobbes leave my office."

"What was she doing with . . . ?"

"I figured you'd tail her and maybe, if you was

smart enough, guess she'd come to see her old boy friend. Well, looks like you was smart enough. Maybe you're also smart enough not to get in my way. I told you once before, Claire Hobbes is my client. We got this business between us, real private business. Understand?"

"Blackmail always is private. That is, until the police become involved."

Aadams stood very close, his face hanging in a lopsided grin. The smell of cheap whiskey almost overpowered Rosen. "The cops? Before you think about calling them, you'd better consult my client. She ain't gonna like that. No, sir . . . not one bit."

"Why're you following me, if you're so sure Claire won't turn you in?" When he saw the detective's eyes widen, he knew why. "You're not through with her, are you? What you got today was only the first installment. You want to keep me from changing her mind."

"Real smart, ain'tcha. We're pretty much alike, I figure. You coming outta nowhere, some kind of ambulance chaser who knows a good thing when you see it. Me, too. I'm sick of working outta a shithole for an office, following deadbeats and cheating husbands. That pretty little blonde is gonna help me get outta all that. Now, if you mind your own business, there might be a little something for you, too. How does that sound?"

"What's it all about? Did you get hold of her husband's second will? Is that why she's paying you off?"

Aadams threw his head back; his laugh came cold and brittle.

Rosen took a step up the stairs, when Aadams struck the back of his head. He turned, arms over his face, a reflex from his days as a civil rights protester. His arms hurt from the blows but, hearing Aadams wheezing, he waited until the other man leaned forward out of breath. Balling his right hand into a fist, Rosen struck Aadams in the face and felt the big man's crooked nose collapse like slush.

"Nice shot," the detective said, not bothering to mop the rivulets of blood running down his chin.

Suddenly Rosen felt his right cheek explode as his body slammed against the wall. Aadams's other fist struck his skull, sending him sprawling across the stairs. He shook his head, but everything was blurry. He heard music, beautiful music, and thought that must be Lemuel Banks playing, perched on Jacob's ladder between heaven and earth, waiting to give him a hand up.

Trying to focus directly ahead, Rosen saw something long and thick swaying in front of him. Was it Aadams's upraised arm or a snake taunting him? A snake, its head poised to strike, yet Rosen was unable to save himself, as if he were a mouse caught under the serpent's spell. Caught, he watched the creature quickly dip to strike him hard, sending him over the edge, falling . . . falling far from Brother Lemuel's heavenly music. Where his own cries for help would never be heard or echo back from deep within the endless black abyss.

Chapter 17

MONDAY AFTERNOON

A roller coaster rattled along the rails, its descent a free-fall sickening his stomach, while his head swayed from side to side. The seat belt was broken, and he hurtled over the front car, bouncing along the track, as the wheels sparked and spun inches from his body. The car rolled over him, crushing his face—hot blood and splintered bones . . .

"Mister, hey, mister!"

The rattling grew louder as Rosen opened his eyes.

"Mister, you all right?"

"Sure." Was that his own voice? It sounded so far away.

He was sitting on the ground, squinting at the sun. Shifting back against something that rattled. Blinking, he looked around. An alley. He leaned against a garbage can in an alley. The old man standing over him—Rosen was sure he'd seen him before.

The old man's face was screwed tight, as if he'd smelled something rotten. "Jesus Christ, you look like shit. Are you all right?"

Rosen nodded, at least he thought he did. He tried to smile, then frown, but couldn't feel his face. Leaning forward, he saw his shirt was splattered with blood. It had dried into a series of Rorschach patterns, which had formed into a violin and a man playing the violin and the man hovering over a rooftop like in Chagall's painting. Was the fiddler moving, or was Rosen unable to keep his own head steady?

"Here," the old man said, "drink some of this brandy."

He felt a few drops roll inside his mouth like ball bearings, suddenly dissolving into liquid fire. "Why don't you add a shot of sulfuric acid?"

"Huh?"

"Help me up."

His body was a fulcrum, either arm leaning against the old man and a garbage can, until he could steady himself. His arms ached, and his breath came tight at the ribs, but his head was clearing. Grabbing the brandy bottle, he took two short swallows. The liquor oiled his mouth like a rusty gate.

He asked, "Don't I know you?"

"You was in last week asking about Hec Perry. I found you here in the back alley a few minutes ago. Come out to empty the trash and saw you lying there. Somebody mug you?"

"What time is it?"

"Almost two."

"I've been out almost two hours. Did you . . ." He leaned against the old man for a moment. "Did you see me or anyone else inside the bar around noon?"

"No. Guess I nodded off for about an hour. Why, was you inside? You ain't saying I'm liable for what happened to you? Don't know a thing about any of this."

"Don't worry. Is there somewhere I can clean up?"

"Uh . . . sure. Use the bathroom inside. Need any help?"

Rosen waved him away and, with minced steps, walked inside.

The men's room was typical of a cheap bar. Cold, with the For Prevention of Disease Only condom machine in one corner, broken towel dispenser in another, and the smell of blue antiseptic mixed with urine. Rosen opened both faucets; of course, only the cold one worked. He wondered if there was any bar in America with hot water in the john.

He splashed his face, then touched his right cheek, swollen to the size of a White Castle burger. He looked into the cracked mirror and grimaced. He'd been beaten worse. His nose had stopped bleeding, the inside of his cheek was cut, but he hadn't lost any teeth. His ribs seemed all right. What about his head? He recited the Kiddush, the blessing over the wine, then one of the first Talmudic passages he'd ever memorized—what to do after forgetting to bless the meal. He whispered the Hebrew words perfectly and smiled, despite the pain, remembering his rabbi's praise: "Even the great Hillel couldn't have said it better."

Rosen straightened his clothing, buttoning his coat to cover most of his bloody shirt, and walked into the bar. Behind the counter, the old man poured two brandies. For the next few minutes they sipped their drinks in silence. A pair of workmen came in, and the old man went down the bar to serve them. He lingered near the cash register, occasionally glancing at Rosen.

It was time to leave. Claire would've been long gone from Hec Perry's room. Anyway, before seeing her, Rosen needed to discover why she was being blackmailed. He'd find out from the source—

Aadams. The last thing the big man would expect was Rosen mixing so soon in his "private business." If he could somehow search the detective's office . . . He knew he wasn't thinking too clearly but maybe he could work out the details as he went. At least he'd be doing something.

The drive to the LaVergne Building took a few minutes. On the way, Rosen realized how hungry he'd become, with no breakfast or lunch. He stopped at a deli and bought a corned beef on rye with a diet cola. The clerk stared at his battered face as if it should've been between two pieces of bread.

Rosen pulled into a space just around the corner on Aadams's street. At the far end of the block stood the LaVergne Building, where the detective's Granada was once again parked. He unwrapped his sandwich. The pickle brine burned the cut on his inside cheek, but the corned beef tasted good, especially considering this was Nashville, not Chicago. He felt better after the sandwich and settled back with his drink.

He'd wait for Aadams to leave, then try to get inside the office; he could jimmy a simple lock. Maybe Aadams would get drunk and leave the door unlocked. Whatever—Rosen would improvise, just as Thelonious Monk and all the jazz greats did. To pass the time, inside his head he played his favorite Monk renditions, beginning with "Between the Devil and the Deep Blue Sea."

By the time he'd finished the set with "Just You, Just Me," an hour had passed. A few vehicles, including a squad car, drove down the street; two bag ladies entered the hotel; and a taxi dropped off a young woman in a leather skirt at the LaVergne Building, probably an employee of the escort service. However, there was no sign of Aadams. What kept him in that hole of an office?

Leaving his car, Rosen stretched his stiff legs and walked back to a corner drugstore. Inside a phone booth, he looked up Aadams's number and dialed the detective. After ten rings no answer. Maybe Aadams had gone for a walk or caught a ride with someone else. Maybe he'd drunk himself into a stupor and passed out on the office floor. Whatever the reason, Rosen was tired of waiting, aching for a hot bath and a long sleep.

Walking into the LaVergne Building, he tried the stairs but his hip tightened in pain. He took the elevator. Like an old man upset at being awakened, the elevator car groaned, then slowly moved, finally shuddering its door open at the third floor.

The corridor was deserted. Rosen approached Aadams's door and knocked softly. No answer. He tried the knob, which wouldn't turn. The lock looked simple enough; with proper manipulation a credit card might . . .

The escort service door opened, and Rosen heard several female voices. Not wanting to be seen, he hurried down the hall to Madame Tallulah's. Her door was unlocked, and a bell jingled as he entered.

A small waiting room was carpeted the color of melted Fudgsicle, its walls barely illuminated by a candle atop a rickety card table. A joss stick smoldered, emitting a heavy peppermint fragrance that permeated the room. On the far wall a door-size opening, covered by neon streamers, glowed faintly in the flickering light.

Through the opening, a woman's voice called, "I feel a troubled soul, one who is in need of Madame Tallulah's help. Come forward. Yes, come inside for the help you've been seeking."

As Rosen pulled aside the streamers, he saw a sign on the wall—NO PERSONAL CHECKS.

The second room was larger and lit by a small chandelier. Ida—a.k.a. Madame Tallulah—sat behind a large wooden desk while intently studying a pile of tarot cards. Directly behind her, beside the dusty window, hung a large velvet portrait called *The Smiling Elvis*.

"I can see from the cards you are deeply troubled." She looked up. "*Oy vay!* What happened to you? Sit down already, while I get something to clean you up with. Such a mess." She disappeared into another room, and he heard running water.

Ida returned with a cloth and a pan of cold water. Washing his face, she said, "A nice Jewish boy getting into a fight. What would your mother say?"

"I need . . ."

"Hold still. I'm almost finished."

"I need to use your phone."

"Why, to call your friends so they can see this face, too? Such a face shouldn't be on my ex-husband."

"Your phone?"

"There in the corner, Mr. Joe Louis."

Rosen dialed Aadams's office. Through the wall, he heard the phone ringing, but again no answer.

"Did you see Aadams go into his office this afternoon?"

She shook her head, then her eyes widened. "Did he do this to you?"

"We had a little disagreement over who was the better singer—Billie Holiday or Ethel Merman."

"That's right, joke about it. He could've killed you."

"Thanks for cleaning me up. I've got to get into

Aadams's office. Too bad you don't have a key." Rosen started to leave.

"Sure I have a key."

He stopped suddenly.

"Yeah. One time he was standing by the door so drunk he couldn't put his key in the lock. I helped him inside—what a *schlep*! I left him on the couch. There was an extra key in his vest pocket. I took it so I could go back and check on him later. I didn't want him dead—think how he'd stink up the building. Well, I got involved with a client and forgot to go back. I never bothered to return the key. It's in one of these drawers." She rummaged through her desk. "Here it is. You really have to go into his office?"

"Don't worry. No one's there."

Ida hesitated a moment, then said, "All right, I'll let you in."

"Just give me the key. I don't want you involved."

But she was already past him. "*Nu?* What are you waiting for, an invitation?"

Rosen followed her into the hallway. After she opened Aadams's door, he slipped past her and put a hand against her shoulder.

"Thanks."

She stepped inside and closed the door quietly, while whispering, "Why take chances? In case that *momzer* comes back, he wouldn't hit you with a lady present. Now get whatever it is you need. I'll be your . . . your lookout."

The floor plan of Aadams's office seemed identical to Ida's. They stood in a waiting room, where a desk took up most of the space. The desk top was bare and covered with dust; obviously a secretary didn't go with the furniture. Two prints hung on the wall—one of Andrew Jackson and the other a

Japanese landscape entitled *Mount Fuji at Dawn*. The door to the second room was slightly ajar. Pushing the door open, he walked inside.

A large metal desk occupied the center of the room. Its chair had been pushed back almost to the window. A half-filled whiskey bottle with two glasses rested on the desk top. To his right, a small bookshelf leaned precariously against the wall; it contained a few law books but mostly abridgments from *Reader's Digest*. Against the opposite wall stood a metal filing cabinet, all three drawers closed. Rosen walked past the desk and tripped over Aadams's body.

The detective lay on his side, knees bent, one hand over his stomach. A knife handle stuck straight out from his diaphragm. It was covered with blood, blood that also covered his shirt. Blood that had collected under his body, soaking the carpet into the color and consistency of mud. Eyes open, almost quizzical, Aadams appeared to be just awakening from sleep, instead of having been put to eternal rest. His nose had been flattened and speckled with blood that had dried long before he'd been killed.

Rosen twisted away from the body and grabbed the desk to steady himself. Feeling the sweat drip down his face, he shivered, fighting to keep down his lunch. Death always sickened him, but this was worse. True—Aadams was probably more deserving than most victims, but he'd died before Rosen had a chance to make peace, even if that had meant bringing him to justice. It was Rosen who'd flattened the detective's nose, and it was Aadams's blood splattered across Rosen's shirt, just as it probably had splattered over the murderer's chest. When they'd fought earlier that morning, had

Rosen been angry enough to kill the detective? Was the difference only a matter of opportunity?

"Young man, you almost done?" Ida walked into the room. "God in heaven!"

He grabbed her. "Don't touch anything." He felt better taking charge of the situation. "Understand?"

She nodded dumbly and took a few steps back, while Rosen knelt to examine the body. Carefully inserting a hand under Aadams's suit coat, he felt some warmth between the arm and rib cage. The detective hadn't been dead long.

"Is there another way to leave the building besides the front entrance?" When Ida didn't respond, he said, "Don't look at the body. Just answer the question."

"Uh . . . yes. There's a back way to the alley."

"Probably how the murderer left." Rosen knew he'd better keep talking, for his own sake as well as Ida's. "Take deep breaths. You're doing fine. You hearing me?"

She nodded, pressing her hands against her cheeks.

He returned to the body. "Down here, where his face and left arm meet the floor, the skin's beginning to turn purplish. He's probably been dead at least an hour—maybe two." He lifted the corpse's elbow; the arm was still flaccid. "No, probably closer to an hour. I could've been in my car, eating my sandwich and watching the building at the very moment Aadams was murdered."

"Do you . . . have to mention food?" Ida's color wasn't much better than the corpse's.

"From the angle of the knife, the coroner should be able to determine the height of the murderer. They must've stood very close to one another, with the way the blade's been driven in."

Ida took a step closer. "I'm all right." She stared at the body. "Then whoever killed him must've been a friend."

"The spirits tell you that?"

"He'd never let a stranger get that close—not with a weapon."

"Good point. You're thinking like a detective."

Rosen examined the desk top. No papers, only the whiskey bottle and two glasses. The glass nearer the victim contained some liquor, but the other was bone-dry. He used a hankerchief to open the top drawer. Under a box of paper clips lay a receipt book. Thumbing through its pages, he found three stubs with the name "Ben Hobbes" written in a caveman scrawl. The first two, each for $500, were dated respectively four and two weeks ago. The last receipt was for $1,000, paid two Saturdays ago—the day before Ben Hobbes was killed.

Could Aadams have been hired by Hobbes to follow Claire? Was that how the old man knew something "evil" was going on with his wife and the church? That last $1,000—a final payment for a completed job, or the beginning of blackmail? If the dead could only talk. Putting back the receipt book, Rosen finished checking the desk. Aadams's gun and holster lay in the middle drawer, and the bottom one was empty.

"Find what you came for?" Ida asked.

"Some of it. Let's hope there's more in the cabinet."

Still using the handkerchief, he slid open the top drawer, marked "A–H." There were about a dozen files of what looked to be old cases, arranged alphabetically. The last was labeled "Henderson, Phil." No "Hobbes," which didn't make any sense, since the receipt book showed that Ben Hobbes had been a client. Either Aadams had pulled the file himself or the murderer had gotten what he'd come for. Looking behind the Henderson file, Rosen noticed a slip of folded paper at the bottom of the drawer. Opening the paper, he saw it was a receipt for photoprocessing. In that same nearly illegible scrawl, Aadams had printed the word, "HOBBES." There had been a file; the receipt must've fallen out when the folder was removed.

The middle drawer, "I–P," had another dozen folders, including one labeled "McCrae, Gideon." The file contained only one page, with McCrae's home and church addresses, along with the names of his daughter and cousin. Was Aadams engaged in yet another blackmail scheme? If the murderer had taken the Hobbes's files, would he have also wanted the one marked "McCrae"? Had he even bothered to look?

Nothing of interest in the bottom drawer, but something just below it on the carpet caught Rosen's eye. Blood. Maybe the murderer's; more likely some of Aadams's blood that had dripped from the killer as he checked the files.

Rosen walked back to Ida, who stared wide-eyed at the corpse. He put an arm around her shoulders and pulled her away.

"Ida, it's a terrible thing to see something like this. No one deserves to die that way, not even a man like Aadams. Sure you're all right?"

She nodded slowly. "At least I'll have something to say when the girls ask over maj-jongg how my day went."

"Forget about everything you've seen here. I'll call the police from a phone booth. If they question you, neither you nor the spirits know a thing about this."

"All right." She trembled slightly. "I'm going back to my office and make us some tea. But no cookies—I don't think I could hold them down."

Rosen led her into Aadams's waiting room, then looked into the hallway.

"No one's there. Go home to have your tea. I don't want you in the building when the cops come."

He waited by the stairs while Ida went into her office to get her coat. They hurried down the three flights into the lobby. Rosen's aching muscles, jarred by the steps, screamed in protest, but he bit his lip and said nothing.

Outside Ida grabbed his coat. "Maybe you think I'm a phoney. *Nu,* maybe the spirits don't exactly talk to me—who am I to be on their social list? But I have a sense about people. Just like I knew all along what a shmuck that Aadams was, may his soul rest in peace, I know you're a good boy. Stay out of this. Don't even call the police—why take chances?"

"I never did tell you my name. It's—"

"I don't want to know. The police might ask me questions. Better I don't know. It's enough you're a good boy. Your mother must be proud of you. You're maybe a doctor?"

"Lawyer."

She smiled. "Almost as good." She hugged him, then quickly walked away.

He watched her disappear around the corner and knew, in all likelihood, they'd never meet again. He'd stay far away from Ida, to keep her from being implicated. She was a good woman and, for some reason, made him think of Ruth Hobbes. She had the same openness, the same simple goodness. Strange, he should've been thinking of Claire; after all, she was his client.

Three murders—Ben Hobbes, Lemuel Banks, and now Aadams—in a little more than a week. Three methods of homicide—poison, bullet, and knife. Three locations—Ben Hobbes's home in Earlyville, the field adjacent to the Hobbes's furniture factory, and the run-down Nashville office of a detective who was probably blackmailing both Ben and his wife. Rosen was certain Claire was linked to all three, through either Danny or Gideon McCrae. If only he could discover why she was being blackmailed. With Aadams dead, she'd be even less inclined to tell anyone, unless someone else knew. There might be someone else. Sure.

Rosen drove the now familiar five-minute journey back to Here's How. He stopped at a service station and, while the attendant filled the tank, called the police as a "concerned citizen" to tell them of Aadams's murder. He arrived at the bar about four-thirty.

A few customers sat on stools chatting with the owner, who leaned against the cash register. Rosen stayed by the stairway near the door and motioned to the owner, who hurried over.

The old man blinked nervously. "I thought you was done here."

"Almost. Do you know if Hec Perry's in his room?"

"Think so. Saw him go up a little while after you left. Ain't you finished with the boy yet?"

"Almost."

As Rosen walked up the dark stairway, he couldn't help wincing, not only from pain, but with the memory of what Aadams had done to him there.

Were his bloodstains on the banister and threadbare carpeting? He hurried up the stairs and down the corridor to Perry's room. The door was ajar.

Hec Perry sat by the window and appeared to be asleep. He wore a torn plaid shirt with the left sleeve rolled up. His dulcimer and an open suitcase stuffed with clothes lay on the bed. Rosen sat near the pillow. On the night table, beside the whiskey bottle, were a needle, an empty syringe, a piece of rubber tubing, and a small plastic bag. Perry's naked forearm, mostly bone, showed a fresh needle mark.

Genesis said that man was made in God's image. Seeing how Perry had ravaged his own body, Rosen grew disgusted. It was more than a waste; it was a sin, the same as when the Temple had been desecrated. Looking away in contempt, he noticed the dulcimer and remembered how Perry had played his strings with the same sweet longing as David's lyre. There was still something holy in the musician, as there was in all men—even the detective Aadams.

Rosen's hand could almost reach around Perry's biceps. He gently shook the other man. It took a few seconds before Perry's eyes focused on him.

"Oh, it's the lawyer. Sorry, no concert today. I don't feel like playing."

"How about singing?"

"Hmm?"

"Talk to me. Claire came by earlier and gave you money. Does she know you use it to feed your habit?"

"Claire's a good friend."

"What about you—are you a good friend? You know, she's in big trouble."

"Is she?"

"She's being blackmailed, and I think you know why."

Perry reached for the whiskey bottle, but his trembling hand almost knocked it over.

"Let me." Rosen poured a stiff drink, which the musician brought to his lips with both hands. "Aadams, the big man who was here the other day, has been blackmailing Claire. Why?"

Finishing the drink, Perry peered into the bottom of the glass. "Why don't you ask Aadams?"

"He's dead. Murdered."

At first Rosen's remark didn't seem to register. Suddenly, Perry threw back his head and stared at the bed. Struggling to his feet, he put the drug paraphernalia into the suitcase and closed it.

Rosen asked, "Don't you want to know how Aadams was killed?"

"No."

"Someone stuck a knife into his gut. The blood must've gushed out like an oil well."

"T-told you, I'm not interested."

When Perry tried to lift the suitcase, Rosen grabbed his wrist, which he could've snapped as easily as a wishbone.

"Where're you going?"

The musician tried to pull away. "I got a gig out of town."

"Where?"

"In . . . Knoxville."

"You're lying. You're afraid of somebody. Afraid you'll end up dead like Aadams. Like Claire's husband."

Perry shivered violently. "Let me go, mister. I can't tell you nothing."

"Not even to help Claire?"

Using both hands, Perry twisted free. "Because I

want to help Claire." He dragged his suitcase to the floor. Its weight almost knocked him down.

Rosen thought about what the bar owner had said; Perry had been out earlier that afternoon. Could he have helped Claire by killing the detective? No, the musician could barely hold a knife, let alone drive it into the gut of a man as powerful as Aadams, even if he'd been drunk. But there was another possibility.

Rosen said, "Claire's pregnant."

"Yeah, she told me."

"Are you the father?"

Perry laughed so hard his brittle bones almost shattered. "Me and Claire, we were never that way." He lifted the dulcimer in his other hand. " 'A damsel with a dulcimer in a vision once I saw. It was an Abyssinian maid, and on her dulcimer she played.' Like I told you the other day, ask the Abyssinian maid."

"Claire?"

Their eyes locked for a moment, then Perry bolted for the door. It would've been easy to stop him, but Rosen let the other man leave, his suitcase banging against the hallway wall. Perry wouldn't talk, not while he thought he was somehow protecting Claire. Maybe staying in town put him in the same danger as Aadams—better he go away for a while.

He'd be back soon. Heroin was a bad habit, and Claire gave Perry something that meant much more to him than friendship. She gave him money.

Chapter 18

TUESDAY MORNING

Holding the Federal Express envelope in both hands, Jesse stood over the bed and glanced at the clock. 10:07. His hand reached down to wake his friend, then hesitated. Enough light seeped around the shade to reveal how badly Rosen's face had been bruised. He probably needed as much rest as possible. Laying the envelope on the night table, Jesse slowly backed away.

He hesitated at the doorway, as Rosen stirred, then settled back into his pillow. Jesse had been home all yesterday reading the Bible when, late in the afternoon, his friend walked stiffly into the house. He'd refused to discuss the beating he'd taken and, struggling upstairs to his bed, fell asleep with his clothes on.

Jesse wanted to learn what had happened yesterday and to apologize for not being there to help. He was responsible for his friend. All along Rosen had known why he'd really been asked to Earlyville—not for the serpent-handling case, but to help Jesse win Bathsheba. However, things were getting out of hand—Ben Hobbes and Lemuel Banks murdered, and now this. He should've been with his friend, yet Rosen would understand why he hadn't come; that was another reason why they needed to talk. In law school, no matter how late at night,

Rosen would sip his tea and listen. Slow to judge . . . always listened. They were both outsiders; they'd always had that in common.

Walking into his study, Jesse sat at his desk and took the Bible from where it lay beside an unopened package of cigarettes. Cigarettes he might never smoke again, just as he might never again drink or take the Lord's name in vain. The nicotine cravings were bad, but so far he'd resisted for nearly two days.

He opened to the verses from St. John he'd reread several times that morning: "And as Jesus passed by, he saw a man which was blind from his birth." Then Jesus ". . . spat on the ground, and made clay of the spittle, and he anointed the eyes of the blind man with the clay, and said unto him, Go, wash in the pool of Si-lo-am. He went his way therefore, and washed, and came seeing."

Jesse leaned back in the chair and rubbed his eyes. He'd been like that all his life, stumbling through the world as blind as a man selling pencils on the street corner. Whatever his parents had considered important—money, power, and, above all, adding luster to the Compton name—he'd been unable to attain. At the courthouse, that statue of the Confederate soldier, his great-granddaddy and the first "great" Compton, seemed always to have pointed his rifle at Jesse's back, prodding him to be like his father. Something he never could . . . never wanted to be.

"He went his way therefore, and washed, and came seeing."

Sunday had changed everything. He turned to Acts and read about Saul of Tarsus being struck blind while on his way to threaten Jesus' disciples, and how God's love had restored his sight. Jesse had been worse than Saul. Instead of cursing the Lord in anger, he'd played the dispassionate social scientist, examining God's church as if it were a colony of ants.

But Sunday changed everything, just as the light from heaven shining upon Saul had changed his life forever. Feeling the power seize him, Jesse had taken up serpents without fear, because he knew, the same as God whispering in his ear, that he'd be safe. He just wanted to be sure the feeling was real, that for him the glory was truly everlasting.

Running a hand over the Bible, Jesse thought of Saul, a Jew who had mocked Jesus. Maybe Rosen wouldn't understand after all. Rosen had been religious, but that had been a long time ago. "A lifetime ago," as he used to say. And the faith in which Rosen had been raised . . . maybe he wouldn't understand. Jesse reopened the book to Acts and continued reading.

The doorbell startled him. Glancing at his watch, Jesse realized he'd been reading for almost an hour. The bell rang again. Usually people just walked into the popular culture center. Sighing, he walked downstairs and opened the front door. His hand froze on the knob.

"Good mornin', Brother Jesse."

Gideon McCrae stood in the doorway. He was dressed in his work clothes, shirt buttoned to the top, with traces of sawdust on his collar and shoulders. He held a Bible with a worn leather cover.

"I come at a bad time?"

"Why, no."

" 'Cause I was able t'get away from the factory. Almost lunch and all. Sheba told me you lived at the college, but it sure is a bigger place than I thought. Had t'ask a few folks how t'get here."

Bathsheba. Had Reverend McCrae come to talk about his daughter? Had Jesse done something wrong, in some way offended him? McCrae neither smiled nor frowned, just waited patiently.

"I can come in, then?"

"I'm sorry, of course."

After entering the hallway, McCrae looked into the center's work area.

Jesse asked, "Would you like to see what we do here?"

"If it's no trouble."

While Jesse waited by the worktable, McCrae slowly walked around the room's perimeter—eyes taking in everything, hands touching nothing. He lingered over some of the old records and the music posters on the wall. Reaching Jesse, he measured himself a small smile.

"I remember some a' them folks back in West Virginia—Pete Whitley, the Granger brothers. Ain't heard 'em in years."

"That's the purpose of the popular culture center, to preserve our Southern heritage. Without this program, a great deal of our stories, music, and art would be lost forever."

"Course, that was in my cuttin'-up days, when I danced 'n' sinned before findin' the Lord."

Jesse's face grew warm. Had he offended the Reverend?

"Sheba said you're doin' some writin' on our church. Said that's how you 'n' she met up."

"That's right."

Jesse glanced down at the table. A file of his notes on McCrae's church lay near a tape recorder, where some of them had been transcribed. Before Sunday, he would've been happy to show the Reverend what he'd accomplished, even ask for an interview. Now he was ashamed. Not of what he'd written—the notes were an honest representation of the church's views, but they'd been written by an unbeliever. The man he used to be, before Sunday, was now a stranger.

McCrae said, "So you've been wantin' t'know the Lord."

"Yes, but it didn't begin that way. I was simply doing research for a book on Southern religion. To be honest, I didn't plan for it to happen."

"Ain't none of us able t'pick the time or place or way we meet the Lord. That's what I come t'talk about. I figgered you might need somebody t'set 'n' talk."

"Oh yes, if you would."

"Well, then, here? We could clear a piece . . ."

"No. One of my students might interrupt. Let's go into my office. We'll be more comfortable there anyway."

Climbing upstairs, Jesse wondered if McCrae could smell the tobacco that, over the years, had permeated the wooden balustrade and doors. He should've put his cigarettes away; what would the other man think? He hurried ahead and slipped the pack inside a drawer just as McCrae entered the room. The Reverend ran a hand over one of the two rocking chairs.

"This here's a Hobbes rocker. Made some of them myself. Ain't no prettier piece a' work than one of these."

"Please sit down. Unless you'd rather take the chair by the computer?"

"No, thank you." He rocked slowly, hands folded over the Good Book.

Sitting beside his desk, Jesse fingered his own

Bible. He didn't know what to say, so he asked, "You enjoy working at the furniture factory?"

"Always liked workin' with my hands. Makin' somethin' useful from a piece a' wood gives a man real satisfaction."

"I'm a little surprised that Simon Hobbes let you remain at the factory. I mean, after his brother's death and the way he feels about the church."

McCrae's rocking chair slowly came to a halt. "I just come every day 'n' do my job. Ain't run into Mr. Hobbes. Seen his wife, Miss Ruth, plenty a' times. She just nods and goes about her business."

"Maybe Claire's insisted that you stay on. You know, she's pregnant, and Ben's will gives her the right to half the company. Nate Rosen says—"

He stopped suddenly. He shouldn't be talking about the case. After all, Rosen believed that the church was somehow involved, and with Reverend McCrae its leader . . . He shook his head and almost laughed aloud. Why was he talking to McCrae as a lawyer and not a fellow Christian?

"I'm sorry, Reverend."

"For what?"

"For a lot of things, I guess. Maybe for my whole life. As a child, I used to pass a pumpkin patch on the way to school. I'd see those pumpkins grow big and firm, then be harvested just in time for Halloween. There'd always be a few left behind. They'd grow bigger for a spell, then slowly soften until they collapsed into a rotting pile. Seed planted, grown the same as the others but, in the end, good for nothing. I feel that's been my life."

Jesse looked down at his Bible, ashamed of his weakness, but he felt the power of McCrae's eyes like a magnet. The Reverend's face was set tight, and his brow furrowed. But those eyes, eyes that could blaze with the righteous anger of the Lord, were soft. The words were also soft.

"I know what's been goin' through your mind, Brother. That's why I gave you a day t'yourself before comin' here. The same kinda thoughts that goes through all that's found the Lord. Thoughts like, 'Did I really feel His power?' That's been troublin' you, ain't it?"

Jesse swallowed hard but could only nod.

"You ask yourself, 'Did it really happen?' That's a question, ain't it?" He lifted the Bible for a moment. "As holy a book as this is, it ain't gonna tell you. Sure, the power's in the Word, but it don't come to you by readin'."

"Then how?"

"No man can tell another what you wanna know. One a' my cousins married a Catholic gal. They had a mass before the wedding. The priest was all dressed up special, like it was a party for God and only he was invited. He'd talk to the Lord, then tell everybody what they was talkin' about. That ain't the way it works. No feller can come between you 'n' the Lord."

"But how do you know?"

McCrae smiled. " 'Reach hither thy hand, and thrust it into my side, and don't be faithless, but believing.' That's what Jesus, after bein' resurrected, said to Doubtin' Thomas. 'Because thou's seen me, thou believes. Blessed are them that haven't seen but believe.' Brother Jesse, what does the Lord have t'do t'make you believe?"

"Is it that you . . . feel different?"

As soon as he'd asked the question, Jesse was sorry. Maybe his questioning showed he also doubted too strongly and that those doubts proved everything was false. However, Reverend McCrae seemed to expect the questions, like a parent patiently explaining something puzzling to his little boy.

"Course you feel different. That's how you know. Sometimes it turns you right around, like a tornado hittin' you broadside. That's what happened to me. Changed my wicked ways, praise Jesus. Sometimes it's real quiet-like. I think maybe that happened to you. Deep down inside you surely do know."

"So you think . . . ?" Jesse hesitated, then, for a moment, closed his eyes. He saw Bathsheba handing him the rattlesnake, remembered what it was like taking it from her. How he'd felt, not fear, but a joy so powerful, drowning and lifting at the same time. "Yes, I know, Reverend. I do know."

"I believe you do."

Jesse should've been heartened by McCrae's words; for the past two days that's all he'd wanted to hear. But something about the way the other man's eyes narrowed troubled him.

As McCrae shifted in his chair, the Bible almost slipped from his hands. "Your friend, Mr. Rosen, I got a strong feelin' he's a good man."

Jesse nodded.

"Bein' a good man ain't enough for the Lord's salvation. 'He that believeth shall be saved, but he that believeth not shall be damned.' You know that's what the Lord says."

Jesse said, "Nate's my friend."

"Your friend but not your brother."

Jesse's hand drummed nervously upon the desk. "What is it you want me to do—disassociate myself from Nate? That would be pretty hard to do. After all, I invited him here to represent you, and now he's defending Claire Hobbes against a murder charge. I wouldn't be able to handle things on my own. We all need Nate's help, if Claire's going to be—"

"Now, don't go worryin' yourself. I'd have t'get over Fool's Hill before sayin' good-bye to as smart a feller as Mr. Rosen. It's just, best remember who your family is. I mean your new family."

What did he mean? Jesse could only shrug helplessly.

McCrae suddenly clapped his hands together, like his cousin, Popper Johnston. "Ever hear two old sisters go at it? First one says some little thing like, 'That was a sorry excuse of a peach cobbler you made for the church social.' The other one replies, 'At least *my* husband kept his eyes off all them pretty young things.' Pretty soon they's goin' at it like a moonshine war, tellin' Lord knows what kinda tales 'bout their family for the whole world t'hear. Lawyers is like that. They start diggin' into something, like your friend Mr. Rosen's doin' right now with Sister Claire, and pretty soon lots a' things come out. Things best left alone."

"Like what?"

McCrae hesitated, looking down at the Bible. "Lots a' things. I want you and Mr. Rosen t'help Sister Claire. But I'm also askin' you t'keep in mind that our church—yours 'n' mine—is doin' the Lord's work. That always comes first. Things sometimes can get twisted around, if folks don't remember what the Good Book says straight out. You understand what I'm sayin'?"

Jesse didn't understand but grew afraid. He'd never seen Reverend McCrae like this. Staring at the other man, Jesse suddenly thought of his mother, the way she sometimes looked at him when he was young and, in her mind, still filled with "potential." When she tried to coax him along the "right path." It was a look that had always angered him. Seeing it on McCrae's face, Jesse remembered something else that had angered him.

"Bathsheba. Your cousin's putting her face on the poster with a rattlesnake. He's planning to hang it all over town. Is that what you mean about things getting twisted around?"

McCrae's face darkened. "That's one such thing. When Popper showed me that paper, I tore it t'pieces. The very idea of showin' Sheba off like she was some carnival freak. What does that say about the rest of the church?"

"I knew you'd feel that way. I told your cousin he wouldn't get away with something like that."

"Popper don't know when t'quit sometimes. He means well. That idea of puttin' a service on television is all right. It'll help spread the Lord's Word. Glad t'know you was lookin' out for Sheba. If you don't mind my sayin', I do believe you're a little sweet on her."

Jesse gripped his Bible, which felt slippery between his hands.

"That's all right, boy. I want you t'know, if you decide to court Sheba proper, you have my blessin'. 'Bout time she settled down with a good man. I'd be right proud to have you as a son."

His knuckles whitened around the holy book. Was he dreaming? It was all coming so fast. After all these years alone, in a matter of days to have a church, a new family, even a wife. Would she marry him? She had to love him, after those two times in the field. Thinking what they'd done, he felt his cheeks burning and looked away.

Rosen stood in the doorway, the Federal Express envelope tucked under his arm. He sat beside McCrae in the other rocking chair.

"Good morning," Jesse said. "Can I get you something—a cup of tea?"

Rosen shook his head and put the letter on his lap. His face looked a little better than yesterday evening. The swelling had gone down, but his hair was disheveled, and his eyes seemed to have trouble focusing. How long had he been standing in the doorway? Had he heard how little Jesse had said in defense of their friendship?

Yawning, Rosen massaged his temples. "Good morning."

"What happened to you?" McCrae asked.

"Don't you preach about the sins of the big city? Well, as they say in church, I'm here to testify, Brothers. By any chance, were you in Nashville yesterday?"

"Why, yes. I went in with Cousin Popper. Wanted t'make sure he changed that order for the posters advertisin' the church meetin'."

"You two were together the whole time?"

"He went on to see them television people. I had some other business 'n' some old friends t'see. We met later in the afternoon and come home five or thereabouts. Why you askin'?"

"Did you actually see those friends?"

"Well, some was at home, and some . . . Why you askin' all these questions. What happened yesterday?"

Rosen leaned back in his chair and, barely blinking, continued to stare at the other man. That stare, as well as the forceful cadence of his questions, reminded Jesse of a courtroom cross-examination. The Reverend shifted in his chair like a witness answering questions he'd rather not.

McCrae asked, "You gonna tell me what happened?"

"No. The incident involves my client and therefore must remain confidential. You want to help clear her of the charges, don't you?"

"Help Sister Claire? Course."

"What do you know about her?"

"I know she's a fine, upstandin' woman who would't hurt a fly, much less her husband."

"I mean about her background."

"She's from Nashville. Don't know nothin' else, 'cept she was troubled in spirit, and the Lord sent her to us."

"Sent her how—UPS or Federal Express?"

Jesse said, "You've got no right to talk like that."

McCrae shook his head. "Brother, you best get used t'the mockery of unbelievers, even from them you thought was friends." To Rosen, "She joined our congregation in Nashville. My cousin introduced us."

"Popper?"

"That's right. He was managin' some group in Nashville. Claire got to know the band members, like Brother Lemuel. He joined us 'bout the same time."

"What about Hec Perry?"

"Don't know the man. Popper just brung her to church one evenin', 'n' the next time she come on her own. First few times she'd sit real quiet 'n' just watch, kinda like a squirrel. Then she joined in the singing' 'n' prayin'. One evenin', a sign come on her. 'I would ye speak in tongues rather than prophesizin', for greater than prophesizin' is he that speaks with tongues.' That's the great gift Sister Claire has."

"How close were she and Lemuel Banks?"

"We're all brothers 'n' sisters in the Lord's church."

"Were they lovers?"

McCrae's mouth dropped, his head cocking slightly. Then he set his jaw and gripped the arms of his chair as if about to stand. Rosen pointed a corner of the Federal Express envelope, like a gun, at the other man, keeping him in his seat.

"This letter contains a report from a forensics lab in D.C. Last Thursday morning I visited Claire Hobbes and took a quick look inside her bedroom. The bed was mussed, and on one of the pillows I found a black hair. I sent it to be analyzed." He tapped the envelope. "I wasn't really sure what the lab would find. I only knew that Claire is a blonde, not a brunette."

"Her husband?" Jesse blurted.

"Ben Hobbes had gray hair cut short. According to the lab results, whoever was in bed with Claire is an African-American. To my knowledge, the only black man that close to Claire was Lemuel Banks. What can you tell me about their relationship, Reverend McCrae?"

The other man no longer paid attention to Rosen. Eyes widening, he fixed his gaze, past Jesse, through the window somewhere far beyond the campus. His head began to shake slowly, denying a truth that only he knew. What was it? Something bad grew palpable in the air; reaching out, Jesse could almost touch it.

Hands trembling on the arms of the rocker, McCrae stood and walked from the room.

Jesse started to go after him.

Rosen shook his head. "Let him go. I don't think Reverend McCrae will tell us what's bothering him, but the look on his face said enough. Yes, the look on his face." Rosen's brow furrowed.

"What are you saying, that Lemuel Banks was

Claire's lover? That maybe he helped kill her husband?"

Rosen remained deep in thought. After a minute he replied, "I don't know yet what Banks's involvement was. If he did kill Ben Hobbes, then his own death must be connected to the first murder. The act of an accomplice, or maybe one of Ben's relatives seeking revenge. Still, I wonder. Did you see the way McCrae looked?"

"If Lem was Claire's lover, that would only strengthen the D.A.'s case against her."

"We mustn't look at things that way. We've got to find whatever is the truth."

"Whether or not it helps her?"

Rosen smiled. "You're talking like a lawyer. And I thought you got religion."

Chapter 19

TUESDAY AFTERNOON

As the sky darkened, the Porsche's wipers flicked occasional droplets big as mosquitos. The drizzle and Miles Davis playing " 'Round Midnight" on the radio put Rosen in a blue mood. He was surprised, because nearing the truth always exhilarated him, and he felt as close to the truth as to the field the car was passing. The field where Lemuel Banks had been murdered.

If Banks had been Claire's lover, there was a connection between his murder and that of Ben Hobbes; solving one would solve the other. And so Rosen was looking for Danny, who, having been in the cornfield, must've witnessed Banks's death. For all of Danny's bravado, he was an overgrown puppy. With a little pushing, he'd tell whatever he knew, and Rosen was ready to push as hard as necessary.

That's why he hadn't let Jesse come along. He wouldn't confide in a man who could no longer be trusted to do his job, who'd only get in the way. Jesse's newfound religion was like a drug—no telling what he'd do under its power. Certainly, his friend cared far less about the case than about his church and Bathsheba. That was all right; Rosen was used to being alone.

Passing the field, he turned into the long winding

driveway of Hobbes Furniture. The mist had floated a gray veil over the factory, nearly dissolving its solid outline. Rosen parked and, dodging several forklifts that loomed through the fog like a pack of wolves, hurried through the building's open doorway. Shaking the water from his sports coat, he glanced at his watch—12:47. The men were back from lunch and, beneath the humming exhaust fans, stood quietly at their stations. Too quiet. One carpenter kept dropping his hammer and nails, while several others occasionally glanced toward the back of the room.

Rosen walked toward the cafeteria, hoping that Danny was still eating lunch. Halfway through the work area, he saw why the men were so nervous.

Wearing a gray three-piece suit, Simon Hobbes stood at one of the stations, pointing to a half-finished cabinet while speaking to three equally well dressed Japanese businessmen. The tallest, with silver hair and glasses, asked an occasional question as his younger colleague scribbled frantically on a clipboard. The third man, wandering with a meter stick around the work area's perimeter, took careful measurements.

Behind them a young carpenter leaned against the wall; his hand played nervously with the brim of his baseball cap. Ruth Hobbes stood beside him, her arm around his shoulder. She wore a sweatshirt and jeans, her thick black hair rippling down her back. She waved at Rosen and whispered something to her husband. Face growing red, Simon grabbed her arm, said a few words and, dabbing his forehead with a handkerchief, turned back to the Japanese.

Ruth hurried toward Rosen.

"Hello, Nate. Nice to see you again."

"Did your husband tell you to give me the bum's rush?"

"Course not, but he is right busy."

"So he's still planning to sell the company to the Japanese?"

For a moment her jaw set; then her face softened and she nodded.

"How can he?"

"You can tell this don't sit none too well with the men. That young feller standing behind Simon—his granddaddy was at Iwo Jima. How do you think he feels? I know it'll be hard, but don't expect me to talk against my own husband."

Rosen shook his head. "That's not what I mean. Now that Claire's pregnant, Ben's will gives her half ownership in the company. Simon can't sell without her approval. You're not saying that she's agreed to the sale?"

"Lord, no, Simon won't even talk to her, let alone discuss business."

"Then how does he expect to do this?"

"You don't know the Hobbes family too well—how pigheaded the men can get. As my daddy used to say, Simon's ass has been workin' buttonholes over this."

"He doesn't believe she's pregnant?"

Ruth shrugged. "If she is, he don't believe the baby belongs to Ben. Besides, he's sure his brother made another will, cutting Claire and her church out. He's called Mr. Garnet a half-dozen times and turned the offices here inside out looking for that piece a' paper. He's sure it'll turn up. Course, them Japanese won't wait forever. Still, Simon's sure he'll be able to sell, like he knows something'll turn his way."

Rosen remembered Claire walking from Aadams's

office, the folded papers in her purse. Were those papers a copy of Ben Hobbes's second will and, if so, had there been more than one copy in Aadams's possession?

"Ruth, do you know where your husband was yesterday around lunchtime?"

"I'm not sure. I'd have to check his calendar."

"Was he in Nashville?"

She thought for a moment. "Why, yes, he was. He drove to the airport to pick up them three Japanese. Left the house for Nashville mid-morning and, I believe, picked them up around three in the afternoon."

"What was he doing in town before going to the airport?"

"Business, I guess. There's a rib place downtown he likes to eat at. Why're you asking me these questions about Simon?"

"I was in Nashville yesterday and thought I saw him."

"Coulda been. Is that why you come out here, to tell Simon you mighta' seen him yesterday?" Before he could answer, she added, "Don't tell me no tales."

"All right. Last time I was here, you said that Danny usually comes in from the cornfield for lunch. I need to see him."

"Danny's a good boy. Maybe he's a little stubborn but, like I said, that's the way all Hobbes men is. I swear he wouldn't hurt nobody." She stared at him hard. "You really think my boy's mixed up in these murders?"

Ruth Hobbes was the most decent person Rosen had met in Earlyville, and the last one he wanted to hurt. But he had to find the truth. No one else would do it.

"Yes, Danny's involved. Maybe he didn't kill anybody, but he knows who murdered Lemuel Banks. He was there when Banks was shot. I've got to talk to him."

"I don't know."

"If I'm right, Danny's witnessed a murder. The killer knows that. How long before he decides it isn't safe to let your son live?"

"Lord—all right. I don't know if he come in for lunch today. We best go see."

Rosen followed her to the cafeteria. The long trestle tables were empty, and the serving tables had been cleared.

Ruth called to the kitchen, "Jenny! My boy Danny come eat here today?"

A scarecrow-thin woman appeared in the doorway. "No, ma'am, and we fried up that catfish just the way he likes it. Peach cobbler, too. I ain't seen Danny at all today."

Turning to Rosen, Ruth crossed her arms. "I don't like this. You're getting me scared."

"It's probably nothing. Maybe he just didn't want to get wet crossing the field."

"I don't like this. What're you planning to do?"

"I've got to find Danny. I'll try the cornfield first."

"I'm going with you."

"I don't think . . ."

"He's my boy, so don't say another word. We'd best go through the kitchen—quickest way out. Besides, I don't want Simon seeing us. No telling what he'd do if he thought the boy was in trouble."

Jenny, the cook, was washing dishes in a large sink. "Miss Ruth, it's still rainin'. If you all are goin' outside, best get in that old closet 'n' fetch a couple raincoats. I believe you'll find some boots as well."

The closet near the back door was filled with all

sorts of work clothes. They each found a navy blue slicker as well as a pair of rubber boots with buckles, the kind Rosen wore as a boy during Chicago's snowy winters. Pinning up her hair, Ruth pulled the hood over her head. While he was buckling his boots, she took a key chain from her pocket and disappeared into the closet's shadows. A minute later she returned, carrying a rifle and a box of shells.

"We keep a few squirrel guns locked back there in a cabinet. Ben liked to hunt the fields early in the morning. Sometimes I'd go with him. When I was a girl, my brothers used to take me, till I started outshootin' 'em. This here's my rifle." Loading it, she added, "If somebody is after my boy, I'll be ready."

Rosen thought about the murder weapon found in the cornfield. "Are any rifles missing?"

"No. You want one?"

He shook his head. "If there's trouble, I'm sure you'll shoot straight enough for both of us."

"That's the Lord's truth." She carefully slid the rifle under her slicker. "Let's go."

They walked through the back door, past four large Dumpsters, then stepped from blacktop onto the field's matted grass. The drizzle continued, making the ground springy underfoot. Rosen liked the feel of his galoshes clumping on the grass. He remembered, as a boy, walking home from *cheder* through a blizzard, his mother anxiously waiting at the door and unsnapping the boot buckles because his own hands were too cold. Then his father putting down the holy book and lifting him onto his lap, warming Rosen's hands between his own. He asked about school, about the beauty of the snow God had made, and he listened to his son's words.

In the distance to his right, Rosen saw the great ridge merging with the horizon, the mist blurring the line between them, so that heaven and earth seemed to be as one. He smiled. Heaven and earth were to be as one when the Messiah came, and justice would truly reign upon the earth. Finally there would be no liars or murderers or victims who needed defending, and he could rest. Maybe then his father would talk to him and, once again, listen. Even a miracle such as that could occur when the Messiah came.

Ruth had walked ahead of him. He couldn't see her face, shadowed by the hood, but sensed her uneasiness in the way she moved. She reached the gate to the cornfield, not far from where Lemuel Banks had been murdered. Rosen wondered what her son really was—a liar, murderer, or victim.

Ruth said, "I don't like this. Danny shoulda come to the factory for lunch."

She probably wanted some small words of comfort, but he didn't know what to say, and he wouldn't lie to her. "Let me go first."

He'd never walked through a cornfield before. The deep green stalks reached his shoulders; tasseled and heavy with corn, they seemed ready to be harvested. He wondered what Danny did here day after day. Did he have to weed between the plants, as one would a garden? Or was his a self-imposed exile, to be away from women expecting too much and a family expecting too little?

He didn't want to leave Ruth to her worries, so he said, "Corn's pretty tall."

"It'll need to be harvested soon. My boy did right well planting this crop. Maybe a farmer 's what he's cut out to be. They's farmers on his daddy's side, way back."

"Not on yours?"

"No, our men mostly worked the coal mines. One a' my people did see corn like this. My great-granddaddy fought with General Lee at Antietam. That's up in Maryland. You ever hear tell about that battle?"

"I think so. It was before Gettsyburg, wasn't it?"

She nodded. "Bloodiest single day of the war. Both sides met in a cornfield like this—tall and green and smelling sweet. When it was over, not one bit a' stalk was left standing. Boys massacred each other. Great-granddaddy was wounded, dragged himself away, and lost a leg. Grandma said he was always bothered knowing he'd have to be buried hundreds of miles from where his leg was."

"He was fortunate to have crawled away from his wound. Other people aren't so lucky. We . . . they carry the hurt inside for the rest of their lives." Rosen knew he shouldn't be talking like that. He said, "War is hell," then shook his head. "Guess I shouldn't be quoting General Sherman to you."

"That Yankee was speaking the truth. I lost me an uncle in World War Two, a brother in Korea, and a son in Lebanon. That last was the worst, but at least I could understand it. A man fights for his country, it's something worth dying for. If anything happens to Danny, I couldn't stand it. Maybe 'cause he's my youngest, maybe 'cause he's still like a baby. Never did grow up. You understand what I'm saying?"

Before Rosen could reply, he heard a sharp crack; at the same time something whizzed past his ear, snapping the broad leaf brushing against him. Ruth pushed him to the ground as he heard another shot. She squatted beside him and drew out her rifle.

He asked her, "You all right?"

She angled a few feet forward in the direction of the gunfire. "My boy's out there. Somebody's trying to hurt my boy."

Another shot cut through the corn. Rosen crawled on his belly toward her. "Ruth, you don't understand."

"Something's moving—there!" Raising the rifle, she fired.

"No, Ruth, don't!"

Reloading, she fired again. In the distance a man screamed.

"Got 'im!"

Turning, she nodded curtly to Rosen. As the man's scream slowly settled into a low plaintive moan, Ruth's jaw slackened and, suddenly, her eyes grew wide. Letting the rifle fall, she struggled to her feet, slipping in the muddy field, and sobbed.

"Lord Jesus, it's Danny! I shot my Danny! Oh, God, no!"

Before Rosen could reach her, she ran toward the wounded man, pushing aside the cornstalks, struggling through ankle-deep mud. "Danny, forgive me! It's Mama! It's Mama!"

Rosen grabbed Ruth's rifle and hurried after as best he could, but lost her in the rain and corn. Suddenly the cornfield opened. He stumbled over another rifle, then noticed different plants, green as the corn but taller and thinner, with long, thin leaves spread wide like a skeleton's fingers. He smelled something acrid, almost making his eyes tear, a familiar odor he couldn't quite identify. The crying grew louder and, moving past several plants, Rosen saw a small wooden shack. Danny lay against the doorway. He wore a denim jacket, soaked by the rain, and cradled his left arm. Ruth sat on the ground beside him, hands clasped together as she stared at the wound.

As Rosen approached, she looked up and tried to smile. "He's gonna be all right, thank the Lord. Just nicked his arm. Ain't that right, son?"

Danny's face was white, his eyes unfocused. His voice seemed disembodied, almost mechanical in its crying.

"Son, tell me you're all right. Please tell Mama you're all right."

Leaning the rifle against the shack, Rosen knelt beside Danny and examined his wound.

Ruth said, "Don't hurt the boy. Please."

The bullet had grazed Danny's arm just below the shoulder. There was an angry tear in his jacket but not much bleeding. Folding his handkerchief diagonally several times, Rosen knotted it around the wound. Danny jerked his head, and his crying stopped.

"Mama," he half whispered, "I didn't know it was you. I just thought somebody was comin' after me. I never meant to—"

"Hush. Don't you worry about nothing. We're gonna get you to a doctor right quick."

He swiveled his head both ways. "No. No, I can't."

"Course, son. You got to."

Rosen said, "He may be in shock, but he's all right. Let's get him out of the rain. We ought to keep him warm."

They carried Danny inside. Rosen grabbed Ruth's rifle before closing the door behind him.

The shack was one large room, illuminated by two windows on either side of the door and a kerosene lamp set on a table. Near the table stood a kerosene heater, which gave off a heavy oily smell, but even that couldn't mask a much stronger odor, one that Rosen now recognized from his college days. They lay Danny on an old couch. Ruth sat beside him, letting his head rest upon her lap, while Rosen looked out the window at the green plants with their thin pointed leaves. It'd been a long time since he'd seen marijuana growing that tall.

There must've been a hundred plants, clustered together in patches of about a dozen and surrounded by chicken wire to protect them from rabbits and other small animals. Each area had been carefully weeded, with troughs dug into the earth to carry off excess rainwater. The entire area was surrounded by cornfields; unless standing in their midst, a person would never realize the marijuana plants were there.

Turning, Rosen let his eyes adjust to the kerosene lamp. A smell like burning rope hung so heavy in the air it almost suffocated him. Drying racks lined the walls, where bunches of leaves slowly withered. Three boxes were stacked beside one of the racks. The top carton was open, revealing small plastic bags filled with the drug. Several sacks of fertilizer lay piled against the back wall, along with shovels and hoes. Kitty-corner to the couch was an orange crate serving as a bookshelf. Rosen pulled out one of the books, *Marijuana—Home-Grown and Proud of It*. The others were of a similar theme—a do-it-yourself guide for the small businessman.

Coughing, Ruth asked, "What is this place?"

Danny looked away.

"Nate?"

Clearing his throat, Rosen replied, "I guess you

could call this a hash house, but not the meat-and-potatoes kind you're used to. Isn't that right, Danny?"

The young man bit his lower lip.

"Ruth, your son's in the wholesale business. He supplies marijuana to other 'businessmen' who, in turn, sell it on the streets of Earlyville. Right, Danny?"

Again Danny wouldn't answer, but this time Ruth turned his face toward her. "Is what Mr. Rosen's saying the truth?" When he nodded, she said softly, "How'd you get into something like this?"

"I don't know."

"You tell me how something like this could happen."

"I don't know, Mama. Marijuana was always here growing wild. In high school a bunch of us would come get us some and smoke it. Weren't any harm."

"How could something like this get on our property?"

Rosen said, "It grows wild all over the Midwest. I remember you once saying how, during World War Two, the army tried to grow plants on your property to make rope? Rope comes from hemp, as does marijuana. The government probably grew the first crop here but, unfortunately for Danny, it's no longer a patriotic enterprise."

Ruth shook his head. "Why, son? Look at the corn you was growing. You've got a fine crop here. You was finally making something of yourself."

Danny sat up, grimacing as he adjusted his arm. "Making something of myself? Who you kidding? Price a' corn wouldn't keep a man in beer and cigarettes, much less give him a living. But this here, Mama, is a real gold mine. I get two to three hundred dollars a pound! And some of the new plants I been working with bring me twice that much. Stuff's so strong they call it 'Bible Weed'—smoke enough of it and you'll see God."

"That's blasphemy."

"No, Mama, it's business. Big business. I grow the marijuana, dry and package it. Look here." Lifting a cushion, he took a shoe box from a hole in the box spring. Grinning, he dumped its contents, mostly hundred-dollar bills, onto his mother's lap. "There's about twenty thousand dollars here, and I started another box hid in the corner. You want me to grow corn? I'm rich, and Daddy said I never did have no head for business. If he could see all this, I wonder what he'd say now."

Danny's grin faded as Ruth brushed the money from her lap as if it were something crawling on her. "Thank the Lord he don't have to see it. What've I done to make you do something like this?"

"But, Mama . . ."

"Don't." She looked up at Rosen, her eyes glistening. "Nate, we're going to the police. I'd surely be grateful if you'd come with us, see that the boy gets whatever rights is due him."

"No, Mama, I can't give all this up!" He tried to stand.

Rosen pushed him back onto the couch. "I'll help, but before we go, Danny'd better tell us all of it."

"What're you talking about?"

"The murder of Lemuel Banks."

Ruth grew pale. "Lord, no!"

Danny grabbed her arm. "Mama, I swear I had nothing to do with no murder. You gotta believe me!"

"What've you done?"

"Please, Mama."

Rosen said, "I think he's telling the truth. But, Danny, if you want to save yourself from the charge of accessory to murder, you'd better tell us who the killer is."

He shook his head.

Ruth put her hand over his. "You've got to, son. Time for you to be a man."

"I'm scared, Mama."

Rosen said, "That's all right. I think I know. The same person who got you into the drug business. You couldn't have done all this by yourself. It takes a combination of flair and attention to detail. Popper Johnston, right?"

Like swallowing medicine, Danny shut his eyes tight and nodded.

Ruth looked up at Rosen. "How'd you know?"

"The district attorney mentioned marijuana had become a big problem in the area. The problem began soon after Reverend McCrae's church was established—about the time Popper came to town. A coincidence? When I helped set Claire's bond, a drug dealer was appearing before the judge. Popper disappeared for a few minutes, just after the dealer left the courtroom. Another coincidence, or were they working together? You remember our lunch last Friday?"

"Yes. With Johnston and Jesse Compton."

"Popper was talking about the anonymous backers for McCrae's televised service. I don't believe there are any. He's backing the show himself to launder all the dirty money he's been making from selling Danny's marijuana. You saw how much cash he had on him when he paid the lunch bill."

"Yeah," Danny said, "it was Popper. When the

church first come to town, Claire went to work in the factory. I tried to date her, told her about the marijuana growing wild and how we could get high. She wouldn't have anything to do with me, but a few days later Popper came to see me. Said he overheard Claire telling Reverend McCrae about the marijuana and how they prayed for me. This all was Popper's idea."

"What about Lemuel Banks?"

Danny swallowed hard. "Popper was with me that day—brought me some new seeds to work with. We was talking just outside the shack when Banks come walking up with his snake bag. Popper didn't wait for no explanation, just grabbed a rifle and lit out after him. I followed close enough to see him shoot Banks in the back. That was just outside the cornfield."

Rosen added, "He threw the rifle at the edge of the field, so the police wouldn't snoop around and find the marijuana. Of course, in this town the Hobbes name would've been enough to keep them away."

"Guess so."

Ruth said, "Then *you* didn't hurt nobody. Why didn't you tell the police? Was it just 'cause of the money?"

"Popper called me an accomplice. Said if he was arrested, so would I. He scared me. I'm still scared."

"I'm gonna take care of you, boy. Mr. Rosen said he'll help us."

Rosen grabbed Danny's shoulders. "Only if he tells the whole truth. Were you involved in your uncle's murder?"

"No! No, I swear I wasn't!"

"There was something between you and Claire. I

saw the way you looked at her at her house the morning after your uncle's death."

He was shaking hard and, despite his wounded arm, pushed Rosen away. "No! I mean, I told you already I tried to take her out."

"That was before her marriage. What about after? Remember, the truth's going to come out."

"All right. I tried to see her—"

"Danny," Ruth cried, "he was your uncle!"

"He was an old man. Didn't matter anyway—me trying. She wouldn't have nothing to do with me. I come on strong one time. I was afraid she'd tell Uncle Ben, but don't guess she never did. Leastways, he never said nothing to me."

Rosen stared at Danny for a long time, then asked, "Did Popper kill him?"

Danny winced. "I don't know."

"Could he have?"

"The only other person who ever used to come around these fields was Uncle Ben. He used to go hunting or just walking, mostly early in the morning. Promised he'd leave my cornfield alone. I don't believe he ever trespassed, but one day Popper and me saw him come pretty close to the fence. Popper got right nervous. After Uncle Ben was killed, I never had the guts to ask Popper, and he never said a word about it. We both acted like it never happened."

Ruth shook her head slowly. "Nate, do you think Johnston killed Ben?"

"I don't know, but it fits. On the night of his death, Ben went to McCrae's church service angry at something the church had done. It sounded personal. Popper Johnston was a church member, McCrae's cousin, and a friend of Claire's. With all the talk about drugs and cults, maybe he thought the marijuana was church-sanctioned. Of course, there's one way to find out."

Danny's shoulder heaved as he wiped his eyes with his good hand.

"The police," Rosen said. "I'm sure Chief Whitcomb would want to join us when we visit our good friend Popper. This time, I don't think he'll be picking up the check."

Chapter 20

TUESDAY AFTERNOON

"Lucky the rain's stopped," the driver of the laundry van said. "This close enough?"

"Yes." Jesse eased himself from the passenger seat, almost dropping his Bible. "It's lucky you saw me leaving the campus. Thanks for the lift."

The driver scanned up and down the road. "Ain't too many houses, and it's a good half mile back to the highway. Sure you'll be all right out here by yourself? I mean, what if it starts raining again?"

"I'll be in the best of hands. Thanks again."

Jesse watched the van drive away, then turned his attention to the old frame house up the road. It seemed different from when services were being conducted. Then it had been filled with the thunderclapped words of Reverend McCrae, joyous prayers of the congregation, and the taking up of serpents by those whom the Spirit had moved. But a building didn't become a church because it had a steeple and stained-glass windows. People, carrying the holiness inside themselves, made it holy. Jesse wanted to believe he was one of those people and, therefore, needed to finish his conversation with Gideon McCrae.

It was just after three. The Reverend said he'd stop by the church after work, about four. Having lent Rosen his car, Jesse had anticipated the walk to take an hour. The unexpected ride in the laundry van had been a blessing and perhaps a sign, like the ravens bringing food to Elijah. He could use the time to pray.

The front door was unlocked. Jesse's footsteps echoed through the large room where services were held. Folding chairs had been neatly arranged in rows for the next service, and the podium, resting on a wooden table, patiently awaited Reverend McCrae's next sermon. Jesse continued down the center aisle and sat where he'd first watched Bathsheba take up serpents.

He turned the pages of his Bible at random; the Book opened to Peter's sermon in Acts: "The sun shall be turned to darkness, and the moon into blood, before that great and notable day of the Lord come: And it shall come to pass, that whosoever shall call on the name of the Lord shall be saved."

Putting the Book down, he clasped his hands in prayer. The sun over Earlyville had been darkened by clouds of suspicion. As for blood . . . both Ben Hobbes and Lemuel Banks had been murdered, and the killer was still on the loose, maybe planning to kill again. This was, indeed, a world of sin, yet "whosoever shall call on the name of the Lord shall be saved."

"Oh, Lord," Jesse whispered, "take me! Take this wicked sinner to Your bosom!"

He prayed as he'd never prayed before. He set before his eyes Jesus on the cross, the selfless love of One who sacrificed Himself so that others might gain eternal life. Selfless love—that's what Jesse so fervently desired, but between his eyes and the crucifix rose the image of Bathsheba. Her body undulated like a snake, arms like snakes around his neck, drawing him to the soft swell of her breasts.

"Oh, Lord, take me in Your arms. That's what I want. That's all that I want."

The Book . . . yes, the words would set him on the right path again. As he fumbled through the pages, he heard the muted sounds of a thump, then a man cried out from somewhere in back of the house. A moment later the house again became so quiet, maybe he'd imagined the noises. Suddenly he heard a man's voice, very distant, then silence once again.

Holding the Bible, Jesse walked past the pulpit, through a small hallway that led into the kitchen. He listened carefully but heard nothing. About to return to the main room, he glanced through the back window and saw a cellar door being closed from the inside. Maybe Reverend McCrae was home early and had work to do downstairs.

Jesse went outside. As his hand moved toward the handle of the cellar door, it suddenly flew open and a short, stocky man, wearing a service station uniform, almost knocked him over. He'd been carrying two brown boxes the size of small orange crates. As they tumbled from his hands, one broke open, dumping clear plastic bags of something dark and crinkled like tobacco.

"Jesus Christ!" the man shouted to someone inside. "He's seen the stuff!"

As Jesse tried returning the bags to the box, the other man pushed him away.

"Leave it alone!"

"It's all right, Gary." Popper Johnston climbed halfway up the stairs and grinned until his teeth must've ached. "It's only Jesse Compton. He's a friend of me and Gideon's. C'mere, Jesse, 'n' sit a spell. Don't be getting shy."

Gary glanced from Jesse to the boxes. "He's seen it, Popper. Ain't no two ways 'bout it."

Jesse shook his head. "I just stopped by to see Reverend McCrae."

Popper asked, "When's Gideon coming by?"

"After work. About four."

"Don't give us much time," Gary said.

Popper laughed. "If you hadn't dropped the cellar door on your foot and screamed, he'd never a' come out here. Just relax. I'll take care of everything."

"This here's a problem, a big problem. Like that other one."

"Shut up. Go on and deliver that stuff the way we planned."

"But . . ."

"Just do what I tell you. I want you to come back this evening about nine. It'll be dark, and nobody'll be around. When you come, bring the truck and a shovel. You'll have to make one more delivery tonight. An oversized one, somewhere way out in the woods. You understand my meaning?"

The other man's eyes suddenly narrowed; then he smiled just enough for his teeth to show. Jesse felt a chill down the back of his neck. He started to back away toward the house, but the other man dragged him toward the cellar. Popper was waiting, a gun in his hand.

"Get yourself down here, Jesse. We're gonna visit a spell."

Following Popper down the stairs, Jesse heard the cellar door slammed shut behind him and a lock snapped into place. His eyes adjusted slowly to the room's interior. There seemed to be two sources of light—one at the top of a wooden stairway directly ahead of him and the other a lamp on the desk to his right. A plywood wall ran the length of the room behind the stairwell. The foundation walls were bare concrete.

"Welcome to my office," Popper said, sitting on the cellar steps. "Take the guest of honor chair, over at my desk."

Jesse noticed two more boxes stacked together in the corner beside the desk.

"This used to be the root cellar, where firewood was delivered," the other man continued. "Somebody turned it into a proper basement, which Gideon lets me use as my office. I take care of church business and, as you saw, any that's my own. Place don't look like much, but a lot more money goes through here than most of them fancy offices in Nashville."

Jesse looked at the boxes. "You're selling drugs, aren't you?"

"Welcome to the real world, professor! Too bad you ain't a botanist. We'd have a lot more to talk about." He pulled one of the boxes to the front of the cellar steps, opened it and took out a plastic bag. "Know what this is?"

"Marijuana."

"Ever use it?"

Jesse shook his head.

"Didn't think so. Anyway, you never had anything like this. We're talking sinsemilla, the Rolls-Royce of grass, the emperor of shit. Stronger than hash. Why, you work in the fields with this stuff, and just the resin you lick off your hands'll put you in orbit." From his shirt pocket he took out a small gold-plated lighter and what appeared to be a hand-rolled cigarette. "Here, try a joint."

Again Jesse shook his head.

"You sure? It'll make things a whole lot easier on you. A helluva lot better than a last cigarette."

"You're going to kill me, just as you killed Lemuel Banks."

Popper lit the joint; it smelled like burning rope. "I have to. You know what they say, a man can only hang once."

"So," Jesse half whispered, "I'm going to die." Deep in his belly he felt the fear trying to scratch its way out, but he kept it down. He was going to die. That wasn't so bad—soldiers died for their country, fathers died rescuing their children from fire, even people walking across the street died from being hit by a bus. At that very moment, somewhere in Earlyville, a man might be dying under the wheels of a bus. Everybody had to die. How much better to know it was your time, to have a Bible in your hands and know that Jesus waited for you on the other side, His arms offering eternal salvation. After all, that very morning Gideon McCrae had assured him of . . .

Suddenly the fear clawed at his throat. "Is . . . ?" He coughed hard. "Is Reverend McCrae involved in this?"

"Gideon . . . Mr. Holier-Than-Thou? Not on your life! He don't know nothing about this, and that's the way it's gonna stay. That's why I have to kill you, Jesse. Can't have you telling nobody." He held the joint in front of his eyes and giggled. "Sure you won't try this? It's good shit, man."

"What about Bathsheba?"

"Now she's some work of art, ain't she?" He took a deep drag on the joint. "No, Bathsheba's no part of it. I don't know what's going on in that girl's head. She could probably use some of this, but then, so can we all. I'll tell you, ain't too many men lucky enough to combine such profitable business with pleasure. I kicked around a powerful long time, sometimes counting my last few nickels to get me a hamburger. Ain't so no more. Now folks . . ."

Jesse sighed softly, closing his ears to Popper's rambling. He was going to die, but it was all right. He opened his Bible and began to read passages at random. "'But first must he suffer many things, and be rejected of this generation.'" Yes, he'd suffered quietly all those years. There'd be one more moment of suffering, when the bullet went into him, but it would be quicker and more merciful than the slow painful nails He had endured.

Bowing his head, Jesse prayed, the words pouring from his heart too quickly for his lips to form them. He prayed for his mother—that she would somehow know he had at last found peace. He prayed for his friend, who'd come to Earlyville simply to answer a call for help. Jesse hoped that one day Rosen would find his way, if not to Jesus, then back to the God of his fathers.

Only when he tried praying for Bathsheba did the words slow, stumbling from his lips. He tried thinking of her as she sat beside him in church, eyes wide and hands clasped upon her lap as she listened to her father's sermon. The image was so perfect, he even saw her breasts lightly rise and fall with each breath. Her heavy breasts, and her long legs wrapping around him in the grass. No, he wasn't to think of those things anymore . . . not at a time like this. Grasping the Bible so that it almost folded in half, he shook his head hard. He crossed two fingers and stared at them until they became the crucifix and he thought no longer of his own passion but the Passion of Christ.

He sat straight in his chair and rested the Bible

on one knee. Popper had finished his joint and stared at his watch as if it were conversing with him.

"I know, I know," Popper whispered. He looked at Jesse. "You said Gideon'd be coming to church about four. Can't waste any more time. You understand. It's just business."

"Go ahead," Jesse heard himself say, but he read the words through the cover of his Bible as clearly as if they were a sampler on the wall: " 'Except a man be born again, he cannot see the kingdom of God.' "

At last Jesse was at peace and waited calmly for the bullet. He waited for a long time and, when it didn't come, stared at the other man. The gun barrel wavered between Jesse and the stairway leading up to the house; Popper cocked his ear in that direction.

"Shh!"

Jesse heard the flooring above them creak with several sets of footsteps. A moment later someone tried the door at the head of the stairs.

Popper aimed the gun at Jesse's head and whispered, "You keep quiet, or I'll—" He stopped suddenly and swallowed hard.

They both knew what he was about to say and how ridiculous it would sound. There was nothing Popper could do. If he shot Jesse, whoever was upstairs would hear and call the police. And if Jesse was going to die anyway, what was stopping him from calling out? It was so ridiculous, Jesse felt his own cheeks tingling with the other man's embarrassment.

Above them the basement door shook harder, and Popper eyed his only escape route, the cellar door, which his accomplice had padlocked from the outside. The gun trembled in his hand as his eyes grew wide with fear. Jesse leaned forward, hands open, about to say that he wouldn't betray Popper, that he had no intention of escaping his fate.

Slapping Jesse's hands away, Popper shouted, "Keep away, or I'll kill him!" The gun exploded, the bullet shot wildly into the ceiling. "That's right," he screamed at the basement door, "you keep away or I'll kill him!"

"You don't understand. I don't want to hurt you."

"Keep away or I'll kill him! I'll . . . Jesus!"

A loud crack as the basement door clattered down the steps, hitting the floor and skidding against Popper's legs. He kicked it away, then pulled Jesse to the floor directly below him, next to the open box of marijuana, and put the gun barrel against Jesse's head.

A voice from the top of the stairs said, "This is Police Chief Whitcomb. What the hell's goin' on down there?"

"Holy shit," Popper said.

"If that's you, Popper Johnston, I'm placing you under arrest for the murder of Lemuel Banks. You can come upstairs quiet-like on your own two feet, or we can carry you out. Which is it gonna be?"

"I got me a hostage down here! You mess with me and I'll kill him!"

"The hell you say."

There was silence for a minute, followed by the scuffling of feet across the floor above them. Doors slammed, and voices shouted to one another. The soft droning of a police siren slowly grew into a wail as a squad car approached the church. Popper's foot tapped spasmodically on the cellar step, his gun hand trembling, so that Jesse felt the cold metal pulsate against his temple.

He heard heavy footsteps walking down the stairs. Chief Whitcomb stopped two thirds of the way and sat on the steps, a shotgun balanced on his knees. Behind him, Rosen also sat down.

Turning, the police chief said, "Told you to stay upstairs. I'm responsible for your safety."

"I appreciate that, but I'm sure I'll be—" He stopped suddenly, seeing Jesse.

Their eyes locked, and Jesse smiled. "Hello, Nate."

"I wasn't expecting you down here. Don't worry, you'll be all right."

"I'm not worried. Really, I'm not."

"That's right," Whitcomb said. "Popper Johnston's the one needs to be worried, unless he drops that gun right now and gives himself up."

Popper pushed the gun barrel against Jesse's head. "I ain't doing no such thing. I'll kill him if you come any closer . . . swear I will! Ain't going to jail or no electric chair. I'd rather get it over with here and now."

Whitcomb patted his shotgun. "That can be arranged, though it's not my druthers. You really want your brains splattered against that wall?"

"Ain't you forgetting one thing? I got me a hostage. You back off, get me a car and a head start, then I'll let him go."

"Where the hell do you think we are, New York? We don't do none a' that hostage bullshit here. If you're wanted by the law, then the law come gets you."

"I'll kill him!"

"Maybe so, but suppose I do like you say and let you go. Suppose your getaway car runs over a couple schoolkids, or you shoot a little old lady in the next town, or get caught three months later and go on the news telling everyone what a candyass the police chief of Earlyville is. No, sir, can't have that. If you do shoot Jesse Compton here"—Whitcomb shrugged—"I'll apologize to his mama, but at least I'll have your body to show for it . . . that is, all except your face, which'll be scattered across the room. Tell you one thing, when the pictures of your remains come out in the paper, dope dealers'll think twice before stepping into my town. Maybe we'll put one of them pictures on a Just Say No poster. Now, boy, my patience is wearing thin. What's it gonna be?"

Popper moved the gun away, but only for a moment, while he wiped the sweat from his brow. With his free hand, he lit another joint and inhaled deeply.

Jesse looked up the stairs to his friend. Rosen appeared calm, a tight smile across his pallid face, but his hands clutched his knees, knuckles probably white. No doubt his mind was racing, analyzing what was going on and wondering if he should interfere with Whitcomb in order to save his friend. Jesse was touched at Rosen's concern and, at the same time, slightly amused, the same way he felt toward the actions of Whitcomb and Popper. It was as if he were a parent watching three little children playing cowboys and Indians. They played so seriously, yet it was only a game—not real. The same way life on this earth was unreal when compared to the promise of eternal life.

Popper relaxed his grip somewhat. Clearing his throat he asked, "Suppose we make a deal?"

"Ain't nothing you got I want. Danny Hobbes is willing to swear that you killed Lemuel Banks."

"I mean about all the dope dealing in Earlyville. I can give you the names of everyone who's dealing for me, even some contacts I know in Nashville. You'd make a name for yourself. It'd look mighty good come next election.

Whitcomb shook his head.

"Why not? I'm giving you something big! Who gives a damn about some nigger holy roller getting killed?"

"No deals."

"You ain't even asked the D.A. You gotta at least ask him."

Whitcomb almost sighed. "If it'd been just Banks, you might have a chance. But you made a mistake killing somebody important like Ben Hobbes. That's a capital M murder. You gotta pay the price in full for that."

"Ben Hobbes? What the hell you talking about?"

"He used to come walking by his nephew's cornfield, the same way Banks did. The night of his death, he was mad as hell at the church. Told his wife it was doing something bad. Well, you're a member of the church, and take a look at what's going on here. I believe you killed Ben Hobbes just like you did Banks, before he could tell the police about the marijuana. You all use strychnine in your church service; that's what killed Hobbes. I bet you got yourself a box of rat poison down here somewhere, with strychnine on the label and your fingerprints on the box."

"As well as the prints of half a dozen other church members! You're crazy. You ain't got nothing but some circumstantial evidence that'd be laughed outta court."

"Think so? You ain't seen the D.A. at work. Besides, I don't think he's gonna need too much of a case. Folks around here sure liked Ben Hobbes, almost as much as they hate dope dealers. You ever seen *Easy Rider*?"

Popper's forearm, the one holding the gun, tightened against Jesse's shoulder. Taking a drag on his joint, he sat very still for a long time, then, with his free hand, lifted a bag of marijuana from the box beside him, tore it open with his teeth, and poured the dope into a little mound back inside the box. He repeated the process another eight or nine times, emptying all the bags while humming some rock and roll song.

"Name that tune, Whitcomb," he said, giggling.

"Can't quite place it. I know it ain't by the Judds."

Popper laughed so hard the gun almost fell from his hand, and his grip on Jesse loosened. Whitcomb inched the double barrels of his shotgun so that they aimed straight ahead. From the way the two men were positioned, Jesse knew he'd get most of the buckshot. He saw Rosen jerking his head as a signal for Jesse to roll to the floor and give the police chief a clear target. It'd be easy. Jesse would be safe; he'd see Bathsheba tonight. Maybe she and the town would think he was a hero. But the cost would be another man's life.

" 'Born to Be Wild'!" Popper shouted, still laughing. "From *Easy Rider*. You remember them buzzing down the road on their cycles, the music blasting? Yeah, that was me in the sixties. I was a wild one. Sex and drugs and that good old country rockin'."

Jesse glanced from Whitcomb's shotgun to Rosen's face, white as ivory. He had been so resigned to die, the thought of living seemed like a betrayal of faith. Not knowing what to do, he prayed.

He tried clearing his mind of everything but the image of the crucifix. It was easy at first; then came the thick odor, making him cough and burning his eyes. Popper had lit the pile of marijuana, which smoldered and raised a dark heavy cloud into the room.

"If you're gonna pull the trigger," Popper said, "then this is the way I want to go. One mind-blowing, cosmic-raising, psycho-fucking vegetarian orgasm!"

The more Jesse tried to catch his breath, the more smoke he inhaled. At first he thought he was, after all, going to die from asphyxiation. However, in a little while he began to relax as his breathing became more regular. Popper kept talking and Whitcomb was shouting something, but the words stretched from their mouths to his ears like thick gobs of taffy. His vision blurred; were his eyes open? He seemed able to step from his body and examine himself, prying his eyelids open until pennies spilled from his sockets, pennies with his picture, not Lincoln's. Falling around him, they piled up to his waist.

He shook his head hard, scattering the pennies, and waded through them until reaching a stream, the place he'd fished as a boy. He cast his line and watched it drop lightly below the surface; then he became a fish following it down toward the bottom. He swam freely as a fish, his tail flapping and fins speeding him through the undulating current. He was laughing and heard her laughing all around him, her voice muted by the water. And though all around him, he swam to where the laughter originated. He swam to her.

She was lying naked in the field, her slender arms and long legs stretching endlessly across the grass. He was a fish flopping over her breasts the size of mountains, over her tanned thighs and shoulders, while she laughed. He was laughing with her, slipping from her grasp as she tried to embrace him. Slowly her body, the field—everything—darkened into night. Still her laughter rang in his ears.

Sometime later the blackness dissolved into gray, then light. There was no longer laughter but a slow steady wail like a baby crying. He was shaking . . . someone was shaking him, calling his name.

"Jesse? Jesse, come on, snap out of it." Rosen was kneeling beside him.

Blinking, he looked around and saw himself sitting on the lawn in front of the house. Two squad cars were parked in the street near Jesse's Porsche, while an ambulance waited in the driveway. Its siren was what Jesse had heard.

"You all right?" Rosen asked.

"Yes, I think so. What happened?"

"You've just experienced your first extralegal mind expansion. As Popper might've said, 'Better living through chemistry.' "

Jesse swiveled his head. "Popper. Where is he?"

"Gone."

"Gone? You mean he's . . . ?"

"No," Rosen said, laughing. "Not dead. He's already on his way to police headquarters. You three are all right—even Chief Whitcomb over there."

Shifting his weight, Jesse saw Whitcomb leaning against the front door. Two policemen supported him on either side as his head lolled forward and his words slurred. The policemen were biting back their laughter, while another officer, barely able to keep his camera steady, took a series of Polaroid photographs.

Rosen said, "I think it's going to be a long time before Whitcomb forgets this case. At least he's busted the major marijuana dealer in town."

Jesse asked, "Are you all right? You weren't affected by the marijuana?"

"When the smoke started rising, I went upstairs for help. The police dragged the three of you outside. See your Bible on the ground over there? You were clutching it like a baby. I also found this." He opened his jacket; Popper's gun was tucked under his belt. "Do you want to try getting up?"

"Uh-huh. I'm all right. I—"

He stopped suddenly, seeing Gideon McCrae standing over him.

McCrae winced before speaking. "Policeman over there told me what happened. Told me 'bout Popper bein' a killer, about how he used the church t'hide his drugs."

"It's not your fault," Jesse said.

"Ain't it? All the time, I'm tellin' folks to watch out, 'cause like Jesus said, 'Shall grievous wolves enter in among you, not sparing the flock.' And all the time the meanest wolf was standin' at my side. My own cousin. T'think he killed Brother Lem and Ben Hobbes."

Rosen said, "He denied murdering Hobbes."

"One more killin' don't much matter, him bein' my own blood."

His own blood? Jesse blurted, "Is Bathsheba all right?"

"Guess so. Don't know where Sheba is. Generally goes off on her own, afternoons she's not workin'."

Rosen stood. He started to speak, stopped, then furrowed his brow for a long time. Finally he asked, "What did you call your daughter?"

McCrae blushed violently. The word seemed to crawl from his mouth. "Sheba."

Jesse said, "It's just an abbreviation for Bathsheba."

Rosen was staring at the Reverend. "Is that all it is?"

McCrae tried to look away but seemed unable to. "You know, don't you?"

"I think so. The question is, how much do you know?"

Jesse struggled to his feet, leaning against his friend for support. "What're you both talking about?"

Rosen's hands gripped him hard, too hard to be just for support. "You feel up for a ride?"

"I . . . uh . . . I guess so."

"Good. Reverend McCrae, you'd better come, too." They took a step, but Rosen stopped to pick up Jesse's Bible. "Here, Jesse. I think you're going to need it."

Chapter 21

"There's one thing lawyers have in common with men of God," Rosen said while driving down Jackson Street.

Jesse sat beside him, with Reverend McCrae in the backseat. Still not completely sure of who murdered Ben Hobbes, he spoke to each as a *chavrusa,* study partner, while constructing a hypothetical case.

"Both lawyers and religious leaders strive with a certainty of purpose that often defies logic. Reverend McCrae genuinely believes only his church has the correct path to salvation. Whether right or wrong, he has a right to that belief as a matter of faith. Lawyers are supposed to be different, men of reason. But we're not, and that's been the trouble with this case all along."

Jesse asked, "What do you mean?"

"Once the police assembled the evidence pointing toward Claire Hobbes as the murderer, the D.A. assumed she was guilty. Neither he nor Whitcomb entertained the slightest doubt and, therefore, made no attempt to investigate other suspects."

"But now they have Popper Johnston. He must've killed Ben Hobbes, just as he killed Lemuel Banks."

Rosen shook his head, not to refute Jesse but to keep his train of thought. "I wasn't much different from the police. Once taking Claire's case, I was committed to her acquittal. I never considered myself the type of lawyer who defended anyone, no matter how dirty, as long as the fee was big enough. I didn't always believe Claire, but I never seriously doubted her innocence."

"You were right."

"Was I? Maybe, but so were the police."

"How can you both be right? You're not making any—"

"Bear with me. We're almost there."

Parking around the corner from Claire's house, Rosen took Popper's gun from the glove compartment and slid it back under his belt. The three men walked down the alley. Claire's garage door was up, the car and truck parked side by side. Rosen walked between them, placing his hand on the Corvette's hood, which was warm.

"The first problem was that of an alibi. The evening of the murder, her neighbor saw Claire's car returning home shortly after nine, before Ben Hobbes. Claire swore she arrived home closer to ten, after her husband. Of course, the D.A. planned to use the neighbor's testimony against her. I worked to find another possibility—that night, while everyone was busy caring for Lemuel Banks, someone took Claire's car keys from her purse."

"Popper," Jesse suggested.

Rosen shrugged and put his hand on the wooden table near a pair of work gloves. "Then there's the question of why her fingerprints and not Ben's were on the milk carton. The police's answer was simple—she poured the milk and put the poison in it. But Claire said that her husband fixed his own milk and went upstairs before she arrived home. Only then did she touch the carton. Why weren't his prints on it?" He tapped the table where it had been discolored. "I had a lab check what made this stain. Milk laced with strychnine. On the night he died, Ben Hobbes brought home lumber to build some kitchen shelving. He must've been wearing these work gloves. He leaned the lumber against the sink, poured the milk, walked back into the garage and put the glass down while taking off his gloves and leaving them here."

"Of course," Jesse said, "that's why the carton didn't have his fingerprints. So far, you've given a jury more than enough reasonable doubt. The D.A. wouldn't dare bring a case against Claire to court."

Rosen opened the door to the house and led the other two men inside. They walked through the kitchen and hallway into the living room.

Jesse whispered, "We shouldn't be in here. Both cars are in the garage. Claire must be home."

"I'm counting on it. Remember this?"

He walked to one of the windows facing the backyard.

Jesse said, "Whitcomb pointed this out the morning after the murder. The killer tried making it appear that someone had broken in. You said it was an attempt to fool the police. Popper could've done it."

"I wouldn't trust Popper Johnston with the proceeds from a Girl Scout cookie sale, but he does qualify as an expert on crime. If he wanted to make this look like a break-in, he would've done a convincing job. This was the work of a rank amateur." Rosen shook his head. "Jesse, when you give a multiple-choice test, don't you tell your students to go with their first response?"

"What're you talking about?"

"That's what I should've done—gone with my

first instinct. Listening to Ben Hobbes on your tape, not what he said about the threat, but the way he said it. At first the police blamed Claire. Maybe she was in love with Reverend McCrae and, under his Svengali influence, killed her husband to gain his estate for the church. Later Simon Hobbes swore there was a second will disinheriting Claire. That was a strong motive. For a while I thought a private investigator named Aadams had found the will and sold it to Claire. Now there's a drug connection between Popper Johnston and Danny—and Ben Hobbes may have discovered the marijuana field a few days before his death. The police are ready to believe Popper killed Ben to protect his dope. You are, too."

"Sure I am."

"What about you, Reverend?"

McCrae stood a few steps from them. He looked Rosen in the eyes but his chin trembled slightly. He didn't answer.

Rosen continued, "I don't think Popper did it. He wouldn't have risked waiting a few days to poison Ben. He'd have shot him right away, as he did Banks. No, I should've gone with my first instinct. On the tape, the bitterness in Ben Hobbes's voice. He felt betrayed as a man. Something so humiliating he couldn't say out loud what happened, but you knew what he was talking about, Reverend."

This time Rosen waited and, after a long time, McCrae finally answered. "I can't . . . I can't say nothin'."

Jesse shook his head. "I won't believe the Reverend's involved in murder." He turned to McCrae. "You can't be. Everything that's changed in my life is because of you."

"No. Any good that's come is 'cause you seen the Light. Ain't got nothin' t'do with me."

"But, you can't—"

"Wait," Rosen said. "We're not done yet. Not until we've seen Claire."

The three men walked back into the hallway, and Rosen led them upstairs. Hearing Claire's voice from inside her room, he paused at the top step to listen. She was reading something—one of her poems.

"You're filled with so much charm and grace,
A perfect smile upon your face.
But if to me any perfection's due,
It's only in my love for you."

She continued reading verses so bad they were almost laughable, but Rosen didn't laugh. There was a fervor in her voice, and for a moment he wondered if Bess had ever felt that way about him.

Claire finished, cleared her throat . . . did she say something softly . . . and began another one. No, it wasn't her voice.

"Who'll take a thread of sunlight
And weave it for my glove;
Who'll bring a rose in winter
And be my own true love?"

Jesse leaned against the wall and moaned softly while, beside him, McCrae stood perfectly still. Reluctantly they followed Rosen into the bedroom.

A smell, heavy with perfume and sweat, filled his nostrils. The same odor as when, days ago, he'd first examined her room. Only this time there was another scent intermingling, something from

McCrae's church. The image before Rosen's eyes was as incomprehensible as an abstract painting with colors the shades of blood; what it whispered the body heard long before the mind understood. The room was whispering something to him now, something that bristled hairs on the back of his neck.

"Yetzer ha-ra," it whispered in his father's voice. "The evil impulse" . . . the one that lowered man into beast.

Taking a step forward, Rosen turned his head. The whispering stopped, while the room came into focus. Claire sat on the bed, legs drawn under her, holding a sheaf of papers, her poems. She wore a frilly white nightgown with a strap fallen from her shoulder, revealing the dark cleft between her breasts. Her hair was loose, a few strands teasing one cheek. The soft curve of shoulders and her throat were pinkish, reminding him of a rabbit, as did the frightened look in her eyes.

Her lips trembled but said nothing. Instead, she held the poems like an offering, just as the children of Israel, dirtying themselves in sin, had made offerings to Baal in the desert.

Lying beside Claire, under the covers with an elbow propped on the pillow, Bathsheba stared at him, her mouth twisted into a small smile. Her face was framed perfectly by coal-black curls, and her eyes were as dark. She touched Claire, who nuzzled like a cat against her hand.

Looking past Rosen, Bathsheba repeated the verse.

"Who'll take a thread of sunlight
And weave it for my glove;
Who'll bring a rose in winter
And be my own true love?"

Jesse stood transfixed by her gaze, the image before his eyes carved so deeply into his mind it might never fade away.

But McCrae's face was more chilling. It showed no anger, no rage about to burst like a thunderclap upon his daughter. There was nothing, nothing but a great stillness deeper than sadness. Rosen had seen that look once before, when his own father had closed the door between them, and he'd endured that same feeling. Every now and then it came back to him, like the slow pulsing pain of a bullet lodged near the heart, a bullet too cruel to kill quickly but one that could never be removed.

Rosen said to the two women, "Tell me about Ben Hobbes's murder. The truth this time."

Claire shook back the hair from her face. "What makes you think I know anything more than I told you?" Her blue eyes shone back clear and empty.

"I ignored my instinct, that this was a crime of passion, because I didn't believe you could do such a thing. I was wrong, because I was right."

She laughed nervously. "What?"

"You didn't do it, but your . . . lover did. Reverend McCrae's world and the one I once lived in are circumscribed by rules carried down from Mount Sinai. In those righteous worlds nothing evil is permitted to enter, like the proscription of Leviticus: 'If a man lies with a man, both have committed an abomination.' "

Bathsheba cocked her head. "You call it evil, just 'cause the love's 'tween two women?"

"No. It's true I didn't think of you as Ben Hobbes's murderer, because I couldn't comprehend you as Claire's lover. Maybe your father believes evil is inherent in this kind of love, but I don't. I've seen too much of the world beyond my father's walls. It's the way you've twisted what you call love. *Yetzer ha-ra.*"

She leaned forward, revealing most of her breasts. "Tell me all the evil I done."

"You were the one, not Popper Johnston, who took the keys from Claire's purse and drove to her house. Claire had told you about her husband's habit of drinking a warm glass of milk, that only he drank from the acidophilus carton. You brought the strychnine from the church and put it into the carton. Your clumsy attempt at a break-in was to protect Claire."

"Why would I do all that?"

"Because he knew you were Claire's lover."

She said nothing, only tilted her head up as if daring him to continue. He wanted to stop, for Jesse's sake and McCrae's, and because he wanted to leave the room, which nearly overpowered him with its smell of evil. But he had to continue; there was no one else to do it.

"Ben Hobbes suspected his wife of having an affair, so he hired a Nashville detective named Aadams to follow her. Aadams discovered the truth about you two. Claire had a history of rejecting male lovers, like Danny or the owner's grandson at the restaurant where she used to work. Even Hec Perry said their relationship wasn't physical. That's why Ben was so upset when he confronted McCrae at the service. Your lesbian affair only confirmed what he'd believed all along, that the church was some sort of perverse cult taking control of his wife. He, too, was a religious man, and that's why he couldn't say aloud what had happened. Maybe Ben Hobbes would never have told, but he would've stopped your affair and tried his best to destroy the church."

Bathsheba stirred, like someone in a peaceful dream, and the covers slipped down to reveal her dark round nipples. He tried not to look at them. Watching his struggle, she grinned. "Ben was gonna send Claire away 'n' get rid of the church, too. Couldn't have none a' that."

"No." He felt the sweat sliding under his collar. "That's not all you did, is it?"

"You tell me."

"When I first arrived in Earlyville, your father said his house had been burglarized and your room had been 'messed with.' My guess is that Aadams did the job and found evidence of your affair."

"What evidence?"

"The papers Claire's holding in her hands. For a while I thought Aadams had found the second will that Simon Hobbes was so sure existed. What he'd really found were those love poems to you. I'm sure when the police lab examines them, they'll find some of Aadams's fingerprints. He blackmailed Claire into buying them back, but you wanted to be sure. Or was it that you started to like killing?"

Claire crinkled her eyebrows and cuddled next to Bathsheba. "What's he talking about?"

Bathsheba stroked the other woman's hair, and said to Rosen, "She ain't much for details."

"Claire didn't know about your plan to kill her husband. You never expected her to leave your place the night of the murder. You didn't know that your father had convinced her to go home. Otherwise, she would've had an airtight alibi."

"Go on, Mr. Lawyer. What else I done?"

"Yesterday afternoon you went to see Aadams at his office. Aadams never let any man close enough to threaten him, but he was different with women. He saw you, started thinking about your body, and when he pulled you toward him, you stuck a knife in his belly. Then you took the file on Ben Hobbes."

Rosen waited for Bathsheba's confession, but she only stared at him while petting Claire like a cat. The room grew silent for a moment, yet he thought he heard something stirring, soft as Bathsheba's stroking. It made him take a step backward against his friend, who pushed him aside.

"Why me?" Jesse whispered hoarsely to Bathsheba. "If you wanted . . . her all along, why did you do those things with me?"

She shrugged. "You bein' Claire's lawyer, thought I'd find out what was goin' on. Then it just become fun. A man can love one woman 'n' still go whorin'. Ain't that right, Daddy? Ain't that what you used t'do before gettin' religion?"

McCrae clutched at the chest of drawers and sagged into a rocking chair nearby. "All that's happened been my doin'. The Lord's laid a curse on me, a righteous curse."

"Why?" Rosen asked. "Because your daughter's black?"

"You know that, too?"

"When I found that hair in Claire's bed, and the lab report said it belonged to a black, I thought that Lemuel Banks was her lover. But there were enough clues pointing to Bathsheba. You call her Sheba, like the biblical queen. Hec Perry wouldn't tell me much about Claire, but he knew the truth—he kept quoting a line from Coleridge about asking the 'Abyssinian maid.' Both women were Ethiopian and black. Besides, Jesse said Bathsheba wouldn't talk about her mother. I suppose an interracial marriage wouldn't help a minister gain too many converts."

"Marriage?" Bathsheba laughed hard. "Daddy

never did marry my mama. She was pure when she first met him. Then after I was born, he left her—didn't want no nigger baby. Left her to a whorehouse. That's where she died."

McCrae pressed his hands together. "I loved her."

"You used her, then throwed us both aside. It was right fine growin' up in a whorehouse, seein' what men did to Mama, 'n' what they did to me. All they ever used was their fists and that thing between their legs. Those last few days, when Mama got sick, you never did visit her."

"I was a wicked man but, findin' the Lord, I figgered He gave me a second chance. I come for you, child. Raised you as mine."

"You never told the world who she was, 'n' who I am."

"No, I didn't, 'n' now I'm bein' punished. Thought I made it up by raisin' you a good Christian."

"It takes a good Christian to have a good Christian hate. The same kinda hate you got for whores like my mama and queers like me. I got me a good hate, too."

"My fault," McCrae repeated, shaking his head slowly. "All along I shoulda known, you was a bad seed planted in bad soil."

Her lips curled. "I knew you'd say somethin' like that."

Gently pushing Claire away, Bathsheba threw back the covers and stood. She was completely naked, and Rosen narrowed his eyes, as one would from too much light. He'd never seen a more beautiful woman, nor anything quite so perfect. And seeing her, he knew what all his years of studying the Torah had never really taught, how Jezebel had turned Ahab to false gods and murder.

Rosen watched her reflection flow into the full-length mirror as she passed. Standing before McCrae she moved a hand gently, but he winced as if slapped. Instead of touching him, she reached for the chest of drawers and opened the top one, which was already ajar. It seemed an innocent movement, but McCrae's body jerked to attention, and he stared at the drawer. A second later Rosen shivered, while the smell that had filled his nostrils suddenly grew stronger.

Bathsheba shifted something inside the drawer and, opening a burlap bag, thrust her hands inside. McCrae stood, kicking away his chair, while she drew out the long, thick diamond patterned body of a rattlesnake. She curled it around her back, like a towel, holding her right hand just below the snake's head. Walking past her father, she stood between the bedroom door and the three men. The snake flicked its tongue, and its tail moved listlessly, the rattle whispering its evil in Rosen's ear.

"You all come too early. We was fixin' to let this here fella crawl around a spell. Sure is a pretty sight. Claire likes the way light shinin' through the window makes his back sparkle. She wrote a poem about it. Me, I just like cuddlin' next to my girl, arms tight around each other, listenin' to him on the floor below us. Gives Claire goose bumps and makes her want me that much more. Don't it, darlin'?"

Claire had crawled to the edge of the bed, eyes widening and fingers twisting loose strands of hair.

Bathsheba asked, "Should I do it now?"

The other woman nodded. "Then come here. Come back to bed and hold me while we watch."

As Bathsheba crouched onto the carpet, the snake's rattling grew louder. It was only a few feet from Jesse, who fell heavily to his knees, like a slaughtered steer, and held out his hands.

She asked, "Want him, Jesse? You feel the power over you and think you can tame the devil? Go 'head, darlin', go 'head 'n' try."

She caressed the snake, her lips kissing its forehead, then let it slowly slither over her shoulder and through her hands. Its rattles shook angrily. Watching Bathsheba, Rosen felt a great chill spreading through his body. His numbed hand clumsily drew Popper's gun from his belt.

She laughed. "You gonna shoot me, Mr. Lawyer? You don't see Jesse cryin' for help."

Rosen reached for his friend, who wouldn't be pulled away. Sensing its freedom, the rattler coiled, wavered for an instant, then reared back its head.

As the snake moved to strike, a hand flashed between it and Jesse, grabbing the rattler below its head and forcing it back. McCrae's hand didn't quite grasp high enough to keep the snake from lunging forward. It missed his arm but, swinging around in a wide arc, plunged its teeth into Bathsheba's shoulder. She stiffened, eyes snapping wide, and cocked her head toward the creature.

Rosen hesitated, afraid of shooting the woman. But McCrae already had opened a pocket knife, grabbed the twisting rattler and nearly sliced off its head. Tossing the snake aside, he pushed his trembling daughter to the floor and held the blade over her.

Bathsheba looked up through half-closed eyes. She whispered weakly, "Daddy."

Leaning over her, he cut into the wound between the bite marks and sucked the poison. Spitting it on the floor, he shouted, "Call an ambulance!"

He went back to work on the wound. Jesse knelt

on the other side of Bathsheba, covering her with his jacket. Then he took her hand in his and held it tightly, as if he'd never let go.

The telephone was on the night table beside the bed. While calling for an ambulance and the police, Rosen watched Claire. Like a child, she looked frightened without understanding why. Climbing down from the bed, she started toward Bathsheba. Rosen pulled her back and, in doing so, his hand rested on the gentle swell of her belly. Her hand closed over his. She looked up and smiled.

"I'm gonna have a baby—Ben's baby. Did you know that?"

Rosen stared into her eyes, at that moment innocent as a baby's. "Yes," he said, and made another call.

Having dressed Claire in a warm quilted robe, Ruth sat beside her in bed, the young woman's head nestled against her shoulder. They could've been mother and daughter—the way they whispered, Claire smiling shyly, took some of the chill from the room. Some, but not all.

Jesse remained on the floor where Bathsheba had lain, before the paramedics, accompanied by her father, had taken her to the hospital. His hand brushed against the carpet. Rosen was sure that, looking into his friend's eyes, he'd still see Bathsheba's reflection.

He considered helping Jesse to his feet but, instead, sat beside him. Saying nothing, he waited patiently for a sign of recognition in the other man's eyes. Finally, Jesse blinked hard.

Rosen asked, "Are you all right?"

Jesse looked around the room, as if seeing it for the first time, then shook his head slowly. "All right? I suppose I'd have to know who I am to answer a question like that. I know who I was—great-grandson of the man who rode with Nathan Bedford Forrest and an unworthy bearer of the Compton name."

"Maybe you'd better take it easy."

"Actually I do know, not who, but what, I am—a common fool, plaything of God above and His most wondrous creation below, woman. Can I dare dignify myself as a tragic hero? How low I've fallen. All that's left is the ending. How would it end in a play, Nate—a walk offstage and a pistol shot as the curtain falls?"

"Maybe in a very bad melodrama. But that's not for you."

"Why not?"

"Because you haven't died today."

"Oh, really?"

"Really. In fact, maybe you've been born, because you finally felt what your family and work kept hidden—the pain of being alive. The pain of losing someone you love, the pain of losing your God. You want me to feel sorry for you? Well, you've come to the wrong place, because I've been there."

"I was such a fool. She . . . how she shamed me."

"Sure, and you're the first man that's ever happened to. You should write a book."

Jesse ran a hand through his hair. "The church, everything I believed in was a lie."

"Maybe for you the church lied, because it was always Bathsheba first. As McCrae might say, it wasn't really the Spirit coming over you."

"Was it all a lie?"

Closing his eyes for a moment, Rosen saw himself as a boy watching his father rocking back and forth, deep in study, then years later—his father's face as he closed the door between them forever. "You admitted once that you really asked me here to help you win Bathsheba. Well, I came here for more than just the case. I wanted to see if there were those whom God touched selflessly, solely from love."

"And Reverend McCrae?"

He shrugged. "I don't know, but I think McCrae truly believes. Maybe that's enough. Maybe that was worth the trip."

Jesse gripped Rosen's shoulder, hesitated, then stood. He helped his friend up and said, "I'm going for a little walk."

"Not off a pier?"

"No, to the corner store. I need a cigarette awfully bad. See you outside in a few minutes. I'd like to talk more tonight. Just like law school, there's a great deal I need to have explained."

"Just like law school, we'll struggle through it together, Chavrusa. I'll stop and pick up a bottle of wine."

"Thanks, but I'll choose the wine. I've already suffered enough."

Watching Jesse leave, Rosen felt a hand on his arm.

"Will he be all right?" Ruth asked.

"Sure, but keep an eye on him for me. Let me know how he's doing. You probably would anyway."

"You're leaving town?"

"I think my friend and I are going to pull an all-nighter, but I'll catch a plane back to D.C. tomorrow. There's nothing more for me to do here."

Ruth glanced at Claire, playing with her hair while curled in the corner of her bed. "I was hoping you'd stay on and be her lawyer. I don't believe that girl had anything to do with Ben's death. She's a child having a child."

"Maybe you're right. There are plenty of psychiatrists who'll agree. Like a child, she did what other people expected of her. She was a dutiful wife to Ben Hobbes, good friend to Hec Perry, devoted church member to Reverend McCrae, and passionate lover to Bathsheba. Don't worry—with her money, Claire will be able to buy the best defense attorney possible. Most importantly, she's got you."

"Still sorry to see you go."

"If you're worried about your son, I talked to Whitcomb. The D.A.'s going to drop most of the charges against Danny in exchange for his testimony against Popper Johnston. He'll probably get probation for possession of marijuana, but you let me know if there're any problems. I think District Attorney Grimes would do anything to keep me out of this town."

Tears rimmed her eyes. "Bless you, Nate. I do wish you'd stay on a spell."

"I'm tempted. I like Earlyville. It's been a long time since I've been in a place where everyone's treated like family. Not since my childhood. It just hurts too much." She tightened her hand on his arm as he continued, "Besides, I've got my own family problems to put in order."

"Your Sarah?"

"Yes, and what used to be my Bess." Almost sighing, he added, "I want to thank you, Ruth. That goodness Reverend McCrae kept talking about, I saw it in your eyes all along. Oh, and you finally got me to like grits."

The laugh caught in her throat as she hugged him tightly, then hurried back to Claire.

Rosen turned to leave. Near the door lay the rattlesnake McCrae had killed. It was a poor dumb creature, a victim the same as Ben Hobbes, Lemuel Banks, and Aadams had been. Like a mirror, it had only reflected the evil impulse in men and women. A poor dumb creature. Still, Rosen gave it a wide berth as he walked from the room.

As that great psychic Madame Tallulah—also known as Ida—would've said, "*Nu,* why take chances?"